The Apara Chronicles (Book 2):

In Your Dreams

By Jeanne Rhodes-Moen

Disclaimer:

Any similarities to actual persons living, dead, or otherwise is unintentional. I have used some actual place names from Asheville for realism.

Some characters occasionally utter words in other languages. See the last page of the book: Foreign Word List for definitions.

Published By:
Jeannius Designs
Asheville, NC 28805
www.Jeannius.com

Visit www.aparachronicles.com

Dedication

To Linda Scott, for seeing me through a degree in psychology in the 80s, which made the main character in this book not only possible, but helps me write stories with psychological depth and emotional believability. Also, thanks for reading my manuscripts and encouraging me with my writing.

And a special thanks to Nicky Rea for acting as my editor, proofer, and mentor, as well as reading through 6 lengthy manuscripts multiple times!

Books in series

HIDDEN IN BROAD DAYLIGHT (MARCH 2024)

IN YOUR DREAMS (MAY 2024)

PERSISTENCE OF VISION (AUGUST 2024)

GOING VIRAL (NOVEMBER 2024)

PHOENIX RISING (2025)

WORLDS COLLIDE (2025)

All books will be released during 2024-2025

About the author

 Jeanne Rhodes-Moen was born in Washington D.C. in 1966. She grew up in Maryland, and attended Hood College, where she received a B.A. Psychology and a second B.A. in Math, Secondary Education.

In 1991, she married a Norwegian and moved to Norway, where she made jewelry based in their traditional filigree fused with her own imaginative style. Her first book, Silver Threads: Making Wire Filigree Jewelry, was published in 2006 by Kalmbach Books, and is currently available as Print-on-Demand and eBook on Amazon.

She and her two daughters moved to Asheville, NC in 2005 after her husband passed from diabetic complications. Since then, she has done a combination of jewelry, lapidary, and jewelry photography.

More recently, she has been using her creative skills toward this series: The Apara Chronicles. A science fantasy book series; of which Hidden in Broad Daylight is the first installment.

Jeanne and her daughters all deal with ADHD, but she finds that it has a positive effect on her creative abilities.

Table of Contents

UNCONTROLLED 1

WHAT HIDES IN BROAD DAYLIGHT: A PRECIS OF BOOK ONE 3

UP IN THE AIR 5

FRUSTRATION, CONCERN, DEPRESSION. OH, MY! 9

ELUSIVE EQUILIBRIUM 13

GETTING TO WORK 25

DO YOU DREAM WHAT I DREAM? 35

BEST OF TIMES, WORST OF TIMES 53

ANNIE, CAN YOU HEAR ME? 65

LAYING THE GROUNDWORK 75

LOST AND FOUND 79

OLD TIMES BECOME NEW 87

RECONNECTING 95

DINNER AND DETOURS 103

CROSSING THE THRESHOLD TO THE TWILIGHT ZONE 113

ROLE REVERSAL 137

LOST MEMORIES 147

LAST SUPPER 153

GENETIC LOTTERY 159

DEATH AND REBIRTH 167

EMERGENCE 173

PROVERBIAL GUINEA PIG 179

LOOSE ENDS 185

ADJUSTMENTS 195

INTUITION VS. EXPERIENCE 203

MILLIE 209

LETTING GO AND REACHING OUT 219

DELVING DEEP 235

DREAM THERAPY 241

BACK TO WORK IN THE REAL WORLD 257

DOUBLE-TAKE 267

IDENTITY CRISIS...279

CONSOLATION PRIZE 285

DOUBLE THE TROUBLE 293

IN VAIN 297

OFFICIALLY 305

REVERSE THE POLARITY 311

THE INVENIR 315

STRATEGY 325

READY, SET: WAIT 331

GO! 335

MISSION ACCOMPLISHED 339

LETTING GO 343

MEANWHILE 345

FOREIGN WORDS LIST..358

Uncontrolled

Marc Girard is in his home office pouring over a new series of natural disaster precogs he's coordinating when he hears a loud pop and the smell of smoke from somewhere in the house.

He paths, *Tess, is everything alright?*

NO! DAMN IT! We're out of light panels and my PK just blew out the last one when Mabel jumped on my chest and woke me up!

Marc closes his eyes, pinches the bridge of his nose and shakes his head in response, pathing, *I'll pop out in a few and get some from Central Supply. In the meantime, you should start wearing your cent-opal pendant while you sleep.*

I am wearing it! Didn't help.

He sighs, replying, *I'll grab extra light panels, then. I suspect we're going to need them until you get your telekinesis under control.*

What hides in broad daylight: A Precis of book one

The nuclear attack on Jerusalem has turned the worlds of both humans and Apara alike upside-down. Many lives were lost and the balance of power on the planet continues to shuffle and realign since that fateful night. What most humans don't know, however, is it could have been, and almost was, much worse. Had it not been for the Apara, Jerusalem would have been but one of nearly a dozen target cities destroyed, including three major cities in the United States: New York, Dallas, and Los Angeles. However, the human world is intentionally unaware of the Apara and their efforts to stop the nuclear devices, but also of their very existence.

The Apara are a group of genetically enhanced humans tasked with protecting and guiding the Earth and humanity until humankind reaches a sufficiently mature level of civilization. At which point, an advanced, alien race, known to the Apara as 'the Benefactors', will approach humanity and make themselves known.

To humans, these thankless, former humans would be seen as monsters, as they were engineered to be dependent on humans, and need to stay anonymous among humanity while living among them, in broad daylight. To most people, these altered beings would be called vampires, but they are hardly the stuff of nightmares, but a group of dedicated protectors, teachers, and even intergalactic diplomats tasked with preserving this world and guiding it into the future. They prefer the name Apara, stemming from the Sanskrit word for 'other', as 'vampire' has such horrific connotations. Their creators, the Benefactors, made them dependent on humans to remind them they are here for humanity and not above it.

While the human population lost between 200-300,000 lives, the Apara lost a little over 3000 of their own, or around 10% of their population. They have maintained a careful balance of their kind relative to humanity's population since they were first created several millennia ago. Now, they must not only regain said balance, but increase their population to compensate for the instability caused by this horrible act. The catch is, only some people can become Apara. The Benefactors choose promising individuals, early in life, and implant them with a unique genetic sequence. Only those with this sequence, who are *also* deemed suitable as adults, can be transformed. Each potential must be evaluated, based on their current life situation, psychological suitability, ethics, and psychic potential. If someone passes all these evaluations, they can be recruited and transformed. Becoming Apara is a gift of great power, but one demanding tremendous responsibility, and has the potential for incredible damage if that power is misused.

While the Benefactors select many as potentials, few are normally called to serve, and never more than a few hundred per century, in balance with the human population. Now, they must make up for their losses, and increase that base number, and those in their database of potentials who are suitable, are unlikely to be enough on their own.

Up in the air

Tess Waterford is one of the newest Apara, transformed the night of the Jerusalem nuclear attack. However, while compatible, Tess lacks much of the early, unconscious training and conditioning potentials are usually given by the Benefactors. In the early years of their lives, potentials receive training meant to help them, should they be called to serve, such as how to use their new abilities, but also to keep them psychologically and ethically stable. They're given certain knowledge about their origin, purpose, and about the Benefactors, the alien race that created them. This information is usually brought forth from their unconscious minds when transformed, such that they understand their own purpose for becoming Apara, as well as the goals of their new lives.

Tess received some of the basic pre-conditioning, up until she was believed lost in the car accident that killed her parents when she was three. After that, she was listed as an "inactive potential", in other words, deceased, and her training was left incomplete.

Ironically, she was also one of the psychically strongest potentials they have seen in the last century, but her lack of in-depth training has made it harder for her to manage her new abilities. Tess discovered the Apara by accident, and due to a particular quirk of her talents, could not be made to forget about them. She worked with them for several months as a human, learning to use what abilities she had prior to her transformation. She also played a major part in stopping the other bombs, as well as a couple of other incidents

No one thought she could be transformed, but an accidental two-way exchange of blood with Marc, the Apara man she'd fallen in love, with transformed her. He was in Jerusalem when the bomb exploded, and barely made it out, teleporting home to Tess, critically injured. As she tried to help him, the blood exchange occurred, transforming her, and allowing her to truly join the Apara, rather than being stuck in between them and humanity; more than human, but not one of them.

Just when she's getting the hang of her new life, Jason Templeton, a potential with serious mental health issues and a history of parental abuse, was mistakenly transformed post-Jerusalem, and went rogue, undoing what stability Tess had gained so far.

***

Ever since Jason kidnapped and neutralized Tess's abilities a few months earlier, she's been working hard to regain some modicum of control, as the antidote opened her psychic pathways and expanded her already formidable gifts. If she gets angry, things tend to break or fall off shelves. If she goes out in public, she must wear a special necklace to keep herself from picking up random thoughts from everyone around her. She's been fighting for weeks to keep her abilities under enough control to leave the house.

Tess's frustration increases daily; the more frustrated she gets, the less she's able to control her abilities. The one ability she's been able to harness is one she's had all her life and never thought of as psychic; the ability to read people; not so much their minds, but their mental states and personalities. That's gotten much stronger since she was turned, and even more so after Jason. Even when she was still human, she knew Jason would be trouble and that there was something deeply wrong with the man, and had even expressed concern he *not* be turned. Unfortunately, those warnings were lost in the chaos after the Jerusalem nuclear terrorist incident, and he was turned anyway. His obsession with Tess stems from a combination of her likeness to his mother, and her natural, psychic shields prevent him from using his innate telepathic abilities to manipulate her, as he could others. He kidnapped her after she became Apara, using a drug that stripped her of most of her abilities. She triggered a subcutaneous antidote, freeing herself, neutralizing his abilities and capturing him. He's currently incarcerated and attempts are being made to redeem him psychologically, as life imprisonment for someone who's essentially immortal is not an option.

The Apara, in an attempt to recoup their losses, have recruited and turned those suitable, but the number of genetically compatible people who were also in appropriate life situations, ages, and also psychologically suitable are limited, and insufficient to make up for their losses. Since Jason turned rogue, they're extra cautious with psychological stability.

They'll have to work hard to find new, highly talented individuals. They must tap a previously unavailable population of compatible humans. These people were found, and genetically tagged during a period with an unusual amount of cosmic radiation hitting earth, which caused mutations, primarily on the X-chromosomes of children conceived during a period of about 8 years, meaning most of these potential transformees are female. These mutations are believed to create extra strong or even novel psychic or other abilities. Unfortunately, the database that contained all the information about these individuals was damaged; all identifying information was lost, leaving a few thousand unidentified gene prints. This also left an age gap between those they've been turning and the next available generation, giving them even fewer to draw upon unless they can find some of the Lost Mission Potentials. It's up to a small group of Apara, including Tess, to find some of these 'lost' individuals, evaluate them, and find any who are suitable to join their efforts to keep humanity from further imploding after Jerusalem, and guide humanity into its adulthood after a rather tumultuous adolescence.

Frustration, concern, depression. Oh, my!

It's a rainy, late-spring day, a few months after Tess's kidnapping by Jason. Marc ports into Inspiration, Inc. while Tess naps after a particularly frustrating practice session with her PK. He knocks on the open office door marked "Lissa Pedersen", to give his 'boss' Liz, an update on his beloved partner.

"Liz, do you have a few?" He inquires.

Liz looks up when she hears the knock, smiling. "Of course. How's Tess holding up?"

Marc sits on the well-used, Scandinavian-style sofa in her office with a sigh. "As well as can be expected. Between being stuck at home for months and having difficulty getting her expanded abilities under control, she's pretty *damn* frustrated!"

"I don't blame her. Peder's been going stir-crazy being stuck in my spare room while he recovers. He's not used to depending on others, but I'm so thankful we found him and the 322 others alive in Sanctuary. Sara thinks he'll recover, but it's gonna take time. And that's what Tess needs to understand as well, it'll take time for her to regain control." Liz reminds him.

Marc leans back on the sofa, concern showing. "She's afraid she'll never regain control, that's the problem. I'm worried her setbacks are going to lead to depression again. I need to find something she can be successful with to counter her feelings of failure. Any ideas?"

Liz sits there, drumming her fingers on the screen of her tablet. "I think I may have just the thing. Remember the meeting we had where she had many ideas about searching out potentials outside our regular system? It's taken a while to create the algorithms, get the genetic sequence from our Benefactors, and the facial extrapolation and matching

9

software is still in the works, but we've put some of her suggestions into action, including outside genetic database searches, and we've found some that aren't in our primary database, including some 'inactives' and a fair number in the Lost Mission database. We're going to need someone to do research on these people, especially on social media, blogs, medical, and school records, for example. Kari keeps telling me how uncanny Tess's intuitive sense about people is. She thinks this would be right up her alley, and she could do it from home. Think she's up to it?"

"I think she'd be thrilled! And it'd keep her out of trouble for a while." He chuckles.

"It's still going to be awhile before we have enough compiled for her to get started. Kari's also been searching certain subsets of previously 'unacceptable' potentials, primarily those who were married, but have since divorced or been widowed, with no children. She's also been looking at some that are above the 30- to 35-year-old cut off. However, I think she wants to begin with those who were in the same category as Tess, improperly filed as inactive or deceased. Kind of a dry run for the big job." Liz clarifies.

There's a knock on the door and Liz's partner, Kari, comes in. "What's up?" Liz asks, the grin draining from her face as she senses Kari's agitation.

Kari closes the door, her mood somber with concern. She sits beside Liz and says, "I came across something that has me worried. Remember how Tess said Jason was looking for compatible women to turn?"

Liz frowns. "Yesssss?" She draws out the word to encourage Kari to finish her thought.

"As you know, we salvaged his drive from the fallout shelter and Tech recovered the data. It was encrypted, but our techs have decrypted most of it. I started going through it and found a file with those he considered 'of interest'. I can't account for two of them. Both were reported missing shortly before we caught him, but no bodies have turned up." Kari says.

Liz curses, "*Faen i helvete!* That means we may have two, unsupervised Apara out there that *bastard* may have turned!"

"I know, and, unfortunately, it gets worse. The last known location for one of them was a psychiatric hospital in central Virginia, as an in-patient. She disappeared from her locked room without a trace."

Liz lets out a lengthy sigh, pinches the bridge of her nose, then looks up and asks, "What was her diagnosis?" She braces herself for more bad news.

"Paranoid Schizophrenia, as well as violent and obsessive behavior. She attacked her boyfriend's mother after he and his mother argued in front of her. She nearly killed her. She said she'd do anything for her boyfriend, including commit murder." Kari explains.

Liz closes her eyes, trying to think. "*Damn!* Get what locaters we have left working on this! Try to track them down ASAP, especially her. If he turned her, she's a particularly high exposure risk, as well as a public menace." Liz taps something into her tablet. "Run a search of police databases for any suspicious killings, in case they're not leaving their feeders alive since we captured Jason! Get me a copy of all her available files: police, medical and psychiatric." Liz pauses, almost afraid to ask her next question. "What about the other woman?"

"She was last screened about 10 years ago when she was 21; average psychic potential, slightly above average IQ, but not particularly strong psychologically. She was easily dominated by others in school. Her local center did not consider Alice a high-priority potential, so they passed on her. But Jason is looking for compatible *women*, and her being easily dominated would certainly suit him fine."

Marc looks alarmed at the news, saying, "If the one is so obsessive, I should get back to Tess. If she knows about Jason's obsession with her, and how Tess beat the crap out of him, she could go looking for her."

"Luckily, no one ever entrusted Jason with the ability to travel to Sanctuary, meaning they shouldn't be able to do that either. Tess should be fine at home, but take precautions when she goes out. She should *not* go out without an escort, and for goodness' sake, *don't* tell her yet! If you get her anxious, she's likely to blow out more than light panels." Liz says and waves him off. Mark ports home to make sure his home and his partner are safe.

Elusive equilibrium

A few days after Marc met with Liz and Kari, Tess and Marc are called in on a planning session about how to increase their numbers. Tess has been moping around the house lately, frustrated over her inability to control her psychic skills, and has been fighting to stave off depression. The morning of the meeting, Marc rolls over in bed and leans close to Tess, whispering in her ear, "Wake up, love. You know we need to go to the office this morning."

"I'm not sure I'm ready. What if I lose control again?" Tess grabs her pillow and drags it over her face.

"You won't. Trust me! *Hell!* Trust yourself!" He pulls the pillow away gently, and leans in to kiss her.

"How can I? Trust myself, that is? I can't even manage basic control! What if I hurt someone?" Her frustration is obvious, both in her words and to Marc's empathic senses.

"You won't, and if you do, we'll heal!" He grins, hoping his sarcasm snaps her out of it.

"What if the person I hurt is one of the human potentials?" Marc picks up on her anxiety like a tangible presence.

"We won't go anywhere near them. We'll port right into the meeting with Liz, Kari, and the others. Wear your necklace if you're worried. I promise, I won't let you lose control! We'll do like we practiced. If you feel yourself losing control, reach out to me, and I'll augment your shields. You can't stay home forever. Besides, everyone wants to see you!" He gently pulls her up into a seated position in the bed beside him.

"*Alright!* But if things get crazy, *don't* blame me!" She says with a huff, and gets up and roots through her closet for something to wear.

"Liz said they have important news, and it sounds like they need your help." He says as she brushes her hair and teeth.

"Oh great! I hope I can do what they need me to!" She walks out of the bathroom dressed in jeans and a blue, button-down blouse. She slips on leather sandals Liz recently brought back from Denmark for her. "I'm as ready as I'll ever be!"

"You forgot something." Marc walks toward her dangling a heavy silver chain with a black, opal-like stone about an inch and a half round, in a simple silver setting.

"I hate that thing! It gives me a headache if I wear it too long!" She says, as he clasps it around her neck, then slides his hands down her back, reaches around her body and holds her lightly.

"Let's take a little trip to the med center after the meeting, and you and Sara can do some re-calibrating. I've noticed you've been avoiding her lately." He mentions casually.

She lets out a huff, then says, "She acts like I'm supposed to be some sort of linchpin for our people; like everything rests on my shoulders, and I feel like I can't live up to that right now!" She lets him pull her into a hug and a light kiss.

"You'll be fine. She said it could take time to get back to a state of equilibrium." He reminds her, leaning down and touching his forehead to hers.

"I know, but I should've reached that stage by now, and I worry I never will." A look of sadness and frustration flashes over her eyes.

"Let it go! Take a deep breath." He commands, as they disappear from the bedroom and reappear in Liz's office. Liz is at her desk, going over something on her tablet with Kari leaning over her shoulder, guiding her through the information. They are the first to arrive.

Liz stands, approaches Tess, and gives her a big hug. "It's good to see you out of the house."

"*Yes*! And just in time! We need your expertise!" Kari says.

"*My* expertise? Not sure what that is, but I'll do what I can!" She forces a smile and tries to look happy.

Kari puts her hand on Tess's arm. "You don't need to try to fool us, especially me. I know you're frustrated and depressed, but I think, if you can focus on something, it may help you get back into the swing of things."

"Yeah, maybe, but you should probably keep me away from humans for now. I don't want to hurt anyone." She ponders a recent night they went out to test her telepathic skills, and she caused three people to have nosebleeds in the middle of a pub in downtown Asheville.

"You can't avoid humans. We're here for their benefit, and I don't think anyone else can do this but you." Liz reassures her.

There's a knock on the door, and three others Tess doesn't know come in, two women and a man, all of different ethnic origins, along with Sara pulling up the rear. Sara gives her a sparkly wink, and Tess hears in her mind *You! Me! After meeting!* Tess rolls her eyes, as the small woman takes her place across from her, staring at her like she's dissecting her aura.

Everyone sits except for Liz. "I think most of you know each other, except for Tess?" She motions toward her. "This is Tess Waterford. She's one of our newest, but don't underestimate her by her relative youth. She's one of the strongest psychic potentials we've seen in a century. Tess, this is Joachim from our Sedona office, Yasamen, originally from the Middle East, but recently assigned to the London office, and Fukumi from Tokyo."

After a round of obligatory handshakes, greetings and nods, Liz continues, "They've been working on some projects you inspired."

"Really?" Tess asks.

Liz touches Tess on her shoulder. "Do you remember your suggestion we look into various genetic databases?"

"Yeah, though everything's been a blur the last few months." Tess is anxious being the focus of everyone's attention and shifts uneasily under their gazes.

"Be that as it may, we implemented your suggestions. We created and ran genetic comparison algorithms of those in the database, both active and inactive, and found a fair number were inactive that shouldn't be.

"Really?" Tess perks up now that she knows she wasn't the only misfiled potential.

"In addition, we did a general search for the genetic tag we all have in common, and found a bunch who are not in the primary or inactive databases." She explains.

"I thought you didn't have the exact sequence?" Tess asks, a touch of enthusiasm sneaking into her voice for the first time in months.

"We didn't, but Sara twisted a few arms and convinced our Benefactors it would be beneficial for us to have that on hand." Liz grins with a nod to Sara.

"Who are these non-database carriers?" Tess asks, curiously.

Liz grins, knowing this will pique her interest. "Do you remember we spoke about the Lost Mission potentials?"

Tess sits up and leans forward, toward Liz. "*Oh*! The ones you didn't have more than genetic prints on? No ID's?" Tess's curiosity grows by the second.

Liz relaxes as she sees Tess's enthusiasm increase. Even before Tess officially joined their ranks, she'd come to see Tess as part of her immediate Apara family, so worries about her. "*Exactly*! Now, we're going through a new algorithm to match those prints with the ones found in the DNA databases with the genetic tags, and hope to have a list of potentials soon. The problem is, no one has followed up on them over the years. Most of them are probably highly gifted. Some of them may even exhibit new or unusual skills when turned because of their specific genetic mutations. The mutations are small and mostly unnoticeable in the first-generation humans affected, but analysis suggests the virus will bring out unusual variations of psychic and other skills. The interesting thing is, over 90% of these potentials are female, as the mutations all occur on the X-chromosome but not the Y. In most males with a mutated X-chromosome, it appears to be recessive, or possibly sex-linked recessive. A few males may manifest when turned, but it will be most common and strongest in female potentials." Liz explains.

"So, what do you need me for? Data searches?" Tess asks.

Kari stares her in the eye, knowing Tess has been feeling worthless since her abilities went wonky. "Tess, you're one of the most gifted, natural, people intuitives I've ever met. What we need from you is to screen these potentials for psychological suitability. You were spot on with Jason and the other potentials we practiced reading recently. At first, we want you to research them online, and in various public and private records we'll give you access to. You'll need to determine if they're alive, in a suitable life situation, psychologically suitable and adaptable, and so on. Social media will be a big part of that. If, and only if, they're stable and adaptable, can we consider contacting them, and bringing them in as potentials. We want to have some idea how they might react *before* we bring them in, in-person. For example, are they likely to accept all of this, freak out, suffer debilitating depression, or go rogue, like Jason? Granted, we won't bring them all in to our company. As you've seen, with people like Li and Andrei, we have people in all walks of life, but we'll be doing the pre-screening and coordinating through a new service we'll offer, job placement among our regional Apara contacts, so this is very important, and no one is more suitable than you to take this on!"

"Isn't that something you can do? I'm still new at all this." Tess stammers out.

"I'll work with you, but your raw skills are far better than mine, and we need you. There are thousands of Lost Mission potentials out there, but doing proper observation and psychological testing will take years. We need your intuitive sense." Kari holds her gaze, hoping Tess will accept she's the best person for the job.

"Tess, you know you can do this. Remember what I told you long ago?" Sara encourages her.

Tess feels dizzy as the memory of Sara telling her how important she'll be rises to the surface. "Yeah... Yes... Sara, I... I do... but what if I screw up?"

"You won't! But we'll work with you, especially Kari and I. We all need you now, more than ever." Sara reassures her with a glint of pride in her eye. Like Sara's favorite Star Wars character, Yoda, she tends to see herself as the Apara equivalent of a Jedi Master, and Tess as her favorite Padawan.

Tess, flabbergasted, can only reply, "I'll do my best." Inside, she feels that spark of confidence burning again, or at least smoldering. Marc gives her arm a slight squeeze and she knows he senses the shift in her emotions.

Kari explains, "So, the first stage is to track down the compatible individuals and research them at a distance. Make notes and recommendations, and then we can go over them together."

"I guess we need to avoid another Jason at all costs." Tess thinks about all the havoc Jason caused, including deaths, and her own personal case of major PTSD.

"Of course! Jason was a mistake made in the haste and chaos of the moment, but we can't ignore the possibility of making such mistakes when trying to replace so many people, especially with people who haven't been properly prepped or followed up on, but without that pool of potentials, we'll fall far short of what we need while we wait for the next generation to come of age." Liz pauses, then continues and sees the 'but what about me' expression on Tess's face. "*You* were the exception, but chances are, even with this influx of genetically compatible potentials, many of them will be psychologically unsuitable or difficult to turn. We're hoping you can help us avoid turning unstable people we might otherwise not catch in our standard screenings."

Tess feels overwhelmed with the job ahead of her, but knows it's important, and notices Sara eyeing her, like she's telling her: 'don't you dare back out of this!' "All I can do is try, Liz, and it's got to be better than staring at the walls at home all day."

"And if you don't feel up to dealing with lots of people, I'll come to you and we can work from your home." Kari gives her a mental hug for being willing to try.

"When can we start?" Tess asks, feeling eager to 'sink her fangs' into a new project.

"I've got a tablet filled with some like you, that were in the inactive files. I want you to track them down in public records and on social media. Sara got her team to create an algorithm that'll extrapolate possible appearances based on the gene prints, but it's still in the beta-testing stage, and will need improvements. First, you can do name searches and comparing appearances. Fukumi and her team are working on an advanced facial recognition program that will interface with the extrapolations. Once we're pretty sure someone is who we're looking for, I'd like you to research them, and get some impressions about their personalities, and any psychological instabilities." Kari explains.

Fukumi, an unusually tall, Japanese woman with jaw length black hair chimes in. "Our facial recognition program will take into consideration age, as well as potential variations in weight, hair color, and other potential cosmetic alterations. It will take the main image generated by the genetic extrapolation program, and use that as a template to check against possible matches. So, if you've tracked down someone in the right age range, with the right name, our system will generate a probability that it's the right person, based on the genetic extrapolation."

"That would be really useful!" Tess remarks enthusiastically.

"So, can I automatically rule out the conspiracy theorists and earlier QAnon crowd?" Tess jokes with a mischievous grin.

Liz rolls her eyes. "We try not to make such generalizations, but considering the make-up of those groups, I doubt they would make good potentials, and would be unlikely to adapt well to being turned, especially the diehard Evangelicals, who would likely view us as demonic." She reminds Tess. "Anyway, I think Sara wants to do a quick follow up on you, and afterwards, Kari should have things ready for you. Kari, will you see to it she has all the programs, utilities, and access she needs on her home computer?"

"Yep. Oh, by the way Tess, our people inside Facebook and other platforms have created moderator-level access profiles for you, like they use when reviewing reported content, so you won't have to worry about privacy settings. You also won't be able to comment or contact using that profile, but if we find people who are good potentials, we'll contact them through appropriate channels." Kari suggests.

"Yeah, I'm not too much of a social butterfly lately, nor do I need another stalker situation." Tess shakes her head.

"Tess, it's not only for your protection, but for ours as well. We must avoid potential exposure risks at all costs, and someone investigating us for looking into them could raise flags where we don't want them!" Liz explains.

Sara stands and walks out, sending a mental *Get a move on it, young lady! I've got a new filter for you to test out!*

Tess rolls her eyes. "Seems I'm being summoned." She nods toward Sara. "I'll swing by when I'm done, Kari, assuming Sara's latest gadget doesn't short circuit and put me in a coma!" She nods toward the others. "Very nice to meet you all. Hopefully, I'll have more time to chat and get to know you another time, but when Sara beckons!"

Yasamen, a Middle Eastern woman with soft brown eyes, and long, black hair down to the middle of her back, smiles at Tess, "Yes, I would enjoy that. You've become well known among those of us who are working with the situation in the Middle East after Jerusalem. It would be nice to get to know you as a person; not just as the 'human', at the time, who made it possible to avoid an even bigger disaster.

"I'm just me. No big mystery there. I just connected some dots." Tess feels awkward over the attention. She follows Sara out and they close the door again.

Liz addresses Marc. "She's really let this get to her, hasn't she?"

The concern is obvious in Marc's eyes. He responds, "Yes, she felt on top of the world after getting the best of Jason, but the complications of the antidote on her abilities are eating away at what confidence she gained. I'm worried about her."

"I know you are. We *all* are. It feels like she's...not *lost* her spark, but it's dimmed to a cooling ember. Hopefully, she'll have some success with this and it will help get her back on track." Liz puts her hand on

Marc's shoulder, then shifts gears, "On with other business. Our other guests have been working on another potential source of transformees. There's a separate, inactive file for those who are alive, but have entered incompatible life situations such as marriage, parenthood, or are beyond 30-35 years old. Joachim took over for Kari on this phase of the project using similar algorithms to track them and see what their current life situations are. Divorce used to be a lot less common, such that once married, that was likely final, but now, there's an increased likelihood some have divorced or otherwise separated, and fewer people are having children. We're still hesitant to consider parents with grown-up, independent children. It would be necessary for significantly older transformees to fake their deaths as their regression to a younger self would be impossible to explain to their families."

"What about adaptability of older individuals? I always heard age was a more psychological adaptation issue, and older potentials are less capable of adapting to the transition?" Yasamen inquires.

"At one time, that may have been true, but more modern society has fewer strictures on age-related social roles. We'll still have to consider it individually, but we may need to consider some older potentials to make up for losses. It's true the de-aging can be hard on some, both physically and psychologically, but Sara suggests keeping them in an induced coma or even putting them into stasis during transformation to avoid any pain associated with greater physical changes." Liz explains.

They continue the meeting, discussing various strategies. In the meantime, Tess and Sara port in to the lobby of Medical. Tess notices it's quieter than when she was here for her unexpected transformation, and when Marc was ready to come home. She looks out the large, floor to ceiling windows in the front of the medical center and notices a new structure resembling a dormitory or apartment complex.

"Sara, that wasn't here the last time. What is it?" Tess wonders.

"Oh, those? We still have long-term recovery patients who need additional care and rehabilitation, or are dealing with post traumatic psychological issues and are not currently up to resuming their duties, so we built separate housing for them until they're ready to go home. That's one reason it's quieter in here, most of the Jerusalem casualties have either gone home, or moved over there where they're cared for by a separate staff. It's new territory for us. I'm hoping we can get some Apara with psychiatric care experience to come aboard here. We've got a serious PTSD and grief problem with some of them." She says, her concern weighing on her.

"I guess you're not used to such mass casualty situations, are you?" Tess walks alongside Sara up the stairs and toward her office. Various members of Sara's staff nod their greetings to Sara as she passes.

"No, mostly, we've dealt with individuals and small groups who were injured in combat zones such as Gaza, or in wars like Vietnam, but never so many as after Jerusalem, and rarely with such extreme damage due to radiation and burns. There were a few back at the end of World War II who got caught in some of the fallout from the bombs dropped on Japan." Sara explains as they arrive at her office. "Have a seat."

"So, what's this new filter? The last experimental one you gave me blew up when I got pissed at Marc for eating the last of my chocolate cheesecake." Tess sits in the guest chair with a thud in Sara's cluttered office.

"Blew up?" Sara tips her chin down and stares at Tess because of her euphemism.

"Ok, so it didn't literally blow up, but it fractured and crazed and my head hurt for two days afterwards." Tess complains.

"Our Benefactors sent some new Cent-opal that's got a higher silication level. It's like working with a 20-amp fuse instead of a 5-amp one. You should be less likely to overload them and blow them to bits. Give me your necklace." She holds out her long-fingered hand.

Tess unclasps the necklace and hands it over to Sara, her mind is rapidly inundated by mental whispers of voices and emotions from some of those still dealing with depression and PTSD nearby.

Sara drops a spherical piece of dark blue, translucent, opal-like gem into Tessa's hand, roughly an inch in diameter. The opalescent, multi-colored points of light dance on the surface of the ball like the lights of a disco ball as she rolls it in her hands. It almost has a warm, yet numbing feel to it. "How's that feel?" Sara inquires.

"Strange. Things just got very mentally quiet. All the telepathic-static has vanished." Tess replies with a quizzical expression as she gives her impressions. "It's almost too quiet!"

"Good! This is a sample I got from them, but we have our techs working on a wearable version we can program and regulate how much to let through. You can take that one home for now, until we get a proper one fitted. I'll need any feedback you can give, both positive and negative." Sara says.

"Thanks. I'm... Sara, I'm really sorry I've been so snappy with you and everyone, it's been difficult, and I'm still having some nightmares about Jason."

"Hm, Marc hasn't mentioned that. Have you told him?" She asks.

"No. He's worried enough as it is." She feels guilty for keeping it from him, but knows she can confide in Sara.

"What were the dreams about?" Sara, knowing Tess's unusually strong abilities, wonders if they were more than PTSD like reactions.

"I keep dreaming he and two women are after me. I'm running from them, but can't port for some reason, and they're catching up with me, making lots of noise and taunting me. Jason's got a look on his face like a predator salivating over juicy prey, bearing his fangs menacingly, like that should scare me!" Tess recalls. "What do you think? Am I going crazy?"

"Probably not. Most likely, it's connected with the PTSD you've been dealing with, though I have heard rumors." Sara is hesitant to tell Tess something that might upset her, but her own intuition says this is something Tess *needs* to know.

"Rumors? Of what?" Tess grows more concerned.

"Rumor is two of the women on Jason's 'wish list' are MIA. Could be nothing, but..." Sara admits

"But he could have turned them and my dreams could be precognitive." Tess face-plants her forehead into her left hand, shaking her head. "*Shit!* Keep me up to date on that, please. I know

Marc and Liz are trying to protect me by not telling me stuff, so I'm counting on you to be straight with me." She pleads.

"Will do Tess, as I always have." Sara puts her hand on Tess's right shoulder. "I expect that to be a two-way street! But Tess, you need to tell Marc as well, just in case they are precognitive warnings, especially if Jason was in them and not in confinement." She walks Tess out of her office and gives her a hug.

Tess sighs, but says, "All right! I'll try to work it in tonight! I don't want him worrying any more than he already does." Tess ports back to the office before Sara can get on her case even more, and heads down the hall from her and Marc's office to see Kari. She has the opal ball in her pocket, and absentmindedly moves it around with her fingertips, noticing how, where she usually felt energetic vibrations from some stones and crystals, it was almost like touching a void where her fingers touched the stone, like it absorbed any such energy, or made it impossible for her to feel it. Her mind is unusually unencumbered by the usual buzz of mental activity around her, and for the first time in a long time, she notices things like her footsteps and other physical sounds becoming prominent over the usual mental cacophony around her. Part of her is happy for the peace and quiet, but it's disconcerting, like she's gone mentally deaf.

As Tess continues down the hall, a human brushes against her as they walk the other way, but Tess hears nothing, where usually, she would have gotten the contents of the person's public mind, and sometimes, even deeper, private, or unconscious thoughts, telepathically. Even at home, she picks up more than she lets on from Marc. She knows he's worried about her and he, Liz, and others have been trying not to overwhelm her with what's been going on since Jason was captured. Unfortunately, Tess feels even worse about herself because she thinks others are losing confidence in her.

Getting to work

Kari's waiting in her office off the lobby. Like Liz's office, there are Scandinavian paintings and knickknacks decorating the room. Standard furnishings in most of the larger offices include a sofa, a low table and additional office chairs for meetings. Her desk is organized to perfection, quite the opposite of Tess's space. She's organizing some additional folders with information that's scattered on the table into a neat, alphabetic pile. She has a fully loaded tablet with all the information they have about the 'inactives' they've discovered are likely alive. Tess saunters in without knocking and plops down on the small sofa along the wall.

"So, what's the mission 'Captain Kari'?" She says sarcastically, kicking off her shoes under the table.

Kari gives her a sidelong glance. "Well, it's like we told you in the meeting, we've got some of the other potentials identified. I've got a list of about 75 'inactives' who were likely misfiled, and any preliminary info we have on them. Your job is to find them, and evaluate anything you can find on them online. You'll have full social media access, public records, IRS or other tax and government records, births, deaths, marriages, and school records; you'll even be able to access hospital and medical records. If you can't get access to something you need to review, call me, and I'll see what I can do. Any foreign language files will automatically translate to English for you."

"Sounds like a big job." Tess is anxious about whether she can manage it.

"No, the big job is going to be the Lost Mission potentials. The inactive ones are limited to fewer than 100 so far, and most of them have some preliminary pre-conditioning and some have full conditioning, but they need to be followed up and evaluated. Many may not be viable due to life situations or unforeseen changes in them psychologically. The LMs are gene coded, but many likely weren't prepared beyond a feeling they have something important to do in life. Sara also said to mention the mutations, while largely not active or obvious among the humans, could increase the risk of some psychological and learning issues, so you'll have to watch for that. In addition, there are thousands of Lost Mission potentials in the database, and we need to track down and evaluate as many as we can." Kari explains.

Tess sinks into the sofa as she sighs, saying "Okay, *that's* a lot! What psychological issues am I looking for? Things like Schizophrenia or what? And learning issues?" Tess is getting more excited as her interest is piqued.

Kari picks up a mug of tea, takes a sip and jumps into an explanation, since Tess is showing some enthusiasm. "Well, the learning issues could include variations on ADHD, autistic spectrum disorders, sound processing disorders, and dyslexia, for example. As to the psychological, we're not sure, but some of the genetic sequences analyzed are likely to affect neurotransmitter levels and receptors; whether they impair them or enhance them is another matter, but there could be issues with bipolar disorder, depression, mania, possibly even some with more serious disorders such as schizophrenia." Kari puts her half empty mug down on a coaster on the table. "Some disorders may be manageable, such as depression; something you're all too familiar with." She gives her a knowing stare. "And some things may be corrected when turned, such as some chemical or hormonal imbalances, but some issues may not, especially if they have long term, behavioral issues, such as anger management, violent behavior, sociopathic tendencies, and similar issues which could lead to the abuse of our abilities."

"Okay, I'll do what I can, but I'm no psychologist! I'm going on gut reactions." Tess says.

"I know, but in the centuries I've worked with other people readers, you're the best raw talent I've ever seen!" Kari says. "I'm trying to get a list thrown together of people with backgrounds in psychology and human behavior you can consult with, but some of the ones who were our best people in those fields, were either injured or died in Jerusalem, or are slammed helping out at Medical with all the PTSD and other issues."

"Yeah, I was pretty good at it, but now? I'm too distracted by mental chatter to focus half the time! I'm losing my edge and I'm not sure I'll ever get it back!" Tess balls up a random bit of paper she has in frustration.

Kari tilts her head to one side as she focuses on and reads Tess's mental state. She's frustrated because she can barely get a hint of what is going on in her head or with her mood, as though Tess has become more two-dimensional to her. "Tess, speaking of reading people, now don't take this the wrong way, but I'm having a hell of a time reading you. Any idea why?"

"I'm not trying to hide anything, if that's what you're worried about? It's probably this." She fishes the blue opalescent marble out of her pocket. "Sarah's having me test out a raw, unmodulated piece of the latest Cent-opal. I have to admit, it was nice to walk down the hallway and not be bombarded by incessant mental chatter and static from everyone, but I didn't think about it preventing others from being able to read me as well!" Tess says as she rolls the marble on the coffee table in front of her absentmindedly.

"May I see it?" Kari extends her open palm, and Tess gently tosses it to her. "Interesting. It almost has a calming effect as well. I've never seen one outside of a wearable unit before."

"Yeah, tech is still working on that. This is a raw piece they shaped and polished. Sara asked me to test it out and give her feedback. That's probably why it works that way, no controls; it dampens any unconscious, and some conscious psychic abilities. I'll have to let her know." Tess pops out her tablet, opens her notes app, and writes her observations while they're fresh in her mind.

Kari picks up a box from under the table and gently stacks the folders in it, putting the tablet on top, and what looks like a USB thumb drive in with it. "Get started with these. Basically, confirm identities, life status and evaluate. That's it for now! I should have a preliminary list for genetic matches to names from the LM database soon, but get your feet wet with these. You'll need the appearance models and eventually, the facial recognition interface for the LM potentials. Until then, here!" Kari hands her the box. "There's a flash drive with security bypass algorithms that will let you bypass firewalls and privacy settings. Plug it into the USB port on your computer and it'll use those as needed. I'll be by tomorrow to install the more advanced apps."

"Alright! I'll go dump this in our office until Marc's ready to head out. I'm gonna catch up with Amy and a few others. It's been a while since I've seen them face-to-face! Telepathy, email, chat, and zoom don't always cut it!" She hefts the box and leaves.

Tess walks down the hall, turns a corner, and literally runs into a petite Asian woman with glasses, and the contents of her box scatters everywhere.

"Oh! I'm *so* sorry, ma'am! My mind was elsewhere! Let me help you with all that!" The young woman says nervously. Tess senses her anxiety, and the woman doesn't feel like a typical, adaptable potential. She feels more like the type who would scream if someone quietly says "Boo!"

"It's alright, you weren't the only one distracted!" Tess smiles reassuringly at her. They both reach for the flash drive and accidentally brush fingertips. Immediate and overwhelming anxiety hits Tess, and she senses amorphous fear she can't quite makes sense of coming from the woman. The woman grabs the rest of the folders, and a lot of loose papers that have fallen out, and stuffs them in the box. She stands, adjusting her glasses, which were sliding down her nose from bending over. "Again! Sorry, ma'am!" She says and rushes off, leaving Tess a little stunned and confused. Tess picks up the tablet and makes sure it still works. She wonders why she had such a strong reaction to this young human woman. Understanding hits her when she reaches into her pocket and realizes she left the opal marble with Kari.

"Well, guess I have two reasons to go back and bother Kari!" She says under her breath, as she looks at the mish-mosh of papers and folders. She turns around and heads back. Kari's at the reception desk talking to a visitor from one of the local charities they work with. Tess paths to her, **When you've got a sec, I need your help.** She sends a mental image of the mess in her box. She goes into the side office and sorts what she can. About 10 minutes later, Kari comes in.

"What *did* you do?" Kari snaps, annoyed.

"I didn't do anything other than collide with a new gal, Asian woman, human, coming around a corner, and splat! Everything went everywhere!!" Tess takes Kari's question too personally.

Kari leaves through the pages in one pile and pulls out three that don't belong. "Let's see if we can't get these sorted and back in order."

"Kari, *that* woman, who is she? Is she a potential?" She sends a mental image of the woman.

"*That's* Annie Deng, transfer from the Hendersonville office. As to potential, yes, and no..." Kari doesn't elaborate further, but goes back to sorting papers, including turning them all in the same direction.

"Yes, and no? What the heck does that mean? The reason I'm asking is I forgot my little gem there and when I touched her, I got a rush of anxiety and fear from her. She's quite nervous. Does she know what we are or something?" Tess asks.

Kari sits, still straightening out papers in folders. Tess resumes her place on the sofa, realizing she has no idea what papers belong where and it's best to let Kari do it. "You and she have something in common, Jason. Jason considered her an easy target. He fed on her repeatedly, but kept her aware to feed off her pain and fear as well, then blocked the memories, unblocking them next time he fed. She was the one Steve mentioned Jason fed from, but it was only after Steve recovered, we got the entire story." Kari rolls her eyes. "We're still evaluating how much psychological damage he did and whether she can still be turned or if his abuse made her unacceptable."

"Ah, does she know or not?" Tess asks.

Kari sorts papers into separate piles on the table, but pauses to look Tess in the eye, "Not consciously. Jason compartmentalized the knowledge in a mental box. Every time he went after her, he'd 'open the box' and..." Kari shrugs.

"That's *damn* well torture! He's such a sadistic bastard!" Tess hands her a few loose papers from the bottom of the box for Kari to put where they belong.

"No *kidding!* It was shortly before he took off. Steve reprimanded him and had her memory examined and properly blocked. She transferred here after Jason went after you so we could evaluate the damages, but things have been so hectic since, we haven't had much time to do it!"

"Well, something's up with her. She's calm and polite on the surface, but she's a freaking ball of nerves inside. I didn't get anything specific, only amorphous feelings of anxiety and being afraid of something. I'm not even sure she knows what." Tess says.

"I'll be sure to check on her. She may be having some leakage from the block. Thanks for letting me know. See! You're still able to do this!" Kari flashes her a knowing grin, and continues to sort the last of the papers into piles, then puts them back into their folders.

"Only because I forgot *that* here." Tess points to the opal sphere. "Kari! If I have to depend on something to control my abilities, it's going to be easy to miss stuff!" She says in a huff.

"Then, get it under control! I'm pretty sure half of your control issue is a loss of confidence. You handled Jason under the worst of circumstances, and now you've come down from your psychological high. Is it hard to control such strong abilities? *Yes!* But you're capable of doing so! If anyone here can, I'm sure *you* can." She puts her hand on Tess's.

"Maybe if everyone would stop treating me like a fragile flower! You all clearly don't believe I can do it. Marc and Liz keep talking about what they should and shouldn't tell me. He doesn't know I know, but even with my filter on, I was picking up on his mind without trying. If Marc can't believe in me, how can I?" Tess's mood is oscillating between depression and irate anger.

Some books on a nearby wall shelf suddenly slide from vertical to horizontal on the shelf and a stone bookend slips off. Tess instinctively reaches out and catches it telekinetically, gently lowering it to the floor. "See! If it weren't for that sphere there, I'd probably have thrown those books across the room!"

"Stop that! You're feeling sorry for yourself, again! *Hey*! I've got an idea! After you left earlier, I asked Liz and the meeting is likely to go on for a while. How about you and I take a break and go get some lunch?" Kari suggests, trying to distract Tess from her self-pitying tendencies.

"I don't know. I don't go out much these days." Tess admits.

"All the more reason to do so. Stick that back in your pocket and you should be fine." Kari says, pointing at the sphere. "Besides, Liz and I were supposed to go out for lunch, and now she's stuck in the meeting, and you're stuck waiting for Marc. Come on! I hear 12 Bones is having an all you can eat barbeque buffet special for their anniversary." She knows Tess has a weakness for their food, especially the jalapeno cheese grits and ribs.

"Okay! *Twist* my arm! But I need you to spot me. If I show any signs of losing control..." Tess looks at her anxiously.

"I'll get you out of there." Kari grins.

The two women port into a dark corner outside a large, brick building, and walk to 12 Bones, one of Asheville's better known Barbecue restaurants. They get in line, which stretches about 10 people long outside the building, and at least as long inside. They join the queue, pay for the special buffet, and get their food, ranging from pulled chicken and pork, to blueberry chipotle ribs. Tess indulges in one of their specialty craft beers, even though the alcohol has no effect on her, and the two women find a table outside. They sit, eat, and talk, though they must limit their discussions to more mundane subjects, as there are other tables full of humans nearby. Tess relaxes and is enjoying herself, but when they're almost finished with their plates and are considering going back for seconds, they both get urgent alerts. An alarm goes off on Tess's phone, followed by a near desperate telepathic shout from Marc, breaking through the dampening field of the Cent-opal.

TESS! WHERE THE HELL ARE YOU? Marc paths.

Calm down! I'm out with Kari having lunch at 12 Bones! What's up? Tess paths, focusing hard to overcome the dampening effect of the opal. She's more than a tad annoyed, thinking he can't even trust her to go out without him.

Tess is about to snap back at Marc when she sees the look on Kari's face as she takes a couple of hurried bites to finish and puts her napkin on the table with a 'we need to go look' expression.

What is it? Kari looks like she's about to freak out. Tess paths.

Tess, I need you two back here NOW! I don't want to upset you, but Jason's gone! Marc paths, trying to maintain some modicum of calm so Tess won't lose it.

WHAT? She screams mentally. Kari grabs her by the arm and the two of them go behind another building and port before Tess can get a reply. They are back in the main office, in front of Marc, who has an expression of extreme relief.

"Tess, I was so afraid you'd been taken!" Marc comes over and embraces her, making her squirm.

"No, we went to lunch since you all would be a while. How the *hell* did he escape? I thought they were keeping him knocked out and neutralized?" Her anxiety level and heart rate rise rapidly.

"He was. *He* didn't escape by himself. He was rescued." Marc says, shaking his head.

"Let me guess, two women, both unregistered transformees; one with very short blonde hair, and one with curly, dark, red hair halfway down her back?" Tess gives him a look implying he better be straight with her, or else!

"Yes, but how did you know? We just got the surveillance video in." Marc sounds confused.

"I've been dreaming about them. Well, them, and Jason, chasing me and I'm unable to port or get away, like I've been neutralized again."

32

"*Merde!* Why the hell didn't you tell me about this?" He demands.

"Because I'm *tired* of you questioning my sanity and stability, or whatever the term is in your mind!" She sits abruptly in a nearby chair.

"You've been reading me? I would have thought I'd notice." Mark asks, worried.

"Get over it! I've been picking up on you for a while! Even with the filter on. You and Liz constantly trying not to overburden me with things. Trying to keep me calm, except I knew about them, anyway! It's like I was sitting at a dinner table with you and Liz on each end, talking over me and thinking I wouldn't hear! I couldn't turn it off!"

Mark squats down in front of Tess to make eye-to-eye contact instead of looming over her. "Okay, yes, we didn't want to upset you more than necessary. We did it out of consideration, not distrust."

"Well, it felt like you two thought I couldn't handle it!" Tess mutters.

"We've got all the confidence in the world in you, but you went through a major ordeal, and then the new abilities on top of it! You may not be human anymore, but you're still subject to human psychological reactions. You've been showing stress and trauma-related symptoms since his first attack on you in the copy room, and Jason taking you exacerbated them, especially after finding out he was the one who tried to *kill* you on the Parkway! Not to mention the effect of the whole Jerusalem mess. We can talk about this more when we get home, but right now, we need to grab your things and get you home." He nods to Kari, who runs into her office and grabs the re-sorted box for Tess and hands it to her.

"Yeah, why's that?" Overtones of annoyance radiate from Tess.

"Because, as far as we know, Jason never learned how to get to Sanctuary, and we've blocked him from all the physical portals. Once he recovers from the neutralizer, he may come after you again."

Tess blanches at the thought. She sighs deeply, takes a couple of slow, deep breaths, and when she speaks, her tone is more moderated. "Okay, considering my dream, it may be best to go where he can't. I just... well..." She trails off.

"What?" He sits in the chair next to her and brushes hair out of her face.

"I'm tired of being locked away for either my or other people's good, that's all. I thought being more powerful would be a good thing; that it would make me feel safer, but it made things worse." She pouts.

Mark tips her chin up to look her in the eye. "No one thinks you're dangerous. You merely need time to regain your equilibrium. Unfortunately, Jason now complicates that; because you're having trouble controlling your abilities, he could get the upper hand if they fail you when you need them most, and because of the PTSD, there's a chance he could make it even harder for you to keep control, like in the restaurant." He leans in and gives her a light kiss, then stands and pulls her up out of the chair. He puts one arm around her, and his other hand on the edge of the box, and they vanish.

"Wasn't that rather risky? Porting out of the lobby? What if a potential had seen?" She asks.

"Don't worry, they're all in the lunch room right now. Emergency meeting. Why don't you go get some rest? You should be safe here, and I've got to get back." He says.

"Keep me posted." She watches as he vanishes. She realizes she should put the opal gem-ball aside for now, so she can hear any calls from Marc, or so she will feel 'them' coming if they get into Sanctuary. She walks over to a tall bookshelf in the living room filled with some knick-knacks and trinkets and finds a small, lead-pewter box that belonged to her grandmother, and puts the marble in there. She feels the effects of it lessening as soon as she closes the box. She puts it up on the mantle, above and to the left of the stone fireplace in the living room, and its effects lessen gradually as she walks away from it.

Do you dream what I dream?

Tess picks up the box Kari gave her and puts it on her computer desk in the living room. She unpacks it, and sits at the computer to check her email and Facebook. On a whim, she looks up Annie Deng, but her page is set to private. She pulls the flash drive out of the box and plugs it in. After a minute, the page refreshes and she can view it from an admin profile. Annie doesn't have a lot of friends in her friends list. Tess scrolls down past some innocuous posts of cat videos and Star Trek memes and finds a post about her nightmares.

> **I've been having a lot of bad dreams lately. Not sure what's up. Someone's stalking me in them, and I never quite see their faces. It's like it's blurred out so I can't recognize them. They're shouting and chasing me. Wish I could find a way to stop these nightmares. I guess they mean something, but I don't know what.**

There are a couple of comments from friends, but nothing other than a "hope you figure them out" and "I hate nightmares!" type comments.

As Tess continues to scroll down her page, a new post pops up at the top. She scrolls up and sees Annie's posted from her phone.

> **Going home early today. They called us all in to a meeting in the lunchroom. A carbon monoxide monitor somewhere went off and they had to send us all home until it could be checked over by experts! They said to plan to come in tomorrow, but in the meantime, we get half a day off with pay! So, I'm not complaining! Maybe I can catch up on some sleep tonight!**

Tess says aloud, "Interesting excuse! Carbon monoxide! I'll admit Jason is noxious and full of hot air!"

As she sits there, her Facebook chat pops up, and it's Marc. "Thought you were going to get some rest?"

"I am. I was checking stuff before I do and got distracted." She says, annoyed he's checking up on her.

"With what? Not trying to track Jason by yourself, I hope!" He types.

"Hell no! I'm not that crazy! I ran into one of the newbies today and got a vibe off her, so was checking her Facebook to see if I could figure out what I picked up." She types.

"You mean Annie Deng? Kari told me. We've got people on watch at her place in case he returns to old habits. Now, go rest, and I'll yell if there's anything." He insists.

"YES SIR!" She types, with an emoticon with its tongue sticking out.

She logs off and plops down on the overstuffed sofa with lion foot legs, and forces herself to sleep, but tosses and turns trying to get comfortable. After a while, she dreams. She sees the two women and Jason. He's awake, but still neutralized. She doesn't recognize the place, so it's not the fallout shelter this time. She can sense he's pissed off and frustrated because his abilities are still stunted. One of the woman hands him a tablet, and he flips through digital pages. Occasionally, he says something to the women and one of them makes notes on her phone. In her mind, she sees women's faces flash by, but too quickly to recognize, though she thinks some look familiar. Before she can put names to faces, she awakens to a kiss on her forehead. Marc's home again.

"Any news?" She sits up slowly, blinking as the afternoon sun flashes through the window.

"We've identified the women. Alice Thompson and Philipa Ball. They've been on the missing person's list for a few weeks, so he apparently turned them a while back." Marc believes it's best not to mention Philipa was taken from a psychiatric facility; the exhaustion in his eyes is obvious, and he inquires, "Are you okay? You seem restless."

"Just dreaming." She sighs.

"Any more with them in it?" He asks.

"Yeah, but I lost most of it when you woke me up." She gives him an annoyed glance.

"Sorry, didn't know! Have you eaten?" He heads toward their kitchen.

"Yeah, remember, Kari and I went to 12 Bones. That should hold me for a while, and you know I fed last night, here, so I wouldn't be tempted when we went in to work today." She pauses, then asks, "How long will he remain neutralized?"

"Probably a couple more days, according to Sara. By the way, she wants to know if you have any feedback on that raw filter." He inquires.

"Yeah, I've made a few notes. I'll holler her way tomorrow. I put it aside for now in the little lead box up on the mantle since there are no controls on it. I didn't want to be psychically blind in case Jason or the others find their way here." She explains. "I guess I'm stuck here until further notice, or as long as he's on the loose?"

Marc sits next to her on the sofa, and puts down a tray of various cured meats, cubes of cheese, and some of her favorite mini-quiche snacks he'd made earlier in the week. "You know it's for the best. He'll be even more pissed at you than before, and I doubt he'll fall for something similar next time." He pats and rubs her leg.

"I feel helpless. I'm stuck here because of him and because I can't control my *fucking* abilities! I feel *useless*!" She says, and a picture on the wall rattles and tilts off balance. "*AHHHHRRRRG!*" She groans in frustration.

"You'll get it, but you have to give yourself time, *love*." He holds up one of the mini-quiche snacks to her face and tempts her until she opens her mouth and eats it.

"I'm frustrated! If you believe Sara, I'm supposed to have some important role in the future, but I can't even manage my own, *damn* abilities! How am I going to live up to it all?" She asks.

"Did you ever consider you've already played an important role?" He suggests.

"Yeah! If it weren't for me, a lot more than Jerusalem would have gone *boom*!" She repeats what she's been told over, and over again, waving her hands animatedly. "However, if I've already fulfilled my so-called destiny, now that I'm 'indefinitely lived'," She repeats his own term for being virtually immortal with a twisted smile. "what the hell am I supposed to do with the rest of my very long life?"

Marc smiles. "You can begin by taking a break and not worrying about it for a couple of hours." He pulls her closer to him on the sofa, and turns on the TV. He puts one of Tess's favorite movies on and makes her watch it, hoping it will help her de-stress. When it's over, he yawns, stands, and holds a hand out to her. "I don't know about you, *love*, but I'm exhausted. I'm going to bed. Join me?" He grins at her and looks her up and down suggestively.

She smiles subtly and then chuckles. "No offence, but I'm gonna pass. I slept a couple of hours waiting for you to get home, and my mood isn't exactly conducive to other bedroom activities. I want to get going on what Kari gave me to do. It might distract me." She says.

"Are you sure you don't want to be distracted in other ways?" He tries again to tempt her.

"I'm sure, but I'll give you a rain check!" She tilts her head and gives him a soft grin.

"I'll hold you to that!" He says, and heads upstairs and off to bed.

Tess goes to the kitchen for something to drink and some of those mini quiches. Marc reheated extra and left them on a plate for her, 'just in case'. She comes back, pulls out the tablet and syncs the files with the desktop computer, then pulls out the stack of folders and makes room for them by clearing away the clutter she normally has on her desk. Once it finishes syncing, she opens the database on her computer, where she can see everything on the big screen, and puts away the tablet.

"Let's see, guess I'll start at the beginning." She says aloud and goes through each subject, one by one, confirming the person's alive and healthy, looks at their life status in terms of marriage, family, medical, and psychiatric history, when available. She looks at the person's social media, job evaluations, school records, and more and ranks them on a scale from one to ten in terms of suitability for turning. Everything will depend on observation in the end, and whether they are psychically and psychologically viable.

She goes into a hyper-focus and works until about 4 am. Her eyes blur and she can't focus. She's had enough, so puts everything into a neat pile. She spies Mabel looking like she wants to jump up and make a bed out of her folders and says, "Oh! *No*, you don't, Mabel! These are *NOT* yours! And no chewing on the papers either!" She puts the folders up above some books on a shelf, hoping it might keep them safe from Mabel, the paper piranha. She puts them up, shuts down the computer and gives Mabel a little attention and dinner, hoping she'll forget about the papers. She ports to the bedroom and slips under the quilt with Marc as quietly as she can, but not quietly enough.

"*Finally* decided to join me?" He says, lethargically yawning.

"Yeah, I got about a third of them done. Kari said she should have a preliminary identity list from the Lost Mission files soon, so I want to get as much done as possible on this project." She finds his yawn contagious and yawns as well.

Marc pulls her against him and puts an arm around her. "Anything interesting?"

"A few good potentials, but mostly average types, and some have families or are otherwise not suitable. Kari gave me this as a dry run for the real job, the Lost Mission files. Those will be much harder. At least, these 'misplaced' potentials have some pre-conditioning and files about their likely potentials and stability. The Lost Mission potentials are unknowns." She settles and rests her head on his chest.

She drifts off to sleep, and soon dreams. She's in what looks like an abandoned building, with wallpaper peeling off the walls, and some cracked glass panes in the windows. The carpet is stained, and the only lights are from plug-in lamps. Jason's there, sitting at a laptop, reviewing Facebook profiles of women. She can't see the details well enough to see faces or names. One of the women comes up to him, giving off anxious vibes and tells Jason something. He gets angry and throws a mug across the room, smashing it into a million pieces, and puts a dent in the plaster-board wall where it hits. He stands and paces. Suddenly, the woman turns and walks toward Tess, passing through her. *Damn! It's not a dream! I'm out of body again!* Upon realizing that, she's yanked back into her own body, and wakes with a start.

She reaches over and shakes Marc's shoulder. "Marc, *Marc!* Wake up, please! It's important."

"Wh...what is it, Tess?" He opens his eyes slowly, yawning.

"They *aren't* dreams!"

"What's not?" He yawns again and focuses on her.

"What I *thought* were dreams about *Jason* and company were not dreams! At least not all of them! They're real time, out-of-body observations." Tess explains.

Marc props himself up on one elbow. "Are you sure? Can you tell where they are?" He realizes this could be the break they need if she can tell them where Jason and the two women are. He gently rubs her arm to calm her.

"I couldn't tell. When I finally realized I was out of body, I snapped back, and woke up. I don't remember 'travelling' there either, just seeing them. I think they're in some old house or apartment; rundown, and he's looking for others to turn, 'strength in numbers' is the thought that comes to mind. This time he was upset. Let me try something." She closes her eyes and replays things before Jason got angry. "He was upset when one of the women told him something. I think the other woman was telling him something about 'protected'. Something, no, someone is protected and will be hard to get to." She stares off at nothing.

"We have several potentials under guard; they don't know it, but we have people keeping an eye on them, just in case." He explains.

"Like Annie Deng?" She asks.

"Yes, she's one of them." He admits, sitting up.

Tess focuses. "Is it possible she's remembering some of what Jason did to her? I only got flashes of things, but it could fit with her remembering."

He pats her on the leg. "No one at work, except you, has picked up even a flicker of memory from her, but you're a lot more sensitive than most. Perhaps it's in her unconscious memory?"

"Could be. I'd check her out again, but I'm stuck here." She reminds him.

Marc knows she's safer at home, in Sanctuary, but also knows Tess won't let this go without a fight. "Maybe we can arrange something, if we port straight into the office and I don't leave your side."

Tess lets out a sigh and her shoulders relax. "Thank you! I'd like to do that today. I think he's still neutralized, so we should do this before he can port."

"*Deal*! Now get some sleep so you can be more in control of your abilities!" He says, gathering her close to him. "I want you to fill Liz and Kari in on all of this! No omissions, got it?" He reaches behind her and pulls the patchwork quilt back over them, then curls one arm protectively around her, so he'll know if she tries to get up and go do something on her own.

In the morning, Tess gets up and finds something comfortable to wear; black jeans and a Weird Al, concert T-shirt she recently found in her storage boxes. She grabs the opal sphere and the box and sticks it in a small purse. Marc comes up behind her, reaching around her, and pulls her close. "Ready?"

"As ready as I'll ever be." She says.

They port into their office, and Liz comes running through the door a minute later. "*Tess*! What the *Hell* are you doing here?! You're supposed to stay put at home!"

"Relax, I'm not going to leave her side, but we needed to come in so she could get a read on someone." Marc explains.

Liz stands there, arms crossed, and says, "A read on whom?"

"Annie Deng. I had a run in with her, literally, and when I touched her, was overwhelmed with a flood of emotionally charged images, and I think Jason was in them." Tess explains.

"Kari mentioned your collision. Did she explain to you what he did to her?" Liz asks, one eyebrow raised.

"Yes, he's one *sadistic asshole!* I need to try to get a better read on her, one that's not so jumbled." She explains.

"They're all coming in after lunch. We're issuing new IDs, with trackers in them, and we'll be implanting them with trackers as well, though they won't be aware of that part." Liz grins.

"Jason plans to turn more women." Tess says, matter of fact.

"We suspect that, yes." She sits on the arm of Marc's office sofa, thinking Tess was asking *if* he is planning to turn more women.

"*No,* Liz! No suspicions, he *is* planning to do so. I thought I was dreaming about him and the women, but I think I was out-of-body again. I saw them looking over profiles, and one woman told him something about them being protected, and he got *angry.*" She explains.

"If true, we may need to speed up plans for some of them. We can't guard everyone all the time. What do you need in order to read Annie?" She asks.

"Why don't I help with the implants. If she'll be unconscious, perhaps I can read her unnoticed." Tess suggests.

"Okay, Sara will be doing them. But I want Marc to stay with you, both in case Jason gets past our security and, in case you lose control." Liz says.

After lunch, the few human employees trickle in for their new security passes. They're diverted into the side office where Tess, Marc, Kari, and Sara are. About 1:18, Annie Deng shows up. Sara slips into her mind and holds her unaware while she injects a micro-tracker into her back, near the vertebrae in her neck. "Alright Tess, I've done my part." Sara nods to her it's her turn.

Tess puts the opal sphere back in the box and puts it across the room. She touches Annie's cheek gently. After a minute of making facial contortions while she focuses, she gets something. "She's been dreaming of Jason coming after her. She doesn't remember consciously *yet.* But the dreams are increasing her anxiety level. She had one last night. She was running down an alley and runs into a dead end, and turns around and Jason's there, gloating, playing with her. She was doing well while he was locked up, but the dreams came back right before he got out. Kari, any idea where her psychic strengths lie?" Tess inquires.

"We think she's got some kind of precognitive ability, possibly some stronger healing potential, but with Jason, there may be an unconscious link between them as well. He could snap her in and out of awareness whenever he fed on her." Kari looks angry.

"Well, that would make sense then. Her unconscious mind is aware he's loose and warning her, but the barriers you put in her mind are keeping the warnings in her subconscious as forgotten dreams." Tess frowns.

Tess sits back, away from Annie, and gets an unfocused look. "*Damn* it! That's what I saw. Annie's one of the profiles he was looking at. She's definitely on his radar. Has she been paired up with anyone for turning?" Tess looks up at Kari, questioningly.

"No, after her encounters with Jason, we've been observing and evaluating her to see if she can be turned, but haven't been able to make a final decision yet. I could use your help there!" Kari gives her a stare.

"Well, if she's on Jason's list..." Tess trails off, looking sideways at Annie. "I think, eventually, she'll be ok if turned, but she'll have to remember about Jason. Leaving that in her subconscious will cause all sorts of trouble."

Liz comes in, having heard the conversation from outside the office. "I may have to do it myself. I've turned many over the years, but we'll have to find her a partner of some kind eventually. In the meantime, I'd suggest we help her through this. Sara, send her on her way to work. We'll work on a solution together." Liz suggests, glancing at the others.

They send Annie back to her cubical, unaware of anything that's happened. Liz heads back to her office, but Tess lightly grabs her by the arm before she can leave the room. "Liz, I don't think you should turn her."

"I may have to. We don't have anyone paired up with her yet. Hell, we haven't even begun because she may be too *damaged.*" Liz says.

"I get she may be damaged, but if she's out there on her own, he's going to turn her one way or another, and then she'll really be damaged. I really don't think *you* should do it, however." Tess shakes her head.

"Yes, I know, that's why I may have to! I don't want to randomly pair her up with someone. She won't react much better to some stranger than she has Jason." Liz replies.

"It's not that. She needs to feel safe and protected, and you won't be able to do that. You have too much on your plate to have her back 24/7, and even if she's turned and Jason loses interest, she'll still be dealing with PTSD symptoms, and she needs someone to be there for her full time, like Marc is for me, until she can work through it all; someone who can help her heal psychologically. She'll need to remember it all, or it'll eat away at her from the inside out." Tess firmly insists.

Kari chimes in, "Tess, where are you getting all this from?"

"I don't know, I just know it! Maybe from reading her? It just fits!" Tess turns to face Kari.

"Told you, you're the best!" Kari says with a grin.

"We're still dealing with the fact no one's lined up for her and it takes time for people to find each other and form natural bonds! I don't like randomly assigning someone." Liz sits on the edge of Kari's office desk with an exasperated expression.

Kari sits beside Liz, facing Tess. "Tess, maybe you can help?"

Tess looks at her, startled. "What can I do?"

"Your people intuition, get an impression of what she needs, and maybe we can look for it. We've been transferring people in and out of centers to match potentials and Apara up. We've gotten several new people in but can also look for someone with the traits you think she might need in a partner." Kari suggests.

"Maybe, but I've never done anything like that. Perhaps if I go talk to her, I can get a better feel for her." Tess suggests.

"Not without me!" Marc worries about Jason grabbing her.

"Marc, really? With everyone here? Isn't this place shielded?" Tess is annoyed at her overprotective partner, even though she knows she's being illogical.

"Yes, it is, but I don't want to risk him getting to you again." Marc admits.

"I'll be fine around here. I may not *need* to talk to her, just be nearby and get a "feel" for her personality. I wasn't looking at that before. I was looking at her dreams and whether she knew anything consciously." Tess says.

Liz chimes in. "Go on, Tess, I'll keep Marc busy." She gives her a wink, and Tess heads on over to Annie Deng's department. She walks in and sees a familiar face acting as department supervisor today. Her old friend, Amy, is in charge, so she makes an excuse to socialize with her.

"Amy!" She stretches her arms out for a hug.

"*Wow*, girl! You've been AWOL a while! How're you doin'? Heard you put my self-defense training to good use!" Amy smirks and motions for Tess to sit with her at her desk.

"Yeah, knocked him clear across the room!" She plops down in the proffered chair.

Amy switches modes and paths to Tess, *So, how're you holding up? Hear he escaped? Think he'll come after you again?*

It's possible. If I could only get control of my abilities, I probably wouldn't have to worry about him.

You will! It takes time. You should see me trying to get my precog skills under control. Not that I'm allowed to play the lotto anymore, but I've been practicing by predicting the winning numbers. Amy paths with overtones of exasperation.

And how's that going? Tess inquires.

Well, I get the numbers, but not for the right week! I might get them for two or three drawings ahead, but not the week I'm aiming for! It's so frustrating! It was Liz's suggestion, but it's gonna make me crazy! She mentally laughs and shakes her head.

Hey! I've been meaning to ask; have you heard anything from Charlie lately? Tess gently puts her hand on Amy's arm and looks her in the eye.

Not much. We email occasionally, but girl, that's a dead end and ya know it! Now that I'm Apara, and he's human. I just haven't figured out how to break things off permanently with him yet. Amy sighs.

He's over in Israel, isn't he? Tess asks.

Yeah! He took off over there as soon as he could. He's got friends and extended family over there. He felt obliged to help with the recovery team and refugees, so he volunteered to re-up if he could be part of the recovery and rebuilding force. Didn't even talk to me beforehand! Just as well, I guess. Like I said, there's no real future for us, so it's best we 'drift apart' now, rather than me having to relocate or something in a few years, so he doesn't realize I'm not aging. Besides, it made it a hell of a lot easier to say yes to Liz when she triggered my subliminal knowledge and told me the Apara need me. Amy goes distant for a few seconds, then paths, *Does Marc have any cute friends looking for a partner?*

Tess grins. *I don't know, but I'll ask him if you want me to!*

Amy gives her a sideways glance. *Nah, I'll just grin and bear it for now! There's so much on all our plates right now! Speaking of which, I heard you're up to your eyeballs in work these days.*

Yes, indeed! That's part of why I'm here! I'm more worried about one of your charges here, Annie? Tess paths.

Yeah, she's a nervous little thing. Why would he be after her? Amy paths.

He was caught feeding on her and torturing her psychically down in the Hendersonville office. She doesn't remember anything... yet, but it's trying to surface, and I'm pretty sure she's on Jason's wish list. Tess paths, rolling her eyes.

Maybe I should give her some self-defense lessons? Amy paths sarcastically.

Don't think it will do much good. She needs turned ASAP, but no one has been lined up because they weren't sure... still aren't sure how stable she is after his BS. Tess paths. *Can you do me a favor?*

Of course! What are buds for? Amy says.

Can you make an excuse to go out and leave me here? They're going to wonder why we aren't 'talking' and I need to get a read on her. Tess explains.

Sure. I need to go get some lunch anyway. Want me to grab you something? I'm heading to the deli down the street. Amy paths, getting up and saying aloud "Tess, can you keep an eye on everything here? I need to run out for a few."

"Sure, I think I can handle this crowd." She laughs, and paths, *Oh! I'd love one of their egg salad specials.*

Tess settles in, acting busy in Amy's cubical, while reaching out with her mind to get an overall impression of Annie. She makes notes about personality traits, but when she scans deeper, she senses Annie flinching mentally.

Crap! I think she felt that. She thinks, and pulls back when she's overwhelmed by the dream she had a few days earlier, of being chased by Jason, two women, and feeling like she was human again. *Damn! That was Annie's dream! Not mine at all!* She thinks. She looks over at Annie, who has her head down and is shaking. She paths to Kari, *I need you! Tried reading Annie, but think I may have triggered something in her.*

I'll be there shortly! Kari paths. Two minutes later, she comes in the door to the department and nods to Tess. *I feel it. I'll see what I can do to tuck those back in her unconscious mind.* She puts a hand gently on Annie's shoulder. Annie stops shaking, but otherwise doesn't react. After a minute or so, Kari gently shakes Annie's shoulder. "Wake up, sleepy head!"

Annie starts awake. "*Oh no!* I'm so sorry! Didn't mean to fall asleep! I haven't been sleeping well lately! Please don't fire me!" She begs apologetically.

"Don't worry Annie, it happens to the best of us." Kari smiles reassuringly at her and heads over to Tess.

All tucked away! You seem flustered. She paths to Tess and sits.

Yeah, sorry. I triggered a dream she had, but I had the same dream! It caught me off guard, and I'm still learning the nuances of memory redaction. Thanks for helping. Tess paths.

No problem. Was it what she was thinking about? Being chased by Jason and his 'harem'? Kari asks.

Yeah. I thought it was me, but now I understand why I felt 'neutralized' in the dream. Somehow, I was picking up on her dream and she, naturally, felt human and vulnerable. Didn't you say she was fairly precognitive? Tess asks.

Yeah, her rating is rather high. Are you thinking her dream may be a premonition? Kari asks.

Well, the two women were there, which is something she shouldn't be aware of, so I'd say there's a good chance it's a precog. Tess paths.

I'll get Liz to up the observation and security around her place. The new implant will help us keep track of her otherwise. Did you get anything that will help us find her a partner? Kari asks.

Not much, unfortunately. I got caught up in that dream of hers. The only thing I picked up, well, is I think she prefers women. Tess paths.

It's possible! That would be like Jason to try to dominate a woman who would reject him! I'm sure he thinks he can 'convert her' to liking men. Kari paths, annoyed. *If Liz ends up turning her, however, she'll have to make it clear that the relationship is NOT going to be a romantic one!*

I think everyone around here knows Liz is spoken for. Tess paths, nudging Kari in the shoulder. *On the bright side, that sure cuts down on who we need to consider! What percentage of our people are lesbian or bi?*

It's higher than in the general population. Without the religious oppression of non-binary people, as well as our extended lives, I'd say about 15-20% of female Apara are either lesbian or bi, but you're right, that certainly reduces the number of potential partners for her. Plus, we prefer to have a senior partner, usually someone who's been with us at least 50 years, but we may have to reduce that. Kari paths.

Ok, do we have an overview of our current people and their preferences? Tess asks.

Overview, yes, but their preferences are not generally noted as we haven't had to match so many new people. It's always been considered non-essential, personal preference information. I'll talk to Liz; maybe she can put the word out to the other centers for single women looking for a female partner. I'm sure there are some who were left alone after Jerusalem. Kari suggests.

Okay, sounds like a start. I'll figure out a way to learn more about her in the meantime. I looked at her Facebook, but there wasn't much. Will see if I can do some research on her. Tess says.

If anyone can figure it out, it's you Tess. She switches over to verbal mode. "Have you started on the misfiled cases yet?"

"Yes, I went through about a third of them last night!" She yawns, as she'd had little *actual* sleep after that.

"And? Any luck?" Kari asks.

"A few" She switches back to pathing. *Unfortunately, most are either married, have children, are low-level potentials, or have psychological issues that might cause trouble. I'll get you a summary from my notes of what I've done so far, okay?*

Sounds good. Tired? Kari notices Tess has trouble keeping her eyes open.

Yeah, haven't been sleeping well. Napped yesterday, then was awake until about 4 am, and once I fell asleep, I ended up taking a little trip to see Jason and his minions while out-of-body! And, NO! I don't know where they are! I zip there, zip back, and can't see where it is or how to get there. Hell! I can't control it yet; it happens spontaneously! She paths with overtones of frustration.

Yet, you're able to zoom in on him, even though I assume he was cloaked? Kari asks.

I guess so, though I don't know how I find him. Maybe his cloaking doesn't work if the viewer is out-of-body? She suggests.

Possible, but I'm betting it may have to do with your run in with him at the restaurant and the strength of your skills. Kari says.

Probably, but what good are all these 'super powers' if I can't control them? She paths, and Kari senses overtones of sadness and sarcasm.

Tess! Stop playing 'poor me' games! Whether or not you believe it, your psychic abilities are stronger than nearly anyone here! I'm sure you'll learn to control them eventually. I knew you were special the moment you walked in the door for your interview, but I didn't know how special. She paths, frustrated she can't get Tess to see herself as everyone else does.

Tess is quiet for a minute. *Sorry, I've been feeling sorry for myself. I guess old human habits die hard.* She paths.

Amy returns with food from the deli. "Lunch time! Oh! Hi, Kari! If I'd known you'd be here, I'd have grabbed one of those salads you like!" Amy says cheerfully.

"That's ok. I need to borrow Tess, but I'm sure she can come back when we're done?" Kari says aloud.

"Yeah, and if not, I'll catch you online tonight. I'll be on there a good bit working on a project for Liz and Kari." She sends a mental image of file folders two feet high with Mabel sitting on top, and grabs her egg salad special from Amy's deli bag.

Amy nearly does a spit take with her latte at Tess's mental image. "Ok, stop by any time and I'll probably catch you tonight if you can see your screen to chat!" She gives her a wink.

Tess follows Kari back to her office off the lobby. "Have a seat. I want to show you something." She opens a chart in a program on her computer. This chart shows the average psychic skill levels and one standard deviation above and below of all the Apara currently in this office." The chart shows a red zigzag line crossing the screen with each peak or valley being a unique skill. Above and below are blue lines that nearly parallel the red line, and a black line overlapping the red line, but is not an exact match.

Tess studies the chart, wondering what Kari's on about. "What's the black line?"

Kari patiently explains. "The average skill ratings for all Apara."

Tess sighs, putting her hands up in a questioning mannerism. "So, what about it?"

"Want to see how you compare?" Kari grins and raises one brow.

"I guess so." Tess says unenthusiastically.

"Technically, it's already displayed, but I have to zoom out." Kari uses her fingers on the touch screen to zoom way out, where a green, zigzag line with high peaks in PK and people reading show about two and a half standard deviations above average, while some abilities are closer to one standard deviation above normal

"That's me?" Tess sounds incredulous.

Kari grins and nudges her with her elbow. "*Yep*! Now, this is potential, not necessarily where you're at. It's based on a combination of genetic models and your practical evaluations. Plus, it doesn't even cover out-of-body travel. I don't think I've ever met another of us with that skill!"

"How can my scores be so much higher than everyone else's?" She asks.

"No idea. Maybe Sara can do some genetic studies, but I've never seen potential like this before now. Granted, you may have some competition with some of the Lost Mission folk, but you're so far above most of us in potential, we may not even have an accurate overview!" Kari faces her.

"There's got to be some reason for that. It's not like I was particularly psychic when I was human, not before Marc gave me psi-amp that first time." Tess says.

"When things calm down, I'll get Sara to do some research on your DNA, as well as a new round of tests, but I don't want to hear you put yourself down anymore. Yes, you have control issues, but considering your potential, you're doing *damn* well! You must be more self-confident and trust yourself and your abilities." She says.

"Tell that to Annie! I nearly put her into a PTSD attack." She sighs, feeling guilty.

"And you did what had to be done, you called on someone who could help you do something you're not proficient at yet. Marc must work with you on that. You need to work on those skills too, so in the future, if you notice a situation like Annie's, you can fix it before it gets out of hand." She explains. "Speaking of Marc, Liz says they're done, and he's eager to get you back home."

"I guess I'd better go meet him." She says with a thoughtful pause. "Thanks Kari, for the help and enlightenment." She heads toward the hallway Marc will be coming down from Liz's office.

"Thank God! Are you okay? I've been sensing anxiety and all sorts of negatives from you for the last half hour! You had me worried." He puts one arm protectively around her and pushes her along to their office.

"I'm fine, it's the same old control issues." She leans into him, and he hugs her with one arm.

"Ready to go home?" He asks.

"Guess so. I should probably get a nap before I tackle more of the misfiled potentials or I'll miss something. If you consider out-of-body time non-sleep time, I don't think I got more than about 2 hours sleep. I know we don't always need as much as humans, but even though I ate an egg salad sandwich a few minutes ago, I'm beat and *starving!*" She says.

He gives her a knowing squeeze. "Well, let's get home and while you nap, I'll run some errands, okay? I'll get something good to eat for when you wake up?"

"Don't suppose we could grab a Quarter Pounder on the way home? Maybe even two?" She grins.

He rolls his eyes, but gives in. "I guess so! We'll have to port in some place no one will see us and walk in, since we don't have the car."

They get to their office, gather their things, and port out, popping in behind a small crop of trees by a church near a McDonald's. Tess ends up ordering two large Bacon Quarter Pounders, fries, and a large Dr Pepper. Marc gives her a dirty look. "You're *not* going to go back on a full-time diet of junk food!" He growls at her.

"Cool it! Not like I'm gonna get fat or have to worry about my cholesterol. Sometimes, I need some comfort food. Besides, Sara said the increase in my abilities burns lots of calories." She stuffs a handful of fries in her mouth, staring at him, silently daring him to continue his chastisement.

"*Okay! This* time, but I'd prefer you eat healthy most of the time! You may not gain weight, but I still think that stuff slows down your brain cells when you eat too much of it." He puts his hand on the small of her back as they walk down a side street and find a dark corner to port home from.

Best of times, worst of times

Once home, Tess finishes her meal and notices Marc putting something up by the door. It looks like an additional control pad. "What's that for?"

"Extra security. It extends the blocks used on the portal door to the entire house, so Jason or anyone unknown can't port in should they find their way to Sanctuary." He explains.

"Do you think that's likely? It's not like anyone's gonna teach him." She asks.

"We've underestimated him too many times already. I'd rather be safe than sorry, and I'll feel better when I have to go out, knowing *this* will keep you safe." He walks behind her and massages her shoulders and neck. "Weren't you going to nap?"

"Yeah, about to. Don't let me sleep too long." She says as she trots up the stairs to bed.

Marc watches her ascend and ports out to run his errands.

A few hours later, Tess wakes to a house full of delicious aromas. She sticks her head out and follows the scents to the kitchen, but Marc has latched it from the inside. "Marc? Whatcha cooking?" She asks through the door.

"It's a surprise! Why don't you go take a hot soak while I finish up in here?" He suggests, hoping she doesn't port in and ruin his surprise.

She shrugs, heads back upstairs to the bathroom off their bedroom, and finds he's put out towels, and a fresh bottle of mint scented bubble bath for her. She fills the oversized tub with hot, bubbly water, and soaks. She becomes uncharacteristically relaxed and picks up the nondescript bottle. There's a handwritten label on it in a handwriting she knows all too well, Sara's. The concoction has mint in it, but also a variety of soothing herbs meant to relax muscles and reduce stress. She's nearly asleep in the tub when Marc knocks on the bathroom door. "Dinner in 30!" He says in singsong tones.

Tess drags herself out of the tub. Every muscle in her body has unknotted itself and relaxed fully. *Geez, Sara should market that stuff! She'd make a fortune!* After drying off, she goes into the bedroom and there's a red dress laid out for her. Under her breath she says "Marc, what the hell are you up to?"

She hears his path with overtones of amusement. *Get dressed and come down, and you'll find out!*

She shakes her head and slips the dress over her head; it's a perfect fit. She looks down where the dress had been and there's a gift box. She opens it and it's a necklace with a gold filigree heart with a red stone in it with a six-rayed star in the middle. She carefully takes it out and looks closely at it, and then puts it on, brushes out her hair, and heads downstairs. As she reaches the stairs, she hears voices, and pauses.

"Come on down! Everyone's waiting for you!" He says with a hint of amusement.

As she gets further down the stairs, she can see Liz, Kari, Peder, Marc, Sara, and Amy waiting for her. "What's this all about?" She asks.

"I was going through some files recently, including updating yours, and noticed we missed your birthday. You and I were both unconscious at the time! But with that, Jerusalem, and then Jason, we never celebrated, and I thought you could use a night with friends." Marc hugs her, pathing, *Hope you like the necklace! I had it custom made for you! The stone is a rare, gem-grade star ruby from the mines in Franklin! You don't see that grade too often anymore, just tourist grade stuff. By the way, Western North Carolina is the only place in North America where you can find star rubies and sapphires.* He pulls back and sees happy tears forming.

"Thank you!" She whispers in his ear, feeling rather overwhelmed.

Amy chimes in. "You should have seen your face when you saw all of us! I was so sure you were going to pick up on the surprise from my mind earlier today. I did everything I could think of to hide it from you, including mentally humming the loudest songs I could think of! Marc's been planning this for the last week, ever since he discovered we'd missed your birthday." She explains.

"Yeah, I noticed your mental radio was on hard rock this morning. Figured it was just your mood. As to my birthday, I thought about it when I realized I'd missed it, but I doubted you guys even did birthdays! And besides, other than being turned and Marc surviving Jerusalem, I didn't think it was appropriate to celebrate anything after everything that happened." Tess sits on the sofa next to Marc.

"I know what you mean." Liz glances at her brother, Peder, with a gentle smile. "We do celebrate 'birthdays', but after the first century or so, most of us stop doing it yearly and move to decades or half centuries or whenever we happen to remember." She laughs. "Some even choose to mark the anniversary of their turning rather than their actual '*birth*-day', and some don't do either! But we thought it would be nice for you to have an evening here at home with all of us." Liz smiles.

"It's wonderful! Thank you! I've been stuck here at home so much; it means a lot to me. Guess I won't be doing any of those searches tonight, Kari." She says, and Kari rolls her eyes.

"I'm sure you'll probably triple your effort tomorrow!" Kari jokes.

Marc and Liz head to the kitchen and bring out serving platters and bowls of food. Braised leg of lamb, pan fried duck breast, young, boiled potatoes as well as potatoes fried in duck fat and garlic, one of Tess's favorites, candied carrots, French green beans, mint sauce, Norwegian lingonberries mixed with sugar, fresh French bread, and homemade sweet butter. There's even a steaming bowl of Sara's homemade, wild mushroom soup. Everyone moves to the dining room table. Marc sits Tess at the head of the table in a place of honor for her belated birthday, and everyone fills their glasses with a French red wine Marc brought back from a small, private winery in Bordeaux.

Sara's the first to chime in with a toast, "To Tess! A special young woman who's touched all our lives and this world deeply!" Which is followed by chants of "Here, here!" by the rest of them.

Tears glisten in Tess's eyes as she looks at all of her friends. "Who'd have thought I'd finally have friends and family among a bunch of *blood-sucking* vampires!" She says sarcastically, but they all know she doesn't mean to insult them. She's only expressing the irony that she's finally found where she belongs by leaving the human world behind.

They spend the next hour eating, talking, and laughing. It's the first time in a long time Tess can relax and enjoy the company of friends. She stops worrying about her shields and control, and enjoys her evening. It's been a long time since she felt this 'normal'.

Marc, Liz, and Kari clear the leftovers off the table and return them to the kitchen. Tess grabs one more ladle of Sara's soup before Marc can take it away. A few minutes later, they come back out with dessert plates and desserts on a rolling cart. There's a chocolate cheesecake with almond brickle and white chocolate drizzle on top, a deep dish of Norwegian caramel pudding, (a dessert like flan), and a cherry pie with cream filling made from sweetened condensed milk.

"*Damn!* It's a good thing I can't gain weight!!" Tess laughs as she takes in all the decadence before her eyes!

Marc puts the cheesecake in front of her and adds a single candle. "We'll go with one candle, as this is the first birthday you're celebrating among us, and age doesn't really matter anymore!" He lights the one candle and waits for her to blow it out.

"Thank you! All of you! Before I worked here, and even up until I was turned, I felt lost, like I didn't belong anywhere. Now, I feel I've found my true family!" She blows out the candle, smiling.

Marc hands her a knife and cake server, and she cuts pieces, puts them on plates, and passes them around. The pie and caramel pudding are sent around for each of them to serve themselves. Tess looks at every one of them around the table and is thankful for the day she called for an interview, and the day she discovered what Marc is.

Liz tells stories about Marc, Peder, and Kari in their early years, including a time Marc accidentally ported into a pile of manure on a pig farm in Marseille. They're all laughing hysterically, when Tess freezes and gets a stressed expression. Her heart races and her body is wracked by tremors. Sara's the first to notice something's off, followed by Marc, who senses her emotional shift. Before they can say anything, she drops her fork and it clangs loudly on her plate, silencing all the chatter in the room in the blink of an eye.

"Tess! What is it?" Marc jumps up out of his chair and squats in front of her, hands on her upper arms. "Look at me! What is it?" He demands.

"Ca... Can't see you! Only seeing... them... following me... *no*! *Not me*! *Annie*! Marc! It's Jason, and those women! My... scratch that! *Annie's* dream!" She stutters out.

"What? Is she having the dream again and you're picking up on it?" He asks, uncertain what is happening.

"NO! REAL TIME! HAPPENING *NOW*! HELP HER! *PLEASE!!*" Tess tears up and breathes rapidly as if she's experiencing Annie's fear first hand.

Sara nudges Marc out of the way. "Tess, it's Sara. Do you know where they are?" She asks calmly.

"No, somewhere with old buildings, but I'm not sure where!" Tess gasps in sympathetic terror. "She's *so* afraid! He's *playing* with her! Getting closer and then letting her *think* she's lost him, then making noises; banging pipes, and taunting her. Oh, *God*! He's no longer neutralized! He's whispering to her mind! Halfway opening the box. She knows it's him, and she's afraid of him, but not why." She blurts out.

"Okay, I want you to take slow, deep breaths now. I want you to imagine your mind is like the lens on a camera. You can zoom in or zoom out on what you're seeing and feeling. Zoom out and see if you can give us some details that tell us where she is." Sara calmly reinforces her words telepathically.

"I don't know if I can, but I'll try." Marc gently rubs her shoulders from behind, reassuring her he's still with her.

"It's okay, you can do this, we're all here with you. You're safe, but we need to help Annie now. Imagine turning that lens and zoom out. What do you see?" Sara asks.

Tess imagines the lens on her DSLR camera, turns the lens, and zooms out so she no longer sees with Annie's eyes, but see's Annie. "She's somewhere with a lot of old buildings and some newer. Some paved roads and some dirt. There's a larger brick building nearby, and some buildings are covered in colorful graffiti. She's passing a building that's completely covered in bright drawings, and she's running toward the large brick building; there's more graffiti there too, she's trying to get inside, but can't find any un-locked doors. She hears them taunting her... 'Annie! We're coming for you, Annie!'. They're laughing. She's running around the end of the big building, trying all the doors and...she's *inside*! She pulled the door shut and locked it. She's trying to find some place to hide, going upstairs! She's trying all the doors! So many doors. She's in an empty room. High ceilings, slanted roof, skylight."

"Where could that be? We need more information about the location of the buildings. Try to zoom out more? Get outside the building, from above maybe? See if there're any landmarks?" Sara suggests.

Liz utters, "*Helvete!*" and ports out.

"I'll try." Tess pulls away and passes through the skylight, rising up higher. She's less frantic, like she's no longer in Annie's head, and she can see all around her. "Down by the River; I think she's somewhere in the River Arts District."

Amy chimes in. "Annie has a studio behind Riverview Station. She draws, paints, and does multimedia. She showed me some pictures of her work one day on her phone."

"That's it! The big building's Riverview Station! The one by 12 Bones! It was hard to recognize from my out-of-body perspective! She's in the right wing of it, second floor, if you're looking from the side the river's on. She's in a vacant studio." Tess says, her eyes shifting focus again and her heart rate skyrockets. "They're in the building, banging on anything metal. They know where she is, but they're still playing with her, trying to terrify her so he can.... Oh, *God*! I touched his mind! I think he's going to sexually *assault* her and turn her!" Tess panics and hyperventilates, her own Jason triggered PTSD kicking in.

Liz ports in again with her tablet. "*Uff!* Forgot to assign some-one to watch her outside of home! I knew I shouldn't have left this at the office!" She says, glaring at Kari, who'd insisted she leave work at work for the party. "Did Tess get a location?"

"Riverview Station." Marc says.

"Confirmed! Her tracker location is a match!" She rapidly taps on her tablet, to alert a security team to head there.

"*TESS! LISTEN* to me! We know where she is now! You can let go. Liz is sending people to help her." Sara says in an effort to calm her. Marc is behind her, kissing the top of her head gently.

"I'm not sure how!" Tess begins to hyperventilate. "I don't want to leave her alone! She's *terrified!*"

"It's okay, several of our people have ported into the building and are searching for her. Can you tell us where Jason is now?" Liz asks.

"He's gone. They left as soon as our people arrived, but... *oh, shit.* He reopened the box. She *knows* what he is now." Tess gasps.

"Well, you did say she'd have to remember eventually." Kari comments.

"Tess, I want you to imagine yourself zooming out again, fur-ther than before, and move your focus across town to North Ashe-ville, where your portal home is. Annie's safe. Our team is there, and as soon as we get you where you belong, Liz, Kari, and I will join them and help with damage control, but right now, you need to separate yourself. Can you still sense her fear?" Sara puts her hand on Tess's shoulder to reassure her.

"Yes, but not as strongly." Tess says.

"Do you see your North Asheville home?"

Tess looks down from above, and floats down in front of the house, where Marc's car is. She thinks briefly, *I'm a freaking superhero coming in for a landing!* "Yes." She says aloud, noticeably less distraught.

"I want you to picture yourself going through that door, and as you do, your connection to Annie will stop. Can you do that?" Sara suggests.

"I think so." She pictures herself going through the door; not an open door, but *through* the wooden door. The next thing she knows, she's jolted by her astral body slamming into her physical one. Her breathing slows, and her eyes focus on Sara's face. "I'm back! I can *see* you again!" She hears an audible sigh of relief from Marc behind her, he leans into her, and holds her. Tess is drenched with sweat from head to toe and trembling.

"What the hell just happened?" Marc asks.

Sara drops into a nearby chair with an audible thud, almost as worn out by Tess's ordeal as Tess herself. "If I had to make an educated guess, she had a combination of telempathic contact with an out-of-body episode. Possibly more remote viewing, but I'll have to review the logs."

"Logs?" Tess asks, weakly.

"Yes, we've had special psychic sensors around your home since the fallout shelter incident. They monitor psychic activity to help us help you control it. I'll have to download the data and review the energy patterns, but I'm guessing, from the way you could zoom in and out, and saw all around you that you were out-of-body again, but also in contact with Annie telempathically." Sara explains offhandedly, like it should be obvious.

"But I was awake this time! How could I have been out-of-body?" Tess breathes in quickly, sucking in moisture dripping from her nose, and wipes tears from her face.

"My guess is Annie's fear and panic made her connect to you again, telempathically, and drew you to her astrally. That's why you couldn't see us. You could only see through your astral self, or through Annie's eyes, in other words, from her perspective. I'll have to do some research, but that's my gut instinct." Sara says.

"Geez! Sure hope that never happens when I'm driving! I swear! I couldn't see any of you! I could hear you all, though, and feel you, Marc." Tess consciously tries to breathe slowly and evenly, but her heart is pounding.

"Marc, get her a bag from the fridge. After that psychic expenditure, she surely needs to feed, and then I want her in bed, asleep! I'll be back after we get Annie settled down to check on her." Sara says. Marc immediately goes and brings back a bag of blood, and Tess obediently feeds, her pulse returning to normal, and she's increasingly sleepy. "Get her to bed, and Marc! I *do* mean *sleep!*" She says with a lopsided smirk.

"Will do, Sara." He helps Tess up, but she's wobbly. He puts his arm around her and ports her to the bedroom.

Liz, Kari, and Sara port out, leaving Amy and Peder waiting for Marc to come back down. Peder has been sedate and quiet all evening, still weak and recovering from Jerusalem. About 20 minutes later, Marc walks down the stairs, looking worn and deflated.

"Marc, why don't you have a seat. I'll deal with the dishes and put the leftovers away." Amy says, putting her hand on his shoulder as she passes him with a stack of plates in her other hand.

"Thanks." He sits next to Peder in emotional exhaustion.

"Sucks being an empath sometimes, doesn't it, old friend?" Peder asks.

"Why do I suspect this won't be the last crisis we have like this?" Marc makes a pained laugh under his breath as he closes his eyes and takes a deep breath.

"Because we all know Tess has potential like we've not seen before, but you love her, and will help her in any way you can, as I was there for Lissa when she was dealing with things over the years. It's what you do for family." Peder takes a sip of wine.

"*Oui, mon Ami!* Now that I've found her, I'd do anything for her!" Marc claps his old friend on the shoulder.

"And after what she did for Lissa and I, we would as well!" Peder reassures him.

The two old friends sit there sipping wine silently. After about 25 minutes, Amy comes out and joins them, carrying another slice of cherry pie. "So, had to move stuff around in your fridge but got everything put away. I want this recipe!" She says, digging her fork into it and shoving a chunk in her mouth.

"I'll get it to you when my head stops spinning." He smiles weakly, a little nauseous now that his adrenaline's returning to normal. "I'd hoped to have a trouble-free gathering of friends to-night, but I guess it wasn't in the stars!"

"On the other hand, it sounds like she saved Annie from that jackass! I still can't believe he got turned after what he tried with Tess!" Amy says in a huff, sitting down and indulging in her pie.

"Things happen in chaos." Marc says.

"I know, but still. After what he pulled, I was ready to go full com-bat on his ass!" Amy says, letting her southern accent out to play.

"I'm glad you taught Tess some self-defense, even if she did use it on me one night." He laughs.

"*WHAT*?! She never told me that!" Amy's mouth gapes, and she laughs.

"It was way before you were turned. She found out about me, I tracked her to her apartment, and had her pinned at the door. I was going to redact her memory, and she nearly put her heel through my foot!" He shakes his head and grins.

"Cool! She's a fast learner!" Amy grins at Marc and Peder. "I should get going. Peder, do you need help porting home or will you be okay?" Amy asks, knowing he's still limited after his injuries.

"I'm gonna keep Marc company until Sara and Liz come back. I may have to finish that other bottle of wine I noticed!" He jokes.

Amy ports out, leaving the two old friends to each other's company.

Almost two hours pass and Sara, Liz, and Kari port in, looking exhausted.

"Peder, Liz wants me to take you home." Kari says, and he carefully stands, joins her, and the two port out.

"How's Annie doing?" Marc asks.

"Heavily sedated for now. Jason somehow prevented her memories from being blocked again, so now we've got a proverbial Pandora's box to deal with. She was pretty freaked out, and nearly catatonic when we found her. We got her calmed down, but she's not sure whom she can trust right now. When Tess has rested, I think I'd like her to talk with her. Their subconscious link may engender trust." Sara explains.

"Do you think that's wise? I don't want to see Tess sucked back into Annie's fear and terror." Marc says, concerned.

"Annie's going to be on some anti-anxiety meds for a while, and Tech should have a new Cent-opal filter for Tess by then. They're putting it in a bracelet this time because it's a larger piece of stone, besides, I suspect Tess is going to be wearing that necklace you gave her instead." Sara has a glint in her eye. "I'm going up and check on her." Sara goes up the steps carrying the tools of her trade.

"You doing okay, Marc?" Liz sits by him at the table.

"I'm exhausted, frustrated, and wondering what's next!" He exclaims.

Liz kicks off her shoes, leans back in her chair and puts her feet on the chair opposite her under the table. "You have your hands full with that one!" She grabs Peder's half-full wineglass, and sips it.

"But I wouldn't have her any other way!" He downs the last of the wine in his glass. "If you're hungry, I can reheat some leftovers for you?" He asks.

"No, I should head home to Kari and Peder. I think we're all exhausted after tonight." Liz stands, grabs her shoes in one hand, and pats Marc on the shoulder with the other. "She's worth it." She says with a soft grin, and vanishes.

Marc takes the last glasses and Amy's plate in and washes them. When he comes back out, Sara's sitting at the table staring at her tablet. "How is she?" Marc asks, sitting down near Sara.

"She'll be fine, but every time we have one of these sudden bursts of psychic energy, she stretches her capacity to new heights. I was reviewing these logs. Definitely an out-of-body trip combined with telempathic linkage. She was either seeing through Annie's eyes, or via her astral self. I've never seen anything quite like it among our kind!" Sara clicks the off button on her tablet. "I'm not sure if her abilities have any concrete limits, other than her own self-limits, if you know what I mean?"

"Unfortunately, I tend to agree. Should I let her sleep until she wakes again?" He asks.

"Yes, as long as she needs to. We can keep Annie sedated until she's ready. She doesn't exactly have psychic 'burn' this time, but her synapses are hyper stimulated, and they need to settle down. I put a dampening field generator on her nightstand. I'm hoping that will keep her from taking a jaunt along the astral highway for the next couple of days." She stands and stretches, then ports out, mid-stretch, leaving Marc alone in a very quiet house as Mabel has already gone upstairs and curled up with Tess in bed.

Annie, can you hear me?

Thanks to Sara's dampening field generator, Tess sleeps heavily for several hours, waking around 3 pm the next day. She looks around, but Marc's not with her. She reaches out tentatively to find him, and after a good bit of effort, senses him downstairs, talking to Liz. She sits on the edge of the bed, feeling odd, like her head is wrapped in cotton. Her red dress is hanging over a nearby chair, and realizes she's wearing one of her sci-fi tees. Her filigree necklace is lying on the nightstand; her old Cent-opal pendant beside it.

"Hmmm, I don't remember that thing making me all fuzzy-headed like this before." She thinks. She tries to stand, but gets dizzy and sits back down. She reaches out to Marc, but her head aches. She looks around for her cell phone, and finds it in the top drawer of her nightstand, on silent. She picks it up and calls him.

He answers. "Tess? You're awake?"

"Obviously," She says slowly. "but my head's all fuzzy and I'm too dizzy to stand." She can hear Marc and Liz coming up the stairs to the bedroom. "Hi, Liz…" Tess says, sounding stoned.

Marc paths to Liz, *can you turn off Sara's gadget?* He crouches down in front of Tess and takes her hands in his. "You'll feel better in a minute." He says, and as the dampening field gradually reduces to off, Tess snaps out of it.

"What the hell was that all about?" She shakes her head like she's trying to jar her synapses into wakefulness.

"One of Sara's gadgets. She wanted to make sure you slept and didn't take any more astral strolls." He says. "Feeling any better?"

"Somewhat, but still have the remains of a dull headache. I don't remember going to bed last night, and after you served dessert, things are fuzzy." She blinks slowly.

He sits next to her on the bed, his arm around her shoulder. "Not surprising. It was because of Annie. Jason was after her, and you not only linked with her, you apparently went out-of-body at the same time."

"Is she safe? I think I remember someone telling me she is, but every time I try to remember, the ache gets worse." She says.

"Physically, she's safe, but she was nearly in shock when our people got to her. Sara's got her in Medical, sedated." He uses his other hand to brush long strands of hair out of her face.

"She remembers now, doesn't she?" Tess struggles to glean what she can from her memory.

"Yes, Jason permanently unlocked her memories. That's why she's under sedation. When you're up to it, Liz and Sara want you to talk to her. She was inconsolable yesterday, so they had to sedate her." He explains.

"What can I do? She barely knows me." Tess rubs her eyes, trying to clear them of encrusted tears.

"Sara thinks the subconscious link you two share might let you get through to her." Liz explains.

"Oh, hi again, Liz; almost forgot you were here." Tess says. "I'm not sure I can do anything until I clear my head. Sara must have done more than used whatever that gadget is. I feel drugged." She's still a tad dizzy and leans against Marc.

Marc looks at Liz, who nods and vanishes. "Liz went to get Sara. They should be back shortly." He reassures her.

She looks up at Marc. "Annie must have been scared *shitless*! I remember now, Jason was terrorizing her on multiple levels. If I could have beaten the shit out of him from the astral plane, I'd have done it!" Tess slurs her speech.

Liz returns with Sara. "I thought you'd be out at least 2 full days." Sara looks at Tess's eyes, and scans her aura. "Hmph.... Well, you recovered from your little jaunt a lot faster than I expected." She takes out an infuser and inserts a clear ampoule. "This should clear your head, but I want you to eat and feed, and then I'll check you over again!" Sara says, sitting on the nearby chair her dress is hanging over.

"Oh, *God*! That's better! I can think again!" Tess exclaims and stretches.

"I gave you enough to last you for two days, figuring you'd sleep that long, but you've rebounded from your psychic exertion a lot faster this time. That's a good sign." Sara says, returning the infuser to her bag. "I'll be back in about an hour to check you. I need to make sure Annie's staying under. She had a rough night as nightmares broke through the sedation." She explains and ports away.

"Liz, I'll call you soon." Marc says aloud, pathing to her *I need a few minutes alone, okay?* Liz nods and vanishes again.

"You need to feed again. You fed last night, and while I could get you a bag from the fridge, I think something a tad fresher and more intimate might do you some good." He turns her to face him, tipping his own head back. "You know what to do." He says. She nods and gently feeds from him, savoring the familiarity and warmth as it spreads through her, as well as his love for her.

After a couple of minutes, she pulls away, healing the wounds automatically. "You've been mostly stuck on bagged blood between your abilities being out of whack and Jason being on the loose, I thought this might do you some good." He says, gently caressing her cheek.

"It did. I feel better and needed that contact with you. Thank you for the wonderful evening, at least, prior to Annie hijacking my brain and soul. It means a lot to me." She smiles, and he leans in and kisses her gently.

"Now, real food! Plenty of leftovers. Do you want me to fix you a plate and bring it up here or do you want to come down and eat?" He asks.

"I've spent enough time up here. Can you help me downstairs, please. I'm still pretty unsteady." She asks.

Marc helps her up and eases her down the steps and to the dining room table where they'd all gathered the night before. He goes into the kitchen, returning a few minutes later with a plate of cold slices of duck, slices of heated lamb, refried potatoes, and a small bowl of Sara's soup. Tess eats it ravenously.

"Thank you. I really needed that. I guess I must have burned a month's worth of psychic calories last night!" She jokes.

"Why don't you go get dressed? Sara will be back soon to give you a once over." He rubs her shoulders.

Feeling stronger, Tess goes up the steps herself, cautiously at first, but taking them like normal as she gets to the top. She washes up in the bathroom sink, puts on some jeans, adds a bra under her Captain Marvel T-shirt, and goes back downstairs, where Sara's waiting, feigning impatience.

"Well, come on, superhero!" She jokes.

Tess sticks her tongue out at Sara, and scampers the rest of the way down, sitting in the chair nearest her. Sara checks her over, including testing her mind for psychic 'sore spots', but Tess is fine. "I'm impressed!" Sara says. "You've recovered much faster from this exertion than the last few."

"I'm not as singed around the edges, if you get my drift?" Tess says.

"Yes, that makes sense. Your synapses are getting used to the higher levels of energy passing through them. I'd say most of your reaction last night was psychological. *NO!* I don't mean psychosomatic, but a combination of picking up on Annie's terror, and your own reactions to Jason as before. Even if you handled him last time, he's been your Achilles Heel earlier." She explains.

"You're probably right. So, do you still want me to talk to her?" Tess asks.

"Most *definitely*! I'm not sure anyone else will get through to her! But before we go," She grasps Tess's hand and slides a cuff bracelet with a large piece of blue Cent-opal in it. "Hopefully, this one will work well for you!"

Tess gets her shoes on and the three of them port to medical.

They walk down a hall to Annie's room. Sara tells Marc, "I know you want to protect Tess, but I think it'll be best if she sees Annie alone. Annie is not sure who she can trust right now. She's locked herself up in her mind as protection, and considering you're a man, she's more likely to see you as a threat!" Sara takes Tess by the hand. "I'll go in with you and clear the sedation, but I think it will be best if you're alone with her."

"Okay. I'll try." Tess nods.

Sara turns off a device similar to the one she used with Tess, and puts something in Annie's IV to help bring her out of it. She paths, *All yours! Good luck!* and leaves the room.

Tess gently puts her hand on Annie's on the bed, and says, "Annie? Can you hear me? Are you awake?"

Annie groans and contorts her face, and Tess can sense she doesn't want to come out of the safe little corner of her mind.

"Annie, it's Tess from work. We literally ran into each other, one day. I need to talk to you." She gently touches Annie's mind as she speaks, using the unconscious link between them.

"Tesssss?" She says quietly and drawn out, halfway opening one eye.

"Yes, Annie, it's Tess, from work." She repeats.

"Is... is *HE* here?" She asks, timidly.

"No, you're safe from Jason, he can't come here. He doesn't know how to get here. No one's going to let him get near you, *especially* me!" She says.

"I do know you, but not just from the hallway. You were with me when they were chasing me, but, but that can't be! I was alone!" She says, confused.

"Annie, do you know what Jason is?" Tess asks.

"Yes, a *monster*." She says, quietly, as if he might hear her and pop in if she says it any louder.

"Yes, he is, but not in the way you're thinking." Tess says.

"He bit me many times, but I forgot, and now, I remember all the pain and fear. He's some kind of *vampire*!" She thinks no one will believe her.

"Yes, I know what he is, but *that* isn't what makes him a monster. He was a monster before he became a *vampire*." She realizes she's stopped thinking of herself, Marc, and the others as vampires any longer, and prefers the term "Apara".

"What was he before he became a vampire?" Annie asks nervously.

Tess lets out a stifled guffaw and answers, "A *major* asshole! That's what!"

Annie looks at Tess askew, startled by her flippant remark. "I thought maybe you meant he was a werewolf or something else." She says nervously.

"No, to *my* knowledge, they don't exist." Tess says, smiling with nice, normal teeth.

"I didn't think vampires existed either, but *HE IS ONE!* And he's *EVIL!*" She grabs onto Tess's hand and holds on for dear life.

"Yes, but how can I explain this? It's not what someone is that makes them evil or a monster, but who they are. I know other people like him, other '*vampires*', who are not monsters, but it's *who* Jason is that makes him evil and a monster, not whether or not he has fangs!" Tess explains.

"I don't know, I thought vampires *were* monsters?" Annie says tentatively.

"Annie, do you trust me? I was with you, sort of, last night. Not physically, but I knew you were in trouble and helped people get to you to save you from him." She explains.

"Are you a witch or something?" Annie's eyes grow large.

"No, not a witch either. I'm *like* Jason, but I would never hurt anyone. I want to help people, including you." She speaks calmly.

"*No!* You're *NOT* like him! *Not* possible!" Annie says.

"Annie, I need you to stay calm, but I'm going to show you what I am, and I promise, you're safe with me." She says, using her telempathic link with Annie to calm her and soften the shock. "Look at me, *okay?*" Tess says, opens her mouth, and lets down her fangs as slowly as she can manage.

Annie doesn't say anything at first; she stares into space. Then asks, "Did Jason turn you into a vampire? Like the other women with him?"

Tess chuckles. "He *wishes!* No, I became like this a few months ago, but I'm not a monster and neither is the man who did change me. When Jason became like this, there was something already broken inside him, and that's where the monster in him comes from."

"Do you bite people? Drink their blood?" She asks with nervous curiosity.

"Sometimes, when I need to, but I never hurt them and they never even know it's happening to them. What Jason did to you was torture and terrorize you. He fed not only on your blood, but on your fear. This is something he's not allowed to do, but he's gone off the deep end mentally." Tess explains.

"Why did he do that to me? If it's not allowed?" She's uncertain about Tess's revelation that she, too, is a vampire.

"Do you know how children that are abused sometimes grow up to become abusers?" Tess asks her.

"Yes, I have a cousin like that." She admits.

"Jason was abused by his mom, and the person who changed him didn't know that, or how broken he was psychologically when he changed him. Abuse is about having power over another, and when Jason became like he is, that added power became another way he could abuse others, and he chose you to take it out on... well, you and me too." Tess says.

"Did he *bite* you, too?" Her eyes go wide.

"No, I knew him while he and I were both human. He cornered me one day, and I thought he was going to rape me, but someone saved me from him. He also kidnapped me later, but that's a long story. The point is, Jason has power over you, so was coming for you, and was going to change you." Tess gently touches Annie's hand again to reassure her.

"I don't want to be *like* him!" Annie's anxiety peaks and her eyes glimmer with budding tears.

"I get that, but you need to understand being one of us doesn't make someone a monster, being like him does." She says.

"Are you going to change me?" Annie asks in a small voice.

"No, I'm not. She pauses, debating if she should go on. "However, if you were to become like me by someone other than Jason, he'd lose interest in you, and you'd be able to defend yourself against him." She says as calmly as possible.

"But I don't want to be a *vampire!*" She sobs.

Tess cringes as a wave of sorrow and fear hits her from Annie. "I know, and no one's gonna force you to become one, but we must protect you from him, and we can't make you forget about all of this, so one way or another, you'll have to work with us. None of us will hurt you, but you're stuck with us now."

Annie looks at her, confused. "What do you mean, 'stuck'?"

Tess sighs. "If you don't become one of us, we'll still have to protect you from him until he can be stopped! In addition, we'll have to put a mental block in your mind so you can't tell anyone about us. If people knew about us, then they'd come after us even though the rest of us don't do any harm. Also, I'm afraid you can't go home until Jason and his people are caught, or they'll come for you. He hurts those he changes, even more than he's already hurt you, he breaks them, and none of us want you to go through that."

Annie sniffles, looks briefly at Tess's eyes, then away. "If I can't go home, where will I live?"

"I'm not sure yet, but we'll find someone who can protect you in case Jason finds a way to come after you." She tries to give her a reassuring mental push.

"You mean someone like you? A *vampire?*" Annie's anxiety level spikes as she thinks of having a vampire around her all the time.

"Annie, it's for your protection. They won't hurt you, or try to feed from you, but they'll make sure you're safe." Tess explains.

"And when he's captured?" She asks, expectantly.

"We'll have to play it by ear. You may be able to go home again, but we'll still be in your life. We need to make sure the post-hypnotic suggestion continues to work." She says. "And maybe, once you see we aren't monsters, you might even, well, *want* to be part of what we do."

"What, *exactly*, do you do?" Annie's eyes narrow skeptically.

"We try to make a difference in the world, make it a better place." Tess lightly touches her arm.

She's quiet for a minute, processing it all; then says, "I'd like to make things better, but I don't know what to do. It's all so confusing and scary."

Tess says, "Yeah, I know it can be, I've been in your position myself, finding out about all this isn't easy, but give us a chance, okay?"

She regards Tess, determining once and for all if she can trust her, and something inside reassures her. "Okay." She yawns.

There's a light knock on the door, and Sara enters. "Tess, I need to make sure Annie's doing okay."

"Annie, this is Sara. She's a doctor. She's going to make sure you're all right. You can trust her." Tess reassures her.

"Okay. Will you come see me later?" Annie asks.

"Yes, but let Sara look you over, and I think you may get a couple of other visitors from work. You don't need to be afraid of them. *Okay?*" Tess reassures her and Annie nods.

She paths to Sara, *Call me if you need me, but I think I need to go home and pass out for a while. That took more out of me than I expected.*

Do that, and thank you! She's clearly in a better place psychologically. I'll make sure she gets some food before Liz and Kari come by."

Tess smiles at Annie, and says, "Bye, Annie, Sara will call me if you need me." And she walks out the door to Marc, who's been waiting anxiously for her.

Laying the groundwork

"How'd it go?" Marc puts his arm around her and ports home.

"Exhausting! But I think I got through to her. Hopefully, we can find a way to convince her to join us, or she'll end up in the same limbo I was in." Tess yawns.

Marc gives her a long kiss. "You really do belong with us, love. You're kind, thoughtful, and did a lot to help her, but don't forget to take care of yourself. Your aura's all frazzled."

"Yeah, it felt like I took on her anxiety for her, if that makes sense? And now I'm crashing." She says, trembling.

"Of course, it makes sense! I'm an empath, after all." He chuckles lightly. "Has anyone taught you how to ground yet?" Marc rubs her back gently.

"Ground what?" She asks.

"Psychic energy can be a lot like electricity. Get too much in your system, and you overload. Sometimes, like when you're taking in someone else's energy or emotions, you must learn not to keep it within yourself, but to 'ground it' out of your system. Sometimes it's as simple as channeling the energy into the literal ground, or picturing it leaving your body and dispersing. We can work on that, but I you need to sleep, but we can get started." He puts a hand on her shoulder and ports them both to their bedroom at home. "Lie down on your stomach, I want to try something before you fall asleep, it may help you sleep better."

She does, and he begins to work on the muscles in her back, massaging them. "Your muscles are knotted up because you took on her anxiety and negative energy. I want you to picture the muscles in your body as glowing with a reddish energy, which is what

I sense. I want you to picture that energy seeping down through your body, through the mattress and the downstairs, into the ground beneath our home, and then dispersing through the land beneath us until it's no longer noticeable. Picture it becoming progressively less red, fading to pink, and then your energy to white as you drain off all the negative energy and emotions."

"Like this?" She asks.

He follows along with both what she's visualizing in her mind, as well as monitoring her aura for changes. He senses tendrils of red hanging below her, like the tendrils under a jellyfish, eventually touching the ground, thinning, and separating from her own aura and body. He sees her aura shift color from red, to pink, to almost white, before going back toward her normal purplish-blue. "Good! Are your muscles unknotting as the energy drains off?"

"Yeah, they are. It's like they were clenched up, almost like they had an electric current passing through them, but now, the tension's fading." Her back relaxes as Marc continues kneading her muscles.

"Now, imagine positive energy from the sun, nature, and the plants around us replenishing what you drained off. Feel it flowing in through your head and travelling through your body, cleansing away the last remnants of the negative energy."

"*Wow*! My skin's vibrating!" She exclaims as she's enveloped by a warm, golden energy from the top of her head and down her spine, into her legs.

"I can't believe I never thought to teach you this! I guess it's second nature to me, being an empath. I must be able to pick up on other's emotions, but not keep them." He shakes his head.

"Makes sense; you wouldn't want to take on someone else's depression or anger and let it affect you." She takes a deep breath and stretches, feeling better.

"Exactly! We should work more on this, and see if it lessens your tendency to overload, but right now, I think your best bet would be to get some rest. I've got some work to do on some recent precog reports." He says.

Tess looks worried. "Not another 'big event' like Jerusalem, I hope?"

"No, more along the line of some natural disasters we might mitigate if we can pinpoint them and give a heads up before it happens. I need to analyze the different reports and see if I can find repeated patterns or clues so we can narrow down the whens and wheres. Get some rest!" She rolls over on her back, he leans down and kisses her, getting a spark of 'static-like' energy when his lips touch hers. "Yes, we definitely need to lay some groundwork with your energy!" He walks away chuckling; his lips still tingling from the spark of their kiss.

"Yes, sir!" She says, already yawning and closing her eyes.

Marc works this in to their daily psychic practice until it becomes automatic for her to cast off excess energy or negative energy and emotions. It makes a big difference for her and helps her focus, and even better her control.

Lost and found

Tess visits Annie daily, and sees her gradually losing that constant cloud of anxiety when dealing with Apara, except for Jason and his minions, who still trigger panic attacks and nightmares. Now that there are dormitory like buildings near the med center for recovering Apara, Sara collects some of Annie's personal items from her apartment, and moves her into one of the rooms. She'll stay there until other arrangements can be made. Sara spends a good bit of time talking to her and even invites her to help her with minor chores around medical, as Annie did some volunteer work at Mission Hospital a few years back.

A few days later, Kari sends out a mental shout to Tess. *Are you decent? I've got the first batch of names matching Lost Mission gene prints for you!*

Yeah! Give me 5 minutes to drag a brush through my hair and stuff, and I'll meet you in the living room! Tess paths back, as she makes herself presentable, and runs down the stairs as Kari pops in. "Let me boot up my computer so we can transfer those files." She jumps into her seat and boots everything up enthusiastically. She's anxious to have something to do again, and hopefully make a difference.

"Take your time. I wanted to come by and see how you're doing, anyway." Kari pulls up an additional office chair and sits beside her, still holding her tablet and some paper files in her arms.

"I'm okay, I guess. I'm still working on control, but Marc's been working with me on grounding, and that's helping. I'm learning to bleed off overload energy, which helps me with control, too." She absentmindedly taps a pen on her desk impatiently, waiting for her computer to boot up.

"Good! Have you been able to go without your filter at all?" Kari puts the pile of papers and her tablet on the desk.

"Some. Though I still wear it when I go out. Sara would kill me if I showed up to medical to see Annie without it." She laughs.

"How's Annie doing? Liz and I went by the first evening, but Sara thought it best we limit how many of us she's exposed to for now." Kari says.

"She's doing better. Sara's got her working as her assistant when she makes the rounds at Medical. I think it helps her to see those there are not invincible monsters, but actual people. Sara thinks she's even seen signs of her latent healing abilities when she helps." Tess takes the tablet and syncs it to her computer.

"Great! Hopefully, she'll be able to overcome what Jason did to her and join us." She pauses and waits until the database comes up on Tess's computer. "Hmm, remind me to set you up with one of our custom computers. No offence, Tess, but your computer's a clunker by our standards." She laughs. "Anyway, as you can see, we've got the first hundred or so matches for you. I want you to research each of them and if they look like they may be in acceptable life situations, go more in depth to see if they may be viable. A lot of that will rely on social media, but also on medical, psychiatric records, job evaluations, school records and so on, if available.

Tess's stomach growls. "I'll get on it right after breakfast. Would you like anything?"

"Don't suppose Marc made any of his homemade croissants lately?" Kari grins.

"Yes! He was up at 5 am today and made a fresh batch. I'll bring some out." Tess slips into the kitchen and comes out a few minutes later with a small, wicker basket of fresh croissants, a tray with different spreads, lunchmeats, and a crock of fresh butter to go with them. "Dig in! I think Marc enjoys having someone to cook and bake for. I'm so glad I can't get fat off this stuff anymore, cause if I were still human, I'd be a blimp by Christmas." Tess laughs and grabs a croissant, butter, and some rhubarb-strawberry jam.

"Thank you! I thought I caught a whiff of fresh bread when I passed him in the hall at work." Kari laughs, and fills a plate with croissants.

Tess turns around and goes back to the kitchen for hot coffee. "I wish the caffeine still worked on us. Can't quite break the habit of coffee in the mornings, even though it doesn't do anything for me anymore."

"Yeah! The same goes for alcohol. I still like the taste of some of it, but mostly, it's an old habit, though that wine Marc brought back from Bordeaux was exquisite!" Kari says.

Tess pauses, looking thoughtful. "Kari, do you ever miss being human?"

Kari gives her an odd glare. "It's been so long since then, it's hard to remember! Of course, the standard of living back then was so much lower." She pauses a moment, then asks, "Are you having regrets?"

"*Hell*, no! I'm trying to think about how to help Annie take the next step. So far, I haven't met anyone who regrets becoming Apara. Yes, some miss their families or friends afterwards, but beyond that, I'm wondering how we can convince any of these people..." She motions to the list on her screen. "that are suitable, to take that step when they haven't been prepped. How do we convince them to join us? When I first found out, the *last* thing I wanted was to become *like* Marc. I was terrified he'd either *kill* me or *change* me. But the more I got to know him, all of you and what you do, the more I *longed* to be Apara. But I'm not sure how to convince these people. I had to face it all because you couldn't make me forget, but I'm not even sure how to *break* it to someone, let alone convince them to *give* up their humanity."

Kari looks pensive, and lets out a sigh. "It's a good question, and one we don't have an easy answer for. Usually, with fully prepped people, we can trigger their memories and understanding of the situation through subliminal triggers before they're turned, and most are fine with being turned, like they've been waiting to be called for duty, but with the Lost Mission people, who are largely unprepped, I think it's going to vary on a person-to-person basis, and that, Tess, is where you come in. I'll work with you on this, but your analysis of them will help us know what's the best way to approach each of them. Some will respond to logic, some to meeting someone, falling for them, and joining us that way. Others, we may even have to consider turning them without their permission, and doing damage control afterwards. I'd rather not do that, but it may have to be considered in some cases, especially with Jason looking for others to add to his 'collection'." Kari makes a disgusted snort.

"You mean like with Annie, where he went after her, that it might be necessary to turn someone to prevent him from getting them? Do you think we should do that with Annie?" Tess asks.

"No, not Annie. I think she's on the best path for her right now. She's slowly learning we aren't creatures to be feared. I'm not sure who we might have to turn without their permission, I'm speculating we may have to consider it if the circumstances warrant it." Kari looks thoughtful.

"I guess I have lots of work ahead of me." Tess finishes up her last croissant. "Let me see how far I can get this week, and I'll make a list of those I think are worth pursuing, how's that sound?"

"Sounds good. Then we can start with those, review them together, and make recommendations to Liz afterwards." Kari puts her plate aside, grabs her tablet, and stands. "Yell if you need me! I'll come to you, okay?"

"Will do! Say hi to everyone from me!" Tess says and gets to work as Kari ports back to the office.

With that, Tess begins the complex process of researching the first of thousands of potentials who are compatible and may eventually join the Apara. At first, she only looks at whether they're alive, married, have children, or are in jail or otherwise institutionalized. The first few on the list are no-go's. Either they're married, have children, or in one case, was on the list of missing, presumed dead after Jerusalem. Tess moves those people onto lists of 'currently unsuitable' and "permanently unsuitable", depending on their situations. Most of the currently unsuitables are married with no children, so there's a chance they may someday be alone again, and could be reconsidered. By the middle of the week, she's narrowed it down to about 38 out of 107 whose life situations make them viable.

"Now for the real work!" She says aloud. "Trying to figure out if they're psychologically suitable or not."

The first one she investigates is a woman named Linda. She lives in Arizona. She finds her on Facebook, and the first posts in her feed are Bible quotes and conspiracy theories. "Well, that's a big 'HELL NO'!" Tess says aloud, at which point, Marc comes out of his home office.

"What's a big 'HELL NO'?" He asks, smirking slightly as he joins her, drags a chair along the floor, and sits beside her.

"Nothing major. I'm evaluating the ones that are potentially available to join us, and was on the first one's Facebook page." She turns the flat screen so he can see it as she scrolls down. "Bible quotes, conspiracy theories, intolerant posts about LGBTQ, other religions, races, and so on. If we approached someone like that, I'm pretty sure they'd try to throw holy water and a cross, and run screaming into the night! And if they were turned, I doubt they could come to grips with it. Their beliefs would prevent them from adapting, wouldn't they?"

He sighs. "In her case, I agree with you, but more because of clear signs of paranoia and her intolerance for others not like her. It's more than being religious. There are plenty of religious people who'd agree, in principle, with what we do, and some may even accept us once they realize we aren't the mythical monsters or demons seen in horror movies. Other faiths believe all creatures have some purpose on this planet. Don't automatically rule out someone because they are a person of faith. Believe it or not, I know a few of us who still practice their human religions even after hundreds of years, believing someday, they too, may still meet their makers." He pauses, trying to think of how to phrase things. "That being said, I used to think religion was a big factor back when I was turned. I was born around the time of the first witch trials in France. When it came down to it, it was all about power hungry and egocentric men taking advantage of fear and ignorance among the lower classes. It was never really about religion."

"It wasn't?" She asks, never having studied much about this in school other than it happened.

"Yes, the real reason for the European witch trials was an attack on women with power. Women, who were midwives and herbalists, had power over life and death, and the men of the church, the real political power in many countries, couldn't accept that lowly women had power they did not. So, they chose to spread fear and hate among the people, who knew little beyond their lives and their faiths. These women were vilified, and many killed, all because of jealous and power-hungry men. It's not that different from politics in the last few decades, where politicians use people's faith to demonize and vilify those who threaten to take their power away from them politically. In some ways, humans have not changed as much as you might think in the last five or six centuries!" He reaches over and caresses her face playfully.

"*Wow!* I didn't know that, and yeah, that sounds like history repeating itself, doesn't it? Makes me wonder if we'll ever be civilized enough for our Benefactors." She admits.

"We'll get there eventually. However, a lot of times, it's willful ignorance, more than religion itself. People may live in fear the truth is not what their leaders tell them, so they reject anything different. Perhaps, being more educated than average, I questioned that thinking, which is another reason they chose me." He suggests.

"Well, I'm glad they did." She grins.

"Me too. But seriously, think about what I've said. I'm sure there are many out there whose faith aligns with what we do, putting others first and helping the world." He puts his hand on hers and lets out a long, drawn-out breath. "Anything else interesting?"

"I'll, keep that in mind." She says, pensively. "As to your question, I'm starting the psychological evaluations. I finished the availability part last night; narrowed it down from 107 to 38. This Linda gal is the first one I've looked at in any detail, but I really don't see any chance she'd make the cut! 37 to go!" She grins.

He gives her a quick kiss, gets up, and heads off to the kitchen. He heads back to his office, but drops off a plate of mini-quiches at Tess's desk with a grin.

"Thank you!" She pops one in her mouth. "On to the next!" She says as if it were a rallying cry.

Tess goes through about half of them that day and continues the next. She gets to the 24th potential candidate, Susan Lee Burns, and searches Google and social media for information. She narrows her down on Facebook, and looks again at her earlier notes. She thinks, *Oh yeah! The local one! There she is! Susan Burns in Weaverville;* a town about fifteen minutes' drive north of Asheville. She goes through her feed and her likes, and puts her in the likely category. She further researches any other records for her and realizes, *Ah! She's a therapist, meaning she's in a 'helping' profession. She works at the local community health clinic. That's good. No criminal history other than a couple of parking tickets, no sign of earlier psychological issues. Definitely a good one to consider. Sara said we could use some therapists to help at Medical as well!* She ponders and makes a note in her file.

Tess continues through the rest, and by Friday morning, has a list for Kari of 18 good prospects. She paths Kari. *Ready when you are! Got 18 I'd recommend we consider. Do you have time today?*

Yes, we've got a couple of interviews this morning, but I can come by about 10 am. Kari paths.

Tess senses Kari's distracted with people in the office, so she wraps it up with a mental *See you then!*

Mabel saunters in and rubs around Tess's ankles. "*Silly* cat! Hungry again?" She bends down and scoops up the fur ball and carries her into the kitchen to feed her. Mabel is so eager, she jumps down, scratching Tess's arm in the process. "Ouch! Goofy cat!" She looks down at the bleeding claw marks, which quickly heal, and she washes off the blood. "Ugh, that reminds me!" She goes to the fridge for a bag of blood. She wanders out and goes through her notes again while waiting for Kari.

Kari pops in at 10:15 am. "Sorry, I'm late! The interviews ran long!" She complains.

"Is that a good or a bad sign?" Tess asks.

"Let's just say I hope some of yours pan out." Kari rolls her eyes. "So, show me what you've got!

They go through them one at a time. Tess shows her the notes on each of them. Some of them, they look at their social media again to see if Kari agrees with Tess's evaluation. Tess saves the local woman for last.

"And we have a local!" She announces, bringing up Susan's social media page.

"Hm, she looks familiar." Kari stares at her photos. "I know I've seen her before. Let me think."

"Really? She works down at the public health clinic on Biltmore Avenue as a therapist. Have we done any work for them?" Tess asks curiously.

"You know, we did a few years ago. No! Could that be her?" Kari lets out a brief snicker of disbelief and looks at Susan's friends list.

"*Who*?" Tess asks.

"Well! What do you know! *Oh, my*! Colin's gonna be surprised!" Kari grins from ear-to-ear."

"*Colin* who?" Tess gets caught up in Kari's excitement.

"Another of Liz's transformees. He worked here for a few years, and they..." She points to Susan's profile. "*had* a relationship. He was certain she was compatible, but she wasn't showing up in the database. *Now*, we know why! He transferred out West right before you began working here, because she would've soon noticed he doesn't age." Kari explains.

"Do you think he's still interested in her?" Tess asks.

"Let's see; thank goodness for admin access!" She mumbles as she skims a log of Susan's Facebook messages. She scrolls down a little. "*Voila!* They're still in touch!"

"Maybe we should let Liz know?" Tess asks.

"Definitely! Let me transfer the info on these potentials to our main system, and we'll head in. Let Marc know you'll be with me, so he doesn't freak out and call in the troops to look for you." Kari jokes.

After Tess tells Marc she's going in to the office with Kari, the two women port to Kari's office, and walk together over to see Liz.

Old times become new

Liz is sitting in her office, reviewing her notes from the morning's two interviews, when there's a knock on the frame of her office door. She turns around and smiles. It's her partner, Kari, and Tess.

"Hey, what's up?" Liz moves over to the conference area, where the two women join her.

"Tess and I were going over some of the Lost Mission data. Tess has gone through the first 107 we found DNA base matches for, and she's narrowed them down to 18 worth looking into, including one who's local." Kari explains with a wide grin.

"Really? Promising potential?" Liz yawns and puts her tablet down.

"Yep!" Tess chirps. "According to the gene print analysis, she should have a strong, genetic, psychic potential. No way to tell how much conscious or latent ability has developed without meeting her in person."

"Tell Liz the other part." Kari grins broadly, encouraging Tess to get on with it.

"But, the in person might not be necessary in this case." Tess grins and her eyes sparkle.

"Why not?" Liz asks.

"Because you've already met her according to Kari, and you know someone who knows her more than well!" Tess says with an ear-to-ear grin. "Her name's Susan Burns. Kari says she used to be involved with a friend of yours named Colin, *and* they're still in contact on Facebook!"

"Colin? Really?" Liz says with a thoughtful look. "I met her a couple of times. Colin had a *relatively* long relationship with her until a year ago. He had to reluctantly break things off." Liz taps her fingers on the table as she looks at a printout of information about Susan Burns.

"So, *he* had a relationship with someone he thought couldn't be turned?" Tess asks.

"Not everyone's as stubborn as Marc, nor do they have his baggage. But yes, Colin and Susan had a relationship for nearly 5 years. Interestingly, his intuition told him she was compatible, but the database said otherwise. He transferred out to the Seattle office so he could have an excuse to break up with her, though, I think it broke both their hearts." Liz ponders.

"Do you think he's still interested in her? Cares about her? They've stayed in touch through Facebook." Tess asks, curious.

"I'm certain he does. I'll give him a holler as soon as her file's up to date." Liz says.

"*Hva i Helvete?* Liz, you may want to do it sooner rather than later." Kari blurts out, looking down at her tablet. "I just got a notice about a data breach in the Database. If it's Jason, then he's likely looking for recent data and locals."

"*Damn it!* Get our field team to put internal and external sensors at her place that will read any of our kind within 200 meters, and set an alarm if porting is detected." Liz tells Kari, slaps her tablet down on the table, and gets up. "You're right, this *can't* wait! Track down what was accessed while I'm out. I'm going to see Colin now and set things in motion, assuming he feels she's a good fit. In this case, unless there's been some major trauma since they parted, I'm going to leave it up to him to determine her suitability, but either way, she'll need protected." She closes her door and ports out.

"Tess, go with field team 3 and see if you can get any reads on her place or her from objects, like we practiced. The clinic she works at closes at 5, so if she works until closing, you've got a few hours while the team gets sensors in order. He may or may not use his cloaking for this, but we need to know if anyone shows up at her place, other than Colin. I think there's a file for his mental signature in our system since he used to work here." Kari explains. "Then, Tess, your job is to do as much research on Susan's personality to figure out the best way to approach turning her. If Jason knows about her, then we'll have to move fast. We need some idea of how she'll react and what would be the best course for Colin to take."

"Will do! Let me give Marc a heads up. If I take off without telling him, he'll freak, even if I have a whole team of guys with me to keep me safe!" Tess chuckles.

"Take him with you! I don't want to deal with him fretting nervously while you're out." Kari complains.

"Will do! Capt. Kari!" She says with a glint in her eye, and vanishes, heading home to fill Marc in, and then on to meet field team 3 at Susan Burn's home. Kari picks up the files and her tablet and heads back to her desk in the front office, setting things in motion with the field team, as well as finding Colin's mental signature to flag it to 'allow' for the sensors being installed at Susan's home. She digs into the logs for the database and confirms someone accessed the new data she'd sent from Tess's computer that morning. "*Damn, this is a mess!*" She narrows down what was accessed before security lockdown cut him off. *Helvete! He got the info on Susan and 4 others!*" She thinks, furious that Jason has breached their system again.

***

Liz materializes outside a fairly large home on a high hill overlooking the ocean, flowers are blooming, and the air is cool. The sun is lower in the east than in Asheville. She approaches the door and it opens before she can knock.

"Liz! What are you doing here? I'm getting ready to go into the office. Is everything all right? Why didn't you tell me you were coming by?" Colin says as he embraces his old friend and mentor.

"Can I come in? I've got some news I think you'll want to hear." She says. He motions for her to come in, and she heads for the living room. He pops into the kitchen and comes out with two cups of steaming, hot coffee with a touch of cinnamon. He puts the cups down and joins Liz on the sofa.

"So, what's this world-shattering news you apparently need to tell me in person?" He takes a sip of his coffee.

"Well, we've been doing some searches for Lost Mission potentials to make up for our losses, and a familiar name popped up when we matched up her DNA!" She grins from ear-to-ear as she hands him her lit-up tablet with Susan's file.

"You're kidding me! Right? This is some kind of *prank*?" He asks, dumbfounded.

"Nope! You were right all along! She's compatible and likely a high-grade psychic potential since she's part of the Lost Mission potentials." Liz says as he continues to stare at the tablet and scrolls through her file.

"Is she to be turned?" He looks up anxiously.

"I was rather hoping you could tell us if she's suitable?" Liz explains.

He lets out a huff of annoyance before saying, "*Damn it*, Liz! You know she's suitable!" He puts the tablet down and runs his fingers through his medium-length, brown hair.

"I figured you'd know her better than our research can tell us." She acts detached and objective. "You see, there may be some urgency to turn her."

"*Urgency*? Why? Is she sick? Dying? She hasn't said anything about it to me!" He gets more anxious by the minute.

"No, it's nothing like that. I don't know if you've been following what's going on in our region, but we've been dealing with a rogue." She says.

"That Jason fellow? I heard about him. Thought you had him neutralized and locked down?" He looks confused.

"He was. He escaped about a month ago with the help of two women he'd turned and bound to him psychologically." She waits for his reaction.

"Why would he be an issue for Sue? Does he know her? Is she dating him or something?" He asks anxiously.

"No, but he's been attempting to find compatible women to turn, as he did with the two who now work with him. From what we know, he uses violence to break their wills before he turns them. This morning, while Kari and Tess were briefing me on Sue being compatible, Kari got a breach alert for the database. Jason's got some serious hacking skills. I looked at his military record recently. He was in one of those 'unofficial' units that did a lot of special ops stuff, including cyberwarfare. Granted, we're not 100% sure it was him, but it makes sense he'd try to hack the database to find compatible women. Unfortunately, he may have accessed some of the new potential info, including Sue's." She explains as calmly as she can.

"I'll go to her today and figure something out; some way to break this to her." He picks up his smartphone and checks her Facebook and other social media to see if there are any signs of things being amiss.

"I'm guessing that means you're still *interested* in her?" She asks with a lopsided, half grin.

He looks up from his phone and glares at her. "You *know* how much I care about her! How could you even think I *wouldn't* be interested?" He gripes as he notices the sparkle in Liz's eyes as she sips her coffee.

"You know, you really should add some vanilla in with that cinnamon." She tries to keep a straight face, but can't.

"Liz! *You* did this on purpose!" He accuses her.

"*Who*? *Me*? Would I encourage you to volunteer to turn your long-lost love?" She feigns surprise, blinking vapidly, trying to look innocent.

"*YES!*" He says bluntly.

"Oh, well, you've got me! And now, you've got things to plan, don't you? I've got a team putting up sensors at her place. Kari's plugging your mental signature into the system so it won't go off on you, but I'm serious, if Jason has found her info, time is of the essence!" She says seriously. "We recently stopped him from getting one potential he'd been feeding from secretly before he ran off. He was stalking her with his women, taunting her, and we have reason to believe, he planned to sexually assault her before turning her. I know you wouldn't want that to happen to Sue!"

He gets a resolved look on his face as he thinks about what might happen if Jason gets to her first. "*Got it*! You know, all you had to do was tell me she's compatible and ask if I still want to turn her!" He reaches one hand across the table and puts it on top of Liz's.

"I know, but I need to be 100% certain you *really* want to be with her, and aren't taking her on out of a sense of obligation. These Lost Mission potentials have little or no prep, so it may not be a smooth ride with any of them, and we believe a good relationship with their eventual partners is crucial." She explains.

"So, do you think I need to turn her ASAP?" He asks.

"I think the sooner the better. Our sensors are good, but Jason's got the ability to cloak, and with his other skills, I think it's best to get it over with and not take any chances. He's killed before. He intentionally killed three we know of. Luckily, we have people on the local and state police who took care of that. The two he has with him now, obviously, were compatible. One, however, he took from a psychiatric hospital, and she's a real piece of work. Since then, we found one potential he killed before she could be turned by being too rough, and another we found before she could die. She had to be turned because she was in such bad shape. He'd beaten her, sexually assaulted, and fed from her multiple times, but she still refused to give in, so he left her to die. Besides, if he knows Sue's a potential, he may want to get to her quickly, before he thinks we can protect her." She explains.

"Ok, I think she still lives where she did when I left?" He picks up the tablet.

"All the info's in there, and I'll path some other relevant info to you. I'll forward the files to your tablet, so you can look through it all. Make sure you get in touch with Sara. She has a kit put together for cases like hers: psychic enhancer, immunosuppressant,

92

and, if needed, a sedative. Plus, she'll want to monitor her as soon as she's begun transformation. These LM potentials have atypical genetic makeups that may manifest differently than the average potential. And she's the first one we'll be turning." She explains.

"Atypical? Anything to worry about?" He gives her a concerned glance.

"If you look through the file, Sara's genetic simulation suggests she may have some unusual telepathic skills, particularly along the empathic and redactive skills, but more than that, we can't tell. Sara wants to map the genetic changes the virus makes so we can get an idea where her skills may lie or if anything may be potentially dangerous to herself or others, until she gets control of it, and not being prepped means no innate control. She'll also have a Cent-opal pendant ready to limit her abilities until they're mapped, and she gains some control." Liz hurriedly explains.

"And the immunosuppressant?" He wonders.

"Normally, part of the physical prep for a potential includes a desensitization of the immune system to the virus, meaning less of an immune reaction and a shorter, and hopefully easier transformation. That's usually done in the later stages of prep, and most, if not all the LM's likely lack that, meaning transformation could be a rough ride without something to disable the immune system."

"All right, I'll stop at medical on the way to her place, but I'll do my best to turn her tonight, if possible, though I'm not sure how to break it to her." His voice oozes with anxiety.

"You may have to turn her and do damage control afterwards." She says, getting up to head back to Asheville.

"Yeah, I hope she doesn't hate me for the first century!" He puts a hand on Liz's back and pulls her in for a hug.

"Well, you got over it when I turned you!" She gives him a lopsided grin.

"Yeah, but I also had a hell of a crush on you at the time! Didn't know you and Kari were a couple!" He laughs.

"What can I say? I left that part out and let you think what you would." She jokes. "But I'm betting she still has feelings for you if she's stayed in touch all this time. Tess couldn't see any signs in her social media she's seeing anyone, so...."

"I suspected she wasn't, and I've felt awful about that. *Yes*, she's still got feelings for me, as I do for her. And I'll be *damned* if I let that *wanker* get to her first!" He exclaims.

"Good! Let me know when you get to town so I can give the field team a heads-up, so no one neutralizes you and takes you into custody!" She grins, gives a little wave, and vanishes.

Reconnecting

Colin contacts his boss in the Seattle office, informs her about the situation, that he won't be coming in, and will be transferring back to Asheville. He grabs a few things he needs with him, ports out, and reappears in the high-ceilinged lobby of the Sanctuary Medical Center. A blonde woman with short hair, Slavic features, and accent greets him.

"Hello, how can I help you?" She asks.

He says, "I'm supposed to stop by and get a transformation kit from Sara. Is she available?"

"*Oh*? Yes, she's checking on some long-termers from Jerusalem. If you go up the stairs and to the left, you'll find her office. There are chairs outside where you can wait until she's done."

"Thanks." He jogs up the steps and settles in to wait for Sara. He keeps anxiously checking the time, and just when he's about to check with the receptionist again, a dark-haired woman with a tablet approaches.

"Hello, Colin. Liz filled me in. Her gene print was among those Kari sent me when they first identified this batch of LM potentials." She motions for him to follow her into her cluttered office.

The shelves are filled with knickknacks, especially Star Wars themed ones. She opens a cupboard and pulls out a wooden box about the size and shape of a pencil case. "Here you go!" She opens the box. "All in order so you can give them to her as necessary. The blue ampoule is to help open her psychic pathways; the yellow is an immunosuppressant. You can either give it right away, or wait and see how her fever goes. If it goes above 102.5 F, give it to her immediately. There are additional ampoules of this under the top layer. If her transformation lasts beyond a day, administer a new dose every 4 hours. The last, should you need it, is a sedative." She closes the box and hands it to him with a grin. "Good luck!"

"Thank you." He stuffs it into a canvas bag with his tablet and cell.

"I've been reviewing Susan's gene print and ran it through some simulations. You know she's a Lost Mission potential?" She sits on the edge of her desk.

"Yes, Liz told me. Do I need to watch out for anything?" He asks.

"Yes! In fact, call me as soon as her transformation begins. She may present with extra strong or even atypical abilities because of the mutations." She hands him a hinged, silver bangle bracelet with a bluish, opal like stone set in silver. "If you think her abilities are getting out of control, put this on her wrist and lock it. That will prevent any unconscious use of abilities, unless she's extremely strong. If that doesn't take care of it, I've got a couple of others I'll bring with me, as well as a portable dampening field generator."

"Thanks, Liz said it would be a necklace?" He asks.

"We're testing out bracelets. There's more room for control components compared to pendants." She explains.

He sits in a chair in her office. "Any idea what abilities she may manifest other than the standard ones?"

She looks at her notes and then back up at him. "I understand she's a counselor? A therapist? I'd watch along that area. Perhaps strong people reading skills, but I suspect there's something more unusual. From the genes, it looks like a combination of healing genes and telempathy? It's in an odd configuration, so I suspect we'll have to wait and see how it manifests. Do you have my cell number? I've got so many people who yell for me telepathically these days, I've had to filter out a lot of random telepathic calls, so it's better to call me."

"No, but I'd appreciate having it." He says.

"Here's my number." She hands him a card. "If you can, call or text when you're about to begin the transformation so I can be on standby; or call me as soon as it's underway."

"Thanks, I will." He takes the card and puts it with the transformation kit in his bag. He nods to Sara, ports out, and appears in Liz's office.

"Colin! I thought you'd be wooing Susan by now." She grins.

"No, it took a while at Medical, as Sara's still got her hands full." He sits on the back of the sofa, facing Liz at her desk.

Liz leans back in her chair, thoughtfully. "Guess you got the kit? What can I help you with?"

"Yeah, Sara gave me that and the psychic suppressor, but was wondering if you have a company car I could borrow for now? I'd rent one, but I always get weird vibes from prior renters." He grimaces.

"Sure! They're down in the garage. They're all electric or hybrids. Kari has the keys at her desk." She says, "Have you figured out how to break it to her?"

"Been running through scenarios in my head since we spoke, but won't know until I see how she reacts to my being back in town! Any sign of my competition?" He looks concerned, and Liz senses his anxiety for Susan.

"Not yet, but we're setting up sensors with alarms that will inform us if he comes within 200 meters of her place or if anyone ports in! You're all set though, Kari added you to the clearance list, so it won't go off on you."

"Okay, I need to call her and let her know I'm in town, but will keep you informed." He heads over to see Kari about a car and borrows a black Tesla. He gets into the car and fishes out his cell; calls her cell from memory, but it naturally goes to voicemail. *Hm, she's probably in a session.* He leaves her a voicemail. "Sue! It's Colin! I've got a big surprise for you! Call me when you have a second between patients, please." He knows she has his number memorized.

He drives around to see how much Asheville has changed since he left. A couple of new hotels have been built, and a new series of statues have been installed near the Art Museum where the Vance Monument used to be. It was a Civil War memorial that was removed several years back. He stops at a florist's and picks up a dozen of Sue's favorite roses, peace roses, with their yellow color and delicate pink highlights. He gets back in his car and is driving through town when his cell rings. It's Sue's ringtone, a clip from "She blinded me with Science" by Thomas Dolby, and smiles as he answers.

"Sue!" He says happily.

"Colin! I got your message. Been a while since I got a call from you! What's up?" She asks curiously.

Coincidentally, he's driving past where she works on Biltmore Avenue, and reaches an empathic tendril out to touch her mind. "Well, I don't want to tell you over the phone, but I'm in Asheville on business and wondered if I could pick you up from work today? I know you usually take the bus in, so figured maybe I could get you and we could grab some dinner and talk?" He suggests.

"You're in town! Why the hell didn't you tell me you were coming? My place is a mess. "Let me make a couple of calls. I was going out for drinks with a couple of other therapists tonight. It's been a hell of a long week for us. Everyone's having major crises lately. Let me tell them something's come up and I should be done around 4:30 today. We end a little early on Fridays." He can hear a knock on her door in the background, and a receptionist letting her know her next client has arrived.

"Sounds like a deal! I'll see you then! Keep an eye out for a black Tesla; I'm borrowing a company car while I'm in town, and sorry I didn't let you know sooner. Things happened very suddenly, so I had to drop everything and come out. It's been such a whirlwind for me, too!" He explains. "But the whole time, I was looking forward to seeing you once I was done with my business."

"Cool, knowing you're in town makes an otherwise awful week bearable. I'll call you if it's going to be later than 4:30, but park in the main lot if I'm not outside waiting. Gotta run! Next client's here! Bye!" She hangs up in a rush as her client comes in.

With a sigh of relief, Colin hangs up and calls Liz. "Hey Liz! Got a favor to ask. Can you connect my place to a local portal home if you have any available?"

"Let's see…" She trails off as she checks her computer. "Your old locale is taken, but we have one close to the office, right off Sweeten Creek Road, a few miles from here. Will that do?"

"That should be fine, but I want to have it ready, in case."

"There's only one problem, your Sanctuary home is significantly larger, so anyone who visits you there will think they're in a TARDIS!" Liz chuckles as she references the famous time-ship that's bigger on the inside.

He smiles as an idea forms in his mind. "Hmm, that could come in handy! I need to eventually tell her what's going on. That incongruity could help break the proverbial ice." He explains.

"I'm sure it's going to get touch and go since she isn't prepped, but at least you have a real relationship to build on which should help." Liz says. "Oh, by the way, we've got people keeping an eye on her workplace from Limbo." Their nickname for the membrane between the two realities they travel through when they port.

"Great! I'm relieved knowing she's protected, but will feel a hell of a lot better when I have her with me!" He turns left into Biltmore Village, drives onto Sweeten Creek, and heads back toward the office and his 'portal home'. "I'm picking her up from work this afternoon and taking her to dinner, and then will see how things go from there. Are the monitors fully operational at her place?"

"Yah, all set. If Jason or anyone like us other than you sets foot within 200 meters of her place, we'll get a warning alarm." She says.

"Good! I'd hate to run into an ambush at her place tonight."

"You should consider putting a subcutaneous GPS tracker on her, in case she gets snatched. Kari fixed one up after your visit. I'll put it in your new office on the second floor. You'll be more likely to get her in a position to implant it." She says with a knowing inflection.

"Liz, wipe that mental grin off your brain!" He can picture her face in his mind.

"Well, I know you've been living like a hermit since you went out west." She chuckles.

"As has she, but I won't rush anything, especially if she reacts badly. The priority is breaking this to her and turning her, anything else can wait." He turns on the GPS and puts in the address Liz texted to the portal home.

"It might be easier to turn her in bed and explain things afterwards." She suggests.

He lets out a grumble at her suggestion as he comes to a stop at a light. "No, she deserves to know and understand, not only what I am, but why I left, and why I want to turn her. She also needs to know about Jason and how dangerous he is. I'm hoping she'll want to be with me, even knowing what I am, but the situation with Jason may tip the scales in my favor."

"Do whatever you think's best. Sara and our resident people reader, Tess, will be on standby." She encourages him.

"Tess? I thought that was Kari's job?" He asks.

"Yes, it was, and still is. Tess is a relatively new addition, but she's extremely gifted. She's been doing most of the research on the Lost Mission potentials, including evaluations, and clearing for transformation. I'll text you her cell since you've never dealt with her.

"I would have thought something like that would be better for someone more experienced as an Apara?" He pauses as he rolls the name over in his mind. "Wait, is this the human who helped figure out the nukes?"

"*Ja*, one and the same! Though she's one of us now. She's with Marc, so you can call him if you need to reach her. She, herself, was a misfiled potential, though not from the Lost Mission group. Long story, but we didn't think she was compatible, but it turned out she was. Luckily, she still found her way to us through a job ad." Liz laughs.

"Great, I'm glad Marc finally settled down with someone. He's been avoiding that for as long as I can remember!" Colin remarks.

"As have you, Colin. They're a splendid match, as are you and Susan. Keep me in the loop, and if you need me, you know how to reach me. I need to get back to things here." She hangs up.

Colin touches base with Marc by phone. Marc answers, recognizing the number, saying, "Hello, stranger! I hear you've got your hands full today?" Marc insinuates.

"Wow, word gets around fast with telepaths, doesn't it?" Colin chuckles.

"No telepathy necessary! Tess, my partner, told me all about it." Marc laughs. "She's excited Sue will be the first of the Lost Mission potentials to join us. Personally, I think she's hoping for more friends closer to her own chronological age to hang out with!"

"That would explain you're knowing. By the way, thank her from me! I'm grateful to find out Sue can be transformed!" Colin says as he continues to drive down the road.

"Message relayed!" Marc says.

"Hey, can you recommend a good restaurant? The one we used to go to all the time is closed." Colin asks.

"Try *Le Petit Chou* on Lexington. Granted, I'm partial to French cuisine." Marc chuckles, and pulls Tess close as she's come over to him, curious about how everything's progressing with Susan.

"Great, I'll make reservations. We'll catch up soon. I've got to get ready to pick Sue up." He tells Marc.

"Hold up a sec, Tess just came in and wants two words with you." Marc says.

"Okay...."

"Hi, Colin, Kari asked me to look into Susan and see if I could figure out how to approach turning her, and I wanted to run this by you and see if it fits, since you know her better than anyone." Tess says anxiously.

"Sure, I could use a couple of suggestions." He drives past the parking lot for Inspiration, Inc.

"From what I can see on her social media and the discussions she has; she doesn't like to be told what to think or believe. She's an independent personality that likes to work out puzzles based on facts and observations. Either she wants proof, or she wants to figure things out for herself based on the evidence. I guess it's her scientific training to be a shrink? Does that make sense? Does it fit?" Tess is anxious about her first attempt at this part of her job.

"That makes sense. Yep, the researcher side of her would react that way." He flashes back to some of the theoretical discussions they had when they were together, and how she argued, and begged for him to present hard evidence for his suppositions. He smiles to himself.

"I think it would help if she sees the clues and comes to her own conclusions, or has evidence that makes it hard to deny, but if you're too direct, and try to tell her what's what, she'll balk. *Oh!* And don't rush her or she'll fight you tooth and nail!" Tess sounds more confident as she lets her intuitive side take over.

"Yeah, I was leaning toward that anyway. Liz connected me to the only available portal home in the area, but it's one-third the size of my real home, plus she's been in my home many times before. If we end up there, the incongruity will get to her, and I can use that as an opening. I think I can make that work. *Thanks!*" He says.

"You're welcome and thanks for the feedback! I'm new at this part of it, but Kari thinks I should be good at figuring people out. Good luck!" She hands the phone back to Marc and goes back to work with a renewed energy and spring in her step.

"We'll talk soon. You should know Tess was also in a similar boat to Sue, so yell if you think she needs to talk to someone who can sympathize, and we can arrange a meetup." Marc suggests.

"Thanks, old friend! I'll keep that in mind! Liz already suggested hollering Tess's way." He hangs up as he pulls up to the rather small home at the address Liz gave him.

The small portal home is only about 950 square feet, as opposed to his Sanctuary dwelling of about 2700 square feet. "That will certainly be hard for her to explain away!" He thinks. He goes to his bedroom and changes clothing into something suitable for dinner. He spends a little time thinking about how he can present clues he can use to nudge her into accepting what's happening.

Dinner and detours

His cell alarm goes off at 4 pm, he grabs the car keys and heads back toward town to the Public Health Clinic on Biltmore Avenue. At a little before 4:30 pm, he turns into the parking lot behind a very large, red brick building. He finds a spot where he can watch the front door. At 4:38 pm, a tall woman with long auburn hair and hazel eyes comes out of the building and looks around the parking lot. She has a braid down her back, and is wearing professional work clothes. Colin grins, suppressed emotions welling to the surface now that he knows she's genetically compatible. She looks around, trying to spot the black Tesla; then spotting the car and making eye contact with him. He can sense the old, subconscious telempathic connection wake to life again and it's like no time has passed at all.

She rushes over to the car and opens the passenger door. "Going my way?" She asks with a wry smile.

"Why, yes, I think I am!" He reaches out and takes her left hand as she gets into the car and settles into the seat. She leans over to give him a hug, but he catches her eye and leans in for a long-overdue kiss.

"Wow! I needed that!" She feels like electricity is coursing through her, not unpleasant, but like her nerves are vibrating.

"Me, too!" He gives her a lopsided grin. He hands her the roses, watching her expectantly.

"You remembered my *favorites*!" She leans forward to smell the flowers.

"Yeah, I thought you'd like those! Hey! I made reservations at *Le Petit Chou*, the French restaurant on Lexington, how's that sound?"

"*Wonderful*! Last time I was there, their quiche of the day was during morel season. Oh *MY GOD*! It was *so* good! They added in some white truffles, bacon, and Brie in the filling. It was amazing!" She exclaims.

"Great! I don't know if you ever met Marc Girard, from my office, but he's originally from France and recommended them." He backs out of the parking space, and drives out and onto Biltmore Avenue, heading north.

There's a fair amount of traffic, so it takes them a few minutes. They drive up Biltmore Avenue and make a couple of turns until they're on Lexington. They drive around the block a couple of times looking for parking and eventually end up in a nearby parking garage. Before she knows it, he's outside her door, opening it, and helping her out.

She gives him a proper bear hug now that they're both standing. After a minute, she says, "I probably should've changed clothes before going out to dinner."

"You look fine. Besides, your place is clear up in Weaverville. I'm sure they'll forgive you for any fashion *faux pas*! He pulls her against his side with one arm, they head out of the parking deck, and walk to *Le Petit Chou*.

They go into the restaurant and get seated. "So, what's this big news you couldn't tell me on the phone?" Her eyes are sparkling with excitement.

"I'm transferring back to Asheville, effective immediately." He gives her an ear-to-ear grin and waits for her reaction.

"*Really*? Oh my God! That's amazing news." Her first reaction is excitement, but then she wonders how things stand between them. *Does he want to pick up where we left off or just stay friends?*

"Yeah, isn't it though? As soon as they offered, I was ready to come back and the first thing I wanted to do after my meeting with Liz was see you." He can sense her uncertainty in waves of anxiety emanating from her as they look at the menu "Is everything okay?"

"Oh, yeah, it all looks so good! But I think I'll do the quiche again; no morels, but it's always good." She looks at the prices of

104

the full entrees and figures she can't justify spending $35 on the duck entrée that makes her mouth water.

"Sue, don't worry about the prices, *love*, this is on me. It's a celebratory meal! They gave me a bonus for moving back on short notice, so, no worries about the cost." He knows her job doesn't pay well because it's a community clinic. However, he can sense her anxiety is about more than the cost.

"Are you sure? The thing I want is about the most expensive thing on the menu, and I don't want to take advantage of you." She admits.

"Order the duck, *love*. I know it's your favorite! Seriously, it's not an issue." He reaches across the table and puts his hand on hers.

She stares at him, making sure he isn't just saying that to be nice or to impress her, then she breaks into a smile. "The duck it is!"

"Good! I'm going to have the lamb. Hope you don't mind me eating all that garlic?" He smiles his nearly perfect smile that always makes her melt.

"You know I like garlic!" She laughs. "Remember that time I made spaghetti and a full loaf of garlic bread and we were competing to see who could eat the most?"

"How can I forget? You bought a two-pound loaf of white bread for it and used what? Five cloves and a pound of butter for the whole thing?" He laughs and his eyes sparkle as he remembers.

"Well, not quite a pound!" She blushes, shyly. "I can't believe you're coming back to town to live!" She's confused and isn't sure if his kiss in the car was just for old time's sake, or if he wants to rekindle their old relationship. She has an odd inkling about his intensions.

"Is there anything you'd like to do after dinner?" He encourages her to talk, hoping whatever's on her mind might come out. He doesn't want to use his telepathy to pluck it out of her mind if he can avoid it, so hopes he can draw out her thoughts verbally.

"I don't know, hang out more, I guess." She tries to be non-committal until she gleans more about his intensions, trying not to get her hopes up too high.

Sensing her unease, he strikes up conversation. "It's so good to see you again! I think I missed you before I'd even left. It'll be good to be back here again." He smiles reassuringly.

"Yeah, I've missed you too..." She trails off and eats some French bread and butter that's been delivered while they wait for their meals.

"Are you okay? You seem worlds away." He senses swirling emotions from her, ranging from being glad to see him, to undertones of hurt, anger, and fear.

"It's nothing, *really*." She continues to eat her bread and has a sip of wine.

"Somehow, I think there's more going on." He says.

Maybe I should be direct? That's what I'd tell my clients! She thinks. "Do you *really* want to know?" She snaps.

"Yes, I do. What's *bothering* you?" He reaches for her hand, which she pulls away, but he won't let her.

She purses her lips, annoyed as his touch diffuses a little of her frustration and anger, now that she's being open about things. "Okay, here goes! *You're the one* that went away. You *chose* your job over me! Never even asking if I might want to go with you! You may have *missed* me, and I *missed* you, but when you left, it *hurt*! Even though I'm happy you're coming back, I just...." She trails off in frustration and a hint of tears glisten along her lower eyelid.

He finally senses what's bothering her, as her unspoken words echo in his mind telepathically. "You're wondering if I'll leave again. If you can trust me not to hurt you."

She lets out a deep breath. "I let myself get caught up in a deep connection to you and then you were gone. How do I know you won't do that again? For that matter, I don't even know if you want to pick up where we left off, or just be friends." She sounds frustrated and deflated.

"Sue, I know my leaving was hard on you, but at the time, I felt it was necessary. It's difficult to explain, but I promise, I'm here to stay this time, and I *will* explain *everything*." He holds up his hand when he senses she's about to chime in. "Give me a chance! When I left, it was based on

106

information I had, some of which turned out to be wrong, and I'm back here more for you than for the job." He gives her a lopsided grin. "I *love* you, and I want us to be together, but I'd prefer to explain when we don't have a potential audience around us." He glances around at the other tables. "Some of what I need to tell you I don't want anyone but you to know." He carefully puts a slight telepathic spin on it for her to accept and wait until they have some privacy.

She sits there weighing his words, then nods. "I better get the full story, buddy. I invested my heart in us, and I was only now healing from you leaving, when *suddenly*, you're *back*!" She goes quiet as the waiter clears the bread away and brings out their entrees.

Once the waiter has put the food in front of them, Colin says "*Merci beaucoup.*" in perfectly accented French to the waiter, who bows slightly, and walks away." Sue, I'm going to make it all up to you. But let's talk after dinner. We'll take that Tesla I borrowed for a spin down the road and take the parkway back up to your place, maybe even stop at the overlook. Who knows, maybe we'll even see a shooting star you can make a wish on." He smiles, she always had to make a wish when she saw shooting stars.

"*Okay!*" She lets a slight grin sneak through. "But *if* your explanations are up to snuff, you've got some making up to me to do!" She blushes and digs into her duck.

"Don't worry, we're going to have plenty of time to make up for time lost." He says, knowing soon, he won't have to worry about her mortality.

She blushes and changes the subject to something more mundane. "So, is it the same old job, or is it a new position?" She asks.

"Combination of the two. Mostly the same thing I've been doing for them both here and out West, but also some training work; training up a new person we're getting in soon." He takes a bite of his lamb.

"Oh? Guy or gal?" She says with a raised eyebrow.

"A woman." He gets pangs of jealousy coming from her.

"Oh?" She asks.

"Pull your claws in, little dragon! I promise you; you won't have any reason to be jealous." He thinks, *because it will be you!*

"Sorry, I guess everything's got me a bit hypersensitive." She digs into the roasted potatoes that came with the duck.

"Understandable. But try to put it out of your mind." He says.

They finish their meal, then order dessert, sharing a serving of *Mousse Au Chocolat* and *Crème brûlée*. Colin pays the check and leaves a nice tip. He helps Sue up, and they head for the parking garage. As they're walking to his car after getting off the elevator, Colin gets a tingling sensation like they're being watched, but can't see anyone around. He also senses traces of anger and impatience coming from whomever is watching them. He gets her to the car, helps her in, locks the doors and heads out. After they're a few blocks away from the parking deck, the feeling abates. He paths to Liz. *Liz? Do you have any idea why someone would be watching us in town? Are any of your people monitoring Sue?*

No, they've got monitors at her place, and one person making rounds nearby, but no one in town. I figured you'd be with her, so it isn't necessary, why? Liz paths.

Because I had an impression of being watched in the parking deck with hostile overtones, and it felt like one of us, frequency-wise." He paths as he drives down Patton Avenue downtown toward the highway.

Hostile? It could be Jason or one of his tracking her, hoping to make a move. She paths.

Good thing I didn't delay. Not going to let her out of my sight for sure! Let me know if he or anyone shows at her place. We're going to take a drive via the parkway. She and I need to talk some stuff through. I'll keep it 'human' until we get to her place. He paths.

Yeah, you don't want her trying to get out of the car while you're driving, to get away from the big, bad 'vampire'. She paths, sending images of him with goofy fangs hanging out of his mouth, salivating.

Stop that! I don't need to explain to her why I lose it when you send those images! She's already having some trust issues because of my leaving. I don't want her to think I'm laughing at her. He paths.

Sure thing. Will keep you in the loop if the alarms go off. She paths, and then mental silence.

108

Sue chimes in. "So, are we gonna talk or stare at the scenery?" She asks, as he takes the exit to go down 26 East.

"We'll talk, I'm trying to remember how to get to the parkway down near the outlets. Figured we'd start there and work our way up toward Weaverville, okay?" He asks.

She crosses her arms in front of her, defensively. "I guess. It'll give us some time to talk."

He turns off onto Brevard Road by the outlets and drives down past the entrance to Bent Creek Forest and the Arboretum. He turns onto the exit for the parkway and heads back toward Asheville and Weaverville. The sun's already set and a light fog is seeping in around the French Broad River below them.

"So, what was this wrong information you based your decision to leave on?" She tries to kick off the conversation.

He's silent at first, looking thoughtful. "Sue, if I tell you that now, it would be like beginning a book in the middle, and you won't understand the significance of the dialog because it refers to an earlier event. I need to tell you the entire story, from the beginning. I know I suggested we could talk while we drive, but I'd rather wait until we get to your place where we can face each other rather than me focusing on the road.

Sue's frustrated and exasperated, but agrees with him. "I guess so, but I need you to be straight with me then. We need to clear the air before we go any further, now that you're back."

They're driving east and as they're crossing over the highway; Colin gets a telepathic heads-up. *Got alarms all over the place. Will call in a minute. Pretend it's all business and head to the office where there's shielding!* Liz paths.

He hides any outward reaction, and paths back *Gotcha!* Ten seconds later, his cell rings, and he answers it through the touch screen in the Tesla. "Hello? Colin?" Liz's voice comes over the speaker as though nothing is wrong.

"Yes, Liz. What's up?" He asks, as nonchalantly as possible.

"Are you anywhere near the office?" She asks.

"Not too far. I'm driving on the parkway with Sue, but we're coming up on Hendersonville Road, so could get over to the office easily from here, why?" He says, pulling off along the side of the road just before the needed exit.

"I need you to sign some papers tonight so we can officially put the transfer through. I've got to run out, Kari's expecting me home for dinner, but if I leave them on your desk, could you swing by, go through, and sign them? I'm so sorry to interrupt your evening. I know you've been looking forward to it." She adds.

"*Sure*, I'll swing by and get that out of the way, I got a keycard from Kari, so I can let myself in." He says.

"Thanks so much! See you bright and early on Monday." She hangs up.

"Sorry, Sue, unavoidable delay. I've got to go by the office and sign the transfer paperwork, but it shouldn't take long." He turns the ignition again, and takes the exit that'll take to the office.

"Should I just wait in the car for you?" She asks.

"*No*, I've heard there have been some safety issues lately, I'd rather you come in with me.

"Whatever." She finds her purse and phone as they pull into the lot for Inspiration, Inc. Again, he's at her door before she can open it and helps her out. He visually scans the area as if looking for something. "Worried Bigfoot is gonna come out and get us?" She asks.

"No, but there are often bears so close to the parkway, and Liz said they've had some issues with homeless people prone to violence recently. Let's get inside." He takes her by the arm and heads for the front door. He uses a keycard to get into the main building and visibly relaxes once the doors close and lock behind him. "We're heading up to the second floor. They've expanded since I worked here earlier." He unlocks the door to that level and walks down the hall to an office. He opens the door and turns on the light. "You can relax on the sofa." He heads over to the pile of papers on his desk. A note on top saying:

Stall for time! We're trying to catch him and his cohorts at her place. It's *definitely not* safe to take her there! He was inside her house.

Liz.

"Sue, this may take longer than I thought," He holds up a pile of papers in a binder nearly an inch thick. Feel free to take a nap or log into the Wi-Fi. Password is Apara42." He says. She logs in and kills time on her phone. Eventually, she lies down on the sofa and dozes off.

Liz! Status update please! He paths.

They got away, though there were four of them, so he's turned someone recently! It's not safe to bring her home, not even if you plan to spend the night! Liz paths.

Well, I guess it's off to my place, then. Will let her sleep so it gets late, then I can make an excuse for us to go there rather than continue up to her place across town. Wish me luck! He says.

You'll need it! Especially if she freaks out over your TARDIS house. She paths.

Yeah, that and the fact it's the same house she's been in hundreds of times, but with a different façade, in a different location, should be quite a way to kick off our conversation. He paths.

Well, if you get the chance to turn her, you've got the kit with you, right? She paths.

Yes! Meds, Cent-opal bracelet for afterwards, and the GPS chip in case I don't turn her tonight! All in my bag in the car except for the GPS, which I have here on my desk. One way or the other, however, she's going to get the truth tonight. He paths. *Hey, Liz, since I shouldn't take her back to her place, can you get someone to fill a couple of suitcases or bags with some essentials for her? Even if she won't let me turn her yet, I'll have to keep her at my place where she'll be safe. This could be a long weekend. If I don't answer at any point, send someone over to make sure she hasn't put me in stasis!* He jokes, mentally chuckling.

Will keep that in mind! Liz paths. *By the way, Tess said to take things slow and let her logic her way through some fill in the blanks, if that makes any sense?*

Yeah, it does! Thanks, I already spoke to Marc and Tess this afternoon. She's stubborn, and if she's able to piece together aspects of it all without me telling her, she's more likely to accept it. She does NOT like to be told what to think! She prefers to draw her own conclusions and has fought for her own, even when wrong, if pushed. He explains.

He sits at his desk, thinking over what he needs to say and do for a couple of hours. When he's ready to wake her up, he paths Liz, *Here goes everything!*

Whatever Gods there are must like you tonight! She paths and he can sense her amusement.

Why's that? He replies.

There's a water main break on Merrimon Avenue, and a jackknifed tractor trailer on 26 west, just after UNCA's exit, and everyone's going a snail's pace up Kimberly and other alternative routes. To top it all off, the rain the last few days caused a small mud slide on the parkway near the overlook, so you have one hell of an excuse to take her to your place. She mentally chuckles.

That's insane! He says.

We may have had something to do with the water main break and the mudslide, but the tractor-trailer was coincidence. We considered setting something up there too, a fake accident to back up traffic or 'construction', but human nature beat us to it! She paths. *Get going! Will keep my 'path-ways' open in case you need anything.*

Thanks, Liz. This should prove interesting and challenging! He gets up from his desk after signing a few places for show and goes over to the couch.

Crossing the threshold
to the Twilight Zone

He sits on the back of the sofa. "Wakey, wakey! Sleepy head!" He leans down and brushes her cheek with his hand.

"Hm, what time is it?" She stretches and opens her eyes a squint.

About 9:00 pm! It took a lot longer than I thought to go through the papers." He says.

"Maybe you better just get me home and we can talk tomorrow?" She sits up and squints at the light in the room.

"About that, the traffic gods have been wreaking havoc." He hands her a tablet with Google maps showing the long red lines almost every route they could take to get to her place.

"*Damn*! You've got to be *shitting* me! *All* the routes?" She hands him the tablet, shaking her head.

"So, it seems! Three are physically blocked and the alternate routes are backed up with traffic and have been for a while." He explains.

"Well, isn't that just dandy? What am I supposed to do? Crash here for the night?" She asks sarcastically.

"They've set me up with a little place down Sweeten Creek, close to the plant nursery. We could go there, talk, and see if the roads improve later tonight." He hesitates, and then suggests, "Or you could stay with me tonight."

"Oh, *Hell*, why not? Sorry, I wake up grumpy sometimes." She says. He laughs. "Yeah, I can *vouch* for that!" She gives him a nasty look.

Sue gets up and collects her stuff into her purse, and looks at Colin. With a grand flourish of her hand, she says "Lead the way!" and wonders if the wine from dinner hasn't set in a little hard as she stumbles.

Colin uses this as an excuse to steady her and lead her by the arm, back downstairs and to the car, watching for signs of trouble. They get in the car and drive a couple of miles down the road and into a residential area near Skyland, where he pulls the Tesla into the driveway of a small brick house. "We're here." He grins and pats her left leg.

"Tiny place! Hope they get you something with a little more space in it. You'll *never* get all your stuff in there." She says as they go up the walk to the door.

He unlocks it and says, "It's bigger than it looks. Ladies first." He motions for her to go in and waits for the reaction.

About three seconds after she walks in, she walks back out again. "What the actual *hell*? Either I had too much wine and am hallucinating, or your living room's bigger than the whole, damn house!" She says, confused.

"Just go in and have a look around, love. It will all be clear soon." He says quietly, and guides her back in carefully, this time following her in, closing the door and locking it behind him.

"This, *this* is just wrong!" She gets a good look around, noticing familiar furniture, art, and an all too familiar fireplace, realizing there was *no* chimney on the outside of the house. She looks at the mantle, and picks up a picture frame of them together, and one of her alone. She looks over to a bookshelf and finds several books she gave him as gifts, complete with her personalized notes in the front covers. She realizes not only is all his stuff already here, and clearly in a place too small for it all, but it's the same layout, no, the same HOUSE he lived in, in West Asheville before he transferred out West. "*How?* This makes no sense!" She runs down the hallway to the bedroom they often shared. Same bed, new curtains, but everything else is pretty much the same. She sits on the side of the bed and it even makes the same wooden creaks, and her mind stumbles to a mental syntax error of 'halt-this does not compute'.

Colin comes in and gently sits next to her. "Are you okay?" He knows her mind is blown.

"Either I'm still in your office asleep and dreaming, or we're in your old house, but it's not where it used to be and from the outside, it's about a third the size?" She's dumbfounded.

"It's my house. Same one as in West Asheville, same one I live in out west, and before Asheville, when I lived in Indiana and Arizona." He says as though everything is normal.

She looks up at his face, eyes large, and her stomach churns like it's going to reject her dinner at any second. "That's not possible! The same house can't be in all those different places, and you certainly couldn't have picked it up and taken it with you."

"Your right, it's not in all those places, and I didn't take it with me. The house is in one place, and hasn't moved. What's moved is the door." He strokes her hair gently, sensing the distress in her mind at the incongruity of what she's seeing and what he's saying. "You sure you're ready for our talk now? Because this is just the beginning of what I need to tell you, and you're already rather overwhelmed." He says, giving her an option to slow down.

She blinks and shakes off the mental paralysis she's been sinking into. "Oh, *Hell!* I've already jumped down the rabbit hole, might as well give me the full tour of Wonderland!"

"Alright. All I ask is you be patient and keep an open mind. A lot of what I need to tell you, your gut reaction will be to reject, or even be afraid of me, but other than leaving before, I'd *never* do anything to hurt you, and on some level, you know that." He stands, extending a hand to her. He walks her back to the living room by the door. "You might want to take another look outside." He suggests.

She looks at him sideways, pursing her lips in annoyance. "I think I saw what I needed to. The outside was smaller than the inside!"

He unlocks the door and says, "Humor me, please."

She reaches for the doorknob, turns it, and opens the door, and the first thing she notices is it's still light out. "What the...?" She steps outside and her brain freezes up. She turns back toward the door. "Where the hell's the car? For that matter, where the hell's the driveway, the street, and your neighbors?" Her heart rate skyrockets.

Colin steps out of the house and takes her hand again, but she resists as he pulls her along with him. He stares her down. "Trust me. I need to show you something, and then I'll explain."

After a couple of seconds studying his face, she relents and follows him down a dirt path past bushes and flowering vines, and through a gap in a small crop of trees. As she reaches the other side, she gasps. "This isn't Asheville or even North Carolina, is it?" She asks as she stares out over a vast ocean with the sun low on the horizon. Colin snickers, but waits for her to draw her own conclusions. She sits on the grassy ridge overlooking the ocean below. She can hear waves crashing hundreds of feet below her, seagulls screeching and other sea sounds, but no signs of civilization. No cars, planes, voices, boat horns, nothing. "If I had to guess, we're somewhere on the West Coast...yeah, three hours behind Asheville would be evening, and the sun is setting in the West, so unless you knocked me out and that's sunrise in the east?" She glances at Colin for confirmation.

He sits next to her on the grass. "Yeah, West Coast of what would be Vancouver Island!" He confirms.

"Would be?" She looks at him and waits for his explanation.

"I'm guessing you noticed there's no sign of neighbors, roads, or civilization. This is going to be hard for you to swallow, but what I'm going to tell you is the hard truth! Technically, we're no longer on the same planet, but on a parallel Earth where humans never evolved." He pauses and watches her closely for a reaction.

She's silent at first, not sure what to do with that information. "*Bullshit*! How is that even possible? They haven't proven the multiverse exists; how can we be on an alternate earth?" She's confused because it shouldn't be possible, but is faced with the evidence in front of her.

"This is where things may get a little rocky. The technology exists, and while my home is here and has been for a long time, the front door is tied to a destination portal on a dummy home on our

116

Earth, so when I come in the door, I go from Asheville on our original Earth, call it Earth Prime, and cross to this world, to my home around 3000 miles and a world away." He explains it as if he were explaining the workings of some basic machine to a child.

"If I hadn't seen it for myself..." She trails off. "But why didn't it open up to Asheville when I came out this time?"

"Because the portal only works when I, or someone who's programmed in as having access, touches the doorknob. You aren't programmed in, so it reverted to a normal door." He explains patiently.

"But it used to work for me before you moved. I was in and out of here all the time!" She says, frustrated.

He smiles and gives her a sympathetic look. "Yes, but when the portal was redirected to the dummy house near Seattle, it was wiped and reset, so you're no longer on the 'approved' list." He snickers, but that'll change."

"Well, that's just too weird! But what if you want it to work like a regular door?" She asks.

"It will also work as a regular door if I want it to, but right now, let's skip that tangent. We have more important things to talk about than the technical specs of inter-dimensional doors." He stands and reaches down to help her up. She turns and takes another look at the ocean as the sun sinks lower, where shades of orange, red, and purple stain the sea from the impending sunset.

"So, if the portal doesn't work for me, that means I'm trapped here unless you let me out." She asks as they walk back toward the house, a tinge of anxiety sneaking into her voice.

He puts his open hand gently on her back and herds her toward the house. "I wouldn't say trapped, because that implies you may be in danger. In fact, you're here because you're safer here than on Earth Prime right now."

"Safer? Why?" She asks.

"I'm getting to that, but I have to take this one step at a time, and unfortunately, the next one's gonna be a doozy, and you really need to trust me." They wind up the path and approach the house. "Look, that's how the outside of the house actually looks." and sure enough, the outer size matches the vastness inside, and there's even a chimney.

"Yeah, that's more like it...." She shakes her head, getting a slight headache. They walk up the path to the door, and go in.

"Have a seat in the living room. I'll fix some snacks for us. This is going to be a long night." He says and goes off to his kitchen.

She sits on the same old sofa she'd not only sat on many times, but even napped on, and spent more than a couple of intimate evenings on with Colin. She thinks, *This is too bizarre! How the hell does he have this technology? What is he, some kind of secret government agent? Someone from another Earth that has this technology, and brought it with him?* She continues in that vein until he comes back from the kitchen with a large tray and a box. He brings out snacks: fruits, chips, cheeses, and her favorite cream puffs, half-thawed, just as she likes them. After putting the tray down, he pulls out plates, glasses and a bottle of wine, a jug of water, and some of the soda she likes.

"Here's some soda, for now, but you may want something stronger as the discussion progresses." He gives her a weak smile. He walks over to the fireplace and picks up the framed photo of the two of them the day they met at the beach seven years earlier. He sits next to her and hands it to her. She already has a full plate of snacks in front of her, and has downed half a glass of soda. "Do you remember that day?"

She looks at the picture and then at him, her mouth twitches briefly into a smile as she remembers their first encounter. "I'll never forget that day! That big wave washed me into shore and practically on top of you! It was like fate wanted us to meet and pushed me into you."

"Yeah, I think we were meant to meet." He pauses. "I want you to take a good look at the picture and tell me what you see.

She does, but thinks he means her interpretation of how she felt, and her memories. "I was so happy, at least until I got nauseous that night and threw up all over my hotel room." She strokes the picture, remembering.

118

"Yeah, you probably shouldn't have packed a lunch with tuna salad on a 90-degree day. I dare say you had food poisoning." He strokes her arm absent-mindedly. "Look closer at me in that picture and then look at me now, seven years later. What do you notice?

She looks closely at the photo, then at him, and back at the photo again, scrunching up her eyebrows. "*Damn!* You sure age well, don't you? You've hardly changed at all! Maybe your hair's a little different, but, yeah, you look the same. *Hell*, I don't! I've found a couple of stray gray hairs and I'm only 27!" She rambles.

He takes the picture out of her hands and puts it down on the coffee table, then takes both of her hands in his. "There's a reason I don't look much different after seven years. I've looked like this since well before we met." He pulls out his wallet, and takes out a worn, black and white photo with the date on the back: May 21, 1953. He hands it to her face down. "Turn it over." He says.

Nervously, she turns it over and looks confused. "Is this your father?" She asks, suspecting it isn't; part of her intuiting the truth. He doesn't say anything, but brings up the color picture of the two of them, takes the black-and-white picture and places it next to his part of the photo, both of which show a distinctive birthmark on his neck. He waits for her to say what she's thinking, but is loath to say.

"That's *you* too, isn't it?" She gulps, her stomach knots, and clenches as she considers the ramifications.

"I think you know the answer." He says quietly.

"How can that be? That was decades ago! That would make you old enough to be my grandfather!" She blurts out, but then regrets that thought as she wrestles with the connotations. She looks up at him, eyes wide. "What *are you*?"

"What do you *think* I am? Make a guess." He leans back on the sofa.

"I don't know, someone's science experiment? An alien? An earth bound god or angel or...I don't know! A vampire? No! That one's absurd, you like garlic too much, I met you at the beach, I got a sunburn, and you didn't, so forget that one. I don't *know*.

What are you?" She asks again, looking at his eyes and noticing a mixture of sympathy and slight amusement.

He looks down at his hands, again grasping hers lightly. "One of your guesses was mostly right." He grins. "Look at me!" He commands and jerks her hands to make her look at him. As she looks him in the eye, he opens his mouth and his fangs slide down." After a second of shock, she tries to pull away, but he holds onto her hands. "*Calm* down! I told you, I'll never hurt you." He sends her calming waves to settle her.

"*Vampires* don't exist! Not outside fantasy and Freudian symbolism! You must be using some kind of special effects, trying to punk me 'cause you know I read those books." She thinks of her shelf full of paranormal romances.

"I was hoping the fact you're into those might help you accept what I am." He looks at her, silently pleading with her to relax and accept the truth.

Sue's stomach does flip-flops as two different concepts of reality war within for dominance. "I like those stories because they *can't* be real! You know, escapism! It's *safe!*" She rambles with a flush of panic in her voice.

"Or, on some level, you *knew* what I am even back then and your subconscious found something you missed in those books; besides sex, that is." He says with a lopsided, fangless grin. "The reason I left was because I don't age, and it was becoming noticeable. You may have ignored it, but when we were out with some of your friends, they noticed something was off. Perhaps not that I wasn't aging, but they noticed you looked older because I didn't. Eventually, they, and you, would have realized I still looked 25 when I should have been 35 or 40.

"I'm still not sure I believe this, but if you are what you say you are, you could have told me. We could have figured it out together. You could have given me a choice to move with you, or walk away."

"It's not that simple, but let's address the reality of this once and for all." He opens his mouth and lets his fangs drop into place again.

"*Hell no*! You're *not* gonna demonstrate on my neck!" She pulls back into the corner, and wishes she had a cross, just in case he isn't punking her.

"He gives her a 'good grief' look and a sigh, raises his own wrist to his mouth, and makes certain she can see his fangs sinking into his flesh, then pulls them out. He moves closer to her on the sofa and extends his arm toward her, underside up, so she can see the two puncture wounds.

"Shouldn't they be bleeding if you *really* bit yourself? Maybe it's some kind of silicone Halloween wounds you slipped on there to make it look like bite marks." She wants to explain it away desperately, yet, on some level, knows that's a lost cause. The psychologist in her thinks, *I'm having a fucking psychotic break! Get a grip! I know this delusion can't be real!*

He sighs. "They're real, but there's a compound released when I bite someone that causes the punctures to seal as soon as I pull my fangs out. *Plus*, even if that weren't the case, unless I make a conscious effort, such wounds heal rapidly because of what I am. Now, don't be afraid, go ahead. Touch them and prove to yourself they're real."

She pauses, debating allowing herself to explore the reality of what *must* be a hallucination, she tentatively takes his hand in hers and uses her other hand to explore the welts. She soon discovers, not only do they not rub off, but she can see them healing in front of her own eyes. "Holy *Hell*!" She looks up and into his eyes with a mixture of fear and clinical fascination. "You aren't *punking* me, are you? Why the hell didn't you tell me before? I should've known! Not years later telling me, 'oh, by the way, I'm a blood-sucking vampire and was the whole time we were together!'" She snipes at him, anger overtaking her fear.

"It's not a matter of choice. There are others like me, and our existence can't become known or we'll have half the world out to stake us or otherwise destroy us! By the way, staking doesn't work, I'd recover! So don't get any ideas!" He grins. "Some percentage would seek us out to live their 'dangerous fantasies' or want to dissect us for our healing and longevity secrets!" He's frustrated, and leans back against the sofa, letting his head fall back on the backrest.

She slips and thinks, *What would it feel like? I've wondered so often when I read my books. Would it hurt? Would it feel good? What would it do to me? Where does fantasy end and reality begin?*

"If you want to know, all you have to do is ask." He catches her glance and her confusion.

"*Know* what? *Ask* what?" She stares at him.

"What you were thinking about." He catches her look of understanding that he heard her thoughts. He sits up and looks her directly in the eye. "Yes, I heard what you were thinking! No, I don't always read your mind. It won't hurt unless I'm careless and don't block the pain, which I'd never do, and yes, under the right circumstances, it can be pleasurable. No, you won't become like me if I bit you one or a hundred times; nor will you become my Renfield, thrall, slave, minion, halfling-vampire or whatever else your stories tell you. Our connection would strengthen as it would with any other form of intimacy: physical, intellectual, or emotional, but it's not some sort of supernatural hold on a person. I feed two to three times a week! If everyone I fed on became my minion, I'd probably go over to bagged blood permanently!" He says, exasperated.

She narrows her eyes and gets an odd look as her curiosity kicks in. "Is that even an option? Seriously? What do you do, raid blood banks?" She asks incredulously.

He laughs and shakes his head. "We have our own channels for sourcing bagged blood. Don't worry, no humans are harmed in the process!"

She pauses, screwing up her mouth as she weighs his words, then tentatively says, "I guess I'll have to take your word for it."

He looks at her with his head cocked to one side in question. "However, if you want to know what it feels like, I *can safely* show you, *if* you'll just *trust* me."

She crosses her arms in front of her chest defensively. "I don't know, part of me is kinda tempted, but for all I know, it's a trick to get me to give you permission and that's all you need to drain me?" She says flippantly.

"Really? We don't hurt humans when we feed! We don't do anything that would risk the exposure of our people to the human world. And hurting humans or leaving corpses everywhere would certainly point a finger at us." He sighs in frustration.

"But why are you telling me this *now*, when you didn't tell me years ago?" She pleads.

He composes himself, knowing he must be calm and straightforward, because she must believe him about Jason. "Because you *need* to know. You're in danger. *No! Not* from me, but from someone like me who doesn't play by our rules. He's what we call a rogue."

"Why would I be in danger from him? What's the probability of running into one *vampire*, let alone two?" She huffs.

He pauses, contemplating how to tell her the next part. "Sue, he was in your home tonight, looking for you." He says bluntly.

Her mouth drops open at his revelation, then closes again as she weighs her next words, "One, why would he be looking for me? And two, how do you know he was in my house?" She's unnerved by this revelation.

"Back up for a second, or it won't make sense." He says calmly but firmly.

"Okay, I'm listening." She says impatiently.

"There was another reason I left and why I never told you what I am. We can't tell most humans, except for a small percentage who are genetically compatible." He explains.

"Genetically compatible with what?" She dreads the answer.

"The virus that transforms us into what we are." He pauses. "Compatible people are quite rare, you see; maybe one in a couple hundred thousand are compatible with the virus, and only they can become like me." He pauses to let her simmer on that fact.

She ponders that momentarily, swallows, and looks him in the eye. "Am I compatible?"

He breathes a sigh of relief as she makes the connection. "And this is where the wrong information I mentioned comes in. When we got to know each other, my intuition said you were compatible, but according to a database my people maintain, you weren't. If you had been, I could have told you and, well, offered you the chance to join me." He explains.

"Join you? As in, move away with you, or are you talking something more drastic?" She gulps audibly.

"I would have wanted to turn you, that's what we call it, to transform you to be like me, so we could be together for as long as we want to be, even centuries." He explains.

"I *know* what the *hell* turning is from books, TV, and stuff! Would I have even had any say in it?" She shakes nervously.

He senses her anxiety grow, but isn't sure if it's fear or something else. "Yes, I could have told you my secret, explained it all, pitched my offer, and if you absolutely refused, I could have made you forget the whole thing, and distanced myself from you, then you could have gone on with your life. I would have done my best to convince you, but know if I forced it on you, you'd make me pay for it for *at least* a few *decades!*" He smirks. "Do you remember my boss, Liz? You met a few years back, she's like me as well. This morning, she informed me that when they were working on identifying compatible people in a 'damaged database', they discovered a match with your DNA, so my intuition was right. You *are* compatible." He gives her a look that melts her heart. She can feel his longing to make her like him, and it tears her soul in two. Part of it wanting to run away in fear, and another part wanting to just jump, head first into her fantasies, and let him change her.

She looks at him wide eyed, a mixture of fear, horror, and anger in her eyes. "Oh, *shit!* You're going to turn me, aren't you?"

"It's one option, but even if I don't, I must keep you here where you'll be safe, because our rogue Apara, Jason, is seeking out other women to transform. Apparently, when Liz was being briefed, a warning went off that the database system had been compromised, and the hacker thrown out of the system, but *not* before accessing the names of five of the newly discovered compatible potentials, one of which was you, and you were the only one from this area where he's active. The rest were from area's he's not familiar with. The only person who would've been hacking us is Jason, looking for other compatible women he can target, and you don't want Jason to turn you."

"Not to suggest if I were to be turned, I'd let anyone but you do it, but what is the issue with this Jason guy?" She asks, curiously.

He gently lays a hand on her arm hoping she doesn't pull away. She doesn't, but she flinches. "First, there wouldn't be any question of your letting him do it, he just would, and from what we understand, he precedes it with violence; physical, sexual, and psychological, until the woman breaks and gives in to him, then he'll turn her to relieve the torture and pain."

She furrows her brows, thinking of the rape and abuse victims she's counseled over the years and their PTSD, depression, and other issues related to the abuse or assaults. "Check! Don't want that!" She says. "What the hell is his problem, anyway? Is it all some kind of power trip or something deeper that drives him?"

"From what Liz told me, he had a previously unknown history of abuse by his mother, which led to him becoming an abuser himself. He was aware of certain psychic gifts prior to becoming one of us, including what we call 'telempathic persuasion', or the ability to use telepathy and empathy to make someone do, feel, or believe something. He apparently had that ability before he was turned, and used it to get women he wanted to sleep with him, as well as other things. Long story short, he's a control freak and breaks the women he turns. At least that's what Liz told me." He explains.

"And if the woman doesn't break?" She thinks about how she'd never give in to such a monster.

"We know he's killed some women, both compatible and not. Some of those killings were vicarious. The women resembled people he had issues with. One was an accident where he was too rough, and she died before he could turn her. We do know of one woman who would not give in, so after beating and sexually assaulting her repeatedly, and draining her significantly, he left her to die. Liz said they found her in time, but the only way to save her life was to turn her, because the damage was too extensive. Even so, she had to be put into a deep sleep for nearly a week while she healed physically. She isn't completely psychologically healed, but she's accepted her life as one of us." He explains.

"Geez! So, you're saying this guy discovered I'm compatible and came after me without even knowing who I am? Just because I'm *compatible* and *female*?" Her anger rises.

"Yes! That, you're attractive and local. The others are in areas he's not familiar with, including other countries. He's dangerous, he never learned to come here, and all the physical portals are programmed to reject him." He explains.

"Couldn't I just *leave* town? Go into hiding somewhere?" She asks.

"Unfortunately, now he could find you anywhere. If he was the one I sensed in the parking garage tonight, then he's sensed you." He pauses, holding up his hand to stop her interrupting him. "Let me explain, everyone has what one might call a mental signature. It's how someone 'feels' to a person with telepathic abilities. Once you have that pattern in your mind, you can find them anywhere in the world." He explains.

"Then I'd keep moving, stay ahead of him." She pleads.

"Won't work, and I'll show you why." He stands, giving her a mischievous grin. "Don't take your eyes off me." He says, then vanishes.

"What the *fuck*? Did you turn invisible? Where are you?" She's frustrated and frightened. A couple of seconds later, his warm hands are on her shoulders from behind and she tries to lunge away, but he holds her where she is.

"I'm right here, and there's no need to fear me, but you should fear him. Anytime you are on 'Earth Prime', he could home in on you, pop in like I just did, and pop out with you again, and there's not a damn thing you could do to stop him." He says, moving back to where he was.

"Are you telling me you teleported? Not just turned invisible." She asks, anxiously.

He rocks his head from side to side as he tries to think of how to explain it to her. "More or less. It's not like Star Trek, where one is disassembled on a molecular level and reassembled somewhere else. We're able to travel via the veil or membrane between the two worlds, and can emerge on either world, but to come out in this one, one must be taught how to find the right 'frequency', and he was never taught how to come here. He may, someday, learn, but for now, you're safe here. He can neither sense you, nor get here as it stands now, but go back home, and he'll be there in minutes." He explains, stroking her hand to keep her calm.

The reality of her potential peril sinks in. "Even if you're there with me?"

"He'll think twice about attacking when we're together, but could use his cohorts, and apparently, he's up to 3 now, to distract, while he or one of them nabs you when I'm distracted. Or, he could just wait until you go into the bathroom or another room alone." He gives her a sympathetic look, knowing she's begun to comprehend the gravity of her situation.

"And how do you know he was in my home?" She asks nervously.

"When Liz found out about the hack, she ordered a team to set up monitors around, and *in* your home, to monitor for signs of anyone like me visiting you. It wasn't intended as an invasion of your privacy, just a protective measure. My mental signature and a few others like Liz's were added as exceptions, but any other of my people approaching your home would set off the alarms back at the office. After the run-in in the parking deck, I assume he thought I was taking you home, and went to lie in wait, so we detoured to the office first, and then here." He notes her anger and fear of him has almost completely dwindled away.

"To keep me safe?" She asks.

"Yes." He replies.

She gives a brief bark of ironic laughter. "*Normally*, I'd be *pissed* to all hell someone was in my home setting up surveillance of any kind, but I guess it's better than becoming his minion! If they knew he was there though, why couldn't they catch him?"

"*Alas!* He has a few skills. I understand he had covert military training from earlier, and he's got a natural ability to disguise or cloak his mental signature and anyone with him. It still showed up as an energy signature indicating someone like me was there, just non-identifiable. We can sense when someone else is porting in, so he just ported out before anyone could get to him." He explains.

"How long do I have to stay here?" She finally accepts the reality of her situation, and thinks, *I'm up the proverbial shit creek when it comes to this Jason guy. How could someone like me fight him off? Oh, God! I can't go through that! Not after seeing what it's done to so many other women to be abused or assaulted!*

"That depends on you, and when we catch him." He slides closer to her, stroking her leg gently.

"If you caught him tomorrow?" She suggests.

"He *and* his minions would all have to be caught and secured. We had him once, but didn't know about the women, two at the time, and one is schizophrenic to *boot*! They rescued him, and it's been about a month since then. We could catch him tomorrow, or it could be years from now. Beyond that, there's a choice for you to make." He explains.

"And that is?" Her heart rate speeds up.

"I'm not letting you put yourself in danger. I thought I'd lost you when I left. You weren't the only person who was heart-broken by that!" He squeezes her hand. "As long as you're human, he'll come for you, so as long as you're human, you must stay here, where you can be protected."

"What about my job? My home? My life?" but thinks, *What life?*

"I can't protect you at work, or anywhere where I can't shadow you closely. My home is your home for as long as you need it. We can deal with your existing home. Didn't you inherit it from your parents? You own it, right?" He asks.

"Yes." She answers.

"Sentimental value?" He asks.

She shrugs. "Some, but I never lived there growing up. It was a more recent, retirement purchase for them. It's basically just a place to live."

"So, it wouldn't be something you couldn't part with?" He asks.

"I *don't* know, maybe." She answers, noncommittally.

He pauses, and then uses his hand to tip her chin up to look at him. "There are a few options, but we don't have to worry about rent. We'll pick up the costs such as utilities, upkeep, property taxes, for as long as you need to be here."

"You keep using "*we*" as in '*we'll* pick up the costs'?" She asks.

"Ah, it's not just me and Liz. Most of the people I work with are like me. Inspiration, Inc, besides the charitable web front, is what you might call a recruitment-clearing house. We hire compatible people so they can be evaluated, and *if* we need new people, we know who to choose and not to choose." He says.

"Then what happened with this Jason guy? Did he fly under the radar somehow?" She inquires.

"You know the Jerusalem bomb, naturally?" He asks.

She gives him an annoyed look. "Oh yeah! That's half the reason we've been so busy. People are terrified it *could* happen here next."

"One thing my people do is try to stop bad things from happening. Some of us have precognitive skills. Some of my people discovered something was coming, and eventually, they figured out it was a massive terrorist attack with nukes." He says.

"You mean one nuke in Jerusalem, don't you?" She asks.

"Do you remember the initial rumors there were other cities at risk?" He asks her.

"Yeah, but then Homeland Security announced it was only Jerusalem and other cities were safe, especially here." She recounts.

Colin snickers. "They *lied!*" There were bombs being assembled in several other cities, including New York, L.A., and Dallas. *We* either directly stopped the terrorists, or tipped off the authorities. I was part of the L.A. team." He explains.

"So, you're saying your people saved the world?" She gives him a weird, incredulous look like she's not sure if she should believe him or not.

"Yes, in fact, the two people who cracked it work here at the Asheville locale. Remember, I mentioned Marc?" He asks.

"The one who recommended *Le Petit Chou*?" She recalls.

"Yes. He and his partner, Tess, solved the puzzle that led to tracking the terrorists and their plans. Tess was still human at the time." He says.

"So, she knew about you all? I thought you weren't *supposed to tell* anyone?" She asks, questioning his story about telling her now, but not earlier.

"Tess was a unique exception. She followed Marc and caught him feeding, and attempts to make her forget didn't work, so she had to work with us. Anyway, she figured out some missing clue, which let Marc break the codes and figure out what they had planned." He says.

"But not in time to stop the bomb there, too?" She wonders.

"We tried and found it well before it would have gone off. Unfortunately, the one thing no one foresaw was a proximity detonator with a 15 second delay, where a remote could be used to shut it off if they needed to, but none of us knew that. 15 seconds after one of us found it, *KABOOM!!* We lost over 3000 of our people that day, and in the aftermath, some of those already on our radar were turned to make up for losses. Jason rated highly for intelligence and psychic abilities, so he was turned in that first round. Tess also joined us, but that's a more complicated story."

She blanches at the thought of so many vampires even existing, let alone being killed. She looks thoughtful, then asks, "You said part of it depends on me; what are my options?" She finally summons the courage to ask, though she suspects she already knows the answer.

"Jason wants to be his minions' creator, almost their 'god', so they would do anything for him, almost worship him. That's why he left the one to die who wouldn't break. Even though she survived, he has shown no interest in getting her back, nor has he attempted to get any already transformed women, with one exception, Tess, who he knew while human. He apparently tried to use his abilities on her, but she wouldn't succumb, so he was personally obsessed with her. In the end, we believe as long as you're human, you're in danger from him, but if you *aren't* human, he'll lose interest." He speaks calmly, almost holding his breath, waiting for her reaction.

"You're saying if I let you turn me, he'll stop coming after me?" She asks, cautiously.

"Yes, we believe that would be the case." Colin grips her hand in his, looking pleadingly in her eyes, hoping she might willingly choose to be transformed.

"So, I could go back home and to work then? If I become like you?" She asks.

"Home, possibly, work, is going to be more complicated. You must learn to control both your appetite, and your abilities, or you'll be a danger to those around you, and a danger to us as you could expose us. While you may be able to go home, it could also get extremely uncomfortable if your new skills, particularly telepathic or empathic skills aren't controlled. You once told me about your neighbor, Ben...?" He says, trying to remember his last name.

"Ben Reeder?" She fills in the missing name.

"You told me he often comes home drunk and shouts at what? Photos? Imaginary friends?" He asks.

"More like ex-girlfriends who've long since left, and the TV. He watches a lot of right-wing news and their stories rile him up." She rolls her eyes.

He shifts on the sofa, putting his other hand on her leg. "And you said you've heard crashes and other sounds that could be him throwing things?"

"Yeah, but he's never done anything to me." She admits.

He sighs and shakes his head. "Doesn't matter. I've experienced that type of person before, and my abilities are controlled; it can be like you're literally inside his head, experiencing his anger, hate, or drunkenness. It can be disorienting and disturbing, and he's just one of a dozen or so nearby neighbors. Without control, you'll pick up on anything emotionally charged from sex, to anger, to suicidal depression, and everything in between."

"Either way, I'll end up back here 'for my own good'." She sighs.

"Yes, but as one of us, you'll eventually be able to go out on your own. Until you get your abilities under control, however, work, especially working with people who are psychologically unstable, could be difficult for you, but it all depends on how quickly we get you trained and your abilities mastered." He pulls her into a hug and then lets her go again.

"Working with unstable people *is* my job!" She blurts out in a huff, then continues, "If I don't show up, I'm gonna get fired, and then won't be able to get a new job." She complains, feeling trapped no matter what she chooses.

"If you become one of us, *that will be* your new job. We'll find something your skills are suited for, either at Inspiration Inc, or somewhere in the area. We've got people working as teachers, scientists, doctors, and many other jobs where they can make a difference." He says.

She looks thoughtful before answering as diplomatically as she can. "I need some time to process all of this. It still doesn't feel real to me. I'm sure I'll have more questions, but right now, I'm reaching my limit, and am about to crash. Can we talk more in the morning?" She's having difficulty keeping her eyes open.

He stands and reaches a hand down to her. "Yes, of course. Let me help you to bed." He says.

"It's okay, I can just sleep on the sofa, done that before!" She says.

"Yes, when we first met and you fell asleep watching a movie!" He laughs. "But there's no need for you to sleep on an uncomfortable sofa."

"Don't take this the wrong way, but if I follow you to bed, how do I know I won't wake up with fangs? And even if I don't, and we resume old habits, I'm not sure I'll be able to make an objective decision." She flashes on herself waking with fangs, going to work, and attacking one of her least favorite clients.

"I'm not sure any of this can be objective. I love you, and I know, on some level, even with all I've dumped on you tonight, you still love me, too. That must count for something!" He sits and pulls her close.

Fuck it! She thinks, and says, "I'll sleep with you, but just sleep, that's it! I need to think clearly about all of this and I can't do it otherwise!" She blushes, but takes his hand and lets him help her up.

"One of these days, you're going to get over your shyness about sex!" He says.

"Why do you think I indulge in those books! I can live there, vicariously experiencing what makes me blush and stammer in real life." She says.

"If you end up letting me turn you, I'll show you what you've been missing in life!" He chuckles. "Come on, I'm exhausted too. I promise, only sleep tonight!"

They head off to his all too familiar bed. She's awkward at first, lying there, knowing, finally, what he is. Eventually, her mind eases and she sleeps with her head on his chest like old times.

The next morning, she wakes up, curled against him, head tucked under his chin, feeling the warmth radiating from him. It's still dark outside, so she picks up her cell. It's still on Asheville time, 8:03 am, or west coast time, *5 am? Ugh,* she thinks. She moves just enough to rouse him from his sleep. "Morning... I've missed waking up with you by my side." He kisses the top of her head.

"Hmm, me too." She mumbles against him. She leans back so she can look him in the eye. "Hey! How come you're not stone cold? I thought vampires were supposed to be cool to the touch, but, well, you're hot! Well, in more ways than one!" She jokes, feeling almost normal again.

He pulls himself up as he rolls her onto her back. "Of course, I'm not cold! I'm very much alive! Parts of me more than others!" He jokes as he pulls her closer to him and she can tell exactly where his warm blood is concentrated.

She blushes bright pink and closes her eyes. He chuckles with sultry undertones. "Well, I said I'd only sleep last night, but someone's got other ideas this morning!" He says.

"As tempting as that is, I need to stay objective!" She insists, but inside, her resolve is weakening as this whole situation overwhelms her, making her want to be held, cared for, and loved.

"We'll see!" He says with a lopsided grin.

"Seriously, there's so much about you that doesn't fit the whole 'vampire' thing! You're warm, alive; you eat real food, including garlic, you burn less in sunlight than I do." She gripes.

He props his head up on one arm, smirking. "You're still hoping I'll tell you this is all a big practical joke, aren't you? Is it so hard to believe your own eyes?" He strokes her cheek.

"Yeah, it is! If this is true, then I'm screwed one way or another!" She says quietly.

"Look at me!" He says, commanding but kind. "I'll never hurt you and will do my best to keep you from harm. You need to believe me; this is *all* true. You need to trust me. Your life *depends* on it." He leans his forehead down to touch hers.

"It just doesn't feel real! I keep expecting you to pop those fangs out as fancy prosthetics and tell me you're the same old Colin!" She blurts out.

"I *am* the same old Colin, I'm just not *human*, and I'm a hell of a lot older than you ever realized." He jokes. "You need to accept this."

"It's hard to accept. *Yes*, I see the evidence, and I know what logic says I should do, but I'm scared! You're asking me to make a tremendous leap of faith, and let you change me into something

134

out of a horror story!" Her eyes glisten with budding tears as she realizes how everything is likely to end up.

He thinks for a minute and remembers what Marc said about Tess. "I'm gonna take you to meet someone who you can talk to about all this." He picks up his cell phone.

"Another vampire?" She asks.

"Naturally, but she hasn't been one of us long, and went through some of this herself recently." He dials a number on his cell.

Colin yawns as Marc answers the phone. "Marc, it's Colin. I was wondering if I could bring Sue by to talk to Tess?"

"Sure, but port to the outside of my home. I've got extra security because of Jason, and your mental signature isn't coded in yet, so you'll have to use the door in Sanctuary." He says. "Give us a few minutes, so I can tell Tess to expect you."

"Great, will port over in a few. Sue needs to get ready anyway." He hangs up.

"You want me to meet the woman who's with your friend?" She asks.

Colin sits back down on the bed beside her. "Yeah, she knew about us before she was turned, *and* she's had run-ins with Jason. So, why don't you get ready; there are a couple of duffle bags with some of your clothes and things under the bed. I asked Liz to grab some of your stuff after they ran Jason off from your place." He says.

"Got all the bases covered, don't you? Okay, I'll go meet this Tess woman." She says, and goes off to wash up, brush her hair and get ready. Colin pulls out the bags with her clothes in them. When she's done, she digs through them, finding some comfortable jeans and a plain green top with short sleeves.

Role reversal

Sue comes out dressed, and gets her shoes on. "Ready." She says.

He draws her to him, the room swirls away, and the next she knows, they're standing in a wooded lot outside a different home. The air's warmer, and the sun is high in the sky. "We're still on the alternate Earth, we just ported to Marc's place on the east coast." He explains.

"So, I *just* teleported?" She asks.

He chuckles. "Yes, just ported a few thousand miles in the blink of an eye. Cool, isn't it?

"Yeah, but disorienting as *Hell*!" She's nauseous, like she could lose the contents of her stomach any second.

"You'll get used to it after a while. Your senses weren't built for this kind of travel, so it throws them for a loop." He explains.

She gives him an annoyed look at his comment, but continues. "So, do many of your friends, live here?" She asks.

"Yes, nearly all of us have our actual homes in this reality. It saves us from having to deal with a lot of human minds nearby. Since we all have telepathic abilities, and some have empathic leanings, it can get difficult when you must constantly guard against picking up random thoughts round the clock." He explains.

"I guess it could be. Though there've been times, I wish I could've read my client's minds or known what they were feeling. It would make some cases so much easier!" She rambles, anxious about meeting more of his kind.

He gently rubs her back reassuringly. "I get that. Relax! Neither Tess nor Marc will hurt you, and I'll bet you'll get along with Tess! I've heard she's especially good at reading people!"

Sue isn't sure what he means. "You mean reading their minds?"

"No, their motivations, behaviors and so on. Closer to what you do as a psychologist." He explains.

"That's why I went into psychology. I always knew when something was wrong with my friends or family, and was the one who could get through to people; I somehow knew what was bothering them and could help them deal with it by bringing things out I sensed. It got a little weird with how accurate I got." She reflects on that, the thought of being able to read her clients minds, and how much good she might do with that ability. In the back of her mind, she finds it oddly tempting to let him turn her for that reason alone.

"You probably have some latent telepathy and empathy." He suggests, as though they were everyday abilities.

Marc comes out the door. "Colin, Susan, sorry about having you port outside. We've got extra security set up in case Jason finds his way to Sanctuary and comes after Tess again. Come in. I've shut it down temporarily so you can enter." Marc explains, waiting for them to come closer before going back in through the door with them behind him. Once the door's closed, Marc reengages the security. "So, you're Susan? I've heard about you before, but don't think I ever met you when Colin was at our office! Welcome!" He smiles, and then shouts, "*Tess*! Company's here!"

Tess comes bounding down the stairs in jeans and a Doctor Who T-shirt. "Sorry about that! Hoped to be downstairs when you got here. I'm Tess."

"Call me Sue." She gets an expression like she's trying to remember something. "Tess, you look familiar to me, have we met before?"

"Not that I know of, though I thought you looked familiar when I was looking at your Facebook yesterday, but I'm not always good at placing faces, and I've been going through so many files on people this week, it blurs together after a while!" Tess smiles, and somehow puts Sue at ease.

"Tess, I think Colin and I are going to catch up in my office. I put out some snacks on a tray in the kitchen. We'll leave you to get to know each other" Marc suggests.

Tess motions for Sue to have a seat in the living room and grabs the snacks from the kitchen before joining her. "Marc's been on a baking and cooking binge lately. After being alone for years, now that *I'm* around, he finally has someone to cook for." Tess plops down on the sofa with Sue.

Sue takes a minute to look around at the eclectic mix of antiquities, classic art, and modern things like the flat screen TV and some modern glass sculptures. She looks down at the tray in front of them. It's filled with various pastries Marc made recently, as well as some of Tess's favorite mini-quiches.

"Marc's been making me his food guinea pig! All kinds of recipes he's had for years or wanted to try, but he had no one to make them for except himself, until I *showed* up! *Please,* help me eat them! They're great, but part of me still worries I'm going to get fat!" She laughs.

Sue smiles and takes a fresh chocolate éclair. She looks thoughtful. "Tess, have you ever taken part in any of the psychological services down at the Public Clinic? I'm wondering if I might have crossed paths with you there?" She asks.

Tess looks awkward, but admits, "Actually, I did for a while. I was working at Digital Danger when all hell broke loose. In fact, I'm the one that turned them in, including my boyfriend! Sometimes, I went to some of the free group sessions on Fridays back by the pharmacy."

"That's it! I remember now. I subbed one time for your regular therapist. She was out with Covid. I remember you struggling with the guilt. If you don't mind my asking, did the group sessions help?" Sue asks.

"I think so. I was going to go to some of the other classes, too, but covid messed that up." Tess picks up a warm chocolate croissant and bites into it. "*Boy!* Am I glad I can still eat real food, and not just my 'liquid' diet! I really would've missed chocolate!" She laughs.

"I guess that's a plus, isn't it?" Sue asks, awkwardly.

"Sue, I can tell you're having a rough time with all this, aren't you?" Tess grows serious, as she can sense Sue's anxiety.

"Wouldn't *anyone*? No offense, but I don't know what to think about all this. Vampires are supposed to be monsters, and suddenly, I find out the man I was in a five-year relationship with, and have stayed in touch with is one and was the whole time we were together. And another one I don't even know wants to turn me into one, as does Colin. I'm trapped and there's no way out!" Sue tears up a little.

Tess moves closer and hands her a box of tissues. "Figured you might need these!" She puts the box in front of Sue on the coffee table.

"*Hey*! That's usually my job! I always have them ready in my office for my clients, too!" She dabs her eyes.

Tess watches Sue, and sympathizes with her internal conflict. "Look, I know, firsthand, how suddenly finding out about all this can be. I accidentally found out about Marc. He made me forget, it's a gift we have. But that asshole, Jason; yes, the same one! He cornered me at work one day and I thought he was going to rape me! The fear and stuff brought back my memories from the night Marc cornered me and made me forget, and by the time he tried again, it was too late. Suddenly, I was in the twilight zone, stuck between my reality, and their reality, and it was a mess." Tess shares.

"Is that when he turned you into one of them?" She asks, still sniffling.

"Oh, no! That happened quite a while later. You see, like you, I wasn't in the main database. In my case, I was in an accident as a kid, got misfiled as 'deceased', and put in their inactive files, but I ended up responding to a job ad. I got their attention with some psychic abilities I didn't even realize I had; so, they hired me to figure me out. Once they couldn't make me forget, they couldn't just cut me loose. It's a long story, but believe me, when I first found out, I had trouble believing it was real, and I was terrified!" Tess explains.

"But you became one of them anyway?" She asks.

"I worked closely with Marc, and others, too. I got to see what they're about, and they do a lot of good." She plucks out another tissue and hands it to Sue.

"Thanks, did you want, I mean, when you became one of them, was it something you wanted, or did they find out you were compatible and just force it on you?" Her voice cracks with anxiety.

"No, they didn't think I could become one of them, so I was in limbo. I couldn't go back to a 'normal life'. Not knowing what I did about them, and having the abilities they brought out in me, but I wasn't one of them either. The more I came to know Marc and the others, and what they do, the more I wanted to be part of that. But they all thought it wouldn't work on me. Of course, working so closely with Marc, especially with telepathy and empathy, we ended up getting close, and you know, things happen!" Tess gives her a knowing grin and a shrug.

"Then how'd you end up one of them if they didn't believe you were-compatible." She struggles to remember the term.

"Has Colin told you about our involvement with the Jerusalem bomb at all?" Tess asks.

"Yes, including three that were going to go off in the US! And how you and Marc somehow figured it out." She tries to recall exactly what Colin told her, but she's dealing with a bad case of information overload.

"Long story short, Marc and many others were over there looking for the bomb. The EM pulse scrambles our ability to port. I assume you know what that is by now?" She asks.

"More or less. Colin brought me here that way. I thought I was going to puke, but don't tell him that!" She lets out a small, nervous laugh.

"That's normal for the first few times. I got used to it, though. Anyway, the EM pulse fucks up the guidance part of porting. Some ended up somewhere they weren't aiming for, and some couldn't port at all because they couldn't get their bearings. I sensed Marc's panic, and mentally screamed for him, and because of our close bond, he could use that to get back here, but he was a mess! Burnt and bleeding. Long story short, I fed him my blood by making a slight cut in my wrist, and then tried to clean him up and some of his blood got in my cut, and the next morning, Liz figured out I was transforming; becoming one of them. By then, I really wanted to be Apara, because what we do, well, the world would be in much worse shape without us heading off disasters. I wish we could've stopped the Jerusalem bomb too, but we got a lot of people out, and it's forcing a power realignment that could end up leading to peace." Tess explains.

"That's a lot to take in. Just tell me this, was it worth it? Becoming one of them? Any regrets?" Sue looks exhausted and her aura gives off an 'on the edge' impression.

"Yeah, it was. *No* regrets, especially since I learned firsthand, I could make a real difference even while still human, but now that I'm Apara, hopefully, I'll be able to do even more. *Hell*, Sara, our doctor, thinks I'm supposed to be 'important' in the future. I don't know about that, but, *Hell!* This is better than any regular career I could have had as a human. Marc and I found each other too, and well, after the mess with my ex, knowing Marc has healed a lot of baggage I had after Digital Danger. At the same time, I've healed something in him too, so yes, I'm *quite* happy! Well, outside of being stuck here while Jason's on the loose. That gets *frustrating*!" Tess complains.

"But Colin says if I let him turn me, then Jason won't be interested in me anymore, but you're saying you still have to hide from him?" Sue asks.

"It's a whole, *hell* of a lot more complicated between me and Jason! We both started working at Inspiration, Inc. the same day, as humans. *Pissed* me off on day one!" She says. "He had some abilities he used to make women compliant, and I was immune to it, and that irked him to no end! Add to that I resemble his abusive mom, and it was just a *mess*!"

Sue chuckles. "Sounds like Freud would have had a field day with Jason's mommy issues." Sue relaxes, but some of it is emotional exhaustion. "He really sounds like a grade-A asshole." Sue laughs through her tears.

"Yep, he sure is, and you definitely want to avoid him at all costs!" Tess pauses, and then gently puts her hand on Sue's. "Sue, I know you must come to grips with all this, and make your own decision, and I know the tug of war you're going through inside right now, especially since you clearly love Colin, but I'm going to tell you this much, when you've come to grips with all the facts and so on, don't forget to listen to your heart. I know you love Colin; I can sense that. I know you're afraid; I've been there too. But there's nothing to be afraid of from him. You know who he is, you know how he feels about you, and how you feel about him. You can't ignore that in favor of facts, logic, and fear of the unknown, what you 'should or shouldn't' do or you'll never be happy." Tess advises her.

"You know Tess, you should be a therapist! You really *are* good at reading people!" She takes a clean tissue, and blows her nose. It's ironic being on the other side of the 'couch'." Sue admits.

"I want you to think about how I was when you met me. The emotional turmoil I was in, the self-doubt, the depression, and compare that to me now. I'm finally on the right path, and while I still have my struggles, I know I really can, and have made a difference. Now it's my job to find people like you, who can join us, because we need you. We lost so many people and with all the chaos now, we need good people more than ever." Tess releases her hand and sits back in the sofa.

"Thanks, I'll keep it all in mind. I'm pretty sure I know how this is going to play out, but part of me is still afraid." Sue admits.

"I get it. But sometimes, the only way to move forward is to trust someone and take that leap of faith. I had to with Marc when he couldn't erase my memories. It's one of the hardest things to do, especially when you've been hurt. It becomes so incredibly hard to trust again, but the alternative is always living in fear, distrust, and sorrow." She says.

Sue's body visibly slackens as she slowly accepts the reality of it all, and of her likely fate. "You're right. I'm just not sure I'm ready yet." Sue looks her in the eye.

"When you are, you'll know!" Tess smiles.

Sue gives a weak smile and wipes her eyes. "I don't suppose I can call you or come visit if I need to talk? I think, in this, you're the therapist and I'm the client!"

"Of course you can! You can call me, or reach me on Facebook chat or have Colin bring you by, or I can get Marc to come get you. I'm kind of in protective custody for now, not just because of Jason, but my abilities are still so out of whack and I've had a hard time controlling them. I think they're a little afraid if I go out on my own and get pissed off, I'm going to become the neighborhood poltergeist!" Tess jokes.

Sue's expression shifts as she remembers a study she once read about supposed poltergeists and emotionally unstable adolescents, and asks "Poltergeist? Wait, your telekinetic?" Sue asks.

"Yep, it's one of my stronger skills. Reading people, PK, and I recently discovered I can go out-of-body! No real control though, yet!" Tess shakes her head.

"It's still pretty cool! Would you be willing to show me some PK?" Sue asks, her professional curiosity kicks in.

"I'll try, but if you end up with chocolate éclair up your nose, don't say I didn't warn you!" She laughs. Tess focuses, and with a flourish of her hand, an éclair rises off the tray and floats over to Sue, who takes it out of the air.

"*Wow*! That's amazing!" She's fascinated to see real evidence of telekinesis.

"Just be glad I didn't get upset and explode the éclair!" She laughs and makes a face, puffing out her cheeks, and crossing her eyes. Tess goes over to her desk, and writes on a piece of paper and hands it to Sue. "Okay, here's all the ways you can reach me: phone, email, social media."

"Thanks, I suspect you'll hear from me soon." She stuffs the paper in her pocket.

"Sue, since you're a psychologist, I have a favor to ask of you? I mean, since you know about all this now, since I can't ask anyone who doesn't." She rambles.

"Are you asking me to be your therapist? Because you seem pretty, damn well-adjusted to me!" She smiles.

"Oh! No! I've just got this enormous project, evaluating people in a humongous database, and I'm doing it on blind intuition! I could just use someone who knows what they're doing to bounce stuff off, now and then. And don't let looks fool you, I'm not that well-adjusted!" She snickers.

"Sure, Tess. It doesn't look like I'm going anywhere for a while, no matter what happens. I'd be happy to help!" She smiles and looks up to see Marc and Colin coming out of the other room.

"You two getting along?" Colin asks.

"Yeah, we are. Thanks for introducing us." Sue says, looking at Tess and smiling.

Colin can see she's been crying, but knows it's part of the process. "We should head back. Marc was telling me Tess has a lot of work to do, but if you want to come back later, just say so." He waits for her to join him.

"Sue gets up, as does Tess. "Sue, come here a sec…" Tess gives her a big hug, which Sue reciprocates, choking back a few tears.

"You know, if this all gets sorted out, and you ever want a job in counseling, they could use someone like you down at the clinic!" She quips.

"Thanks, but I suspect I'm gonna have plenty to do here, if what Kari and Sara keep saying is true." Tess walks Sue and Colin to the door, along with Marc, who turns off the security to slip them out.

Colin ports them back to his home across the continent. "You've been crying?" He uses his hand to trace and wipe dry some tears.

"Yeah, what do you expect?" She asks.

He pulls her into a hug. "Did it help? Talking to Tess?"

"Yes, but I just wish I knew what I'm getting myself into. You know, I just realized, I don't even know how old you *really* are!" She stares at him, trying to find any clue to his real age.

"I didn't want to freak you out, so I let that part slide." He admits.

"Well? Spit it out!" She demands.

"I'm around 450 years old. I'd have to do the math. I lose track! I was turned around the same time as Marc. We were both turned by Liz, so we're kind of like brothers." He sits with her on his sofa.

"And here I thought you were about 5 years older than me when we met, and *that* felt like a big deal." She laughs at the absurdity.

"No jokes about robbing the cradle, please! Not like I can find a human my age!" He says with a grin, showing a little fang.

She cringes when she sees the sharp tips of his fangs. "Those things still freak me out."

He laughs. "Come on! I know you've thought about what it would feel like. Even from here, I picked up on some of your day-dreams after I left, because you slipped me in when you imagined the guys in your books." He nudges her in the shoulder.

"That's so *damn* embarrassing! I don't think I want to know what else you picked up on!" She cringes. "Listen, I need a little alone time to process things. I'm gonna go lie down for a while. I don't suppose you have anything for a headache? I always get them after crying." She closes her eyes and winces silently.

"No headache meds, but I can help you. I'll follow you to the bedroom, and ease your headache, then I've got some work to do. You can rest, and 'process'." He says.

They go down the hallway to the bedroom, and he helps her under the covers. "I'm going to block the pain. If it comes back, let me know and I'll pop out and get some regular meds for you." He caresses her cheek and temples, noticing the tension vanishing. Before she knows it, her pain is gone, and she falls into a deep sleep.

Lost memories

Sue wakes later that afternoon to a massive thunderstorm when a nearby lightning strike rouses her and shakes the entire house. She lies there in bed, trying to get her heart to slow down, and thinks about everything she's learned so far, including all she and Tess talked about. The storm gets louder and another nearby strike startles and distracts her. Colin checks on her when he senses her reaction to the loud thunder.

"*Hey*! Are you okay?" He comes in and sits on the edge of the bed. "How's your headache?"

"It's better, but that's some storm!" She flinches as another bright flash is quickly followed by house-shaking thunder. "Never been fond of storms!"

"Are you hungry? I can go grab something from the kitchen and bring it here?" He asks.

"*Oddly*, I'm craving another of Marc's éclairs!" She laughs.

"I'll see if he can send some over later." Colin smiles, and takes her hand.

"Colin, I know you want me to say it's okay to turn me, but things still feel so surreal. It's difficult to reconcile the five years we were together with what you are. My *God*! How could I *not* have known, or suspected things were off? There must have been clues you weren't a normal, human man!" She throws up her hands in frustration.

"There were, but I think you chose to ignore them. At least, the visible evidence I wasn't aging." He suggests.

She gets an odd expression, like she's debating asking something. "When we were together, did you ever erase my memory about anything?

Like, did you ever indulge in a 'midnight snack' and make me forget?"
She has a sinking feeling in the back of her mind.

He turns down his eyes, sighing, then makes eye contact again.
"Yeah, I've *tasted* you many times before." He says seriously.

She looks up at him, mouth open. "When you say tasted, you
are talking about biting me, *right*?" She's confused by some sexual
overtones she's getting from him.

He hesitates briefly. "Yes, I bit you many times while we were
together, and believe it or not, you enjoyed it." He admits.

She gives him an annoyed look, wondering if he's just acting
like a typical male egoist, or if she really had enjoyed it. "So, was I
aware you were biting me? I'd have thought that would be hard
for you to make me forget? Especially if I 'enjoyed' it, as you say I
did." However, she's got a sinking feeling he's telling the truth.

"Hear me out, please! Mostly, my people partner up with others like ourselves, with a few exceptions. Occasionally, we find
someone compatible and take our time easing them over to be
with us. Sometimes, some of my people do have short trysts with
unknowing humans, but they rarely last, and when we first got together, it was a nice diversion, but soon, deeper feelings awoke in
me, and my intuition kept telling me you're compatible and we
belong together. Unfortunately, according to our database you
weren't, so I was forbidden from telling you what I am, but I
found it nearly impossible to leave you. Among my people, feeding from each other is a form of intimacy, and I found it difficult
to keep my fangs to myself. Let's just say I bent the rules. I used
my telepathy and other abilities to create a schism in your mind,
like a hidden partition on a hard drive. This was an unconscious
part of you that knew and accepted me for what I am, and while
you were conscious as well, only your 'partition personality' was
fully aware of my nature and remembered. Technically, you still
didn't 'know', but some part of you was aware and reveled in it."
He pauses, trying to sense her emotional reactions, but he draws a

blank. "I know you probably see this as a betrayal, but I wouldn't have gone to such lengths if I didn't care about you. I would have just fed from you, made you forget and left." He explains, holding his breath, waiting for her to react.

"I had dreams about being bitten by you after you left, though I assumed it was some symbolic shit about feeling... betrayed. Oddly, it's part of what pushed me more toward the books." She admits.

"Part of you felt the loss of *that* element of our relationship, and found it again vicariously through books." He suggests, looking pensive for a few seconds before suggesting, "Maybe, I can reintegrate the partition memories with your regular memories; restore your memories to your conscious mind, so you can remember all we had. It may make it easier for you to reconcile." He lies down next to her, and props his head up on his arm, waiting for her response.

Lightning, rapidly followed by thunder distracts her briefly, but she forces herself back on track. "I don't know about letting you root around in my mind. You might find stuff I don't want you to find in there, private stuff."

"If you mean you're already tempted to let me feed from you, so you know what it feels like, or you're a hair's breadth away from crying because you ache to have me inside you again.... Yeah, I already know." He gives her a lopsided smirk and takes her hand in his.

"It's *really* not fair you can read my mind!" She pouts.

"That wasn't mind reading, I just know you way too well. I saw your reaction when I pulled you close this morning and heard you gasp as you thought about just how close I was." He leans in and gives her a light kiss. She responds without thinking, and he pushes his mind into hers. Her eyes flutter and roll back as he seeks the unconscious walls he'd created years earlier around the part of her that knew what he was and reveled in it. He pictures the memories swelling like water, reaching the tops of the walls, cresting over them, and washing away the walls all together; once hidden memories wash into her conscious mind, mingling with all the other memories of their time together. She's sleeping, but is oddly at peace, so he pulls her close and dozes while her mind heals and her memories merge.

About an hour later, she wakes. A quiet groan escapes her throat. "Hey there, are you ok?" He kisses her forehead.

"Don't suppose you got the license number of the freight train that went through my brain?" She opens one eye and sees his grin.

"Yeah, I'll turn myself in for mental hit and run later! What do you remember?" He asks.

"It's a jumble, like it's still trying to organize itself in the right order, but...." A mixed sigh and groan come from deep in her throat. "Does everyone you feed from react like *that*?" She's a little jealous of those two or three people he feeds from each week.

He chuckles and runs his fingers through her hair to push it out of her face. "No, the people we feed upon are completely unaware of the process. We divert them somewhere to where we can safely feed on them, and they are put into an oblivious state where they are unaware of what's happening. Some say they don't even create memories while in that state; we feed, heal, and send them on their way, adding some vague filler memories if necessary. There are those who prefer to feed during sex, choosing people who want a one-night stand, taking the edge off any fear they might have, feeding from them and then altering their memories. In those cases, there's often some reaction, but not like when there's an emotional bond involved, like we've had for years. We're in sync, emotionally, mentally, and to some extent, psychically. I told you, there were times I'd pick up on your book-induced fantasies from across the country and worlds. Made me want to say screw it and show up at your front door, but I couldn't; not until Liz told me you're compatible. Then my resolve to stay away evaporated like dry ice on a hot sidewalk."

"There's really no way out of this, is there?" She looks him in the eye. "Either you turn me, he turns me, or he kills me in the process?" She asks.

"Unfortunately, that pretty much sums it up; me, or him. Even if you stay here but remain human, you'll be with me and connected to my people because you've already known too long for me to erase it from your memory. You'll *never* have a 'normal' human life, no matter what." He caresses her face gently.

She looks him in the eye in one last attempt to convince herself of his sincerity. She takes a slow, deep breath, closes her eyes, and tips her head back to give him access. "It's you." She waits for him to bite her.

He leans in, and she feels his warm breath on her neck, but he doesn't bite. He kisses her throat over the artery gently, and then wanders up to her mouth. He moves across her cheek and whispers in her ear, "I love you, and I'll turn you, but not right now." He kisses her deeply and makes love to her. She knows there's no turning back, especially as she feels him as part of her again, and their bond ignites with a fire from deep within. As she nears a peak, he bites her, but only feeds a little, and her reaction is as she remembers, explosive, as his fangs slide into the soft, pulsing artery, giving them both what they've longed for.

Afterwards, more relaxed than she can remember being for a long time, she asks, "Is it just me, or didn't you do it?"

"It? If you mean turning you, no, not yet. We're going to spend a night out, your last night as a human." He grins and rolls over to kiss her.

"But won't he come for me?" She asks anxiously.

"Not if we stay together and are in public. I thought maybe we could try the new Korean place on Biltmore near the Orange Peel?" He asks, as he holds her against him in bed.

"Okay, if you think it's *safe*?" She asks.

"I'll have Liz send extra security to watch over us, covertly, of course! Maybe he'll show up and they can catch him!" He suggests.

"Even if they do, I want you to do it. I know, somehow, we belong together, and I'm not going to fight the inevitable any longer." She says.

He leans down and kisses her forehead. "I know. I felt that when you offered me you neck. Get a little more rest. We'll have our night out, and then, it's likely to be a long night, if not a long couple of days." He says.

"Oh, *damn*! I didn't think of that! I need to let the clinic know I won't be in!" She frets.

"Don't worry about it. I'll get our doctor to call it in and say you're too sick to come in or to call, and may be out for a while. Sara can be quite convincing in such situations." He says.

"She slowly drifts off, the stress completely gone from her body, drained away, leaving only peace as she sleeps knowing her decision's been made.

Last supper

She wakes and the sun's a little lower in the sky. She rolls over and finds a low-cut dress with matching shoes laid out for her on a nearby chair, as well as clean towels and shampoo, so she can take a bath before dinner. An hour later, she wanders out into the living room, and he's dressed equally as well. He extends a hand to her, and when she accepts, he pulls her to him, spinning her in to his embrace, and kisses her. "Ready?"

"For my proverbial last supper?" She asks.

"Sue, this is more than an ending! It's a night on the town! A night to remember! The end of your human existence, and the *beginning* of the rest of your very long life with me!" He pulls her against him from behind.

"I'm as ready as I can be!" She leans into him.

"We better get going before they give our reservation away." He opens the front door, and they're back in South Asheville, the Tesla's in the drive, and all the neighbor homes are there again. They walk to the car, and he opens the door for her. They head out to dinner.

After they find a parking space, they walk arm in arm to the new Korean restaurant near the Orange Peel, an entertainment and concert venue. They pass a long line outside the Peel waiting to get into a concert. They get to the restaurant and go in. They're seated in a private booth and order the house Bulgogi special they can cook at their table. They're oddly quiet while they eat, both thinking ahead to what's yet to come.

Colin's scalp tingles and he furrows his brow, closes his eyes, and mentally scans the surrounding area. He can sense the security guy Liz assigned outside in his car, and he can sense someone else, someone Apara. He can tell from the psychic energy emanating from them, but he can't identify them. He pulls out a pen, writes a note on a paper napkin, and slides it over to Sue. It says, "Don't react, but we're being observed, and not by our backup. Imagine your mind open to me, and 'listen'!"

She looks at him questioningly and hears in her mind. *Sue, if you can hear me, scratch your nose.* She thinks that's odd, but scratches the side of her nose anyway. Again, she hears his voice in her mind, *Either Jason or one of his women is nearby. I can tell they're there, and they're like me, but their mental signature is generic, no identity. I'm must give our backup a heads up, but I think we should give them a show to convince them you're off the market.* He paths.

I am off the market, you're going to turn me. She thinks.

Until I've fed from you, my blood crosses your lips, and you become infected with the virus, he'll see you as a viable target. I'll guide you with my mind when we leave, just go with it, and don't be afraid!

Guide me with your mind? She thinks.

He hears her unspoken thought even though she's not actually projecting telepathically. *Yes, I'll temporarily take over your motor control, like when I'm hijacking someone to feed on. You'll be fine. I'll leave you aware though, so don't fight me or it won't look authentic. Trust me!*

Are you going to turn me in front of them? She thinks, anxiously.

No! Not unless they force my hand, I won't do it until we get home where we can do it in relative comfort. I'm hoping it's one of his women he's sent to watch you, and she'll get careless when she thinks she's let you slip through Jason's fingers, and just maybe, we can catch her off guard and bring her in. He reaches over and holds her hand to reassure her.

Colin reaches out to their backup, Jesse, sitting in an older, black Trans Am in pristine condition, a car he's had since his human days in the 1980s. *Jesse! We've got company somewhere nearby!* He paths.

Huh? I can't sense anyone! Are you sure? Jesse paths, sits up straight in the seat and gets ready for action. While the car itself appears to be a 1980s Trans Am, he's replaced the inner workings with more modern technology, and it's deceptively fast and maneuverable, making him appear less of a threat until the chase is on!

154

Yeah, it's very faint, and 'generic', but definitely not human; probably one of Jason's people. I don't think it's strong enough to be Jason, himself. There aren't any overtones of anger, but someone's watching us. I just can't pinpoint where or who! Colin paths.

I'll relay this to Liz, she's got a team on standby, maybe we can catch one of them this time. Jesse replies telepathically.

NO! At least, not right away. I've got something else in mind! I'm going to pretend to turn Sue in the alley, and hope the woman reports it to Jason. Maybe we can even draw him out. I won't really turn her until later tonight, but want to make them think she's off the market, and perhaps catch one or both of them in the trap. Don't interfere unless they try to stop us or grab Sue. We need her to relay the info to Jason. The woman should be caught off guard and THEN you can grab her. Colin commands.

Okay! Whatever you say. It's your call, but I'm letting Liz in on your plans, just in case... oh, and congrats! He paths with a mental grin. *She seems like a winner.* Jesse paths.

Indeed, she is, my friend. Colin replies, and breaks the connection.

When it's time to leave, Colin pays and tips the waiter, and nods to the owner, who gives him a slight, knowing smile.

"What's that about?" She asks.

"He's one of us, like me. He expressed his approval of my company for the evening. I told him we were celebrating, and he understood. We're welcome back for a special meal when you're one of us." He says.

"Just how many vam... people like you are there in this town?" She looks unsettled.

"There are quite a few. Asheville is one of several psychic hot spots in the country. They're natural energy centers which attract compatible people because they can sense the energy, and it feels 'right' to them." He smiles and catches her eye. *Don't be afraid.* He paths. Her mind goes still, and she walks out the door on autopilot, down the street a short distance with Colin's hand firmly on the small of her back. They turn down an alley and into a dark corner. Sue hears in her mind, *This is what happens when we take a feeder. The only difference is you'll remember what happens. We need to put on a show for our audience, just follow my lead.* He paths.

Her eyes open wide as he tips her chin back, numbs her neck, and bends in, sinking his fangs into her artery. He lingers for a while, as though he's drinking a lot of her blood, but she can tell he hasn't taken much. He withdraws, heals the wounds, and pulls her against him. Sue, it's time to take this to its natural conclusion." He says out loud. He leans in to kiss her deeply and paths *I'm going to bite your lip, so when I pull away, they'll think I've given you my blood! It won't hurt, I promise.* He gently bites her lip and spreads the blood on her lips. He pulls away so the observer can witness the blood on her lips. He says aloud, "Now you're mine forever!" and telepathically quips, *I know, it's corny, but we just need them to believe it! Feign weakness!*

She feigns a swoon, and acts drunk. She hears in her mind *Clearly one of his women, the cloaking slipped when she realized what she was witnessing and realized Jason would be pissed she let it happen. Just keep up the act a little longer!*

Jesse paths, *Yo, Colin! I see a woman coming from the opening of your alley. She's got her cell out and is telling someone something. From her reaction, they're not happy. She's telling them she did her best, but didn't know you were going to turn her there in the alley. The voice on the phone is male. He's telling her to come back immediately and he hung up on her. She's stuffing the cell back in her pocket, but isn't in any hurry to rush back to him. I think she's crying.*

Can you catch her? Take her back to Liz and the others? Colin paths.

Yeah, I'll pull the big guy comes to the rescue of crying girl act. I've got some neutralizer on me. So, she shouldn't be a problem. Jesse paths with a mental grin, and heads off like he's just walking by the steps where she's sitting. He stops to lend a sympathetic ear, and sits next to her. She's too upset, and inexperienced; she doesn't notice the energy coming from him isn't human. He hands her a tissue, and puts his hand on her arm. She looks up with a start as she realizes he's injected her with something, and she crumples into his arms. *Got her!* He paths with an ever-broader mental grin as he lifts her, and puts her in the back seat of his trans am, starts up its updated electric engine, and drives nearly silently away with her off to a secure location, pathing to Liz to meet him there.

Colin says, "You can stop pretending now. She passed on the bad news to Jason I've 'turned you' and you're now 'off the market'." He says with an ear-to-ear grin. "If you'd been my feeder, I'd send you on your way now, none the wiser!" He grins, showing his fangs, but perhaps something a little more exciting now no one's watching!" He pulls her closer and kisses her. They stand in the alley, kissing and caressing each other for a few minutes until the screams of fighting cats further down the alley startle them. "Maybe we should find someplace more appropriate?" He laughs.

The world swirls out again, and they're both in his bed. He cups her face. Just like old times, except this time, it's for good," He says. They make love, and as she nears her peak, he sinks his fangs into her throat painlessly, and draws hard, causing residual waves of pleasure that slowly give way as she fades in and out of consciousness, as he drinks more than she could normally afford to lose. He withdraws his fangs, kissing and healing the wounds, and then bites his own wrist. She hears in both her mind and with her ears "Your turn". She feels him push something warm and wet against her mouth. She instinctively parts her lips, drinking in the salty, metallic, sweet liquid. "That's it, no turning back now. Drink as much as you can. You're safe now." He says reassuringly. She feeds until she no longer feels the driving urge to do so.

"Can't keep my eyes open!" She slurs out.

"Then don't." He says and reaches over to grab something from his nightstand.

There's a slight pressure on her arm, and she wakes briefly. "What?" She asks.

"Something to ease your transition. When this is over, you'll be one of us, and Jason won't come after you again!" He puts two more infusers against her arm, the last one makes her sleep.

Genetic lottery

After a few minutes, Colin carefully crawls out of bed, gets dressed, and gently dresses Sue in a mid-length, nightshirt and underwear from her duffle bag, and pulls a blanket up over her. He grabs his cell and calls Sara. She answers, "Sara here."

"It's Colin, it's done." He says.

"Did you give her the infusions?" Sara asks. Colin can hear her moving things around in the background as she speaks.

"Yes, all three. I know you wanted to monitor her as early as possible, so you're duly notified she's in transition and it's all clear for you to come now." He says, sounding chipper and relieved now Sue is finally his.

"I assume you're decent?" Sara asks sarcastically.

"Yes, ma'am! Though I'll shower after you get here. I assume someone should be with her at all times?" He asks.

"Yes, we don't know what her transformation will be like. It's a bit of a genetic lottery with the LM potentials. The mutations could cause unpredictable reactions to the virus. It's best to keep an eye on her!" Her last words come across both on the phone and in his bedroom itself, as she ports in carrying a box and a medical bag filled with various equipment. "Go on then, I'll watch her. How long ago did you give her the infusions?"

"About 20-25 minutes ago." He heads off to shower.

Sara busies herself checking Sue. She sets up a monitor to scan Sue's physical and mental states constantly. She picks up her cell and calls Liz. "Liz, I'm over at Colin's and have monitors set up on Sue. It's early, but I'm already seeing unusual readings. Can you pop by medical and ask them for med pack fourteen? As well as a proper sleep inducer. I suspect she'll shake off the sedative soon enough."

"Alright, should I get Tess and bring her along?" Liz asks.

"Up to you. Let her know it's begun. We'll need her more when Sue's through her transformation.

"Gotcha. Marc told me Sue and Tess hit it off, so it might be comforting if she's there should Sue wake. Will be along in a few. I need to give Kari a heads up I may miss our supper. She's picking up fresh moose lapskaus in Bergen, but I'll tell her to put it in the fridge for another night." She hangs up.

Sara scans Sue's changing DNA and compares it to her earlier simulation. So far, the changes are about an 85% match with her simulation.

A few minutes later, both Liz and Tess pop in. Liz asks, "How's she doing?" The two women come over next to her, as she's sitting in an armchair by the bed.

"Her transition is slow and irregular. I see the usual changes we see with most Apara, and some are following the simulation I ran prior to her turning, but there are some changes it didn't predict. The added changes are slowing down the entire process, so we may be in for a long haul with her."

"Any sign of problems?" Liz peeks over Sara's shoulder at her tablet.

Sara shrugs. "Beats me. This is new territory. I have to assume our Benefactors knew what they were doing when they gene-tagged these people, but I'm just not sure what's *normal* for them." Sara leans back in her armchair. "Tess, I'm glad you came along after all! With the rate her transformation's going, I'd suggest we set up a schedule and take turns monitoring her. Are you up to that?"

"Sure. I just need to let Marc know I may be here for a while." She sits on the arm of Sara's chair. "I've never actually watched anyone turn before. *Hell*, I wasn't even present for most of my own!" She laughs, remembering how Sara knocked her out before she could object.

"You can keep me company through my watch now, and then go home or rest here, that way, you'll get some idea what to watch for.

Liz interrupts. "Just pathed with Kari. She got an extra-large batch of lapskaus, so I've asked her to bring it over here, and we can all share it." Liz leaves the room, and comes back a minute later carrying a chair from Colin's dining room for Tess to sit on. She pulls out a soft packet and gives it to Sara. "They want to know if you think you'll need more because they'll have to synthesize more of the immunosuppressant if you need it."

"I don't know for sure, but I'll holler their way in a few." Sara pulls out a small sphere and puts it on the nightstand next to Sue. "This should keep her knocked out for a while. I'll pop over and talk to my staff since you two are here. Colin should be out any time. Tell him I'll be right back. Liz, check her temperature every ten minutes while I'm gone. That should tell us if the immunosuppressant is working on her!" Sara ports out.

Liz lets out a long exhale before saying, "I hear you two really hit it off."

"Yeah, we crossed paths at her clinic after Digital Danger. I've got to admit; I'm looking forward to having someone besides Amy from my time period to hang with. No offense Liz, but..." She trails off.

"No offence taken. Even though Kari's a few hundred years younger than I am, she and I share more in common in some ways than I share with you and other new ones. I'm glad you're finding your own friends, as well as you and Marc finding each other." Liz says.

The bathroom door opens and Colin comes out in a bathrobe. "Liz? Tess? Where's Sara?"

"Off dealing with something at Medical. I'm glad Sue was willing to let you turn her. I'm so happy for you!" Liz stands and gives him a hug.

"Any change?" He walks around the women to sit in Sara's chair. He leans over and feels her cheek. "She's feverish." He says, concerned.

Liz pulls out a scanner and checks. "Hmm. She's running a fever, all right. Despite the immunosuppressant. It's 103 F. I'll let Sara know." She sends Sara a rapid path with the information, and immediately, Sara pops back in with a concerned expression.

Liz can sense her worry "What is it?"

As you know, with those who are prepped, our Benefactors desensitize the potentials to the virus over time, so the immune system won't fight it as hard. Either they didn't get that far with her, the immunosuppressant is useless, or possibly both." She says, as she scans Sue with one of her gadgets. She turns to Colin and says, "Get dressed and go to medical; tell them we need a freezer box full of ice. If her temperature gets too high, we'll have to put her in the tub with ice to cool her down. The high temperature won't hurt her in the long run, but it will certainly make her miserable, and possibly give her hallucinations or seizures."

Colin walks quickly to the bathroom after grabbing clean clothes and changes, pathing to all three women, *Heading there now!*

Sara goes ahead and infuses Sue with another ampoule of immunosuppressant, and spends a few minutes monitoring a device, giving her a hyper-detailed EEG reading.

A few minutes later, Colin pops back in next to Sara. "How is she?"

"Fever's down for now, which means the immunosuppressant works, but it doesn't last long. I've told my staff to synthesize more. I suspect, if this is going to be normal for LM-potentials, we'll need to build up a stockpile of the stuff!" Sara makes notes on her tablet, and circles some areas on the EEG type graph flowing in one window on her tablet.

"What's that?" Colin leans past her and strokes Sue's cheek.

"I'm watching changes in her brain activity, and there are areas activating all over the place from the virus. Some are normal, and some I've not seen before." She says, clinically, but there are undertones of concern.

"Anything dangerous?" Colin sits on the edge of the bed, gently stroking Sue's hair, which is sweat soaked from the falling fever.

"It's hard to say. We'll have to wait and see what manifests. This is as new for me as it is for you." Sara snaps, unused to not knowing what's going on medically. "I think Kari just ported into the kitchen. Why don't you three eat, and let me focus on Sue?"

Liz comes over and touches Colin on the shoulder, pathing. *Come on! Kari brought moose lapskaus from Norway, along with lingonberries. Let's let Sara do her job!*

The three of them go out to the kitchen and each fill up a bowl with the moose lapskaus, a Norwegian stew made of meat, potatoes, and carrots. Kari also brought mashed, sugared lingonberries, which are often served with wild meats, and freshly made flat bread and potato lefse, a Norwegian, tortilla-like, bread wrap. Liz, Colin, and Kari sit around a table to eat, and Tess takes a bowl in to Sara.

She quietly goes back into the bedroom, and closes the door. "Sara, I brought you some lapskaus. Figured you might miss out if I didn't."

"Put it on the nightstand, child! Thank you. I suspect it will be a long transition." Sara turns off the screen on her tablet and puts it down on the bed, grabbing the bowl of stew.

Tess sits on one of the chairs from earlier. "You're worried, aren't you?"

Sara faces Tess. "*Alas!* I didn't think the day would come this soon when you'd be using your skills on me! *Yes*, I'm concerned, but mostly because I don't understand what's happening to Sue, as it's different from normal transitions! Everything may turn out just fine, but I hate feeling helpless with my patients! We've had thousands of years of routine transformations, but we're entering a period when anything goes. Not knowing what to expect makes me uneasy."

"Sue's a strong and stable woman considering what she's been thrown into. I'm sure she'll be able to adapt to whatever transformation throws at her." Tess reassures Sara.

"I know she is, as are you, young-one! But some things are out of our control and sometimes, no matter how strong one is, things go wrong; but, enough negative thoughts. We'll just have to wait and see how it goes!" Sara eats her lapskaus and continues monitoring Sue's progress. Tess keeps her company, as she suggested.

They continue to give her the immunosuppressant, but each time, the fever returns more rapidly, and within twelve hours, it no longer has any real effect, and Sue's temperature rises unchecked.

"Tess, I need a cold bath drawn! And we need several buckets of ice. We must force her temperature down!" Sara looks worried as she reads the current temperature of 105.5F.

Tess fills the tub, but paths to the others, *Bring buckets of ice up! Setting up an ice bath to bring Sue's temperature down!*

Colin ports up carrying two buckets in each hand, and dumps them into the tub, porting to Sue's side, gently picking her unconscious body up, and carrying her toward the bathroom. "Do I just put her in or ease her in?"

"Try easing her in. We just need to cool her down, not put her in shock!" Sara snaps as she adds in more water and checks the temperature.

Colin eases her in, feet first. Even under sedation, her feet flinch, and she shivers as he lowers her gently into the ice bath. "Why won't her fever stay down? I thought transformation fevers rarely went above 102F!"

Sara looks flustered, and checks Sue's forehead temperature. "Part of the preparation for potential transformation is a desensitizing of the immune system to the virus. I'm guessing they never got that far with Susan, which means we need to keep that in mind in the future for other LM potentials. The immunosuppressant's losing effectiveness quickly, so I'll have to change up the formula and find one that works better."

"Will she be okay?" Colin sits on the floor next to the tub and holds Sue's hand gently, stroking the back of her hand with his thumb.

"Yes, eventually. The virus has created a strong foothold, but her body is fighting it tooth and nail. The virus will win out, but it's going to be a rough ride, and based on these readings..." She taps the screen of her tablet. "it may take several days, unless we can crash her immune system." Sara continues reading the data

flashing across her screen and shakes her head, muttering something in a language no one present knows, but everyone present
understands Sara's not happy about the situation. Sara turns to
Tess. "Monitor her temperature! I'm going back to Medical to see
if I can find anything else that might help." She vanishes after
handing Tess her tablet and a scanning device.

Kari and Liz stand in the doorway, watching, holding each
other, worried not only for Sue but also for Colin, should anything
go wrong. Liz paths privately to Kari. *If this goes badly, I'll have to
make sure Colin doesn't lose it. Maybe we shouldn't have rushed it. I
know it couldn't be helped with Jason nipping at her heels, but I
never expected things to get so touch and go.*

Kari paths in return, *Give it time! You heard Sara! She'll get
through this and recover; it just may be a rough one. And I'm sure
Colin knows it's still better than Jason getting her.*

*Sorry! I know, but even though Colin's not one of my core family,
I turned him and feel responsible for him. Like any parent, I don't
want to see my 'offspring' or their loved ones suffer.* Liz lays her
head on Kari's shoulder as they watch them cool Sue down.

Tess watches the tablet and notes Sue's temperature is dropping. As it drops below 102 F, she breathes a sigh of relief. "She's
out of the danger-zone now. Give her about ten more minutes in
the ice bath, then we'll get her dried off, and get her back in bed."

Colin slumps, not only exhausted from the ordeal, but he's quite
pale from giving Sue so much of his blood while turning her. Tess puts
the tablet down and ports out, returning ten minutes later. "Let's get
her out of there and strip those wet clothes off her. Sara told me to put
light clothing on her; underwear, a t-shirt, and no covers."

Colin carefully lifts her out of the water. All the ice has melted, but
the water's still chilly. He holds Sue up while Tess, Kari, and Liz re-
move all her cold, wet clothing, either by hand, or porting it off and
into a pile in the sink where the water can drip away without making a
mess. They dry her off and Colin carries her back to the bed, laying

her on top of a quilt. He grabs one of the duffle bags of her clothes, and pulls out a clean t-shirt and underwear, and proceeds to dress her, letting her lie there on the bed. He stands, then nearly falls over.

Tess helps stabilize him. "Colin, you need to feed! I went out and got you some bagged blood. I figure you probably don't want to leave Sue under the circumstances, but you need this, not only for yourself, but also for her when she's through transformation. You'll want her to feed from you."

Colin looks at Tess, too tired to speak, but nods and follows her over to a chair at a desk in his bedroom, where Tess has a small cooler with three bags of blood in it. "If you need more than that, I'll get it for you! Sara will be back shortly, but she said you need to rest while you can while she's resting quietly."

Colin finishes a bag of blood, keeping the others for later, and crawls into bed with Sue, careful to keep some distance so his body heat doesn't increase her temperature. He leans over and gently kisses her forehead, and loosely holds her hand as he falls asleep, realizing Sara dosed the blood with a mild sedative so he's forced to get some rest as well.

Death and rebirth

Tess, Liz, and Kari settle in Colin's living room. Sara comes out from the bedroom after setting up a remote monitor so they can keep track of Sue's transformation while Sue and Colin rest.

"It's going to be a long process. All three of you don't need to stay here. I need one of you here to monitor her while I run back and forth to check on the new immunosuppressant batch being produced." Sara says, looking rather run through the ringer herself.

Liz stretches and yawns. "If it's all the same to you, I'd like to stay. He is one of my former charges, after all."

Kari rubs Liz's back. "And if Liz is staying, so am I!"

Sara looks expectantly at Tess, who looks up, obviously worn out, but says, "Not like I have anything better to do but stare at the walls and my computer screen at home! I'll stay too! Just need to check in with Marc and let him know I'm okay!"

"All right then! I'd suggest you take turns getting some rest! I'll make sure more blood is sent over in case any of you need some." Sara nods at the three women and vanishes.

Sue and Colin both sleep for several hours, and gradually, Kari, Liz, and Tess drift off in the living room, only to be woken by the monitor alarm going off and a shout both verbal and telepathic from Colin for help. By the time the three of them get to the bedroom, Sara's already there, helping Colin hold Sue in place while Sara attempts to put something in her mouth. Sue's having convulsions and her fever's spiked again. Sara infuses her with three different concoctions, and after about five minutes, Sue settles and becomes still, except for her rapid breathing. Colin, despite having fed and gotten some sleep looks haggard.

Sara puts her hands up to her face, rubbing her eyes, and then puts a hand on Colin's arm. "I've given her the new immunosuppressant, a sedative, and an anticonvulsant." She looks at a tablet and shakes her head. "She's still only partially through the colonization stage of the virus." When everyone looks a little confused, she elucidates. "Stage one is when the virus colonizes the body by entering the cells, multiplying, and spreading to all the other cells. Stage one is about 73% complete, and it runs concurrent with Stage two, where the virus rewrites the DNA. Usually, they overlap closely, but her body is fighting the virus so strongly, more energy is being put into producing extra viral particles so the colonization can complete. This is also the most active stage of the immune reaction." She leans over and feels Sue's forehead to confirm her fever is down, but still relatively high.

"What does all this mean?" Colin asks, clearly worried.

"The immune system usually weakens once most of the cells are colonized and completely gives up once the DNA is rewritten in all the cells, prior to the final stage, transformation. I'm not seeing any reduction in her immune system's aggressive defense. The DNA rewrite is closer to 48%. Normally, there's usually only about a 10% lag between colonization and rewrite, but we're seeing 25%. We'll have to see how this new version of the immunosuppressant works, but if she ends up with another fever spike and seizures, we may have to consider more drastic measures..." She trails off.

Colin's expression tightens with stress and he blanches, even though he recently fed. "*Drastic*?" Colin asks. "Like what?"

"Once the cells are colonized and mostly rewritten, we may have to consider stopping her heart, which will put her into stasis, and her immune system will zero out as well." Sara plops down in a chair next to the bed in frustration.

"You mean killing what's left of her as a human?" Colin asks, his voice rising in stress.

"She'll be *fine*! It may mean a couple of extra days for her transformation, but she won't be in any *pain* or discomfort that way. And every time she seizes, there's some measure of brain damage that needs extra time to heal. If we reach that point, I'd prefer to take her to Medical, but if you want to keep her here, we can, but it may be difficult to watch." Sara puts a hand gently on Colin's shoulder, waiting for his reply.

"Can I accompany her if you take her there?" He asks as he plays with Sue's sweat-soaked hair.

"Of course, but she'll be in stasis for at least a couple of days. You'd be better off getting some rest and just visiting rather than camping out there!" Sara says.

"Let's play it by ear." Colin looks at Liz to see what her reaction is.

Liz paths, *Trust Sara's judgment. You won't be doing any good sitting around there until she's breathing again. She won't know you're there until then.*

Colin nods curtly to Liz. "When will we know if she needs to go in?"

"I'd like her colonization rate to reach 94% before we pull the plug. Her brain was the first to be colonized and rewritten, which creates a protective effect should she go into stasis, even now, but I'd prefer to wait until we reach that point unless her seizures become more severe. I want you to give her a new dose every two hours. I've got to head back to Medical, but call me if her temp creeps up toward 105 again, or if she seizes." Sara vanishes, leaving Colin, Liz, Kari, and Tess there with Sue.

They take turns sitting with her and administer the immunosuppressant every two hours. After about twelve hours, her fever rises sooner and higher by the time the next dose is due. Sara comes back and checks her status. "Well, she's up to about 89% colonization, and 70% rewritten, but at the rate she's going, she'll likely seize again before she hits the optimum 94%. I'd suggest we put her into an induced stasis now, and avoid another round of seizures. It will extend her transformation, but it will be a lot easier on her." She waits for Colin's decision.

Colin closes his eyes and takes a slow, deep breath. He opens his eyes and looks at Sara, and gives her a curt nod. "Do what you think is best. I certainly don't want her to be in more pain or distress than necessary."

"Then come over here, take her hand, and lightly link with her telepathically to reassure her. I don't want her to go into a panic when I do this." Sara reaches into her bag and brings out a clear ampoule, putting it into the diffuser, but adds a needle attachment. "I must slip this into her heart. It will block the nerve impulses telling her heart to beat and paralyze the heart muscles, forcing her into stasis. Have you made a choice?"

"Can I keep her here for now?" Colin asks with a forlorn look in his eyes.

Sara's sighs and turns to Tess. "Can you be on call and get over here if they need you?"

"I'm sure I can work something out with Marc." Tess chimes in.

"I may bring Annie with me next time, so she can help in the future. She's got some latent healing skills, and I think it will help her to witness this process as well, but I think she'll feel more comfortable if you're here. Especially if I need to pop back to Medical for anything!" Sara turns to Colin. "Are you ready? You need to help her through this! Part of her will think she's really dying and may panic."

Colin climbs onto the bed, lies alongside Sue, takes her hand in his, and closes his eyes, reaching into her mind. After a minute, a dream like venue unfolds in his mind. It's misty, but he can make out a figure in the distance, and heads toward it. He gets closer and can see Sue's face. She looks exhausted. He goes up to her and gently puts his arms around her. "Sue, it's me, Colin." He says.

"Colin? Where am I? I thought I was lying in your bed, but this seems more like some movie version of the afterlife?" Sue turns around and holds him tightly.

"You *are* in my bed, but this is a dream, though I am here with you. You're transforming, but it's a rough one. Your fever's been high and you've had seizures." He holds her, rubbing her back.

"Seizures? That doesn't sound good." She looks up at him.

"They won't do any permanent damage, but Sara's worried about the strain on you psychologically. Do you remember me telling you how sometimes my people can appear dead, but they're in a kind of healing stasis?" He tips his forehead down toward hers.

After a pause, he can tell she remembers. "Yes, but what's that have to do with me?"

Our doctor is worried about putting you through more rounds of seizures, so she wants to put you in stasis. You'll be fine, I promise! Your immune system is fighting so hard against the virus, your body is being put through Hell. But if you go into stasis, your immune system will be shut down and the virus can complete its job."

"Are you saying I have to *die*?" Tears meander down her cheeks, and the dream room gets colder as her temperature rises again.

"By human standards, but you'll revive again in a few days, I *promise*." He kisses her on the forehead and hugs her tightly.

She's shaking, but asks, "Are you sure that's *necessary*?"

"It'll be a lot easier on you. You won't be in pain, or have to deal with fever, or seizures anymore. You won't be aware of time even passing while you're in stasis, but if we don't do it, you'll be in pain and potentially have to deal with brain damage, albeit temporary. I'm so sorry this has been so hard on you. None of us knew it would be this rough. You're the first from your group of lost potentials to be transformed." He says softly.

"It's okay. As long as it's over soon, I'll be okay, and with you." She tries to sound brave and strong.

He looks at her, and kisses her in the dream venue, then holds her close as he paths to Sara, "Do it! She understands. I'll stay with her as long as I can."

Sue's heart slows down and grows irregular. She suppresses the instinctive panic and holds on to Colin until her heart fully stops, the dream world dissolves, and Colin opens his eyes, tears running down his face and into her hair. She's no longer breathing. He listens, but there's no heartbeat. He tries to touch her mind, and while she's silent, it's not an empty void. She's there, in some form, waiting to re-emerge like a butterfly from a cocoon.

Emergence

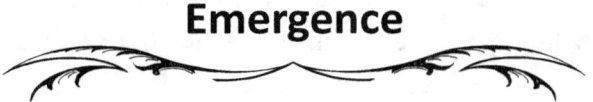

Two days pass, and Colin is getting increasingly impatient. He checks on her frequently, even when lying there in bed waiting for her to show any renewed signs of life. Colin stays by her side as much as possible and settles into a reclining backed chair in her room. The wait and worry exhaust him, and as much as he wants to stay awake, he drifts off into a deep, emotionally tumultuous sleep.

He wakes to glaring light making it difficult to keep his eyes open. He closes them again and smells salty, sea air, hears waves crashing, seagulls screeching, children giggling, and playing as they run from the waves breaking on *the beach?* He thinks, confused. He cannot remember how he came to lie on a sunny beach somewhere! He shadows his eyes with his hands, slowly opens them, and allows them to adapt. *What the Hell? Folly Beach, South Carolina?* But before he can think any further, a large wave crashes close to him and a young woman with red hair and a Styrofoam boogie-board crashes into the sand at his feet and practically rolls into his lap, laughing.

"Are you alright?" He reaches a hand out to her to help her right herself.

"Oh! *Yeah!* Sorry about that! BIG WAVE! Kinda caught me off guard! Sorry if I got you all wet." She laughs and brushes sand off her bathing suit and legs. "Mind if I just sit here for a few? That knocked the wind out of me."

"Sure! Do you realize you're getting quite a sunburn?" Colin comments as he sees and senses the burn on her shoulders, back, and face.

"Yeah! I put on waterproof SPF100, but with my skin, I still burn. I've got some good aloe-based cream I'll use when I get back to my hotel room." She smiles. "Hey! I don't know what it is, but you look familiar to me. Have we met before?"

"I wondered that myself. I'm not from around here. Came in from Asheville for the weekend." He hands her a spare towel. "Why don't you drape this over your shoulders until you can get some more sunscreen on!"

"Asheville? I'm living there too! Well, just moved to Weaverville. I'm finishing up my masters in psych at Mars Hill. Oh, *thanks*. It sucks I burn so easily, but it goes along with the red hair." She takes the towel and throws it over her shoulders. "My name's Susan Burns, though most call me Sue." She smiles at him and is oddly at ease with this man."

"Hmm, appropriate name with that sunburn, 'Sue burns!'" He chuckles at his own pun. "So, you're a budding psychologist?" He asks.

Sue groans at his pun, but says, "I'm trying! I'm finishing up my masters for now, but I hope to eventually get my PhD!" She smiles and looks Colin straight in the eye.

"Name's Colin...Colin Davenport, it's very nice to meet you, Sue." He experiences an intense sense of déjà vu. *Susan? Sue, Weaverville?* He flashes on her sitting on the hillside overlooking the ocean at his home in Sanctuary, then of the two of them in bed together. Other visions flash through his mind and he feels dizzy. He looks back up at her and she's looking at him oddly, with her head cocked to one side.

She swallows hard. "I do know you... somehow... and I know *what* you are!"

His eyes go wide as he realizes she knows exactly what he is. "How?"

"This has all happened before; years ago! This was the beginning of everything!" She exclaims.

More images and visions, along with feelings bombard him. "*Years* ago? How's that possible?" He's disoriented.

"I think I'm dreaming. These are memories, but now, they're no longer playing back as they were at first. My washing up in that wave at your feet, the whole sunburn thing and introductions." She pauses and looks up at him. "I'm going to be like you someday. You're going to change me. No! You already *have changed* me!"

"What the hell are you talking about?" He suddenly can't see the beach or anything around him, but flashes on himself feeding on Sue, and giving her his blood. He's momentarily overwhelmed by the vision and the emotions attached to it all, but when his vision clears, he's looking at Sue and knows he's dreaming too. "But whose dream is this? Yours or mine?"

"It *feels* like we're both here?" She scrambles closer to him, cups his cheek with her hand and looks him in the eye. "You're here too, aren't you? I can feel you!"

He puts his own hand on hers, reaches out mentally, and feels her 'soul' with his own. "It must be some kind of telepathic dream, but that means you must be back!"

"Back?" She looks confused.

"Your transformation was going badly. Sara, our doctor, felt it would be best to put you in stasis; stop your heart, and thus, your immune reaction. You were running a high fever with seizures, remember?" He leans over and pulls her close to him, hugging her.

As he holds her close in the dream, he shakes uncontrollably. He ignores it, holding on to Sue, but soon, the dream dissolves, and he hears Sara's voice. "Colin! *Colin!* Wake up! Sue's out of stasis!"

He groans. "I know!" He yawns. "I was just with her." His eyes flutter open to a look of confusion from Sara.

"With her? Well, you're in the same room and have been for the last few days! I just thought you'd like to know she's breathing and her heart is beating again and there's no sign of fever!" Sara stands there with her arms crossed in front of her chest.

Colin is a little disoriented after his dream. He sits on the edge of the bed and takes Sue's hand, which is once again warm. He breathes a sigh of relief and reaches over with his other hand and brushes some stray strands of hair away from her face. He notices her eyes moving rapidly under her eyelids in REM sleep. "She's still dreaming."

"*Still*? She just came out of stasis. It usually takes a few hours before they reach a level where they can dream! Though she appears to be in REM sleep. Quite curious!" Sara pulls out her scanner and takes readings of Sue.

"We were dreaming together! We were! I'm sure of it!" But Sara holds up a hand to him.

"Write it down and don't tell anyone the contents! When she's up to it, we'll see what she says and compare notes. Then we'll know if you just had a dream about her or if it was mutual." She goes over and finds a notebook and a pen and hands it to him. "Or would you rather have a tablet?" She smirks.

Colin takes the notebook and pen and at his desk and reconstructs as much of the shared dream as he can. He smiles as he remembers her crash landing at his feet on the beach, and how he could feel her with him in the dream. He gets lost in thought remembering the day they first met, and realizes they've finally come full circle. He breaks out of his memories when he feels a small hand on his shoulder and sees a bag of blood dropped on his notebook in front of him. He looks up and Sara's standing there with an eyebrow raise.

"You need to feed. No doubt she'll be hungry when she wakes." Sara pats him reassuringly on the arm.

"How long do you think it will be?" He asks as he tears off the corner of the bag and downs the blood.

"Probably pretty soon. If she's already dreaming, it may not be long before she regains consciousness. We'll go down the hall and wait in the living room and give you two some privacy." Sara motions to the others and they all leave the room and close the door.

Colin walks back over and sits in the armchair by the bed and takes Sue's hand in his. It's warm again, but not hot, and he breathes a sigh of relief. He looks at her face, and despite being a little wan and her hair being a sweaty, tangled mess, she looks more beautiful to him than ever.

He waits attentively for her to wake for nearly two hours, and lays his head on his arms on the edge of the mattress beside her hip and dozes, exhausted, but relieved she's breathing again. A while later, he wakes to the sensation of her fingers playing with the ends of his hair. He sits up and looks at her face and sees her smiling at him. He slides over from the chair to the edge of the mattress and reaches down and hugs her. At first, she hugs him back, but then she tenses up. He pulls back, her eyes are wide, and she's breathing heavily, her mouth is halfway open, and her fangs are showing.

"It's alright, Sue! You're just hungry and my nearness triggered your fangs instinctively. It's normal!" He reaches out both of his hands for hers and pulls her upright. "I'm going to show you how to feed from me now. We'll take it slowly, but don't worry, you won't hurt me." He smiles at her and brushes her knotted red hair out of her eyes.

"I'm afraid..." She admits in a small, lisping voice, rough from disuse.

He puts his hand behind her head, holding eye contact and pulls her toward him. "Just come closer and lean in toward my neck. Once you get closer, your instincts will kick in. Don't be afraid of them, trust them!" He tips his head back, pulls her closer and she feeds from him. There's a slight pain as she doesn't know how to numb it fully, and yet, it's the sweetest pain he's ever felt because it means they're now truly together.

Sue loses track of how much she's taking from him and hears in her mind, *Sue, you need to stop now! If you're still hungry, I'll get you more blood in a minute.* She pauses, and then slowly backs off from him, withdrawing her fangs from his neck. Her face is smudged nearly from ear-to-ear, down her chin and on the tip of her nose with his blood, and he has to suppress a laugh. He reaches down and picks up her left hand and brings it to the wounds on his neck. "Now, picture the wounds healing up, growing smaller, and going away all together."

She struggles to make eye contact with him. "Did I do it wrong? Did I take too much?" She asks in a small, quiet voice.

"It's fine! You're just very hungry after the transition and time in stasis." He pauses and looks her in the eye. "Do you know how long I've waited for this? I was sure you were compatible from early on, and have longed for you to feed from me and make me a real part of you too!" He pulls her close and holds her tight. She can hear him sniffle, and knows he's crying tears of joy, which makes her hug him even tighter. He slowly pulls away from her, smiling, and stands. "I'll be right back!" He walks to the bathroom and fills the tub with hot water, and then returns to her side, scoops her up in his arms, spins her around, and takes her to the bathroom, setting her down on the toilet. "Get cleaned up and I'll let Sara know you're awake. She'll want to check you over."

"Sara?" She must think for a minute, as she's never actually met the woman. "You mean the doctor you and Tess mentioned?"

"Yes, I'm sure she'll want to give you a thorough once over! You're the first one of the Lost Mission potentials to be transformed, and she needs to make sure everything is as it should be." He helps her off with her t-shirt, she slips off her underwear, and settles into the warm water.

Sue's surprised how sensitive her skin is as the warm water conforms to and caresses her body. She watches as Colin heads back out to the living room; she allows herself to slide down into the water and submerge her head and hair, and then sits back up without effort, dragging her hair back from her face with her hands. She realizes, *I've never really felt this alive before!* And she lets out an enormous sigh of relief because she knows, in her heart, neither she, nor Colin are monsters.

Proverbial guinea pig

Sue gets out, dries off, and finds clean clothes from the duffle bag. Her pants are a little loose, but that's not surprising since she hasn't eaten any solid food in several days. She takes the towel off her hair and begins to brush it out when she hears footsteps approaching the bedroom door. Somehow, she knows one of the two sets of footsteps belong to her new friend, Tess, so she puts down her brush and says, "Come in, Tess!" before she can even knock.

Tess opens the door and comes in, smiling. Behind her is a small, dark-haired woman who gives Sue the odd impression of being ancient despite her apparent youth.

"How're you feeling?" Tess asks, coming in and sitting on the edge of the bed not far from Sue.

"Surprisingly good, considering!" Sue says. "Who's your friend?" She asks, skeptically.

"Sara's our doctor. Not that we get sick, but she's there if we need her for injuries or transformation irregularities, and she needs to check you over now that you're awake." Tess nods to Sara.

"You gave us a few rough days, child! I just need to make sure everything is as it should be after your rough transition." Sara comes a little closer with her tablet and a small scanner attachment.

Sue's eyes grow distant for a minute as she struggles to remember something. "I think I remember Colin telling me something about stopping my heart, and seizures?"

"Yes, you had several seizures. Our usual immunosuppressant wasn't sufficient to keep your fever down. I adjusted the formula, but your fever was still out of control, and potential new seizures were likely when we put you into stasis, which, to humans, would appear as death. To us, however, it's merely a period where all our energies are focused on healing, rather than maintaining breathing, heartbeat and so on." Sara comes closer, and cautiously touches Sue's chin to get her to face her. "Hmmm..."

"Is everything alright?" Sue asks, with a concerned look.

"Oh, yes! Though I was expecting a few more surprises." Sara chuckles.

"Surprises? You mean because of the seizures and stuff? Were you expecting brain damage?" Sue thinks about how many ways things can go wrong in the brain due to strokes, high fever, and other potentially damaging influences.

"No, though there may have been some minor damage, you've clearly healed!" Sara pulls up the same chair she'd sat in to watch Sue through the transformation. "Colin did tell you you're *special*, didn't he?"

Sue bursts out laughing. "He's been telling me that since the first time I crash landed in an enormous wave at his feet at the beach!"

Sara smiles and nods. "Yes, but did he explain to you you're from a group of potentials we call 'The Lost Mission" potentials?"

"Yes, he said they found my DNA was in a damaged database, which is why I was not in the main one, even though he was sure I was compatible." She takes a slow, deep breath.

"Ah, but did he explain what that actually means?" Sara gives her a kindly look and waits for her answer.

"Just that I'm compatible and could become one of you. Is there something else? I mean, I feel fine. Great, actually!" Sue worries Colin may have left out some big negatives, so she'd let him change her.

"It's nothing really to worry about. You're the first one from the Lost Mission database. The thing is..., how can I put this? Do you ever read comic books or watch superhero movies?" Sara grins.

"Yeah, but I've had little time to read comics lately." Sue shifts uneasily on the edge of the bed.

"The people in that database were born during a time of some unusual cosmic energy and radiation bombarding the planet, and it caused genetic mutations which will probably give you extra strong or unique abilities, like some superheroes in the comics!" Sara watches her carefully for a reaction.

"What? Am I going to start flying or shape-shifting or something?" She gives Sara a skeptical look.

Sara lets out a long sigh and gives her a slight smile. "Honestly, we don't know all of what may manifest in people like you! You may be just like the rest of us, with base amounts of various psychic abilities, plus the ability to port, redact memories, heal, and so on! However, you may end up with variations of those abilities we haven't seen before or even completely new ones!"

"What? Am I some sort of experimental guinea pig?" Sue stands and paces back and forth anxiously.

Tess speaks up. "Sue! It's okay! We'll all help you through this. I've been through some of this myself!"

"What? But she said I'm the first from this new group! I don't really appreciate being a lab-rat!" Sue crosses her arms and glares at Sara.

"I'm sorry if you feel that way, but someone had to be first, and at least you're with someone you know you belong with! While Tess is not from the same group as you, she's in a similar situation! I don't see any overt signs of new or uncontrolled abilities when I scan you with this. That doesn't mean they won't come, but we have ways to deal with them." Sara sends calming energy to Sue, who eventually comes over and roughly sits on the bed again.

"What *measures*?" Sue asks, irritated.

Sara pulls out a bracelet like the one Tess is wearing from her bag. "Until we know what we're dealing with, this will help you control whatever abilities you have. It works by blocking unconscious use of your abilities, but will still let you explore what you can do." She gently slips it on Sue's left wrist. "Now, most of those turned these days have some subconscious knowledge and training on how to use their abilities. Unfortunately, we don't know if you do or not, but it's likely many of the Lost Mission potentials have little or no pre-conditioning, but we're all here to help you learn."

Sue turns to Tess. "*Ugh!* Why have I got the feeling I've just gotten myself into more than I bargained for?" Exasperation drips from every word.

Tess's face is full of compassion and sympathy. "It *is* going to take time to get used to everything, but trust me, the alternative would have been much worse! Worrying constantly Jason might come after you, or worse, having him get you and turn you himself. Trust me, before you know it, you won't have any regrets about becoming one of us. What would you tell one of your clients when they're feeling overwhelmed?"

Sue's quiet, but Tess can sense her relaxing as she realizes she's just overwhelmed and needs to take the advice she's given to many. "I'd tell them to take a step back, calm down and try to look at things objectively. They should take things in small chunks or steps, and not to let themselves try to take everything head-on. But more than anything, they should be patient with themselves, because getting upset makes everything appear so much worse."

Tess gives her a smile, grabs one of her hands, and gives it a friendly squeeze. "Wish I'd had you here to tell me all that when I had to come to that conclusion on my own. Seriously, I'll do whatever I can to help you through this, as will Sara, Colin, and the rest of us at Inspiration Inc. Remind me to introduce you to my friend, Amy. She's new too!"

Sue turns back to Sara. "Do you have any idea what I should expect or be looking for?"

"I did some simulations based on your DNA and the changes that should happen when turned. It wasn't 100% on target, but you may see it in your chosen field. Likely, you were latently talented even as a human, and it affected your choice of career. Probably some ability that helped you with reading or helping people psychologically, from what I can see." She explains. "I need to take a small blood sample, so I can do a DNA analysis

182

now your transformation is complete. *Oh!* I think someone's eager to see for himself you've come through all this unscathed!" She chuckles and nods toward the footsteps coming toward the door.

"Colin?" She asks.

"He's been anxious about your transformation! He's so happy you turned out to be compatible, but also worried because of the circumstances. You have my number, call me, anytime! I'm heading back to Marc. By now, he's got a backlog of baked croissants and éclairs for me to peruse!" She stands and ports out.

Sara pats Sue on one hand and says, "Get some rest. I know you just 'woke up', but you've been through the biological equivalent of a tempest, and you're likely to tire quickly." Sara paths to Colin. *All looks good so far! Call me if there's anything strange, and I mean anything!* She ports out as Colin opens the door.

The anxiety he's been harboring for days dissolves from his expression, he sits next to her, and gives her an enormous bear hug, rolling her onto the bed so they're lying there, face to face. "Are you feeling better after your bath?" He mentally scans her mood and energy.

She laughs briefly. "I'm fine, though you could have told me I was a freaking guinea pig!"

"*Guinea pig*?" He looks at her confused.

"Yeah, you only told me I was compatible, but not about the rest of it! All the mutations and weirdness!" She screws up her face and looks annoyed, but doesn't stay that way, not when she knows this time, he will never leave her, and they can finally be together for real.

"I didn't want to completely freak you out! I figured all the normal parts of becoming Apara was enough to deal with." He pulls her close again, just holding her, still finding it hard to believe she was compatible and now can be with him for centuries to come. Under the circumstances, he doesn't mention their possible shared dream; afraid it might freak her out. While he's holding her tightly, her stomach lets out a loud, empty growl, and they both laugh. "Guess we'd better find you some real food!

Loose ends

After she eats enough for three dinners, she stands and stretches. "Colin, where's my phone? I bet I have a ton of messages to catch up with! How long was I out?"

"About a week. Your cell's charging over there by the sofa." He points toward an end table.

"A week! Dear Lord! What about work?" She walks frantically over to the sofa, sits with a thud, and grabs her phone. She skims email headers, tossing spam as she goes.

"Don't worry about it! Sara got in touch with them. She said you'd come down with severe pneumonia and a sinus infection. They weren't happy about rescheduling all your clients, but they certainly understood you couldn't come in!" He settles next to her on the sofa and gently rubs the tension out of her nearest shoulder.

She looks up from her phone at Colin, scowling. "But I *do* worry! My clients need me, and I want to go back to work as soon as possible!"

He cocks his head to one side, knowing he must be patient with Sue, as she doesn't yet understand how much her life has just changed beyond the need for blood, and they're now together for good. "Love, we talked about this before I turned you. You need to get control of your abilities first, as well as your needs, or you could put your clients in danger and risk exposing what you, and we are!"

Sue takes a deep breath and lets it out slowly, knowing he has a point, but still annoyed at how everything has turned her life upside down. "I get that, but I was just looking at messages from work, and a couple of my clients have been in with mental health crises, and they don't feel comfortable talking to anyone else.

185

Besides, Sara said my new abilities are probably something related to my work! Maybe I could really help them now."

"Maybe, but we must work on your abilities and make sure you know when to feed, so you don't put any of them at risk or get overwhelmed. Give me ten days, okay? I promise, we'll investigate the possibilities then.

Ten days? I'm gonna hold you to that." She says stubbornly.

"Sue, there's something else we need to talk about..." He trails off.

"Okay, what *else* haven't you told me?" She puts her cell back down on the end table and crosses her arms in front of her chest.

"I'm not sure how to tell you this part, but it's why you're referred to as a Lost Mission potential." He grins cautiously.

"Well, I assume it's because the database was damaged and the information was *lost*?" She looks warily at him, having a sinking feeling she's about to get a new tour through the Twilight Zone now that she's made it through her transition.

"Yeah, well, it's the "Mission" part. Our existence isn't just some random, viral happenstance. The virus was engineered thousands of years ago." He pauses, watching her face, and sensing her emotions shift at this revelation.

"Say what? How could it have been *engineered* thousands of years ago? What the *Hell*?" She closes her eyes and shakes her head slowly, as she nears her limits.

He faces her and takes her hands in his. "The gene sequence that made you compatible is not something you inherited naturally. It was added to your DNA as a child." He watches her as she holds her tongue to let him explain, even though she instinctively wants to argue with him over what seems impossible. "The Apara were created to safeguard this world and to help usher it into a mature civilization." She opens her mouth to ask 'created by whom?', but he holds his hand up and cuts off her question. A group of long-lived beings from very far away, who want to see humans evolve to a state of true civilization, created the transformational virus. They came here thousands of years ago and had the technology to alter DNA. It's a long story and I don't want to overwhelm you any more than I already have, but they changed representatives of various cultures around the world. They gave us our indefinite lifespan, our psychic gifts, the ability to port, and so on. Yes, they also made us dependent on humans by giving us the need for blood. Our bodies can't make it from raw materials. We must have whole blood our bodies convert to keep our blood levels up to normal." He stops talking long enough to allow her to react.

Sue's eyes grow wide and her breathing's rapid as she comes to the only logical conclusion, barking out, "You're talking about *aliens*? *FREAKING ALIENS*! Oh, *dear Lord*! What have you gotten me into? It was hard enough to deal with the whole 'my long-term boyfriend is a vampire and I need to become one so I'll be safe from another crazy vampire', but *Holy Hell*! I think my synapses are *melting* after this little revelation!" She puts her face down in her hands and shakes her head.

Colin reaches one arm around her and pulls her close. "You need to know this, sweetie. There really isn't any easy way to break this to you. Most people who are turned have been given subliminal knowledge of all this which we can trigger, but those in the Lost Mission database, we just don't know if you have the knowledge or not. You see, the team of...we call them our Bene-factors; they pick up children who have promising genetic poten-tial, and evaluate them. Those who are acceptable and amenable to 'helping humanity reach its potential' are given the DNA tag which later makes them compatible, if needed. We have a data-base over all the people who are compatible, as well as names, and other information. Unfortunately, the team that was dealing with your *generation* was lost in a freak accident... in *space*. Eventually, the wreckage was found, with no survivors, but they found the equivalent of a computer with the database in it. Unfortunately, all information other than the raw gene prints was lost for those eight years of the mission. We haven't needed that many new transformees, until after Jerusalem, so never really did anything with it until now. We lost so many of our people we must replace, and we were coming up short. So, efforts have been made to find genetic matches between the database and world genetic registries now they're relatively commonplace."

"*That's* where you all found me? Some random match in a database like Ancestry.com?" She asks as her head is leaning on his shoulder.

"Yes, though I don't have any idea which database they found your DNA in. You were in the first batch of identified potentials." He explains.

"Are you all going to change everyone in that database?" She asks, slowly pulling away so she can look him in the eye. Her own eyes look glassy, like she could cry at any second.

"*Hell* no! Many of the ones in the database are unsuitable for turning!" He reaches down and takes one of her hands in his.

"But I was suitable? And what would have made me suitable or unsuitable?" She asks, quietly.

"There're a lot of things. We never turn someone in an established marriage or with children. We look at their psychological health and adaptability, as well as their psychic potential. We only turn people we think will adapt well, and use their new abilities responsibly." He explains, giving her hand a slight squeeze.

Yeah, Tess mentioned something about that. She said Jason slipped through the cracks, and after Jerusalem, the person who turned him didn't know he was unstable. It can be a risky business trying to figure out who will and won't make the psychological and ethical cut." Sue sits there for a minute, processing it all, when she gets a look of sudden comprehension. "So, this is what Tess was talking about? Having to go through and evaluate all these potentials to see who should and shouldn't be turned?"

"*Exactly*! She's been doing this by the seat of her pants, but Liz and Kari say she's one of the best people-intuitives they've seen in decades." He smiles as he senses her comprehension ease her mind.

"Tess asked me if she could run some of..., I guess, these potentials by me. Though I'm not sure I feel too comfortable deciding to have someone changed without their permission." She's exasperated.

"I know this is hard for you to understand, but every single potential was asked on a telepathic level if they would be willing to put the world ahead of their own lives, and help make Earth it a better place. Only those who were willing were gene-tagged, and only a small percentage of those will ever be tapped for service; at least until now." He attempts to sense if she will accept this or argue, but before he can determine it, she speaks up.

"You're talking about *children* making such a decision at what *age*?" She asks, sounding appalled.

"Usually under the age of two." He answers, knowing she's going to fight him, but he attempts to steer the conversation onto a productive path.

"*Small children* can't make such decisions! They can't even understand complex language! They don't understand what they're *agreeing* to!" She rants, angrily.

"Not the specifics, no. They don't know they'll become what we are, at first, but they understand, should they be needed, they will be helping this world, and that comes before what they may or may not want for themselves. Before now, if we thought someone would react badly, we down-prioritized them in favor of more open-minded, willing potentials. You see, with most potentials, we can show them a visual trigger which makes them remember their subliminal training, so they understand what will happen to them and it's nothing to fear! Usually, when presented with the possibility to finally make a difference, most join us willingly. Unfortunately, with people like you, we don't know how much preparation you had prior to their ship being destroyed." He pulls out a plastic square about five-by-five inches in size. "I'd like you to look at this, and see if you remember anything you may have been taught by them." He hands it to her.

She takes the plastic card, flips it over, and views an intricate design on the card. It resembles a fractal pattern with complex colors on it. She feels disoriented as she stares at it and closes her eyes. She relaxes and lets out a sigh. "You're right! They asked me and I agreed. Eventually, they said I'd be changed to make it possible for me to make a difference, and when it happened, I shouldn't be afraid." *Why didn't you just show me that to begin with?*

"We didn't know how much preconditioning you had, so I wasn't sure it would work. Plus, I didn't have it. Liz brought it by during your transformation and asked me to test it on you when you were done. Do you remember anything else? Anything about your abilities?" He searches her face curiously.

Sue focuses inward, delving deep to remember anything else. "Not really. I remember what you talked about. I remember them asking me if I would help, and I shouldn't be afraid of what may happen, though..." She trails off.

"What? Do you remember something else?" Colin gently puts one hand on her arm.

She looks at him and sends him a telepathic message for the first time. *I remember how to do this! Can you hear me?*

A wide grin spreads across his face. *Yes!* He paths in return, leans over, and gives her a bear hug. *It makes sense you'd know how to path, as that's how they communicated with you as a child. I'm hoping more will come back to you, but if not, we'll teach you.*

Sue relaxes as she comprehends, she was meant to be Apara. She snuggles against him in his embrace, and he knows she's going to be all right.

She pulls away and sits up, speaking aloud. "So, what happens now?"

"Now, you rest. Tomorrow, we'll work on the basics. We'll continue with telepathy, as well as proper feeding and healing techniques. I suspect Liz will have an evaluation set up to check your general psychic skills and strengths, and we'll take it from there." He, too, relaxes now Sue's calmed down.

"What about afterward? I spent years getting my education and degrees. Does that all become irrelevant?" She asks.

"No, in fact, we need people like you." He reassures her.

"Not like you guys are likely to have a high suicidal depression rate!" She quips.

"No, but we do have issues you can help with, especially now." He reassures her.

She gives him a slight chuckle of disbelief. "I thought you told me you all choose people who adapt well and are psychologically stable?"

"Yes, but that doesn't mean we're all a bunch of happy-campers. We have quite a few people who survived Jerusalem who are dealing with everything from PTSD to grief. Imagine losing your partner after *hundreds* of years. We know we're not truly immortal, or at least, not indestructible, but once we've gone through stasis a few times, it becomes routine, and we forget the possibility we *can* die in the course of our duties. It's rare, and usually involves either major destruction of brain tissue or extreme damage, such as in Jerusalem. Vaporization tends to be *permanent*."

Sue gets a thoughtful look on her face and leans back. "I really hadn't thought about that. I guess that would be quite a shock. I remember taking a death and dying class, and one thing they told us is most people, especially women, begin the grieving process long before their partners pass because we know it's going to happen eventually, though it's still often a shock when it finally happens. I can only imagine what it would be like when you get used to the idea someone will *always* be there, and then they're suddenly gone." She shivers thinking about what that must be like.

"We have a lot of people who weren't over there, but lost partners and friends in Jerusalem. Still, others have not completely recovered from their injuries, and are dealing with anxiety, depression, and helplessness, or of not being able to do their part. Some are hesitant to do things that earlier didn't faze them." He explains.

"Because they now realize they *can* die?" She chews on her lower lip in thought.

Colin nods. "Yes! We've seen a big decrease in people willing to volunteer for missions, even though there's still relatively low risk for us, because there's a lingering feeling of mortality hanging over us after so many died at one time."

Sue ponders this and gives a slight chuckle under her breath. Colin gets a confused look and raises an eyebrow in question.

Noticing his look, Sue flushes. "*Sorry*! Was just thinking how it would make a *kick-ass* PhD dissertation to study the effects of mass deaths on a society of relative immortals!"

Colin rolls his eyes and chuckles. "You would see it *that* way, wouldn't you? Well, the dissertation is a no-go, but you could always use some of your time to research how it's impacted us, and how we can deal with it." He raises one eyebrow again, hoping she'll see this as a pro-active challenge for her new life.

She gives him a wicked grin. "Damn, that would've been a killer dissertation! But I guess there's not much point in me going for a PhD now, is there?"

"No reason not to if it's important to you. Though you won't need it to get a job somewhere, and you don't really need to worry about earning a living. Whatever we need, we can get, as our people have nearly unlimited resources." He explains.

"Just how's that possible?" She narrows her eyes, wondering how the Apara make money.

He gives her a lopsided grin as he's about to let her in on one of their 'secrets' and says, "Many investments spanning many years, for one. A little precognitive investing helps too! Plus, we have an entire world to ourselves and the means to find and extract things like precious metals and gems without setting up big, toxic mining operations, and no one on Earth can tell our resources didn't come from this Earth. We have art collections that span the ages, and when we really need the cash, an otherwise unknown work of art or ancient artifact suddenly surfaces, gets authenticated, sold, or auctioned, and that money gets reinvested." He watches her eyes go wide in surprise.

192

"So, you all work without getting paid directly, but share the proceeds of community investments and property? No one's sitting there hoarding a ton of money somewhere?" She asks, flabbergasted that greed is not a thing for the Apara.

"I'm sure there are some who have their own investments, but I think you'll find that the drive toward wealth or power is not what we're about. It goes against our basic purpose. We're about making a difference in the world and keeping it from imploding before it can reach a state of societal maturity. Anything else you want to know?"

She ponders for a minute. "I guess I can always jump in and help Tess with her project."

"Definitely! While Tess is very good at what she does, I'm sure her intuition could benefit from your training and experience. Plus, with so many people in the Lost Mission database who likely have little or no prep or follow-up, the risk of depression and other issues because of transformation, being taken out of their 'known reality', and being dropped into the Twilight Zone, is going to be a lot higher than with people who have had years of preparation for this duty." He senses she's overwhelmed. "Why don't you go get some rest, or otherwise take it easy? I went to your place while you were out and got some of your things, including some of your books, if that helps?"

She chuckles. "I think I'll skip any of my paranormal romance books! But you didn't by any chance bring any of my psychology and philosophy books? I think they might come in handy."

"I'll move the boxes to the bedroom and you can see. If you'd like, we can port to your place and pack up some other boxes of your things and bring them here. We'll figure out what to do with the rest later." He says, offhandedly.

"Oh, yeah. What to do about my place? I guess I won't exactly be moving back home, will I?" She says, absentmindedly.

"Unlikely. I assume we'll live as a couple now, and this is the best place for us to be because of the safety and isolation from undisciplined human minds, but there's no real hurry to deal with your place. As I said, we can take care of the upkeep if you want. You could even rent it out for a while if you don't want to part with it right away." He suggests.

She sits there thinking, and eventually gets a lopsided smirk on her face. He narrows his eyes and tries to get a read on her, but gets an impression of amusement and cleverness. "What are you thinking?"

"I don't know if this is possible, or not, but your, what did you call it? Portal home is ridiculously tiny and incongruent size-wise! My place is closer to yours in size. Is it possible to somehow make my place a portal home, and connect this place to it?" She asks with a cautious grin.

Colin laughs out loud at her cleverness. "You know, that certainly would solve a few things, wouldn't it? You'd be able to live where you have, at least for now, and I'll have a more *congruent* façade to my place."

"For now?" She asks uncertainly.

"Eventually, we will have to relocate when it becomes clear we're not aging, but it's a damn good solution in the meantime. I'll ask Liz to set things in motion. In the meantime, your things can stay in your home for now! It would work as a kind of storage until we can make space for what you want to have on hand here!" He leans over and hugs her again, and then leans back, taking her hands and standing, drawing her up as well. "Go get some rest! I'll get your books. I also brought over your computer and CD collection."

Now it's her turn to lean in and hug him. "Thank you! It's always been those little things you do for me that makes me love you even more." She lets him go, and heads back to the bedroom, cell in hand, to get some rest.

Adjustments

As Colin expects, various psychic evaluations are run on Sue to determine the extent of her abilities. Nothing too unusual shows up, other than she's stronger than average in telempathy and 'people reading', but not quite in the same way Tess is. Sara can see signs of something more, but as yet, she can't see that anything out of the ordinary has manifested. She has minor skills in telekinesis and precognition, but exhibits some unusual healing energy, though they haven't yet observed how it may manifest.

Once her evaluation is done, Colin teaches her some basic skills, and she catches on relatively fast. On the fifth day after her rejoining the living, her cell rings. It's Tess.

"Hi, Tess! So nice to hear from you! I love Colin dearly, but I've been dying to talk to someone besides him the last day or so!" She admits.

Tess laughs, "As much as I'd love to just hangout and have a girls' day, I'm wondering if you're up to helping me out with a few things?"

"If I can. I'm still new with all this stuff, but I'd be glad to try and if it would get me out of here for a few hours, I'm all for it!" She admits enthusiastically.

"Can you get Colin to bring you over here? I've got my files here and my computer, and it would just be easier. I'd like to run some potentials by you I'm on the edge about approving or not, and would love your input, plus, Sara and I were talking and was wondering if you'd be willing to see someone in a professional capacity." She says, vaguely.

"Who? You or someone else?" Sue asks, intrigued.

Tess lets out a stifled guffaw. "We can deal with me later!" She laughs. "This case is more pressing, but I'll fill you in when you get here. By the way, Marc made more éclairs last night. They've been chilling in the fridge!"

Sue sucks in her breath and lets out a long "Ooooo!" followed by, "That sounds fantastic! Chocolate covered?"

"Of course! Belgian chocolate fresh from Brussels yesterday!" Tess says in a teasing voice.

"I'll be over as soon as I can twist Colin's arm! He's still not letting me port too much." She sighs.

"Speaking of porting, tell him Marc has added both of your mental signatures to his security system, so you don't have to port outside first." Tess chuckles.

"Will do!" and Tess can hear her mood pick up over the phone.

About an hour later, Tess senses them porting in and gets up from her computer to greet them. She goes straight up to Sue and gives her a big hug.

"Thanks for coming. How're you doing?" Tess guides her over to the sofa in the living room. She tells Colin. "Marc's in his office if you want to bug him, otherwise, Sue and I have a lot to talk about." Tess says, encouraging him to give Sue some breathing room and privacy for a couple of hours.

"Thanks, but I need to get back to work." He nods to the two women and ports out.

Tess tells Sue. "Well, now we can talk!" She lets out a long sigh. "Wait right here." She goes to the kitchen, bringing out a tray full of chocolate éclairs, hot coffee, some of her mini-quiches, and puts them on the coffee table, along with two plates. "So, how're you holding up?"

"I guess as well as can be expected. Though I feel like I need to get back to work as soon as possible. I just can't shake the feeling my clients need me, and maybe whatever talents I have will come out when I do my counselling. I'd like to get some of them on the right path, or at least ready to deal with another therapist before I have to stop working there." She halfway smiles and stuffs an éclair in her mouth.

"I get it! You *need* to feel useful. Those couple of years after Digital Danger, I went back and forth between burnout and needing to feel useful again. It was frustrating because I felt so lost, and knew I had to get back to work and life, but no one would give me a chance. I was running out of steam trying to find my place in the world." Tess takes a mini-quiche and slowly eases it into her mouth, savoring the aged cheddar and garlic Marc used in them.

"Yeah, Colin's afraid to let me go back. He's worried either I'll get overwhelmed by my clients' emotions and mental issues, or I might lose control and expose what I've become, or worse, I might get the blood-munchies and snack on a client." She sighs.

"You'll just have to convince him to let you go back as soon as you feel ready. In the meantime, I've got a couple of things you can help with." She smirks.

"Helping you evaluate potentials?" She asks.

"That's one thing. There are some I'm on the fence about. I worry some of their past or current psychological, or even cognitive issues could be a problem, but I don't know enough about those issues to judge. I'll show you the files and their psych records soon. However, there's another thing. Liz and Sara asked me to broach the subject with you." She says, hesitantly.

"Like what? What do they need me to do?" She asks, wondering why Tess doesn't just come out with it.

"Do you remember the night you were turned, while you were out at dinner?" Tess asks.

Sue gets a distant look, and then says, "Yeah, as far as I know, I remember it all."

"The woman who was following and observing you and Colin, you're aware of her?" Tess queries.

"I never saw or felt her. Colin just told me we were being observed." She admits with a shrug.

"Well, her name's Millie Jameson. She was in a rough marriage for a few years, and got divorced, and went back to college to get her degree in Communications Studies and Mass Media when Jason tracked her down and took her from the UNC Charlotte campus after an evening class. I've spoken to her, and she doesn't remember much about the first few days other than feeling humiliated, weakness, pain, and then waking as one of us. Jason had her convinced he was the good guy, and we were the bad guys. He sent her out to watch you and Colin and report if there might be an opportunity for him to grab you. By then, she'd already begun to question who was and wasn't the bad guy and was leaning toward it being Jason, not us." Tess explains.

"Well, that's a start. How long was she with him?" Sue asks, making mental notes about what Millie might be feeling after all of this.

"Approximately two months. The man who was doing security for you and Colin caught her after she hung up with Jason, and brought her in to our medical facility. She's been having a rough time reconciling it all. Did Colin tell you what Jason does to women he turns?" Tess asks hesitantly.

"Yeah, he made it quite clear I would not want to be in his clutches." Concern grows in Sue's eyes. "And I've counseled more women who were victims of rape and abuse: physical, emotional, psychological, and sexual, than I ever thought existed, so I can imagine what she may have been through."

"And that's why we would really appreciate it if you could talk to her. It's not something any of us have had enough experience with. Hell, I have enough trouble dealing with the major case of PTSD I've got from Jason myself." She pauses. "But my issues will wait, hers are much more urgent."

Sue nods her head slowly. "Yes, I get that, and I've been dealing with that sort of thing at the clinic for a while; that and anxiety issues after Jerusalem. I'd be glad to talk to her, but if he abused her as badly as you suspect, it may take a while for her to come to grips with the trauma of *not only* the abuse, but what she became because of him. How depressed does she seem?"

198

"She swings back and forth between feeling like she's a monster because he is, and being too numb to think about it. She's anxious, and unsure whom to trust. She would be a test case for you, but there are others he's abused who could benefit from your experience and skills." Tess admits.

Sue gives Tess a sidelong look. "Including you?"

Tess avoids looking Sue in the eye. "Four, including me. One person's still human. Her name's Annie Deng. She worked with him down at the Hendersonville branch. After he was turned, he targeted her, terrorized, and fed on her, allowing her to be aware while doing it, only to stuff the memories back down into a mental box so she'd forget, until the next time he fed from her. The bastard was feeding on her fear as well as her blood."

Sue shifts in her seat and blows out a long breath. "I can imagine how that could affect someone. Does she remember now?"

"Yeah, a few weeks back, he went after her, was going to turn her. She had a studio in the River District, down near 12 Bones. He and two women, not including Millie, tracked her there, stalked, and terrorized her. He planned to corner her, rape her, and turn her. He didn't get far because we intervened, but he did open her mental box and did something to prevent her memory from being suppressed anew. I've been working with her, and Sara's taken her under her wing and is trying to ease her over, but maybe you can get through to her in ways I can't?" Tess leans back in her chair and looks thoughtful as she thinks about how timid and fragile Annie feels.

"And the third?" Sue inquires.

"The third is a woman he abducted and tried to break before turning her. She never gave up though, and when she refused to ask him to turn her, to stop the pain, he and his minions fed on her until she was on the edge of multiple organ failure and discarded her in a construction dumpster like a piece of broken drywall; laughing at her as they walked away. Someone found her and took her to Mission Hospital in critical condition. Our people went in and got her out and redacted memories and records and brought her back here. Couldn't exactly leave any records of those bite wounds! She was too far-gone to save by conventional means, so they turned her and kept her out for a while to heal. She's doing reasonably well now. She's a nurse and even volunteers both at our medical center and at the hospital in Hendersonville, but she's still dealing with PTSD about Jason." Tess sighs. "He's ruined several lives, and even killed some women both intentionally or accidentally trying to turn them. *Hell*, he even tried to kill me by running my car off the parkway while we were both still human."

"Colin mentioned some murders while trying to convince me he was, in fact, the lesser of two evils." Sue grins mischievously. "Though I didn't know about his attempt on your life!

Sue sits, looking thoughtful. "These women need to feel safe again, and empowered. I'm guessing becoming Apara helps. But to empower them, we need to go above and beyond. I know someone in West Asheville with a martial arts studio, but I'm not sure how I can convince him to give them lessons, or if that's advisable, since Apara are so much stronger than humans. Maybe Annie, but you said she's still human and a potential target for Jason." Tess nods. "Which means she's *here* for her own protection, so going to a studio in West Asheville probably wouldn't be a smart move." She says, thinking out loud.

"If it's martial arts or self-defense you want, I know just the person. My friend, Amy. She was in the Army and was raised doing martial arts. She even taught it in the Army. She taught me a few moves early on when we both first met Jason, and he gave off that nasty, stalker vibe of his." Tess says with a wide grin, remembering kicking Jason across the fallout shelter when he kidnapped her.

"Do you think she'd be willing to give lessons?" Sue asks.

"She'd do it in a heartbeat! Before we were both turned, one of her web projects was for a company doing just that. She's quite passionate about it and has even suggested giving Annie lessons in passing." Tess sits up straighter and looks enthusiastic at the prospect of getting Amy involved.

"Okay, can you talk to her about it? And I'll see if Colin can get Sara to come by and fill me in more on their cases, but it sounds like Millie is the priority, right?" Sue feels better now that she may be able to do what she does best, help people in crisis.

"I'll holler Amy's way when we're done, and I'd love to get you two together." She pauses, thoughtfully. "She's been pretty much my only contemporary friend here until you were turned. There are a couple of others from Inspiration Inc. who were turned after Jerusalem, but I don't know them well. Amy and I began working there at the same time, while human, and became friends right off the bat. Originally, it was me, Amy, and Jason hired at the same time. It's really nice to know you're here, too. I love Marc dearly, and Kari, Liz, and Sara are all like family, but they're still old as dirt, relative to me, and sometimes I'll say stuff that just misses the mark with them, like they don't quite get the cultural references." Tess sighs.

"When all this settles down a little, we should have a girl's night. I was supposed to have one of those the night Colin came back to Asheville and swept me off to the Twilight Zone." She chuckles. "Now, I understand he had little choice, but it really turned my life upside down, and I could use a night to blow off steam, and maybe get away from his overprotective doting." She laughs out loud.

"*Cool!* I'm sure we can work something out, though it may have to be in Sanctuary. I'm getting better control of my abilities, but Marc's still paranoid Jason's going to kidnap me or do something to avenge me kicking his *ass* a while back." Tess notices Sue's mood has lightened since she arrived despite the serious and depressing nature of what they've been discussing. "Now, about those potentials..."

Intuition vs. experience

Tess gets up and motions for Sue to follow her over to her computer, where she's got two comfortable office chairs. Her computer is booted up with a database showing a file with a person's face, and information on a page, with various links to other information. There's a tall stack of physical folders on the desk, as well as a tablet.

"Here's my dilemma. A lot of the Lost Mission Potentials have various learning disabilities or even possible mental illness or cognitive issues. I'm not sure how such things will be affected if someone is turned, and if the pre-existing issue will be a problem even if it's corrected when transformed." Tess explains as she shuffles through the folders on the desk trying to find the one she wants to look at first.

"That's a tough one. I really have no idea if such things would be fixed by turning. Does Sara have any idea? I got the impression she's the go-to person about transformations." She grabs a couple of folders slipping out of the pile as Tess digs through them.

"I know. It's all up in the air, which makes it even harder for me to judge, because I don't know much about the actual disorders, and how they affect people and their thought processes, emotions and so on! I can get a hunch someone will probably adapt or be good or not adapt and be a problem, but then I worry about these things too." She lets out an exasperated groan as two folders fall on the floor when she tries to pull out three folders from the bottom of the pile. She reaches down and grabs one folder off the floor. "BINGO!" She lays it out in front of Sue. "Okay, this potential has a history of bipolar disorder. Sara says she believes being transformed will fix the actual disorder, but do you know if it creates any issues which may persist?"

"You're going to have to look at each case individually for what we call comorbid disorders. These are other disorders which often exist alongside each other, but no causality. For example, many people with bipolar disorder can have anxiety and panic disorders, and are a stronger risk for suicide. Some of these may not go away even if the bipolar is 'cured' by transformation. Naturally, I don't have any evidence when it comes to transformation, but have seen some of these things persist in some medicated bipolar patients, while they improve in others." Sue explains in a way she hopes Tess understands.

"Okay, so maybe if I weed out those with a bipolar diagnosis, you could go over them with me? I just don't feel comfortable going by intuition alone when the documents show diagnosed issues." Tess sighs and digs for another folder.

"Sure, I'd be happy to." Sue says as she watches Tess juggle the pile of folders.

Tess lets out a long sigh and grabs about the top five inches of folders and hands them to Sue. "If you can hold those, I think the other two I want are in this pile here!" She continues digging through the rest and pulls out two folders. "Okay, this one is dealing with ADHD. Sara says this one should mostly correct when transformed, but are there any pros or cons you can think of with people who have ADHD?"

Sue looks thoughtful. "That one's more complex. There are positives and negatives. You'll need to watch out for signs of anger control issues, depression, poor self-image, dyslexia, and OCD. On the other hand, properly managed, people with ADHD are often highly intelligent, creative people, who can come up with unique solutions, as they often think outside the box!"

Marc comes out of his office and paths to Tess, *Sounds like you, love! Not the anger management, dyslexia, or OCD, but the rest of it, positive and negative rings a distinct bell. In fact, on your original evaluation, it said you displayed some signs of ADHD, but that isn't uncommon in potentials.*

Tess paths him the wordless, mental equivalent of sticking her tongue out at him. He chuckles out loud and runs up the stairs to the bedroom.

Sue notices Tess's expression as she watches Marc jog up the stairs. "Everything okay?"

Tess shakes her head like she's shaking herself back to attention. "Yeah, yeah, just a snide comment from the peanut gallery! Marc thinks I fit that description, and says my *evaluation* even mentioned I have ADHD symptoms."

"That's not necessarily a bad thing. Who knows, it may be what helped you see what Marc and everyone missed before Jerusalem. That's what I was trying to explain; many people with ADHD become entrepreneurs, artists, inventers, and problem solvers! It can be a real gift!" Sue stares at her until Tess makes eye contact.

Tess lets out a huff and says, "I guess that means it's not an automatic disqualification?"

"No, it's *not*! In fact, it can be a bonus if being turned corrects the attention moderation control. It's not so much about not being able to focus or being hyperactive. Have you ever had times when you focus on something so hard, you can't pull yourself away even though you need to?" Sue grins and raises one eyebrow.

Tess lets out a huff and replies, "Hasn't everyone?"

"Probably, but does it happen to you often, while other times you get lost in thought, and can't stay on task?" Sue says as she absentmindedly scans the information in the woman's folder.

Tess sighs. "I guess I see your point."

"I think you may even want to prioritize some of them unless you see issues with anger management. Depression, anxiety, and self-image issues can be treated. OCD and dyslexia can be moderated with therapy or learned strategies, and some of those things may even correct themselves as well!" She closes the folder, putting it on top. "Didn't you say you have one more you wanted to discuss?"

"Yeah, it's probably the one I understand least. A fair number of these people were diagnosed with various forms of autism as children, such as Asperger's, Kanner's Syndrome, and Pervasive Developmental Disorders. I've also seen a fair number of references to something called Auditory Processing disorder. I tried looking them up and sort of get it, but most sites keep saying the terms are obsolete, and they just call it Autism Spectrum Disorder now?" Tess is glancing at some handwritten notes she'd made and stuck in the ASD folder.

"Yes, they changed it to ASD because it's a big spectrum of symptoms, and impairment can be anywhere from mild to profound. I think you'll have to look at how they function on a daily basis. Some of them are highly intelligent, but have issues with social development, and interpreting social cues, other people's emotions and don't tolerate sudden, unexpected changes, while others, you would have a hard time noticing their issues. Girls and women are better at, how shall I put it? Camouflaging their symptoms and compensating for them. As to the Auditory Processing Disorder, APD may be one form of a broader issue with autism." She pauses, trying to think about how to explain it to Tess.

"Oh? Like what?" Tess asks.

"Some theories suggest autism may be an incomplete step in evolution. As I mentioned, many autistic people are up in the gifted and genius levels intellectually, but they have difficulty processing input and expressing themselves. One theory, especially with the auditory issues, is while normal people can be in a room with a bunch of people and distinguish foreground conversation, such as we're having, from background noise, some autistic children really struggle with this. It's one of the reasons speech-development is often delayed. Some of these children were once deemed mentally incapacitated, or, as the term was, retarded, but inside, their minds were functioning above normal levels. The thought is there may have been a genetic mutation or variant for high intelligence, but somewhere in the sensory or input processing department, things are getting scrambled or become overwhelming." Sue watches Tess for signs of comprehension.

"You're suggesting they may be very intelligent, but it doesn't always appear that way, and they have trouble processing things from sounds to social cues, and other information, which makes them out of place in society?" Tess asks uncertainly.

"Pretty much. A lot will depend on how much of those processing errors might be corrected with transformation, or, heaven forbid, made worse somehow. We may not know, however, until we have an actual case, and even then, just as with ADHD, no two cases are totally alike." She explains.

Tess sits back and thinks for a minute, but then her eyes light up with an idea. "Sue, if auditory processing is an issue, would telepathy bypass that? Or would they experience the same issue with that? Like hearing everyone's mental chatter at once?"

"That's a profound question. Unfortunately, I don't really know. It could go either way. Empathy, for example, could help them understand social cues better, if the empathic input itself doesn't overwhelm them. Maybe we can get together with Sara and go over some of these things, but I suspect we may just have to test out a mild case your intuition says will adapt, and try it. If turning them bypasses or corrects the input issues, they may process things much better than most people." Sue yawns. "Sorry! I get tired so quickly. Maybe we can pick this up again tomorrow?"

"Yeah, I think that would be good. You've given me something to work with. I can sort the ones with these disorders or disabilities into categories, and then sort them into least risk to most risk, I think." Tess says as she runs through all the information again in her mind.

Sue stands and stretches while pathing to Colin she's ready to go home. "Listen, one thing you must remember is some of these disorders are themselves 'comorbid' disorders. You will need to make a category for complex cases who may have both autism and ADHD or ADHD and bipolar disorder, or several issues. They may be the ones that are hardest to analyze because their eventual reactions to being turned will be the most complex."

Colin ports in behind Sue and massages her shoulders. "Ready to go home?"

"In just a sec." She replies to Colin, and then turns back to Tess. "Get it?"

"Yeah, better now you've given me a crash course in this stuff. I'd appreciate your help evaluating some of the individual cases, but I can see how some disabilities may not always be negative now." Tess stands, leaning over and gives Sue a hug. "Thanks!"

Sue smiles and yawns again before saying, "You're welcome!" And the two of them port out, leaving Tess to ponder the new information and figure out how to use it when evaluating potentials with possible cognitive issues.

Millie

The next day, Sue's cell rings and she sees it's Tess. She answers cheerily. "Good morning! Ready to look at some of your potentials today?"

Tess is quiet for a second. "We'll have to put that on hold for a day or two. Sara just hollered my way. Millie had a meltdown last night and tried to use her fangs to rip open her wrists."

"*Holy Hell*! She tried to kill herself?" Sue asks, concerned.

"Sara's not sure if she was really trying to kill herself or if she was doing it as... what was Sara's term?" Tess is quiet for a minute while she tries to remember.

"Are you thinking of self-harm? When it's done to hurt oneself out of frustration or anger, but not intending to die?" Sue asks cautiously.

"*Yes*! Sara says she knew she'd heal, but she just kept slicing her skin open with her fangs! I know you're barely getting up to speed as one of us, but are you up to a professional visit this morning? I'll go with you! She knows me." Tess frets as she thinks about Millie's situation.

"Of course. I'll do whatever I can. Give me a little time to get ready. I assume she's at Medical?" Sue asks as she walks around the bedroom, finds something professional to wear and tosses it on the bed.

"Yes! Great. Thanks! I can deal with some stuff, but this is above and beyond my pay grade. Not that we get paid!" Tess lets out a half-hearted laugh. "I'm heading over there now to touch base with Sara, holler when you're on your way." Tess says, hanging up and pulling on her shoes and a clean t-shirt.

Sue looks at the phone for a second, thinking Tess sounds distracted and frantic. She gets dressed, then grabs one of the smaller canvas bags they'd brought back from her place, and dumps the odds and ends out of it and onto the bed. She throws her cell into it and runs out to find Colin at the dining room table, going through some things on his tablet. He hears her coming and looks up, smiling, but his smile fades quickly as he senses her serious mood.

"What's going on?" He asks.

"I need a notebook and some pens or pencils. They need me over at medical for a psychological emergency." She says, going over to an antique roll-top desk with several large drawers and a China cabinet on top. She finds an unused lined tablet in the top drawer and several pens under the roll-top and slips them into her bag. She stops suddenly, in front of Colin. "Are you going to port me over there, or can I?"

"If you feel you're up to porting there by yourself, you can, but I'll gladly port you there if you want me to." He says, standing up.

"*Hell* with it!" She says and ports out, reappearing in the lobby of Medical with its floor to ceiling windows and winding vines and plants running up the walls. Excited to be useful again, she runs up the stairs without even stopping to talk to the woman at the front desk, and heads straight for Sara's office. As she gets closer, she can hear and sense Tess. Tess's mood is anxious, as well as guilty she hadn't somehow prevented Millie's latest breakdown. She stumbles into Sara's cluttered office, out of breath, and leans against the frame of the door as there's no place to sit.

"*Sue!*" Sara says as she scans her aura mentally. "Colin let you port on your own today?"

Breathing heavily, Sue gathers her wits and says, "More or less! He was wishy-washy about it so I just said 'Hell with it' and ported out! How's Millie?"

"She's resting. I sedated her after her incident last night, so we have a little time to strategize before you see her." Sara says, and clears junk out of two chairs in her office, making room for both Tess and Sue to sit.

The women spend some time discussing the situation, and Sue suggests it's probably because of a combination of a delayed stress reaction to Jason, as well as feeling like she has become some sort of abomination.

They discuss how to approach the situation, and after about an hour, they go over to the locked room where Millie's sedated.

Sara stops the other two women from following her in. "Wait out here. I've got her under a sedative plus a wave generator to make sure she stays out. It will take a few minutes to bring her out of it, and I want to see what kind of state she's in."

Sara walks into the room, putting on a light on a dim setting so Millie won't wake to blindingly bright lights. She checks Millie's energy and senses for any underlying emotions from her unconscious mind. She can sense Millie's dreaming and peeks in on her mind. Millie's dream is of her being in a basement in an abandoned house. It's dark, but she can still see. A spider crawls across her bare foot. Her reaction is exaggerated like she might be phobic of them. She feels something heavy and cool on her leg and reaches down to feel it. She sees glints of metal in some dim light from a barred window across the room and realizes she's been chained to a wall next to a large bin that smells like moldy potatoes. In the dream, she hears the telltale sounds of sex above her and the voices of her captors, Jason and the other two women. She gets a whiff of something that grabs her attention. She's not sure what it is. It smells metallic, yet sweet, and she strains to reach it as a new hunger flairs up from within. She knows it's between her and the stairs, and she *needs* it, but try as she might, the chain around her ankle keeps her goal just out of reach. The hollow feeling inside is like a hunger or a craving. After trying for several minutes, she's frustrated by failing to reach the dark bag on the floor, slinks back to her corner, and curls up into a ball, rocking herself in the dark.

A few minutes later, the sound of sex stops, and she can hear whimpering and crying, but also sadistic laughter from Jason. The door to the cellar opens and blinding light floods in for a few seconds as she hears Jason drag someone behind him down the steps and throws a simpering, half-naked woman toward her. Millie tries to resist, but is starving and instinctively feeds. Jason stops her just short of taking too much, shoving her hard against the wall, banging, and bloodying the back of her skull, but doesn't say a word to her. He takes the terrified woman back upstairs, slams, and locks the cellar door behind him. Millie is nearly in shock over what she's just done and what she's become. She curls up into a ball and sobs, her body's wracked with tremors.

A few minutes pass and she can hear water running above her and down through the drain-pipes in the cellar. When the water stops, she can hear voices again, and focuses, her now enhanced hearing zooming in on them. She hears Jason telling the woman, "Put your clothes on bitch and stop sobbing! Not like anyone else would show you a good time!" Millie hears continued, but muffled sobbing, then silence, and she can sense Jason is no longer in the house.

Sara realizes Millie is reliving some of her first waking moments after being turned by Jason. *No wonder she's a mess!* Sara thinks. She takes the small ball sitting on a concave pedestal on the night table, and flips off a switch, making the wave generator slowly power down. She pulls out an infuser from a drawer across the room and holds it to Millie's arm, infusing something to clear the sedative from her system. She pulls up a chair and sits beside the bed and paths to Tess and Sue. *Gonna take a few minutes! She was having a nightmare when I came in, so I'm pulling her out gradually so it's not too much of a shock.*

After about five minutes, Millie begins to stir and her eyes flutter open, having trouble focusing.

"Take it slowly. It's just me, Sara, here with you. You were having a nightmare, so I woke you up." Sara calmly says.

Millie lets out a long, despondent sigh. "And yet, the real nightmare continues. I was hoping I'd wake up back home, still human, but no such luck!" She says sarcastically, her voice weak and rough as she'd strained it screaming during her crisis.

Sara gently puts her hand on Millie's arm. "I know this isn't what you want, but there really is no way to reverse the process and make you human again. For your sake, I wish there were, but we all must deal with the cards we've been dealt! If it makes you feel any better,"

212

She pauses, considering what she's about to confide in her carefully. "I know quite well what you're going through."

Millie turns and looks at Sara with an expression of disgust and annoyance. "How can you?" She demands.

"I've never told anyone this, not since I was newly turned. The woman who saved me from madness and made me understand this is a gift, not a curse is the only one who knows my history, and how I joined the Apara. It was long ago, in a primitive land, and I was abducted, much like you, and subjected to physical and sexual assault, including having my heart cut out! I was turned, starved, and released to punish my people for denying the power of the man who changed me. So, yes! I can relate to what you've been through, and I know you can get through this, just as *I did*." Sara says with quiet force that makes Millie sit quietly in thought for a minute.

"I guess it *is* a little like what I went through. How long ago did that happen to you?" She asks, quietly.

"Now, Millie, even among Apara, there are times you don't ask a woman her age!" She grins ear-to-ear, making Millie choke back a chuckle. "Let's just say I'm probably the oldest person you're likely to meet anytime soon and I try to keep that number a closely held secret!"

Millie sniffles and says, "Okay, but how did you get over it?"

"I had help. A woman named Isanda took me in and helped me to understand what I am, and I don't have to be the monster my creator intended me to be. I was lucky she found me and helped me, and I know two other people who would like to help you." Sara gives her a lopsided smile.

Millie shifts uncomfortably in her hospital bed. "Who?"

"Well, one you've already met, and one you've seen, but never spoken to. Tess is here, and she's brought a new friend." Sara says, but paths to the two waiting women, *Come in, ladies!*

The door slowly opens and Sara senses Millie's anxiety amp up until Tess's smiling face sticks through the open door. "Hi, Millie. Sara said you could use a friend today! So, I brought an extra one." She reaches back and drags Sue into the room.

Millie's eyes go wide when she sees the woman she'd been sent to watch on Jason's behalf. "*You!* You're the reason I'm here!" She gasps out.

"No, Jason's the reason you're here." Sue walks over toward the bed cautiously, trying to watch Millie's reaction. She grabs a chair, pulls it up beside the bed, and tries to look non-threatening.

Millie looks uncertain and battles with who to blame for her current situation. She knows Jason is ultimately to blame, but he did something in the early days that made her averse to blaming him for anything. If she even thinks of blaming him, memories of pain flood her mind along with feelings of extreme guilt. After a minute, she cringes inwardly, but says, "I know, but it hurts when I..." And she visibly cringes and winces as she thinks about how much she hates him, part of her expecting punishment for such thoughts."

Sue shivers as she feels Millie's warring emotions and paths to Tess, *All this actual empathy is going to take some getting used to. I'm used to reading expressions and body language, but to actually feel someone's emotions makes it damn hard to stay clinically objective and detached.*

Tess paths in return, *Yeah, it took me a while, too, and I still have issues because I can't always control it. It's very important to know your own feelings before you go into a situation like this, so you can tell what your feelings are versus the other person's.*

Sue adjusts herself in her chair and takes a deep breath before continuing. "Millie, I'm here to see if, maybe, I can help you through all of this. I..." She pauses, trying to think of how to phrase the next part. "I realize Jason gave you reason to think we're the bad guys, that he is 'blameless', and saved you from us, right?"

Millie looks at Sue uncertainly for a second, frowning, and then nods curtly.

"However, I suspect part of you has already seen through that, perhaps? But I understand something about him makes it hard to accept." Sue feels the twists and turns in Millie's mind as she battles with the reactions Jason instilled in her during her time in his captivity.

Slowly, Millie looks up and opens her mouth to speak. At first, nothing comes out, but then, she shivers again and says, in a quiet voice, "I'm not sure what to believe anymore! Objectively, I know he manipulated me through the things he did to me! How he treated me, but I still find it hard to fight this irrational loyalty I've got to him. I can't help feeling he's going to be angry with me for letting myself get captured. I know he told me you all were the monsters, but I'm more afraid of his reaction than I am of you!" A stray tear dribbles down her cheek, and she inhales to stop her nose from running.

Tess touches Sue on the shoulder lightly and paths, *He probably used fear and his telempathic persuasion ability on her to make her feel a connection to him. It sounds like her rational mind knows otherwise, but his subconscious manipulation, for the moment, is stronger.*

Sue replies, *I agree. You say he had those abilities while still human?*

Sue can sense the equivalent of telepathic eyes rolling, as Tess continues pathing. *Oh, yeah! He apparently used it for years before being turned and was pissed at me because I was immune to his 'charms'! I doubt Millie had a chance against his abilities, especially now he's Apara!*

"Millie, I know it's difficult to separate gut feelings and logic, but Jason has a way of manipulating people, especially women. From what Tess has told me about him, he's a control freak, and likely did something to ensure your loyalty. I know it's difficult to break those unconscious, gut reactions, but you need to try, *okay*?" Sue says, concern palpable in her voice, and visible in her eyes.

Millie is sitting up, back against the headboard of her bed, arms crossed, scowling. "I've *tried*! But every time I think about him not being..." she takes a deep breath and has shades of pain in her eyes, as her voice quivers, "the good guy, it hurts, almost physically! I know he did something to me! I just can't remember much from those first weeks. It hurts to even *try* to recall what happened!" Tears run down her cheeks, and her breathing is ragged.

Sara is standing behind Sue, and chimes in. "Millie, do you remember anything about being in a basement, chained up?"

An extremely brief flash of recognition crosses her face and fades just as quickly. "No..." She cringes and everyone in the room feels echoes of near physical pain from her trying to recall what Sara mentioned, followed by a sense of relief when she stops, and says she doesn't recall anything.

Sara paths the content of Millie's dream to Sue and Tess in a flash of information. *I believe those are actual memories from just after he turned her. She was dreaming about it when I came in.*

Sue mentally nods to Sara. *I wonder if that's connected to the pain she's feeling. Suppressed memories? Some kind of aversion conditioning, perhaps?*

Sara squeezes Sue's shoulder. *Do what you can now, but I suspect this will take time.*

I agree, but there's something about that dream. It's so emotionally 'charged', yet suppressed. We need to find some way to bring those memories to the surface without causing her undue pain. Sue paths, while pondering how she might reach this young woman and help her. She turns back to Millie. "I can tell this is hard for you right now, and I don't want to push things and cause you pain, but if you can, be open-minded that *we're good guys.* None of us want to hurt you, but only help you! I realize, this is going to take time, but I want you to know you're safe here. Not only won't we hurt you, but Jason won't be able to come for you either."

Millie looks thoughtful and relaxes marginally. The thought, *If Jason can't come here, he can't punish me* flickers at the edge of her consciousness. She looks from Sue to Tess, and back to Sara. "I'll try." She yawns. "Not sure why I'm so tired! I slept a lot, but it doesn't feel like I got any rest." She slides back down in her bed, fluffing her pillow, and putting it down behind her head. "I think I'd like to sleep some more." She says, looking at Sara pleadingly.

"Alright, you rest. Annie will come along in a few with blood and some food for you." Sara turns to the other two women and mentally shoos them out the door.

They walk with Sara back to her office and sit in the waiting chairs. "This won't be easy!" Sue says with an extended sigh.

"That's why we need you! You've had experience dealing with clients who were abused and traumatized. It's way out of my league. We figured if anyone could reach her, you could." Tess says, sounding frustrated.

"Tess, Sara, I'm going to need some time to process my impressions and strategize on this one. I'm used to reading people through normal means, but the layers and layers of thoughts and emotions bombarded me on top of my normal impressions, it was information overload!" Sue says as her stomach grumbles and she has a sudden feeling of need.

Sara ports out and back, handing her a bag of blood. "Intense psychic work, especially when you're new at it, leads to hunger of both kinds, as Tess can attest!"

"I'm still not used to doing this in front of anyone but Colin." She says, embarrassed to puncture the bag with her fangs and feed.

"Just do it, Sue! It's not going to phase either of us. And it's better you take care of it than lose control." Tess reassures her.

Sue bites into it and drinks it down. "I feel better, but I think I need to go home and fumble through all these impressions in peace."

"I'll help you port home. You're too distracted, and it's easy to miscalculate and end up porting into a pond or something!" Tess says, standing up, and encouraging Sue to do the same. She slips her arm under Sue's and they reappear in Sue and Colin's living room.

"Thanks." Sue says, and reaches over and gives her a hug, and Tess can sense her exhaustion.

"Go get some rest. I promise, it will get easier, but when you're first learning this stuff, it's exhausting because you often overkill on the energy trying to make it work. Eventually, you'll learn to use just enough to get the job done, and you should ask Colin about grounding. Marc taught me how to ground out the negative energy after such an encounter and it helped me a lot." Tess suggests. She gives her a small goodbye wave and ports out, leaving Sue to go into her and Colin's house in the alternate world version of Vancouver Island.

Letting go
and reaching out

Sue goes into the house, but Colin isn't home. There's a note on the table saying he had to pop in to the office to talk to Liz. She stretches and walks to the kitchen looking for something to eat. She finds some leftover Beef Stroganoff from the night before, warms it up, sits at the dining room table, and eats while pondering the situation with Millie. There are so many overlapping layers of impressions fighting for dominance in her mind. She gets flashes from the dream Sara observed, but also overtones of suppressed memories to go with it. She gets impressions of pain, and not just from when Jason knocked her against the wall after feeding. She gets flashes of more than hunger and starvation; followed by disgust at having to either feed from some terrified stranger he dragged in or from Jason, himself. Somewhere, even fainter impressions taunt her from touching Millie's mind. She felt overtones of violation and embarrassment, but few specific memories except for enough to tell her Jason had likely sexually assaulted her at some point and somehow suppressed the memories of it.

Anger rises in Sue's gut as she forms a real picture of what Jason must be like, and she's thankful more than ever Colin got to her first. She paces off some of the anxiety she picked up from Millie, and wishes she knew how to do what Tess mentioned, grounding it off. The more she paces, the more the anxiety stresses her out until she slams the wall with her fist in frustration, punching a hole in it. She looks at the hole in shock, not realizing her own strength. Part of her feels better, however, and realizes she's been channeling the same anger Millie has suppressed about Jason. She knows if she can't ground off the energy, she should find some other outlet for it. She goes and changes into some jogging clothes and goes back outside. She jogs down the path to where she first saw the Pacific Ocean, and stands there for a minute, taking in the sunshine, sea breeze, and salty air. She looks around, spies an overgrown path going down the hill. She knows she can port, but needs to burn off the energy, so jogs down the path, meandering back and forth down the steep slope until she nears the beach below. She spends about an hour running back and forth along the beach, periodically finding rocks, and tossing them out into the surf, imagining she's throwing them at Jason. After jogging, she's overheated, so walks toward the surf, and shucks off her shoes, wading in, cooling her feet and ankles in the water lapping the shore. She looks around, realizes no one's around, so strips off everything but her underwear and bra and wades out into the surf, letting the water slap and caress her as she stands there, trying to do some creative visualization. She imagines the water and the waves washing all the negative energy from her body and mind, and carrying it back out to sea where it won't bother anyone. After a few minutes, she feels much better, like the latent stress, anxiety, and anger from Millie has finally left her in peace. As she stands in the surf, she senses someone nearby, turns around, and sees Colin sitting on a large boulder protruding from the sand. He's holding an oversized towel and has a grin on his face.

"Are you quite done yet?" He smirks at her as she stomps out of the surf and along the soft, warm sand toward him.

"Yes! I think I am!" She shouts and grins as he enfolds her in the towel.

"You *are* going to brush off all that sand before you go into the house, right? Or better yet, port straight to the shower and wash all the salt, sand, and..." He smirks and reaches over and takes a long green ribbon of seaweed out of her red hair. "other stuff off your beautiful body!" He leans in and gives her a salty kiss. "I'll grab your clothes. Go on! Go clean up!"

He chuckles as he walks over to get her sand infested jogging clothes. He turns around, and she's already gone.

She ports into the bathroom and turns on the water as hot as she can stand it, and washes all the sand and salt away. She washes her hair three times, finding not only sand, but also bits of shell, a small starfish and three more bits of seaweed twisted in her red locks. When she's done, she finds something comfortable to wear, brushes out her hair, and heads out to the living room, grabbing her bag from her trip to medical. She hadn't made any notes while there, but is determined to make as many notes as possible while her impressions are still relatively fresh and clear. She gets out to the living room and sees Colin sitting on the sofa, with an expression somewhere between annoyance and amusement.

"What?" She asks, unsure of what's bothering him.

"Whatever did the poor wall do to deserve your wrath, my *dear*?" He inquires, seriously at first, but can't help smirking at her embarrassment.

"Sorry! I just got so *fucking* angry at that *bastard,* Jason for what he's done to that poor woman! I really didn't mean to put a hole in the wall, I'm just not used to my new strength, I guess." She cringes as she looks at the approximately eight-inch area of shattered plasterboard. "Maybe we can put a painting in front of it?" She suggests awkwardly.

Colin shakes his head and chuckles. "I'll fix it, don't worry. Did your sand marathon and swim help?" He pats the sofa next to him, motioning for her to come sit. She plops down next to him, and he wraps one arm around her shoulders.

"Yeah, it really did! Especially the water! I felt like a lot of the anxiety and stuff literally washed away!" She leans into him, and puts her head on his shoulder.

"You're not far off. Tess stopped by the office to let Liz know how things went with Millie while I was there. She mentioned I should teach you to ground, but I think you figured it out on your own, or at least a form of it." He gives her a one-armed hug as she stirs and lifts her head to look him in the eye.

"I did?" She asks, confused.

"Yes, let me guess, you visualized the waves "washing away the stress and energy?" He gives her a lopsided, expectant smirk.

"Yeah, something like that. I pictured them washing it out of me and then dragging all the energy and emotions out to sea, is that grounding?" She asks uncertainly.

"Yes ma'am! It's all about *visualization*! There are different ways to picture it, but it's up to you to find what works best for you. We can work on it more next time you need to, so you don't have to go thrash around in the surf to do it." He chuckles.

"Yeah, but it was fun blowing off steam." She grins. "Now, I need to make some notes about today while things are still fresh in my mind and then I think..." She lets out a big yawn. "I need a nap!"

"Did you eat and feed?" He asks like a doting parent more than a partner.

"*Yes*! Sara gave me blood at medical, and I ate about half the leftover Stroganoff before I attacked the wall, and went for my run!" She grins.

He leans over and gives her a kiss. "Then I'll leave you to your notes. I must do some things Liz asked me to work on. *Unfortunately*, I will probably be up late." He gives her a wistful smile, making her blush.

"Who knows, maybe I'll be awake by the time you're done." She sends him thoughts of what she'd like to do with him.

"Now, *now*! *Don't* distract me, love. I need to get my work done, as do you." He chuckles as he walks off to his study.

Sue watches him saunter off, then digs out her notepad and pen. Her mind is much less jumbled and her impressions clearer after her beach activities. She makes many notes about her interactions with, and impressions from Millie. After about forty-five minutes of writing, she closes it up, and leaves it on the coffee table. She stands and stretches, briefly looking off toward Colin's study door wistfully, but thinks better of disturbing him. It's only about 9:30 pm local time, but she heads to bed, strips off most of her clothes, and gets under the covers. She drifts off to sleep quickly and dreams. At first, it's just random dreams; dreams about old friends and family visiting her, and her having to hide what she's become, or of riding the waves into the beach. Eventually, the dreams change texture, from shallow, personal dreams to full color, full sensory dreams. She feels almost like she's in a three-dimensional space, a *real* space, and she's *not* alone.

She's in the basement of the abandoned house and can see Millie sobbing, blood on her hands from touching the back of her skull where she'd hit the wall. Millie is unaware of Sue's presence, but cringes and pulls herself back into a corner when she hears Jason's voice coming through the ceiling above her. She trembles in fear and confusion, and curls up tighter into a ball on the floor. Time speeds up as shadows shift on the wall opposite the small, basement window, and grow darker. Millie's sobs grow quieter and finally stop, but Sue can see signs of her rocking herself while in an upright, fetal position. This is a clear sign of trauma and self-comfort, an instinctual reaction hailing back to infancy and childhood where a parent rocks a child to calm them. Sue realizes she's dreaming, and moves a little closer to Millie, careful not to disturb her and still unsure if Millie can even see her in this dream. Sue assumes her own mind is processing her own impressions of Millie's dream, along with her own observations of Millie, and her mental state.

Sue carefully moves a little closer, unsure of the rules of the dream world. Would it react like reality? Would Millie see her and react to her presence, or was her own mind just replaying and observing Millie's earlier dream.

She looks around the makeshift dungeon with clinical fascination, noting details she missed when Sara initially transferred the dream memory to her. She hears scratching sounds and sees a mouse scurry across the floor and under an old, wooden shelf. She smells the dankness and a moldy smell from old bins once used for storing a winter's worth of potatoes or other harvested foods. There's a faint dripping sound, and she looks past Millie and sees an old, rusty pipe coming down from the main house; condensation on the outside, running down, and dripping onto the floor. She's weighed down by the oppressive, humid heat of the May evening as it clings to her own skin in this dream realm. For a dream, there's an overwhelming feeling of reality to it.

Sue hears the thump of footsteps coming toward the cellar door, the rattling of metal, and clicking of a key as a padlock is undone, and heavy chains moved to allow access to the basement door. Sue thinks, *Why bother with undoing the chains when they could just port?* But she hears whimpering from Millie on the floor, and realizes the person is doing it for effect! Terrorizing her with torture chamber like sounds and nuances. The door creaks open with a disturbingly eerie sound, followed by footsteps on the old, creaky, wooden steps, and the door makes a sudden bang as it closes behind whoever is coming down. Sue feels terror and dread emanating from Millie's curled up form on the floor and hears quiet sobbing, rapid breathing, and her heart pounding. Sue looks up at the stairs, but the person coming down is not Jason, but a woman with long, curly red hair and a sneer on her face. She descends the stairs with deliberate thumps on the wooden staircase, and Sue realizes it's someone she knows. *Holy Hell!* She thinks. *That's my cousin, Philipa! It can't be! Last I heard, she was in a psychiatric hospital in Virginia. Maybe it's just my imagination filling in details to make sense of what I'm seeing, but this would be something she'd do. But if that's really her, is she Apara, too?* The dream pauses like a video or DVD while Sue thinks about her cousin.

She always did have issues. Even as a kid, she was always somewhat off. She had a fascination with tormenting the weak, be it a kitten she'd gotten for her birthday, or Sue herself when her Aunt Jenny would come over to visit her twin sister, Sue's mom. Philipa was about three years older than Sue, and would act sweet and nice when an adult was watching, but as soon as she and Sue were alone, she would find ways to make her life hell, from pulling her hair, to pulling the heads off her dolls, and making sure Sue got the blame. She also recalls some horrendous temper tantrums Philipa threw when she didn't get her way.

As she hit her teenage years, she began having major anger management problems, as well as delusions. She claimed she knew what other people were thinking, and they all hated her. This type of symptom, along with an incident with her boyfriend and his mother, eventually led to a diagnosis of paranoid schizophrenia and anger management issues. They tried to medicate her for a while, but when she refused to take the medication, she was eventually placed in Chippenham Hospital in Virginia for observation and treatment. Philipa was one reason Sue chose psychology as her field of study. That, and her innate ability to read people psychologically. She hoped to, one day, understand people like Philipa, and find a way to help them. She had thought little about her recently, but remembers her mother mentioning something about her no longer being in Chippenham. She thinks, *What was it she said? I wasn't really paying attention at the time. Was she released? NO! She'd gone missing! Shit! Jason must have taken her straight from the hospital and turned her! God! What a pair they must make!*

As she focuses on the dream again, it moves slowly at first, but resumes normal speed. She watches Philipa stomp down the stairway carrying a tray of food. Sue can smell the stench of it and knows it's semi-rancid. She drops the tray on the floor in front of Millie's terrified form, allowing the food to scatter on the dirty, basement floor.

"Enjoy your *meal*, Millie! Just like you enjoyed your first *feed!*" She laughs sadistically as she turns and climbs the stairs again, making a show of slamming the door and locking it up with chains and a padlock to make Millie feel thoroughly trapped.

Sue watches Millie uncurl a little and sniff at the food. The smell makes her gag, but she can't remember when she last had any real food. She tries holding her nose and eating small bits, but she can still smell and taste it, with her heightened senses making it nearly unbearable. Sue's heart aches just watching this, and finds herself pulling out of the dream, and waking with eyes swollen with tears.

"Oh, *Hell!*" She says aloud. She grabs some tissues and composes herself. She picks up her cell phone to check the time, It's 11:16 pm. Since she's awake, she checks her emails and messages, and notices Tess is online on Facebook. She types in a message.

"Tess? Are you there? I know it's after 2 am there, but if you're up, I could really use someone to talk to!" She can see the read symbol pop down to her message and knows Tess has seen it. She's lying on her side, facing in to the bed while she looks at her cell. Before she can type anything else, she feels a hand on her shoulder and hears:

"What's up? Have you been crying?" Tess has ported in and is sitting on the side of the bed, looking concerned at Sue's state. Sue shifts, turns around, and sits up to face Tess.

"Yeah, but it's not because of anything going on with me! It was a dream about Millie. I think I replayed the dream Sara sent us, but it felt like there was so much more to it. It was so real! Like I was there." Sue says, blowing her nose and wiping her eyes.

"Yeah, that was one hell of a dream! I went back and talked to Sara about it. Imagine being left in the basement after being starved, not knowing what she'd become, and feeding on that poor girl! I can only imagine what may have happened after that." Tess says, leaning over and giving Sue a much-needed hug.

"That's just it, my dream picked up from there. Wait, are you saying it stopped after she fed?" Sue asks, uncertain what is really happening.

"Yes, that's where it ended for Sara and she sent us the whole thing, so I'm not quite sure what you were dreaming. Do you think you can show me what you saw?" Tess asks.

"I don't know how to send it to you like Sara did to us, but I'll try to remember it all and maybe you can *read* my mind?" She asks.

"Let's try it!" Tess says.

226

After a few minutes and a mild migraine, Tess has the new dream engrained into her own mind. "Wow! Yeah, that's *not* what Sara sent us. So much detail, and you saw one of his women, too?" She asks.

"Yeah, about that.... You don't know the names of the women he has with him, do you?" Sue looks hedgy about why she wants to know, and Tess can sense something's off.

"Let me think. One gal's name is Alice Thompson, but I think the woman in yours is probably Philipa Ball. She's a piece of work! Marc finally let me in on the fact she's an escaped mental patient!" Tess exclaims, but her face shifts to one of concern as she sees Sue go ashen.

"Yeah, I know all about Philipa. She's my cousin." Sue admits, waiting to see Tess's reaction.

"What the *actual fuck*? She's your cousin? Oh wait! You do both have red hair and similar eyes now that I think about it! What are the chances of that?" Tess says with a huff of disbelief.

"I really wouldn't know, but if we were all chosen for our psychic potential and stuff, it makes sense. Our moms are identical twins, and both claimed they always knew when each other was in trouble or needed the other one, and claimed they got it from their mother!" She pauses. "*Holy Hell*! She wasn't delusional after all! Well, not completely."

"What do you mean Sue?" Tess looks concerned.

"I was thinking about Philipa in the dream! She used to claim she knew what people were thinking, and everyone hated her. In truth, most everyone did because she was one mean, little bitch! Everyone, including the psychiatrists assumed she was 'hearing voices', a key component of paranoid schizophrenia, and the 'everyone hates me' sure sounds paranoid. Though, thinking about it now, it was probably true. She must have had active telepathic abilities." Sue leans back against the headboard with a huff of realization.

"*Wow*! You could be right, and the fact you were both made compatible may have come from you both carrying similar genes from your mothers. You should mention it to Sara next time you're at Medical." Tess says, excited by this revelation. "You must tell Liz she's your cousin, ASAP! If there's anything you can tell us that might help find or catch her, Liz needs to know it."

"Yeah, I will in the morning. One thing's for sure, Philipa's dangerous! She's got a mean streak as wide as the Mississippi, and no conscience. If she was part of whatever they put Millie through, then it must have been a living hell." Sue says, and grabs her note pad and scribbles down some notes from her dream and a note to write as much as she can about Philipa.

Tess crawls up on the bed and sits cross-legged, facing Sue, and asks, "So, what do you think the dream was? Were you just extrapolating from her dream? If so, you probably wouldn't have seen Philipa. Maybe you're retrocognitive?" Tess suggests.

"Retro...cognitive?" Sue looks at Tess curiously.

"Yeah, it's like precognition, seeing the future, except you're reading the past. We've got a few of those people who often end up working in police crime and forensic units. They're often able to see the violence or even the whole crime psychically." Tess says excitedly.

Sue looks thoughtful. "No, that doesn't feel right. If felt like I was there with Millie, in the basement. All my senses were active. Sound, smell, hearing and I could almost taste what she tasted when she tried to eat the rotten food Philipa left her. I could also feel her emotions; especially her fear!" Sue remarks, trying to remember every detail she could muster.

"You know, it reminds me of something Marc tried with me when I first...well, the second time I found out about him!" She chuckles. "He'd made me forget after I walked in on him feeding in an alley, but it all came back. I think I told you about it?" She looks at Sue, who nods. "Anyway, when he tried to make me forget again, he gave me a drug. *Damn!* I keep forgetting the name! Psiamp! The blue stuff, as I call it! It opens psychic pathways but can also aid in shared dreaming, and he gave me a tiny dose to see if he could get through my native shields. It worked, and we dreamed together. He couldn't make me forget, however, but we did share a dream. Is it possible you were sharing a dream with Millie?"

"I really don't know, though that would explain why I could sense her emotions so strongly and experience the smells and tastes, if I was getting them from her dream or memory somehow. Is there any way we can test this theory?" A touch of her researcher side kicks in.

Tess gives her an odd look. "I'm sure if you brought it up to Sara, she'd figure something out!" She laughs. "However, let's just assume for a minute, you were somehow linked with her; either you tapped into her memories and were viewing them, or you were sharing a dream like she had while we were at medical. What could you do with that?"

After a minute of thought, Sue says, "A hell of a lot! I could know what she went through and her feelings. That would help me craft a strategy to work with her as a therapist! *God*! What I could do with such an ability with some of my clients at the clinic! Some of them were dealing with suppressed childhood memories or other abuse, or other things they avoided remembering because they didn't want to admit to themselves something happened."

"Well, maybe you should try again? See if you can do whatever you did, and find out what he did to Millie, then maybe we can undo the damage. Maybe if you knew, and could help her remember, she could break the cycle of pain and avoidance he created in her." Tess says, but gets an annoyed look on her face. "Just a sec, someone's worried I'm not home!" Tess looks off for a second, her expression changing and looking more annoyed. She makes a long sigh, opens her eyes and half smiles at Sue. "I popped out so fast, I didn't tell Marc where I was going! He can be overprotective sometimes."

"So can Colin! I guess I can try, but I don't really know what I did to make it happen." Sue sighs with frustration.

Tess chuckles and shakes her head. "I know exactly how that is. My whole out-of-body thing! It happens, but I haven't been able to make it happen. It just does, usually when I need it and occasionally when it's a pain in the *ass*!" She says, thinking of her unplanned jaunt to save Annie from Jason a few weeks earlier. "What I will say about some of our abilities, however, is if you try too hard, it won't happen. So, maybe just think about it when you fall asleep again, and if you need it, it'll happen." Tess shrugs.

Sue sighs. "I guess that's all I can do for now. That, and be aware of what it might be next time it happens. Which do you think it is? Am I just observing her memories, or do you think it's shared dreaming? If it's the latter, maybe I could use it kinda like a form of regression therapy."

Tess looks at her oddly. "You mean like they do with past lives and stuff?"

"No, that's not really a legitimate use of it! The proper use is often for remembering suppressed memories or even details in the unconscious mind. For example, if a woman is assaulted, and can't really remember what the guy looked like except he had dark hair. Sometimes, regression hypnosis can take them back and help them look objectively, and notice things they didn't con-sciously remember. Unfortunately, it's a legally gray area for court use, but has its therapeutic advantages. Sometimes, you can even use it to take them back through the event to recall it, and walk them through it, giving them an alternate ending to empower them. For example, if I could have been in there with Millie and encouraged her to be strong, break her chains, and overpower Ja-son or Philipa, that could help her break the hold he has on her psychologically, see?" Sue explains, excited by the possibilities.

"Hm, it's really an interesting concept! Did Millie react at all to your presence in the dream?" Tess asks.

"No, but I tried to stay in the background. Do you think I should reach out to her? See if she can even see me?" Sue suggests.

"I think it's worth a try. If she still doesn't react to your presence, you may just be dealing with her unconscious memories, but if she interacts with you..." Tess trails off, letting Sue finish the train of thought.

"If she does, then maybe I can help her in the dream world! Not to mention, if we could set up a safe space in her dream, where she knows he can't really hurt her, we can work through some things. Thanks! Whatever it is, it really helped to talk it through!" She yawns, tired once again. "Maybe you'd better get home before Marc pops in here looking for you!" She snickers, remembering she's just wearing a t-shirt and underwear under her blanket.

Tess gives her a mischievous look. "*He wouldn't dare!*" She says with a glint in her eye. She leans in and gives Sue another hug and vanishes.

Sue lies in bed, pondering the dream with Millie in it, trying to figure out what it was. She loses track of time, and as she's lying there, she hears footsteps trudging down the hallway as Colin heads for bed. She can tell from the unevenness of his footsteps, he's exhausted, will likely stumble into bed, and be asleep quickly. She glances at her cell and it's already about midnight local time.

He opens the door, looking bleary-eyed. "Still awake?" He asks as he comes over and sits on the edge of the bed, leans over, and kisses her forehead.

"Well, not still. I slept for a while, but had a crazy dream and woke up." She says.

"Were you talking in your sleep? I could have sworn I heard voices." He says as he undresses for bed.

"No." She shakes her head emphatically. "That was Tess. I hollered her way after the dream, she popped in, and we talked about it."

"Must have been some dream!" He comments as he slides under the covers and rolls on his side toward her.

"You could say that, yes! The truth is, I'm not entirely sure it was a dream." She comments.

He yawns and gently caresses her cheek. "What else could it have been?"

"That's what Tess and I were discussing. Sara shared a dream she'd observed from Millie, and I assumed I was just replaying it, but it was more of a continuation. It was so incredibly detailed and real! I think, somehow, I was either reading her unconscious memories, or Tess suggested I may have been dreaming *'with'* her?" She finds herself yawning in response to Colin.

Colin's quiet for a moment, and looks like he's trying to remember something. After another minute, he drags himself up out of bed, and stumbles to a small desk in the bedroom, grabbing a small notebook from a drawer. He returns, sits on the side of the bed, and opens the notebook up, reading what's written in it. "Do you remember much from when you woke up after transforming? I know you were out of it, but do you remember dreaming anything?"

"I'm not sure. It's all a jumble. I remember waking up, you hugging me, getting really hungry, and nearly skewering my tongue when my fangs popped out for the first time..." She trails off, looking embarrassed. There was something, though. I remember waking up and thinking about when we first met at the beach and thinking how we got from there to here." She smiles at him. "I remember thinking about what if I'd known what you were back then or something. Like I said, it was a jumble, like time was mixed up and while I was back there, part of me was from the here and now. Does that make any sense?

Colin gives a brief bark of laughter and shakes his head in bemusement. "I was sleeping until just before you came to. Sara woke me from a dream about you, and the strange thing is, I was sure you were there with me. It was about the day we met." He hands her the notebook. Sara told me to write it all down and we could compare notes once you were up, but you were so upset over the whole 'guinea pig' thing, and I didn't wish to add to your burden. However, you might want to read this and see how it compares to your own memories."

Sue takes it from him, with a curious expression, and reads his notes. As she does, her own dream flashes back to her, including the part about her knowing what he is and how she'd become like him some day. She puts the notebook down on her stomach and lets out a "Huh..." and rolls over on her side, propping her head on her arm and looking up at Colin. "So, if we both had the same dream, but from our own perspectives, and we interacted, what would you call that? Tess mentioned something about her and Marc sharing a dream after taking some blue colored drug, psiamp, I think?"

"Yes, we use it for shared dreaming, usually when one of us needs to share knowledge quickly. We'll share a dream where one will teach and the other will learn. You can cram days' worth of normal learning into a half an hour dream." He explains.

"Yes, but she said they used that medication..." She trails off.

"Yes, it helps create a psychic link that usually results in a shared dream space. You had some of that drug, but that was at the beginning of your transformation. It was one medication I infused your arm with, but it should have been out of your system by the time you woke up." He reaches down and takes her free hand, caressing it gently.

"Why give it to me then? I mean, we weren't trying to share any dreams or anything." She looks perplexed.

"That's not the primary use for psiamp. As the name implies, 'psi' as in psychic, and 'amp' as in increasing. It's often given to people when they are turned to help bring out their new abilities. Sara thought it would be a good idea to give it to you preemptively, because you're a Lost Missioner. But I never took any, and the shared dreaming usually requires both parties to take a small dose to create the interactive link." He looks pensive as he explains this to her.

She lies there, thinking while he crawls back under the covers. "Colin, do shared dreams ever happen without using psiamp?"

"You mean spontaneously?" He asks, reaching down and taking her hand in his. "Yeah, they can. It isn't that common, and it's almost always with closely bonded couples. Distance is often an issue, for example, we were in the same room when you came out of stasis. I've heard of very rare incidents when it's happened to partners who are physically separated because of work or something, but then time zones and sleep times are a factor. Why?"

"Tess and I were talking about how it could either have been me tapping into Millie's unconscious memories and replaying them, without her present in the dream, or it could have been a shared dream. She also mentioned something called retro...cognition, but we ruled that out because of all the sensory details like smells, sounds, tastes and even the sensation of the humidity clinging to my skin." Sue explains, while gripping Colin's hand tighter.

"I really don't know what you were doing then. It isn't like you had any real bond with Millie. You've barely crossed paths with her and hadn't interacted with her until you visited her at Medical. However, Sara did say your gene print indicated some type of funky telempathy or people reading." He looks over at a lamp and flicks it off telekinetically. "Did you interact with her..." He yawns again. "at all in the dream? Did you try talking to her at all?"

"*No!* I was just trying to be a good observer! I thought it was a replay of the first dream, so I kept my distance and just watched." Sue leans closer and snuggles her head against his shoulder.

"If it happens again, try talking to her in the dream or get her to change it. If all you're looking at are memories, then nothing should change. Maybe you can go to medical tomorrow, and ask her if she had any similar dreams?" She hears his breathing transition to a sleep rhythm, and lets him slip into much needed slumber.

Sue ponders his suggestions and finally dozes off a little after 2:10 am.

Delving deep

At first, Sue has a few random dream fragments; nothing unusual, just the regular rehashing of her recent existence. After a while, she finds herself back in the dank, and now dark basement. The room suddenly lights up briefly, followed by a loud rumble, and the sound of heavy rain hammering the metal flashing on the window wells outside. Water seeps in through a crack in an outer wall, and a cold puddle of dust-filled rainwater creeps toward Millie. She tries to move out of its way, but her chain restricts her movements. Eventually, she's sitting in a shallow pool of cold water, shivering. Sue feels waves of despondency emanating from Millie.

I wonder if I can influence this scene at all? She thinks. She closes her eyes, pictures the floor dry again, and Millie dry and warm. She opens her eyes, and while there's still water on the floor, there's now an elevated bulge on the floor under Millie, water around its base, but she's high and dry. *Well, that's an interesting turn of events! Wasn't quite what I was going for, but it's a start! And if these are inflexible memories....* Her thoughts trail off as she hears a small exclamation of surprise from Millie. Sue looks at Millie, who's staring back at her, eyes wide and unblinking. Sue picks up mixed emotions coming from her. At first, she's afraid of Sue, wondering if she's another of Jason's gang, but another part of her has a vague sense of recognition, like Sue was somehow known, yet didn't belong here.

Sue carefully squats down on the floor a few feet away from the frightened woman, trying to make herself less threatening. "Millie, you can see me, can't you?" She asks quietly, and watches her reaction. After a few seconds, Millie nods nervously. "It's okay, I'm not going to hurt you; I want to help you. Do you know who I am?"

Millie purses her lips together, trying to remember. She whispers quietly, afraid Jason or the others will hear her. "Look familiar but can't remember."

"It's okay, I'm not surprised. My name's Sue." She watches Millie carefully, sensing her emotions. Sue's fear lessens as Millie realizes her name rings a bell. "I know you're afraid Millie, and I know you've been hurt by the people upstairs. But it's all going to be okay. You'll get out of here and you'll be safe among new friends."

She looks around nervously, then says, "Tried to escape! I'm trapped! They *did* something to me. I'm a *monster*, some sort of *thing*! They made me *hurt* a woman! I *bit* her! I think I would have *killed* her if they hadn't stopped me!"

Sue sits all the way down on the water-covered floor, ignoring the dampness. "I know what happened. It wasn't your fault. Jason did this to you. He made you this way. None of it's your fault!"

"I don't remember how it happened, but I remember pain!" She grasps her throat with her hand where he bit her. And I remember other pain I thought wouldn't end, and laughter, but not good laughter. Laughter that only comes from...." She trails off as she gets a shooting pain through her mind.

Sue finishes her thought. "The kind a sadistic bastard makes when his victim is in pain and suffering." Sue watches as Millie's lower lip trembles and her eyes tear up.

"Help me?" She begs.

Sue's unsure of where to go from here, but says, "I'm trying to help you. Would it help if I told you you're already safe some place far from here, and this is just a dream; a nightmare where you're remembering what happened?"

Millie looks at her strangely. Her first reaction is to reject this notion because everything feels so real, and yet, part of her inexplicably senses some truth in what Sue is saying. "If I'm safe, then where am I?"

"You're in a hospital room, sleeping. We met there earlier today, along with two other women, Tess, and Sara. Do they sound familiar?"

Sue focuses on the floor drying up between them and edges closer to the terrified woman, watching for any reaction to her getting closer.

"Tess? Sara?" She asks and shakes her head as she gets an image of their faces in her mind. "Yes! I don't know how, but I know them."

"Tess brought me to see you today, and we spoke, but you got tired and needed to rest. We're both sleeping and dreaming together." Sue edges another few inches closer.

"I don't want to dream this! Don't want to remember! It *hurts!*" She cries.

"I know, but you need to remember some of it so you can move on. That way, you can break the power Jason has over you." Sue looks at her compassionately. Millie startles as she hears the thumping as earlier, the chains rattling and the locks being opened. Millie scrambles down off the bulge and into the dampness of her corner. Philipa stomps down the stairs and glares at Millie.

"Who the Hell are you talking to? Are you going insane, Millie? I know all about insane!" Philipa walks over to Millie and grabs her by the wrist and wrenches back one finger at a time on her hand, causing her intense pain.

Sue's own memories of Philipa flood back into her mind as she remembers her doing something similar to her, forcing her to give up her cookies as a child. As Sue's anger swells, she lunges forward, grabbing Philipa by her long, red curls, which oddly appear almost blood red, though their real color was closer to her own auburn. "Leave her alone, Philipa! I won't let you torment her like you did me!" Sue pulls back her arm and punches Philipa in the jaw, knocking her across the room, and into an old wooden bin along the wall.

Millie stares in stunned silence, seeing the 'red-haired demon', as she thinks of her, lying in a pile of shattered wooden planks. "How'd you do that?" She gapes and moves forward, but hides defensively behind Sue's legs.

"I probably shouldn't have let her get to me. Philipa's always been a bully, but she's hardly invincible!" Sue stares at Philipa's prone body lying crumpled in the pile of shattered wood. She realizes this little dream may be therapeutic to herself as well. She turns to Millie, reaches down, and gently draws her up. "I need you to look around you and remember this place. You can't move on as long as it haunts your subconscious mind and forgotten nightmares. This is the past, Millie. And you have the power to leave this place now."

"How?" She asks in disbelief.

"I want you to picture the chain and the manacle on your ankle rusting in the water on the floor. Picture it getting ever more rusty, crumbly, and weak, until it's so weak you can just walk away, and it disintegrates." Sue watches her focus, will it to happen, and her will manifests, causing the iron bonds to rust.

The manacle becomes lighter like it's losing density, then falls away as rusty dust as she steps forward. She opens her eyes and looks down to see her ankle is free, but bloodied, and in pain.

She gently touches her on the arm, and says, "*Millie*! The pain is all in your *mind*! It's a reminder of the pain you felt here in this place, but it'll heal, just as *you* will. *Picture* it! The sores healing up, returning to normal skin, the pain fading and disappearing." Sue urges her, intuitively finding the words Millie needs to hear.

Millie glances down; her ankle is healed, and the pain is gone. She can hear the door to the cellar being ripped off its hinges as someone rages down the stairs. It's Jason, who looks over and see's Philipa in shambles. His anger peaks, and he lunges toward Millie as though he can't see Sue between them. Millie's cowering behind Sue, but Jason moves belligerently toward her.

Sue turns to Millie. "He *can't hurt you* anymore! He's just a shadow of the real Jason. And like any shadow..." Sue turns toward Jason and walks right through him to the stairs. "He has no substance, and no power over you. *Come*! We're *leaving*!" She extends her hand toward Millie, whose mouth is hanging open in shock.

Millie closes her eyes, reminding herself of what Sue just told her, *he's nothing but a shadow.* Jason grabs at her, thrashing his arms around, but Millie walks right through him, taking Sue's extended hand. Millie turns back and is surprised to see Jason now encumbered with the shackle, still trying to reach her as she walks up the stairs with Sue. As they get to the wide-open, cellar door, the dream dissolves.

Sue shifts, rolls over in bed, still mostly asleep, only to be woken up by her cell phone going off. She clumsily picks it up, squints at the brightly lit screen, and notes it's a little after 4 am locally. She closes her eyes again as she answers it on autopilot. "*Sara*? Is everything okay?" She yawns and feels Colin lay his hand on her back in concern.

"I'm not sure. Millie just broke out of another nightmare, but this time, she's insisting you helped her escape from 'the dungeon' and that I call you and thank you for her! Do you have any idea what she's talking about?" Sara sounds unsettled, which is unusual for her.

"Yeah, tell her she's welcome. I'll be by later today and we can talk about what happened. It's..." She lets out a long yawn. "4 am here and I haven't exactly slept well so far! Oh, and Sara, I think I found my *unusual* talent." She yawns again. "I'll fill you in when I get there later!" She fumbles with her phone and hangs it up, putting it on 'do not disturb'. She rolls over toward Colin and smiles gently when she sees him peering back through half-opened eyes. "I'll fill you in on everything in the morning, too. I'm so damn exhausted; I think I'd fall asleep mid-explanation." She lays her head on his warm chest, he curls his arm around her, and draws her tightly against him. She drifts off to sleep knowing she helped Millie, and it feels good to be useful again.

Dream therapy

Colin wakes first, and is about to wake Sue when he senses her deep exhaustion, but also peace of mind and satisfaction. He carefully disentangles himself from her, pulls the blanket back over her, and lets her sleep. He heads to his home office and continues his work from the night before.

Around 7:12 am West Coast time, Sue's awakened by multiple pings from her Facebook Messenger. After the fourth ping, she rouses, wipes the sleep from her eyes, and picks up her phone. Her lock screen has several notifications telling her Tess has sent her multiple messages this morning while she was sleeping. She opens Messenger, and finds Tess is more than eager to know what happened the night before.

The first message reads, "YOOHOO! SUE! ARE YOU AWAKE?"

When Tess doesn't get an answer, she continues, "You've got Sara and medical all abuzz over whatever you did last night!"

Getting impatient, the next message is, "*What* in the world happened? Have you talked to Liz about *Philipa* yet?"

Finally, Tess realizes Sue must be unavailable, and messages, "*UGH!* Guess you're busy or still sleeping or something! Holler one way or another when you get my messages! I'm dying to know the details! Sara wants to see you *ASAP*, BTW!"

Sue checks the time and sees it's barely after 7 am where she is, but 10 am Asheville time. She lets out a long yawn, stretches, and sends Tess a brief reply. "Just crawling out of bed. *Damn* long night! Totally wiped out! Will fill you, Sara, Liz, and everyone in as soon as my head stops spinning! Give me about an hour to get myself fully conscious and presentable, and I'll port out to you. I want to run stuff by you first, and then we'll go bug Sara!"

Sue leaves her cell phone on the nightstand and takes a quick shower. She finds something comfortable to wear, lightweight pants, and a blue, sleeveless top. She glanced at her phone when she got up and saw the temperature in Asheville is expected to hit 95 degrees today. She grabs her bag from the night before, stuffs her notepad back into it, and glances at her phone. Tess has messaged back with a simple, "Ok, see you soon! Marc made almond croissants this morning!" She heads out of the bedroom, then goes back and reaches under the bed, pulling out several boxes of books Colin brought from her home. She digs through them until she finds some books about trauma, women and assault, and PTSD. She stuffs them into her bag and slings it over her shoulder, noting it feels much lighter than she remembers from when she was human.

Since Tess implied breakfast is courtesy of Marc this morning, she skips breakfast at home, goes down the hall, and leans her head into Colin's office. "*Morning!*" She yawns.

Colin cocks his head to one side with an eyebrow raised in question. "Thought I heard the shower!" He motions for her to come in and join him in his office. She plops down in a spare chair he has for guests. "*So*, you gonna fill me in or what?" He gives her a sideways glance and a lopsided grin.

Sue takes a deep breath and blows it out audibly. "I'm *still* trying to figure it all out, but I think it was shared dreaming. It was based on her unconscious memories, but I could interact with her and I could manipulate the dream! Oh! And you're not gonna believe this! You know how he's still got two women with him?"

"Yes, Liz told me about them when I first came to town for you; said one escaped from a psych ward." Colin puts his tablet down and focuses on Sue. "What about them?"

Sue lets out an ironic laugh. "Guess who the *psychiatric* case is!" She gives him a pained smile.

"Who?" He asks curiously.

242

"My cousin, Philipa! She's been batshit crazy since I can remember and used to make my life a living hell!" She says seriously, but then gets a look of amusement. "And after all the years of her tormenting me when we were growing up, I knocked her on her *ass* in the dream! *Granted*, it wasn't really her; just Millie's memory of her, but it felt *damn* good!"

Colin shakes his head and chuckles. "Are you sure this wasn't just your dream? A little wish fulfillment, perhaps?"

"Yeah, I'm sure! I didn't know she was part of this until I saw her in the first dream with Millie, and then Tess confirmed the names of his two companions. Anyway, between that and the fact Millie woke up knowing I'd been there, I'm guessing we were sharing a dream. Especially since it looks like you and I may have, as well." She grins even wider. "I suspect it may be part of whatever 'superpowers' I got from this whole mess." She says with an element of sarcasm, but he can sense her excitement about this latest turn of events.

"You heading over to talk to Sara about all of this? I'm sure she'll want to give you a once over." He considers offering to port her, but after she took off on her own the day before; he lets her be her independent self.

"Yeah, but first, I'm heading over to Tess so I can go over it with her. I don't know what it is, but when I talk to her, things get clearer! After that, we'll go over to Medical, talk to Sara and Millie to confirm stuff, and see how she's doing after it all! I'm guessing she wasn't doing too badly last night because she told Sara to thank me for getting her out of the basement 'dungeon'" She looks more serious and sighs. "Of course, after initial elation, I suspect we'll have plenty to talk about, and work through. A lot of times, after a breakthrough, initial elation gives way to needing to deal with it all, which means mood swings, depression, anger, and many reactions to a situation. She's not likely to be all-better after one little shared dream! However, I have some idea where to start now." She stands again, getting ready to head to Tess's. "Oh, and then I've got to tell *Liz* about Philipa! I'm guessing that's gonna be like a proverbial Spanish Inquisition, as I'm sure she'll want to know anything I can tell her about my 'dear' cousin.

"Have you eaten yet?" He asks as she heads out of his office.

Sue looks back over her shoulder and smiles. "*Nah!* Tess says Marc baked this morning, so I took that as a late breakfast invite! I'll yell if I need you, or if we figure anything out." She smiles, turns back around and ports away, reappearing in Tess and Marc's living room, where Tess has laid out a spread of croissants and other food on the living room table.

"Hope you're hungry!" Is all Tess says, but Sue knows she's dying for all the details from the night before. Tess can sense the excitement in her aura and motions for Sue to have a seat with her at the table.

Sue takes in the feast before her. "Marc really loves to bake, doesn't he?" She grabs a plate and fills it up with both plain and almond croissants, as well as some ham and cheese to put in the plain ones.

"Yes, he does! I'm sure he'll tire of it eventually, so might as well enjoy the spoils of his current obsession while we can! *So!* What the *hell* did you do?" She gets an irrepressible grin on her face and fills her own plate, adding a little chocolate spread to one of the almond croissants and easing the decadent delight into her mouth.

Sue puts her plate down and gets a lopsided grin that spreads from ear-to-ear. "Tess! I'm pretty sure it *was* shared dreaming, like you talked about with you and Marc! It had to be! They were *her* memories, but I could *sense* her there, *interacted* with her, and could manipulate the dream! Oh! And get this! Philipa showed up again! I think it was a defense mechanism in Millie's mind trying to distract me, push me away, or something, as I was getting too close to the problem, but when she showed up, I don't know, I just suddenly realized Philipa had no power over me any longer! I *decked* her and she flew across the room! *Damn!* That felt so good!" She says, almost giddy.

Tess looks at her with astonishment and interest. "How did Millie react?"

"I think it gave her some courage or hope, and we made some progress, but then she sabotaged it unconsciously by bringing in a new obstacle, Jason. In the end though, I was able to show her Jason had no power over her in her dream, so we literally walked through him, up the stairs, and out of the basement! The dream ended, I woke up, and Sara called me all flustered!" Sue explains, out of breath.

"So, does she remember it all?" Tess asks, while savoring her croissant.

"She remembers something, that's for sure, but I don't know if she remembers it all. I need to go talk to her at Medical, but I'd like you to come with me." Sue gives her a quick, anxious smile.

"Sure, if you want me to! I just need to let Mr. Anxiety know I'll be at Medical so he doesn't call out the Apara-SWAT team to search for me!" She snickers, and wipes her mouth of flaky crumbs. She trots to Marc's home office and sticks her head in the door.

"Hey, I'm gonna go with Sue to Medical and see how Millie's doing. Sue thinks she made a breakthrough with her, but wants me to go with her as backup." She cocks her head to one side, waiting for Marc's reply.

"Make sure you stay in Sanctuary, *okay*? If you go to the office or anything, let me know!" He gives her a concerned glare.

Tess shakes her head. "I *know* the drill! *No* unnecessary risks! *God*! I'll be so glad when Jason's not an issue anymore!" She makes a huffing sound, turns, and heads back to Sue.

"Let me go get ready and we'll head over, okay?" She runs up the stairs to change into something more appropriate for Medical and grabs her bracelet.

Marc comes out of his office, in Tess's chair, and grabs one of the croissants, admonishing Sue, "If she even thinks about leaving Sanctuary without telling me, please path me, or get Colin to. She's stubborn, and I know she thinks I'm overprotective, but I don't want anything to happen to her, okay?"

"Will do, but you need to let her off her leash a little." Sue gives him a sardonic grin. "You *are* overprotective! You want her to get her confidence back, but you keep limiting her like you don't believe she'll be okay without you. Tess is a capable woman, you know? But you've got to drop the training wheels if you want her to believe in herself fully again!"

Marc sighs. "I know, but it's not easy! I don't want her hurt physically, mentally, or emotionally! Maybe it's because when she hurts, so do I... I don't know." He says, awkwardly. "I'll keep what you say in mind, but I do worry about her every time I can't be there to protect her." He hears her coming down the hall from the bedroom, approaching the stairs, and puts a finger up to his lips to remind Sue not to say anything about what they'd discussed.

Sue nods, grabs her last croissant from her plate, saying "One for the road!" She grins and waits for Tess to come all the way down the stairs.

Marc is about to ask Tess if she has her bracelet on and her GPS tracker turned on in her phone, but catches a knowing look from Sue, so, instead, says, "Good luck you two. I'm sure Sara will have plenty to talk to you about!" He stands there, watching, as Tess and Sue port out, leaving him alone with Mabel, who's wrapping herself around his legs, purring, and meowing for food.

The two women port into Medical right outside Sara's office and go in the open door, only to nearly collide with Sara, who's coming out of her office.

"Good morning, ladies! You do know we have a lobby for a reason? What if I'd been running off to an emergency and had to waste time after colliding with the two of you?" She says, trying to sound annoyed.

Tess rolls her eyes. "Sara, if it were that big an emergency, you wouldn't walk, you'd port!" She says sarcastically.

Sara glares at her and Tess feels the empathic equivalent of Sara calling her *Smart-ass!* Sara says aloud. "Well, now that you're here, come on in! Millie was so excited about 'escaping from the dungeon', she couldn't sleep, so I gave her something to help her settle down. *Now!*" She shifts her gaze to Sue. "What in the Benefactors' name did you do, young lady?"

Sue knows Sara is many times her elder, but is taken aback by being treated more like a student again, and not as a professional equal. "Tess and I have been going over it, and we believe I can go into other's dreams, manipulate them, and interact with the person having them. By doing so, I helped her take back control and walk out of the basement where Jason had her confined early on, leaving him locked up in there in her stead!"

Sara gets a thoughtful look on her face. "You didn't need any psiamp, then? Was it spontaneous, or did you make a conscious effort?"

"No psiamp. The first time it was spontaneous, but I talked to Tess about it afterwards and we realized it might be shared dreaming. I went back to sleep thinking about it, wanting it to happen again, and it did, and this time, I had more control! Millie was aware of me, where she wasn't in the spontaneous one." She catches Tess's raised eyebrow and the name *Philipa?* wafts into her mind from Tess; a not-so-subtle nudge to let Sara know Philipa is her cousin.

Sara notices the mental interaction between them, and looks at Sue expectantly. "Have something else you want to tell me?"

"Yeah, my life is all about coincidences lately! First there's the whole thing with being compatible after being with Colin for years, and now, well, Philipa Ball is my cousin..." She trails off, waiting nervously for Sara's reaction.

"Your *cousin*?" Sara sits forward in her chair, leaning closer to Sue.

Sue nods awkwardly, like she's under an interrogation spotlight. "Yeah. She's my mom's identical twin sister's daughter! And she's been a royal *bitch* for as long as I can remember!" She sighs and shakes her head.

"Hmph! Well, that's quite interesting! I wonder if her abilities are anything like yours? You do know you'll need to fill Liz in on this as soon as you're done with Millie, right?" Sara eyes both women seriously.

"Yeah, Tess said the same thing. But right now, Millie's my priority. I need to compare notes and see just how much she remembers and how it correlates to what I remember." Sue says firmly.

"Before we go see Liz, I'll have to let my 'warden' know I'm leaving Sanctuary for a few hours." Tess says, trying to temper her resentment. She knows Marc doesn't mistrust her, but his constant overprotectiveness is really starting to annoy her. Every time he slacks off for a few days, he rebounds and becomes even more overprotective than before.

Sara senses her annoyance and chimes in. "I'll let him know. You and Sue go on over to Millie's room. I'll be along after I run a quick errand and bring her out from under her sedation."

All three women leave Sara's office. Sue and Tess meander down several hallways until they get to Millie's room, and wait on a bench for Sara. Sara rounds a corner and ports out, reappearing in Marc's living room. Marc senses her port in, and comes out of his home office, confused by her unannounced visit.

"Sara? Is everything all right? Is Tess *alright*?" Sara can hear the anxiety in his voice.

"She's *fine*. You need to accept that. Tess is starting to resent your overzealous protectiveness. In fact, she referred to you as her *warden*." Sara stares at him expectantly.

Upon hearing this, Marc drops and slumps in a chair, motioning Sara to sit as well. "Did she really call me her *warden*?" He looks disturbed by this revelation.

"Yes, she did. Now, she loves you, that hasn't changed, but you're going to have to give her some freedom, or she's just going to resent your efforts. She's not that vulnerable human you had to shepherd through our world anymore. She's your partner, *not* your child!" She stares him down.

Marc's surprised by the analogy and the connotations. "I certainly *don't* see her as my child!" He says with indignation.

Sara sits across from Marc. "As I understand it, you've been protective of her since she walked into your life at the interview!

She doesn't need the coddling and constant 'on guard' mentality you have, especially since Jason escaped! That girl can *handle* herself, and you need to let her prove that!"

Marc sits quietly for a couple of minutes. "You're the second person today who's told me I need to 'let her off her leash', as Sue put it. I *can't* help it if I worry about her, but I'll make a conscious effort to let her stand her own ground, okay?" He acknowledges. Sara knows it's difficult for him to do, but senses his sincerity.

"Well, while I'm here, I promised to tell you she's going with Sue to the office to talk to Liz. Sue is Philipa Ball's cousin." She smirks.

"*Merde*! What's the probability of that?" Marc asks.

Sara shrugs, saying, "Hard to say, but Sue's mother and Philipa's mother are identical twins, so the two women likely carry some of the same genes, which might have given our Benefactors a reason to make both compatible.

"But Philipa's *not* Lost Mission." Marc says.

"No, she's closer to Tess's age. In fact, I think there's only a few months difference between them, which would put her birth before the LMs arose. *Still*, the base DNA for talents may have been there, even if Sue's got tweaked by the mutations." Sara explains.

Marc chuckles. "Liz is just going to *love* this! Maybe Sue has some input into any psychological weaknesses her cousin has." He looks thoughtful.

"That would be my hope, as well. Now, I've got to get back to them and wake Millie. Don't worry so much! I've got anti-anxiety drugs that work on Apara reserved for our long termers after Jerusalem, so you'll just have to get over it, and let her be!" She gives him one of her Cheshire Cat like grins and ports back to Medical.

Sara ports directly into Millie's room, and wakes her from the sedative. "Millie, you've got a couple of visitors who'd like to talk to you."

Millie looks a little confused. "Who?" She asks, running straight into a yawn.

"Sue and Tess." Sara smiles as Millie perks up at the mention of Sue's name.

"Oh! *Yes*! *Please*! I want to thank Sue for what she did for me!" Millie sits up and runs her fingers through her short, black hair like a brush.

Sara paths to the two waiting women to come in, and they join Millie. Sara ports out briefly, returning with a couple of extra folding chairs since she, too, wants to know exactly what happened.

The first thing that happens, however, is Millie reaches out to Sue, motions for her to come closer, and gives her an enthusiastic embrace. "*Thank you*! Whatever you did last night, it's like a weight lifted from my soul! I know there are still mental monsters in my closet after everything that bastard did to me, but for the first time, I feel safe again! Like he can't hurt me!"

"That's what I'm here for. You're right, though, this will take time to work through; but you've taken the first, and most important step. I want to set-up times we can meet and work through everything. How much do you remember now?" Sue asks as she takes a seat next to Millie's bed, while Tess and Sara sit back and observe.

"A lot of the early stuff is still a hazy. I remember him grabbing me as I got in my car on the UNC Charlotte campus and then we were in that dungeon of a basement. I know..." She closes her eyes and gets a distressed look. "he attacked me multiple times. Biting me and..." Her voice goes quieter and shakes. "...and...he raped me, more than once. I think I withdrew myself into a safe place in my mind and tried to ignore what he was doing. *He* made sure I was in pain and terrified, and in the end, when he told me he could stop the pain if I just said yes, I did. He drank my blood again and gave me his and the next thing I knew, I woke up, well, you saw! In that basement dungeon from Hell! And I was..." Tears flow and Sue takes her hand reassuringly. "He changed me into a *monster*!" She gasps and her stuttered sobbing increases.

Sue paths to Tess and Sara. *I swear, if I ever deal with that jackass face-to-face, he's gonna regret it!* Waves of fury emanate from Sue as she thinks about the true monster, Jason, and what he's done to multiple women.

Sue turns back to Millie and reaches forward, gently pulling her back into a hug. "Get it out of your system, hon. Sometimes, the only way to move forward is to face things and push your way through them." Sue rocks her gently, rubbing her back in a comforting motion until Millie cries herself out.

Eventually, Millie pulls back from Sue's hug, her eyes puffy and red. "Sorry, I didn't mean to cry like that! I guess it's just been building up for a while. Every time I cried after he changed me, he let that Philipa woman '*play* with me', as he called it. *Torture* is more like it!" Her face shifts from sadness to shades of anger.

Sue looks distant, remembering her own encounters with Philipa and her sadistic 'play'. "Yeah, I can imagine. Do you remember what I did to Philipa in your dream last night?"

Millie almost laughs through her remaining tears. "You *knocked* her on her *ass*! It was wonderful!"

"What else do you remember?" Sue slips the question in, hoping to get Millie to tell her more so she can compare Millie's memories with her own recollections.

"I remember being cold, afraid, and wet." She pauses and looks up at Sue. "And then the water that flooded the basement receded, and that's when I noticed you. I was confused, at first. I wondered if you were one of Jason's *people*, but it didn't take too long to understand you were something else entirely. Something about you helped me not only remember that place, as I'd forgotten it, but showed me I didn't have to be afraid anymore. I remember the elation of walking through Jason and up the stairs to freedom!" She turns to Sara. "I know you said there's no way to make me human again, but I'm still not sure I'm okay with all of this, either. I don't want to hurt anyone." She turns back to Sue. "He sent me to watch you that night, and even wanted me to grab you if your man left you alone. He wanted me to *prove* my loyalty to him, but even if you had been alone at some point, I don't think I could have taken you back to him, not after how he treated me. I may not have remembered all the bad stuff until now, but I think I knew he was not the good guy as he claimed."

Millie's sitting upright on her bed, cross-legged. Sue reaches over to her and puts her hand gently on one leg. "My *man*, Colin is his name, is a *good* guy, and in the end, I let him change me because of Jason, but I think I would have let him even without the threat of Jason looming over my head. Most of those like us *are* good people! I know the mythology and movies say otherwise, and Jason was a really horrid example for your first exposure to this reality, but I'm hoping, with time, you can see it's not a bad thing to be Apara."

Millie looks a little confused. "A...Ap-ar-a?" She asks.

"Yes, that's what we call ourselves. While it's true we are, in the purest sense, vampires, we're far from monsters. We depend on humans, so we do our best to repay them by helping them, and by protecting this world. Jason is the aberration, and yes, Philipa as well. I don't know much about the other woman, but Philipa and Jason are a damn good fit for each other!" Sue lets out a long sigh and shakes her head thinking about the duo.

Quietly, Millie chimes in. "Alice went along with them, but I could tell she wasn't thrilled. I think she was afraid to stand-up to them. She never did anything to hurt me, but neither did she help me, not directly. I think I heard her tell Philipa once she should let me be." She looks flustered as she remembers that moment. "I think Philipa may have hurt her. I heard sounds like thuds, and then I could hear Alice sobbing somewhere in the house. Then Philipa came into my room, and 'played' with me as a cat does a mouse. But I'd rather not think about that right now."

Sue gets flashes of Philipa's actions, she seethes inside, and wishes she could punch her cousin in real life. Sue pulls herself together, forces herself to retract her emotional claws, and turns back to her client. "Millie, I want to set aside regular times we can talk, and if you have an emergency, Sara can holler my way, okay?" Millie nods. "You're bound

252

to have some reactions to the trauma now that you remember more, but unfortunately, remembering was necessary or it would have festered in your subconscious for years to come. Bringing it to the surface is the only real way to deal with it." She reaches inter her bag and pulls out the books she brought. "I'd like you to take some time to read through these. Don't push it, but read what you can. You may not be human anymore, but your psychological reactions still are. You've been through hell because of Jason, but, given time and some work, we can get you through all of this." Sue hands Millie the books, leans in, and gives her another hug. "I need to go for now, but I'll be back soon."

Tess clears her throat. "And if Sue isn't available in a crisis, Sara can call me in. We're all here to help."

Millie clutches the books to her chest and watches as Tess and Sue leave the room. Sara has her tablet in hand and checks over Millie's stats again.

"Sara, thanks for bringing them in to see me. Talking to them makes me feel almost normal again!" She smiles and slides back down into bed.

"That's great! Now, get some rest! Doctor's orders! Someone will be by with food for you in a few, of both kinds." Sara grins as she goes out the door and motions for the other two women to follow her back to her office. They follow Sara in, and after shoving a few things out of the way with her foot, Sara closes her office door with a huff.

"Well, young lady! I'd say you have a *very* useful talent!" She says raising one eyebrow at Sue.

Sue chuckles. "Yeah, it seems that way, and as you suspected, it fits with my therapeutic skills. I just hope I can learn to harness it and access it when I need to! Millie could just be a fluke."

Sara gives her a smug smile. "I *think* not! I set up psychic monitors in her room after what happened last night, and there's more to it than just the dreams. Your energy was interacting with her the whole time, either keeping her calm or nudging her psychologically. I also noticed her serotonin and dopamine levels, which have been fairly low, began to rise as you two spoke. We'll have to monitor neurotransmitters in the future.

The mystery healing aspect of your DNA may be at work, and we'll have to keep an eye on it to confirm my suspicions." She hands Sue a silver and copper linked bracelet with a transparent crystal in the middle. "Whenever you're working with Millie, or any other future patient, I'd like you to wear this. Also, wear it when you sleep. It will monitor your psychic energy so we can get a better hand on what you're doing. "I *will* tell you this much, however. When you told me about the dream from your perspective, I could see most of it in your mind. When Millie was describing things from her own angle, I could see hers. The overlap between the two makes it unmistakably a shared dreamscape."

Sue leans back in her chair, nearly knocking a couple of Star Wars figurines off a cluttered shelf behind her. "Does anyone else here have an ability similar to this?" She asks.

"Not really. We have people readers, like Tess, and others who have more background in therapeutic technique, but I haven't met anyone who could spontaneously enter or create a dream reality, manipulate it, and do 'dream therapy'. Add to that you appear to be having a direct effect on her neurotransmitter levels, and you're in a field by yourself! However, we can definitely use someone with your skills. We're still dealing with a lot of psychological fallout from Jerusalem, and can use all the people we can get with experience in the field." Sara explains.

"First, I need to figure out what I'm actually doing, and how to control it. I'd like to get back to my human clients soon, and get them to a good place before I move on to my new work. Colin said we'd talk about it again in a few days, but maybe you could put in a good word for me with him? Tell him it's okay for me to go back?" She looks Sara in the eye pleadingly.

Sara purses her lips in consideration for a few seconds. "Give us another week of working with you on this. And I want you to wear your Cent-opal bracelet when you work with people. Colin told me you've figured out a form of grounding, but I want him to work with you on it between now and when you go back. I don't want you getting overwhelmed by your clients. You need to be in control when dealing with humans."

Sue nods. "I can do that! Though, I think Colin may still want to be there to protect me, but that's not going to be possible! My clients don't know him and I doubt my boss will let my 'boyfriend' tag along on sessions!" She makes a sarcastic snort.

Sara ponders the situation for a second and then her mouth widens into a wicked grin. "Tell him to go limbo!" She chuckles.

Sue narrows her eyes and looks at Sara like she's gone barking mad. "As in the dance with poles?"

"No! When we port, we enter a membrane between the realities, and while mostly, we go in and out again in the blink of an eye, it's possible to linger in the membrane to observe events in either of the realities. He can essentially port into the membrane and hang around in your office, unseen, so he can help you if you lose control or become overwhelmed. It takes a lot of focus and energy, but if he's determined to protect you, that's the best option." Sara throws her hands out in a 'so there' gesture, and raises one eyebrow waiting for Sue's reaction.

"If it'll get me back to my clients so I'm not leaving them hanging, I'll tell him what you suggest. I guess I'll need some sort of doctor's note or letter excusing my long absence." Sue suggests.

Sara smirks. "I already have one drafted; just need to date it and print it out. As far as they're concerned, you had a nasty flu with bacterial pneumonia and were ordered to stay home until your lungs clear and I give you the okay to return. You could always throw in a mild cough now and again, *just* for show!" Sara cocks her head to one side and winks. She turns to Tess.

"I want you and Sue to team up as much as possible. I think you will each learn much from the other, and your skills are complimentary. You can work with her on grounding as well, as Marc says you've gotten fairly good at it and it's helping both your tendency to overload, and your control, right?"

"Yes, it's made a *huge* difference, which is why it pisses me off he's still treating me like I could lose control at any second!" She utters in a huff.

"I suspect Marc is beginning to understand the folly of his ways, but would suggest you simply remind him you've come a long way, and he needs to stop being your training wheels!" Sara chuckles as she imagines Marc walking close behind Tess, checking everything. "And if nothing else, tell him *I said* to back off and let you handle things yourself unless it's an absolute emergency!"

Tess gets a faint telepathic 'sound' of Yoda laughing maniacally, and shakes her head at Sara.

Back to work
in the real world

Sue and Tess continue to work with Millie almost every day for the next week, and Sue helps Tess go through more of the Lost Mission potentials that have been matched to DNA records. Both Colin and Tess work with her on grounding, and as the day Sara set as a deadline approaches, Sue breaches the subject with Colin.

"Got a few?" Sue asks as she sticks her head into his home office.

"For you, always! What's up?" Colin puts down what he's working on and waits attentively.

"I want to go back to work." She says, and can sense him about to object. She holds up a finger stopping him before he can. "I'm not talking *forever*. I know Sara needs me here, as does Tess for the Lost Mission searches, but I could do all that better if I can get some closure with my clients, and then close the book on that chapter of my life! And as I *told* you, you can watch me from 'limbo' if you must. This *is* important to me! I got an email from my boss earlier today wondering if I would be back soon. I haven't answered her yet, but she told me my clients aren't doing so well with the substitute therapist, and two of my clients won't even agree to meet with her. I'm hoping my new skills might be just what we need to make a breakthrough, and get them on the right paths." She sighs, expecting Colin to fight her.

Instead, he surprises her. "*Okay*, we'll try it your way, if Sara gives you the all-clear! I'll hang out in 'limbo' for a few days just to make sure you don't get overwhelmed or anything, and as Sara told you, you need to wear your bracelets. Make your arrangements with the Clinic, but ask them to keep your load light for the first week. Tell them you still get tired easily, and make sure you don't take on too much! You're going to be using a lot more energy and focus than when you were human, and while you and Tess have been managing Millie just fine, handling a full load of clients is another matter.

Sue relaxes. She smiles and lets out a long sigh. "Thanks, hon! I promise, if I get overwhelmed, I'll let you know before things can go sideways." She gets up, and gives him a hug and a kiss. "I need to go make sure I have clean work clothes and stuff, and let my boss, Cheryl, know I'll be in soon." She leaves him to his work and heads off to the bedroom to inventory her clothes for appropriate work attire. She sits with her laptop on the bed, and emails Cheryl, including what Colin suggested: they should keep her appointment load light the first week. After a little back and forth, they agree she'll go back in three days. They'll use the next day or two to contact her clients and set up new appointments with them for her.

Her first day back to work, she does her make-up to look intentionally wan from being sick, and slips in a few, well-placed coughs, and yawns to suggest she's still recovering. She realizes if she were to go in looking her best now that she's Apara, they'll never believe she'd been sick at all!

When she arrives, she takes time to stop by and says hello to various colleagues and some of the nurses downstairs, who all welcome her back. She goes up to the reception desk on the second floor and gets a printout of her schedule for the coming week, thanks the receptionist, and heads into her office. Colin is waiting in the chair usually reserved for her clients.

"Well, that took a while." He remarks with a grin.

"Colin! I *had* to say hello to everyone! I need to act like I would if I've been sick." She looks down at her schedule. "My first client will be here in an hour. So, if you want to hang out here, that's fine, but I've got to get ready! I need to read the notes from the substitute therapist before they get here, so I *must* focus!" She says as she takes on her professional mantle as therapist again. She sits at her desk and reads through the notes. Colin can tell she's getting annoyed.

"What's wrong?" he asks as he walks behind her chair and rubs her shoulders to relax her.

"The sub clearly doesn't know how to deal with this client, Denise. She was abused as a child, and then had a string of boyfriends who treated her badly. It turned out she's bi-polar, and it's a very delicate balance. But the therapist is going about it all wrong! She's only looking at it from a poor self-image angle, and ignoring the vicious circle her disorder puts her in, see?" She rambles off like Colin should understand, but she can see he doesn't.

"Her bipolar swings affect her self-image and self-control. When she's low or depressive, she believes she deserves to be treated poorly, and when she's manic, she gets impulsive and tends to hook up with one of her exes, or even, occasionally, some random guy at a bar without thinking. This sends her back into a depressive spiral, and half the time, when she's manic, she goes off her meds! Ugh!" She slams the folder shut on her desk, and calms herself down by taking slow, deep breaths, and grounding off her frantic energy.

"I'll take your word for it, love. I'm going to port over to the office for a few and check in with Liz. Send me a path when your client arrives, I'll port into 'limbo' as backup for you." He slides his hand down her back and lingers there for a second before porting out.

Sue spends the remaining time going through a few more client folders. She'll have three today, five tomorrow and only two the day after. She notices on the third day, they have her listed as 'on call'. This is the designation for the person who's available to take walk-in, psychological emergencies. *Oh great*, she thinks. *Let's hope it's a slow day!*

Denise arrives a few minutes late for her appointment. Sue notices before she even comes in the office that Denise is in a depressive swing as the mood hits her like a wave of heavy, cold air. Sue shivers as the depressive wave rolls over her, and Colin nearly materializes, but the door opens, and the receptionist slips Denise in.

"Hello, Denise! How're you feeling today?" She asks, already knowing. She gets strange overtones of Swedish death metal music wafting from Denise's mind; she's dressed in all black, with Goth-style makeup and hair today. *Oh boy, this is going to be a rough session.* She thinks.

Denise looks at her for a long moment, blinking slowly. "My mom said I have to come in and see you today." Denise is 26, but still lives at home because of her unstable mental state.

"Well, it's been a while. I'm sorry, but I was sick, but I'm back now. I've been worried about you. Where are you today on your bipolar scale? I'm guessing, from your appearance and attitude you're in a depressive phase, right?"

"What do *you* think?" She says sarcastically and slouches down in her chair looking apathetic.

"How would *you* rate yourself on a 7-point scale for depression with 1 as not depressed to 7 being very depressed/despondent." Sue can already tell she's on the far end of a depressive episode, but part of Denise's therapy is knowing where her current mental state is and then trying to moderate it. She can see Denise drumming her fingers on the arm of the chair as she's done many times before, but now, she can telepathically hear she's drumming to the death metal song going through her head. She thinks, *Well, that explains that!*

"Doesn't matter. Don't wanna be here today." Denise says, but Sue can sense something else, resentment Sue left her for several weeks. Sue paths to Colin. *I can understand why you want me to have light loads. All these extra layers of perception to consider can be really exhausting!*

Colin doesn't reply so much in words as a non-verbal, 'I told you so' feeling.

Sue focuses on her client. "Denise, before we go on, I want to apologize for not being here for you. If I *could* have, I *would* have. I wanted to come back sooner, but my doctor forbade it. I came down with a nasty case of pneumonia and ended up in the hospital. My fever was so high I had seizures and I was put in an induced coma. Afterwards, they told me I must take it easy or I could end up back in the hospital. So, they only gave me the go

260

ahead to come back today, and you are my *very first client*." Sue senses Denise's targeted anger diffuse as she realizes, Sue hadn't left her intentionally, while part clings to her anger because part of her wants an excuse to feel like a victim. Sue gets an odd impression as she's talking to Denise. It's almost as if she can see a mental PET-scan of the energy flow and neurotransmitters in Denise's brain. She makes a note to monitor it during the session.

"Think you can forgive me?" Sue asks, while trying to catch Denise's eye. Not a simple task as her dyed, straight, black hair with bright red streaks is hanging down in her face, obscuring her eyes as though she were a frightened animal peering out at a predator from inside a bush.

Just for a moment, Denise's eyes connect with Sue's and the emotional turmoil in her mind feels like it smacks Sue in the face. Sue finds she must use a shielding technique Tess taught her to stave off the worst of it, and ground off the rest so she can focus on her client more objectively.

Sue takes a couple of slow, deep breaths to regain her composure and asks, "Let's try this again; where would you say you are on the scale? I'd really like to know how you see yourself right now."

Denise shakes some of the hair out of her eyes and looks at Sue. "Not so good, I guess, like you couldn't tell!" She spits out.

"Oh, I have a pretty good impression of where your depression sits on the scale, but as you know, part of your therapy is for *you* to be aware of where your mental state lies, so you can manage it better." Sue tries sending out calming waves toward Denise, and she senses the young woman's tension level drop a notch. She continues to watch the mental PET scan of Denise's mind. As her mood and attitude begin to gently soften, a handful of red energy nodes in her mental image appear to be blocking or reflecting energy. She's not sure how to interpret it, except initially, the red was more widespread. Now that her mood is moderating, the core nodes of red are clearly visible in the hippocampus, amygdala, and prefrontal cortex regions of the brain. All these areas are associated with depression and anxiety. Her impression is the red areas are blocking normal energy flow, though whether it's actual energy, or perhaps neurotransmitters is hard to tell.

After a minute or so, Denise says, "I guess I'm pretty close to a 6 or 7, depressive." She runs her hand through her hair and shoves it out of her face. Sue can see she's been crying, as her mascara and eyeliner have become smudged. Automatically, Sue grabs a box of tissues and pushes it across the small table between them. Denise pauses, and then grabs a tissue and carefully dabs the moisture while trying not to smudge even more of her makeup.

"You've been holding a lot in for the last few weeks, haven't you?" Sue asks, watching those red nodes, and wondering what would happen if they shrunk and vanished.

"Guess so. Not like I could talk to my mom about any of this. She just doesn't get it's not something I can control by flipping a mental switch!" She admits and tosses the wadded up, damp, and blackened tissue into a nearby wastebasket.

"Sometimes, it's hard for people who've never dealt with severe depression or bipolar disorder to understand. You inherited it from your father's side of the family, right? Isn't it his sister we believe is bi-polar?" She asks her cautiously.

"Yeah, Aunt Stella. She ended up spending some time in a mental ward somewhere after her daughter was born." Denise admits, and Sue feels her energy is less 'spiky', or angry, and defensive. She takes another mental peek and notices the red nodes have grown smaller, and streams of blue are slipping past them, almost like water flowing around a stone damming up a creek has finally been worn away enough to let the water flow past. *Interesting,* she thinks.

"It sounds like maybe she had postpartum bipolar disorder from what you've told me." Sue remarks, as she not only watches, but feels Denise's reactions. *Must remember to note the emotions and ground!* She thinks, a knot forms in her stomach from holding onto too much of Denise's emotional baggage.

Denise lets out a sigh and relaxes a little. "I don't think she ever broke out of that cycle though. She's been fighting it ever since, and her daughter's starting to act like her, too." She admits.

Sue feels a sudden upwelling of fear in Denise related to her admission. "Are you afraid you'll end up like her? Swinging from one extreme to another."

Denise looks down at her fingers holding another mascara-smudged tissue. She's outwardly quiet for a minute, but Sue can sense more energy flowing in her mind as she puzzles out her own feelings. "Aunt Stella was fine until she had Tami. Before then, she had a mostly normal life, from what dad told me. She had boyfriends that weren't jerks, eventually married one, settled down, had a family, and then everything went to *shit!*" She admits. "What chance do I have of having even a semi-normal life if I'm already bonkers like she became *after* having a kid? I can't even attract a decent boyfriend who doesn't treat me like crap!" Denise's eyes glisten as tears flow, and Sue notices the red nodes are becoming less crimson, fading to pink and shrinking as the flow of blue, and now other colors, are less hampered by the nodes, almost like her energy is no longer blocked. She reaches out and tentatively gets a read on Denise's mental state, and while she's still depressed, the very texture of her depression has changed from an extreme, irrationally despondent state, to one much more in line with a normal person who wants to change their life, and make things better.

Sue asks her to rate her depression again. "Denise, I want you to think about how you felt when you came in today and how you're feeling now. Would you say your depression is worse, or better?"

Denise chews on the inside of her lip for a few seconds before speaking. "Oddly enough, it all feels a lot lighter, like a weight has been lifted, yet I don't feel like I'm heading for a manic swing, either. It's weird. I'm still kind of sad and depressed, but I feel oddly *normal.*"

Sue takes another mental peek at her mind and sees the nodes have nearly faded away, and her energy is flowing much more naturally. There are still shades of depressive colors and swirls of energy, but Denise almost feels like a different person. She thinks, *I need to look at others around here and see what their minds look like. Hard to know for sure what all of this means without something to compare it to.* She paths to Colin. ***This session is almost done. I'm glad they didn't put sessions back-to-back! I need time to recover.*** She can almost feel his arms around her as she senses his energy all around her like an invisible security blanket.

"We made some progress today. I want you to keep a journal for the next week, and note your bipolar scale three times a day and we'll graph it next week when you come in, okay?" Sue says with a gentle grin.

"I can do that." Denise says, still trying to control her crying.

"I don't have a client for another hour, so why don't you take a few minutes to compose yourself." Sue says. She takes out some wet wipes, and hands them to Denise. "Thought you might want to clean up your makeup before going out."

Denise lets out a nervous laugh, and Sue knows her mood is lighter without the edge of mania sneaking in. "Thanks! I don't need to look like a raccoon when I go out!"

Sue notices something else. The death metal has faded and been replaced by more ordered and less chaotic music, though she doesn't recognize the tune. After ten more minutes, and a lot of careful clean-up with wet wipes, Denise grabs her bag and stands. She turns to Sue and says, "Thanks. I really do feel better. It's odd though. I haven't felt this way in years!" She remarks, and Sue reaches out and feels a centered within her; a feeling of balance that's new. Sue walks her to the door, but stops her before she goes out. "I rarely do this with my clients." She says as she opens her arms to offer Denise a hug. After a brief pause, the young woman embraces her tightly. "Call me if you need me, and I'll do my best to work you in, but I have the impression you're gonna be okay this week." Sue grins, knowing something's fundamentally different with Denise as she leaves the office; something has irrevocably changed inside her for the better.

Sue closes and locks her door after her client leaves, and flops down into her chair, exhausted. Colin ports in and crouches down in front of her.

"Are you alright, *love*?" He asks.

"Yeah, I think so. It was difficult and different, but I really made a difference today. She was like a new girl when she left. I don't know if it's temporary or permanent, but it's a clear improvement over what usually happens with her." Sue says, as she lethargically sprawls in her office chair.

Colin looks at her for a minute, physically, as well as reading her energy. "You need to ground more before your next client comes in, and you must feed. You used a lot of psychic energy with her and it's taken its toll." He says as he puts one hand on her chin to make her look at him.

She feels odd about feeding at the office, almost like it would be doing something 'wrong', but knows he's right. He stands and pulls her up against him. "Feed from me, and I'll slip out and replenish myself during your break. While I'm gone, work on grounding and clearing your empathic pathways for the next client, okay?"

Sue nods and asks, "Am I going to need to feed between every client?" She sounds deflated, as that would be a major hassle, especially when her schedule fills up again.

He gently uses one hand to cup her cheek. "No, love. It's worse now because you're so new, and because you still must learn to use the right amount of energy. Right now, your skills are more like a sledgehammer; you use a lot of psychic, brute force. As you learn to use them, you'll also learn finesse, and use just the energy you need to. When you get to that point, combined with grounding, and time, your need should decrease significantly."

"Glad to hear it! Otherwise, you'll have to be constantly on call between sessions!" She grins, and she stands on her toes to reach him, feeding from his neck as he holds his arms gently around her. When she's done, he ports out, leaving her to center herself and ground out any remaining emotional energy from Denise.

Double-take

Sue gets through her first two days back at work with effort, finding while she has new senses and skills she assumed would make her job easier, they take a lot of energy and focus to use. She must constantly juggle between using her new skills, and grounding out her energy during, and between, each session. By the end of the second day, however, some of it is becoming more automatic.

On her third day, she has a light schedule, but is also assigned as the therapist on call. She gets to work and pulls up her schedule. Two of her regular clients have appointments this morning, and then her schedule is wide open after 10 am. She sighs, and Colin slips out of Limbo.

"What's up? Is something *wrong*?" He asks.

"No, not really. It's either going to be an easy day, or a hellacious one, and unfortunately, I'm afraid it may be the latter! I'm 'on call' today, which means should they triage any psychological emergencies, I get to deal with them. I rarely mind, but some of them can be rough, depending on their crisis. Add to that, when I deal with my usual clients, I already know them, so I don't have to rely on my 'new skills' as much, but with someone new? Just be on guard if you see mental steam coming out my ears." She chuckles.

Colin comes up behind her, and gently massages her shoulders. "Don't wait for me to know when you're overwhelmed! *Tell* me!" He leans forward and kisses the top of her head.

"I will, I'm just worried about having to deal with someone whose emotions are volatile. I know we've been working on my empathy, and being able to keep myself objective, but what happens if their emotions are literally overpowering?" She leans back, looking up at his face.

Colin crouches down and swivels her office chair to face him. "Maybe you should start any such sessions with your shields up, and *then* ease them down carefully, or read them at a distance *before* they actually come in." He suggests.

There's a knock on the door, so Colin ports back into Limbo. The receptionist opens the door, and lets her know her first client has arrived, and Sue begins her day.

Her first two clients go well, and she's able to make some progress with them, using her new skills to see behind their various defense mechanisms. There are no psychological emergencies before lunch, so Colin brings her lunch from a noodle shop closer to downtown Asheville. During lunch, Sue's able to relax, and laughs hysterically as Colin acts silly, almost inhaling individual noodles, trying to make her relax. Toward the end of the common lunchtime, she gets a call on her office phone.

"Hello, Sue here." She says, trying not to giggle at Colin's antics.

The caller on the other end is the psychiatric triage-nurse letting her know she'll have a 1 pm urgent-care session. She'll be seeing a local teacher named Miranda Bartholomew, whose been suffering from a series of debilitating nightmares about her sister. She's worried about her, as she's not heard from her sister in a couple of months.

After the nurse finishes giving her a synopsis of the situation, Sue replies, "I see, I'll get ready for her. Please send me an email with your intake notes and summary." She hangs up and sighs.

She turns to Colin and shrugs, saying, "Well, could be worse. *Better* a local teacher than someone strung-out, delusional because of drugs, or something. Can you do me a favor and clean up after lunch? I've got to read over the intake notes before my appointment." She motions to the various plastic containers the noodles came in.

Colin nods and packs everything back in the carryout bag, then puts them in a small closet in her office. "I'll go ahead and port into Limbo so I don't distract you." He smiles, and vanishes, but she can still sense his comforting presence all around her.

1 pm rolls around, and there's a knock on her door. The triage nurse sticks his head in and asks if Sue's ready. She nods, opens her notebook, and waits. The door opens fully, and a woman comes in that makes Sue

do a double-take. She looks so much like Millie, she must stop herself from saying, "Millie! What are you doing here?" She glances down at her notes and looks at the name. *Miranda Bartholomew?*

In her mind, she hears an urgent path from Colin. *THAT is NOT Millie! Whoever she is, she's human!*

Sue gathers her wits back up from the floor, and stands, extending her hand to the woman. "Miranda Bartholomew?" Miranda nods nervously. "I'm Sue Burns. I understand you've been having some rather distressing nightmares?" She motions for Miranda to take a seat in the other chair across from her. She mentally scans Miranda, and while there's something oddly familiar about her mind and mental signature, she, too, can sense, and smell the woman before her is human.

She looks at her carefully; Miranda's hair looks similar to Millie's, but while it appears short at first glance, like Millie's, it's drawn into a longer braid down her back. Millie also has a tattoo of a black cat on her left wrist, and this woman has none. She looks a little older than Millie, and when Sue glances down at her notes, she sees Miranda is thirty-two years old. She tries to remember Millie's actual, human age, but can't recall the exact number, though she believes she's at least thirty, and makes a note to look it up. "Can you tell me about these nightmares and..." She glances down at her notes. "*how* they may relate to your sister?"

Miranda looks anxious. "Before I do that, this is all confidential, right? I mean, I'm a teacher at a local elementary school and, well, I don't want this getting back to them or they might hold it against me."

"One hundred percent confidential." Sue reassures her, and notes the woman has insurance, but declined to use it, and is paying out of pocket. "If you're worried about it getting back to the school, don't. This is between you and me!" She says, but thinks, *And my currently invisible boyfriend!* She can hear a mental chuckle from Colin, and pictures him making a 'my lips are sealed' motion.

Miranda relaxes and breathes out a long sigh of relief. "Thanks! There are some things about my sister and me I don't think they'd understand; that's why I came *here*, and took a personal day.

Normally, I'd be off on summer break anyway, but, as you know, schools closed for a while after Jerusalem, and extended the school year by three and a half weeks instead." Miranda rambles, briefly making eye contact, then nervously looking away.

Normally, such a comment about familial relationships not being 'understood', or being held against someone, would set off warning flags of abnormal sexual relationships or abuse, but Sue doesn't pick up any such overtones from Miranda's mind. "Yes, everything was so chaotic after that, a lot of things just stopped for a while. So, Miranda, where would you like to begin? Your *dreams*, or your sister?"

Miranda let's out a relieved breath, and explains, "My sister's been out of touch for almost three months now. Her cell goes straight to voicemail, and there's been no sign of her at her place in Charlotte. I even went there to check on her, but got no answer. She's been house-sitting for a friend while they're out of the country, on a year abroad, so, there's no rent or utilities to deal with, so I'm not sure what to think. She's been going to UNC Charlotte, trying to get her degree, but she also hasn't been to any of her classes lately. Her ex-husband's a *real bastard*, and their split was *not* friendly. I don't know if he's done anything, but something's *definitely* wrong!" She explains.

"Have you spoken to the police, or filed a missing person's report?" Sue asks.

"Yeah, but there's been no updates on her case, and when I called in a couple of weeks back to check, they couldn't even find her case file!" Miranda's visibly frustrated. Sue feels her anxiety rising, and must mentally take a step back and ground off the energy as she attempts to get back to an objective viewpoint.

"Okay, and what are the dreams you've been having? Why do you think they're related to your sister's absence?" Sue asks, making a note on her tablet 'dreams? *Precognitive?*'

"This is where things get kinda *weird*. A few days after I last heard from Melinda, I started having crazy dreams about her, and I don't know why. You're gonna think I'm *nuts*, but I was dreaming about her being attacked by... by *vampires!*" Miranda blurts out.

270

Sue's been leaning back in her office chair, and suddenly leans forward, allowing the back of the chair to audibly snap into its normal, upright position. "*Vampires*?" Sue asks, also sensing Colin's mind focusing in on the woman.

"*You* think I'm nuts, *right*? How could I believe a dream about *vampires* attacking my sister could have any *relevance* to her disappearance, right?" Miranda's expression turns sullen. "I'm *not* crazy!"

"I'm not saying you are! I'm just trying to understand the connection. Do you think your dreams are telling you what happened to her? And if so, are these vampires literal, or figurative? Could they represent people who are figurative blood-suckers, like someone who takes advantage of others, for example?" Sue attempts to read Miranda's mind and get a look at the dreams, but all she gets are dark, shadowy images, which are hard to make out.

"I don't know. I guess I should tell you the part I don't think will go over well at work, as my principal is one of those strait-laced, previous science teacher types. My sister and I are twins, and we usually know what's going on with each other. If one of us is sad, the other will call to check in, or send a funny e-card to cheer the other up! The first dream I had of her after I last talked to her, was a dream of her panicking as some red-haired guy abducted her. Then there was pain, like he'd bitten her, and then things went black!" She begins to tear up, and Sue hands her the tissue box.

Sue paths to Colin. *Are you thinking what I'm thinking? She looks so much like Millie, and Miranda said her sister's a twin! Plus, her sister's name's Melinda. Millie, Melinda! That's awfully close to be a coincidence!*

Colin curses mentally. *I'll be back. Need to go check this out! Just keep her talking. If you need me, path!* The room feels empty without him hanging around in Limbo.

Sue gets up, and fills a cup of water for Miranda. She returns to her seat, and slides it across the table. "Are you still having the dreams?"

"Sort of, but they're mostly replaying the old ones, like flash-backs. There was one recently though, something about being *chained* up in a *basement*." Miranda shivers, and takes a sip of water, then blows her nose.

At the mention of being chained up in a basement, Sue's shoulder muscles tense up, as it all begins to look less and less coincidental. "I'm *familiar* with some of the twin studies and lore. Outside of your dreams, do you ever sense each other?" Sue's stomach goes queasy, and she is increasingly convinced Miranda's sister, Melinda, is *their* Millie.

"Yeah, it's always been a comfortable feeling, like there's some part of her in the back of my mind. I guess you could call it a presence." Miranda fidgets in her chair thinking about it.

Sue wonders if their link is still intact now Millie is Apara, assuming the twin sister and Millie are the same. "So, can you still feel her?"

Miranda furrows her brow and closes her eyes for a second before answering. "Yes, I think so, but something's different."

Sue leans forward a little. "Can you tell me how it's changed, and when?" Sue almost holds her breath waiting to hear Miranda's answer.

Miranda opens her eyes, but they defocus as she concentrates on her memories. "I'd say it changed about the time the dreams began. In some ways, for a while, the connection was oddly stronger, but different. It felt very disjointed and chaotic. I could tell she was upset, and she didn't feel quite like herself, like something had changed within her. Then, maybe about a month ago, it suddenly disappeared for about a week, and then came back, but a lot weaker. I was terrified she'd died when the connection dropped entirely! Now, I feel it very faintly, like she's far away. It's weird though, distance has never really been a factor before. Even when I went to visit a friend in Scotland, it was like she was just a short distance away."

Sue realizes the timing lines up with when Jason took, and turned Millie, and then, when she was neutralized and taken to Sanctuary. *Damn! How the hell do I handle this? What do we do if she's Millie's sister?* She thinks, and hears Colin's voice in her mind.

He paths. *Not a question of if! She IS Millie's identical, twin sister! Listen, I'm with Liz, Kari, and Tess. We're trying to figure out which end is up.*" He pauses briefly. *Damn! This complicates matters even more! Like Millie, Miranda is compatible.*

Holy Hell! How the hell do I deal with this! I know exactly why she's been dreaming about her sister, and about vampires! Sue paths anxiously.

Sue, I want you to reach into her mind, and picture her sleeping. He instructs her.

Sue reaches into Miranda's mind, picturing her nodding off. Miranda, who's still talking about the times she and Melinda picked up on each other from afar, yawns, and begins to lethargically blink until she nods off entirely, chin down and eyes closed, but still sitting upright.

She's out, now what? Sue asks.

This gives us time to talk without her noticing you're spacing out. Tess went over to talk to Millie. She's going to cautiously breach the subject with her, as to if there's any chance Jason knows she has a twin. He paths, and Sue gets the impression of him mentally pulling his hair out.

Sue gasps, *You're thinking he might go after Miranda, aren't you?*

It's a distinct possibility. If he knows she has an identical twin, he may assume she's compatible. Even if he doesn't make that assumption, he could try to use her as leverage to get Millie to come back to him. Colin explains, but then seems distant for a second before returning to the telepathic conversation. *Tess just pathed me, Millie's sure she never mentioned her sister around Jason, but that doesn't mean he doesn't know. We're going to brainstorm on this end. I'll fill you in when we're done!*

Colin, before you go, I'm guessing there's a reason her missing person's report disappeared? She paths anxiously.

Of course. Once we liberated her from Jason, our people had to eliminate any trails to her, just in case someone comes looking for her. This is one Hell of a cock-up, love! Focus on waking her up again, and keep her talking. Just put in the suggestion she doesn't remember dosing off. His telepathic presence vanishes again, but she can still sense his agitation and urgency to get this taken care of.

Sue turns back to Miranda, again focusing on her until she opens her eyes, and picks up where she left off. Once she finishes her current anecdote about Millie, Sue asks, "Have you ever had dreams about your sister like this before? Were they accurate? Literal? Symbolic?" Sue hopes she can find a way to convince

Miranda her dreams aren't real, but a knot forms in the pit of her own stomach as she realizes she may be in over her head.

"When we were kids, our parents separated for a while; I went with dad and she went with mom. We'd often dream about what the other did in school, or what we had for dinner, and other things; then we'd compare notes on the phone or by text the next day. Those were usually quite literal, and accurate." She admits.

Sue thinks, *Maybe I can use my new skills to put her at ease? Hell, if she goes poking around in Charlotte, asking questions, looking for Millie, Jason could get word of it somehow, and then she'll be royally fucked! And now, I know how to put her to sleep....*

Sue looks at her clock, seeing they still have about 20 minutes left in their 'hour'; if there's no one else waiting, she can use her discretion to continue the session beyond the usual length. She says, "Miranda, excuse me for just a second. I'm going to let them know we may run long, okay? That way, if there are any more walk-ins, they won't schedule them until later." Miranda nods quietly.

Sue rapidly messages the triage nurse, and so far, there are no others waiting. She turns back to Miranda and smiles. Once again, she pushes Miranda over into sleep. After a minute, she's sound asleep in the arm-chair. Sue makes sure the door is locked, and closes her eyes. She slips into Miranda's mind, tracks down one of her troublesome dreams, and slips into it. Sue doesn't sleep, but finds herself in the dream, fully aware. It's the one where her sister's abducted. The first thing she notices is the dream is subjective. She's experiencing it from Millie's perspective. She feels Jason grab her and bite her. It's hard to go through it, because she also feels Millie's emotions, and hears her thoughts. It's basically a replay from Millie's memory. Sue thinks, *Well, if Miranda's picking up on even half of the emotional and physical input from this, I'm not surprised she's distraught! Hm, if I could make Millie remember her suppressed memories, maybe I can suppress Miranda's dream memories, so they fade away. Then she won't worry so much, or feel the need to go looking where she shouldn't.* She feels Colin's presence again, hears his mental voice.

What are you up to? He inquires when he notices Miranda's asleep again.

Trying to use my talents to deal with her dreams. She's had a Millie's-eye-view of everything! Quite frankly, I'm worried she may get desperate enough to go looking for her in Charlotte again, and if Jason has her place staked out, he could grab Miranda if she shows up there. She paths.

Wait? Has she had any dreams about all of us since Millie's been with us? She senses his dread at the thought the Apara could be exposed by this woman's dreams.

I doubt it! Since Tess and I have been working so much with Millie, if she'd picked up on that, I'm pretty sure she'd have recognized me, and she hasn't. Sue pauses, then continues, *Since she's compatible can't they just turn her as well?*

He says, *Right now, we need to do damage control. Go ahead and see what you can do with her dreams. We can always unblock them. Liz, Kari, and Tess are putting emergency plans into action. Remember how I said we had sensors up at your place?*

Yeah, so? Sue answers.

They've sent in a team to secure her place, and will go in tonight and tag her with a tracker. Kari didn't have any handy, or I'd be doing it now. He says, and Sue picks up on his frustration over this turn of events.

Sue turns back to Miranda, pondering her next move. *I'm going to try to dim her dream memories; maybe push them into her subconscious. Can you try to give her a suggestion afterwards, not to worry about Millie? Or give her a sense everything's all right with her?*

Colin is silent for a minute, *Yes, I'll also put in a subconscious command for her to go straight home, and stay there for the weekend, until we can come up with a plan.*

Sue lightly scans Miranda's dream memory, and finds dreams of events up until Millie was captured by the Apara, including the basement one. She thinks, *Hm, perhaps being in Sanctuary has weakened their connection?* As she finds the various dreams, including some that are already half-forgotten, she mentally tags them, and telepathically summons Miranda into the dream.

The various dreams about Millie become what look like clear, helium balloons on strings, with the dreams playing inside them. Miranda steps out of a fog and sees Sue holding the strange bundle of balloons. She walks up to Sue with an odd expression. She watches the various scenes playing out in each balloon, and then at Sue.

"What's happening?" Miranda asks.

"These are the dreams about your sister." She almost says 'Millie', but catches herself, and calls her "Melinda," as Miranda does. "I want you to hold this bouquet of balloons. These are the dreams which have been troubling you." She hands them to her. Now, I want you to let them go, a few at a time, and as they rise, and fly away, your memories of those dreams will fade into your subconscious. The further away they get, the more the dreams fade into insignificance, until you can no longer remember them."

"But what about Melinda?" She asks.

"I promise you, Melinda's fine, but you need to let these dreams fade now, for your own sake. Can you take three out, and let them go?" Sue asks with a slight smile.

Miranda takes three out of the bouquet with her left hand, and slips them loose one at a time. She watches them fly away, getting smaller and smaller, and part of her is relieved, like she's just lost some burden on her back. They repeat this until all the balloons have flown off, and Miranda is much more at peace.

Sue paths to Colin. *The rest is up to you. Try giving her a suggestion not to dream of her in the future, or not to remember those dreams. I think, if Millie's in Sanctuary, their connection may be weaker. We can ask to Sara about that.*

Colin does as she asks, as well as giving her a subconscious command to go straight home, and stay there for the weekend. *I just hope this works, and holds, love. If she has more dreams, and they're as accurate as these, we could be exposed, but our priority right now, is to set up some kind of protection for her, on the off-chance Jason comes looking for Millie's twin.*

When Colin's done, Sue turns back and speaks softly to Miranda. "When you wake up, you'll be ready to go home. You'll feel fine, and not be worried about Melinda. You'll go straight home, and stay there until Monday. If anything happens, call me...." She glances at Colin, and he nods his approval at her thought. "at the phone number on the back of my business card I'm going to put in your wallet."

Sue allows Miranda to come out of the dream, and wake in her chair. "Feeling better now?" Sue asks.

"*Yeah*, I *am*. Maybe I was just overreacting. It's *odd*, it doesn't seem urgent anymore." Miranda says, with an odd expression.

"Miranda, you know you can always reach out to me if this happens again." Sue stands, walks Miranda to the door, and opens it.

Miranda turns back briefly, saying, "Thank you, it feels like a weight has been lifted from me." She leaves the office, heads to check-out, and then home.

Sue closes the door quietly, locks it, then turns and leans her back against it, sliding down to the floor in exhaustion. Colin ports in from Limbo, and drops next to her on the floor.

"I must admit, it's a damn, good thing you were working today! If you hadn't been, we wouldn't be aware of Miranda and her dreams." He reaches over and lays a hand on her folded knee, rubbing gently.

Sue's body is lead-heavy from exhaustion. "I think I'm gonna *have* to leave early, unless they have a new crisis waiting in the wings." She lays her head on his shoulder, and lets out a long breath.

"You should. Your aura is muddied and drained." He says as he takes inventory of her energy's ebb and flow.

"Colin, are they going to turn Miranda?" She asks, the words coming out a little sluggishly.

"I don't know, *love*. It's possible, but as you *know* from working with Tess on the LM potential files, there are so many factors to consider.

Sue sits up and looks at Colin. "If they don't turn her, will they make Millie fake her death? I mean, if Miranda can still *feel* her sister, will it do any good?"

"I really don't know. Tess will spend some more time talking to Millie today, and Miranda should be safe once she gets home, as they're rushing to get the security measures in place. We'll have some of our people monitoring her home as well. You and I are meeting with Liz and the others tomorrow to talk all this through, and hopefully, make some decisions." He stands and reaches down to help Sue off the floor.

She leans on Colin in her exhaustion, needing contact. Colin enfolds her comfortingly, and says, "No matter what, they're both in for some rough weather. If we didn't have the complication of Jason to consider, I'd almost say Millie should fake her death, and let Miranda go on with her life. It may be kinder than the alternative, depending on her personality."

"I'm guessing there can't be an exception to the rules, so Miranda can learn about us, and what Millie's become without being transformed?" She closes her eyes with her head against his chest; the only thing keeping her from dosing off is she's standing.

Colin gives her a sad little smile and holds her tighter. "Would that be fair to Miranda? If she won't be turned, dragging her into our world? She's human, and would grow old while her sister stays young? No, if we don't bring her over, we'll find some way to cut the connection, and let her move on with life. She'll get over the loss. We'll just have to see what Liz wants to do after our meeting tomorrow." He sighs. "So, if I release my hold on you, are you able to stand on your own, or should I just port you home?" He snickers.

She slowly glances up at his smirking face, saying, "How would I explain my not being here when no one sees me leave?" She stands straight, stretching and cracking her back, steadying herself on the back of one of the nearby chairs. "I'll touch base with triage, and see if I can leave early. May have to have you come back and port me home, though. I'm beat!"

Colin slips one arm under hers, and helps her to her office chair, so she can get in touch with triage. "I'm going to set things in motion, but I'll be back with the car, for 'normality's sake', as soon as you're ready to leave." He gives her a lopsided smirk and a wink, then ports out, leaving her to wrap up her day.

"Thank *goodness* it's Friday!" She says out loud, after confirming there are no more psychiatric crisis cases waiting in the wings.

Identity crisis

Miranda leaves the clinic after paying for her session, and heads for home south of town. A major accident has traffic backed up on Hendersonville Road, and she's already passed the turnoffs to any alternate routes. Since she's not moving, she checks her traffic app. The culprit is a truck full of scrap from construction that's crashed. It spread debris over all but one lane, and cleanup is likely to be time consuming and labor intensive. Traffic is being manually directed, a few cars at a time, alternating directions, in the one, unimpeded lane. When she looks closer, she has more than two miles before she passes the bottleneck. Unless they get it cleaned up, and reopened quickly, it's going to be at least an hour and a half until she gets home according to her app. She has an urgent feeling nagging at her to get home, so is anxious about the delay, and wants, no, *needs*, to get moving.

Her cell phone rings and she answers it, seeing it's one of her fellow teachers, Barb.

"Hey, Barb, what's up?" She asks.

"Missed you at school today. Are you okay?" Barb inquires.

"Yeah, mostly. Family stuff. Took a personal day." Though she can't remember what family stuff is bothering her, or why it required a personal day.

"Oh, *believe* me, with this extended school year, I feel like taking *every* day as a *personal* day! It's too, *damn* hot in June for school in the *Carolinas*! Even *here* in the mountains!" Barb laughs. "*Listen*, I was wondering, since you're not sick, are you doing anything tonight? I've got an extra ticket to a concert at the Orange Peel and wondered if you might keep me company? Have a girls' night out!" She asks in her usual, upbeat tones.

Miranda pauses for a minute. "Well, I'm on my way home. Thought I'd go straight home, and kinda take it easy this weekend, but the traffic's royally messed up." She pauses, trying to rationalize why she *needs* to get home, when part of her would rather go out with Barb, and have fun for a change. *Barb is always fun to hang around with, and it sure beats sitting in traffic in this heat!* She thinks, then says, "You know what? Screw it! I'll try to work myself over to the left, and make a U-turn. Want to grab some dinner first?" Miranda asks as she turns on her blinkers, and hopes someone's willing to let her merge to the left, make a U-turn, and head back toward town.

"Sure. How 'bout our usual place on South Slope? It's early enough, so it won't be crazy with bands, or karaoke! I've been craving their *Country* Fried Chicken platter!" Barb exclaims.

Miranda's stomach growls just thinking about food, and says, "That sounds *good*! Maybe we can grab a drink before we go to the Orange Peel. Drinks are cheaper there, and I could *use* one to-night! I'll meet you there about 5 pm. I'm gonna run out to the mall and grab a couple of books, since I've got a little time to kill."

"It's a *deal*!" Barb says cheerily.

Miranda eventually manages to merge left and make a U-turn. She heads back up Hendersonville Road toward town, driving out to East Asheville where the mall is. She runs her errands, including picking up a couple of books about creative lessons for kids in the large bookstore there, and heads downtown to the South Slope brew-ery district. It's an area with multiple craft-breweries, restaurants, and shops on the southern side of downtown Asheville. She parks in the parking garage on Cox Avenue, and heads off to meet Barb.

Miranda goes in through the bar part of the restaurant, and stops for a drink. The usual, evening bartender, Vince, is working. She's spoken to him several times in the past. She thinks he's too smart to be slinging drinks. She sighs, thinking he's a lot nicer than her soon-to-be ex-hus-band, but she isn't in any hurry to find anyone new right now.

"Hey, Vince! How about a Blueberry-Ginger Bellini tonight?" She asks, realizing she'll need to be clear-headed enough to drive over to the Orange Peel, and home later tonight, so she'll skip anything *too* alcoholic.

"Well, good evening, Ms. Miranda! Kids at school treating you well?" He grins, and his blue eyes sparkle.

She wonders, *How the hell does he remember everyone's names?* But says, "Just fine! But I need a little break from everything tonight. You doing well?" She enquires.

He comes over, giving her a charming smile, and puts her drink down in front of her. "Yes, ma'am! Here ya go! Should I start a tab for you tonight?"

"No, not tonight, but thanks! I'm meeting a friend from work for dinner and a concert." She picks up her glass and takes a sip, savoring the fruity flavor. She hands him enough to cover the drink, and a nice tip for him. She doesn't feel some of the other bartenders deserve much of a tip, but Vince is always nice and goes out of his way for people. "Keep the change, and catch you next time." She heads toward the restaurant part of the locale. As she enters, her friend Barb, a slightly heavy-set, African American woman in her mid 40s, with a smile that can light up a room, waves at her enthusiastically when she sees her.

The two order their fried chicken platters, then chat and laugh while they eat until it's time to go to the concert.

Barb chimes in. "Where're you parked, anyhow?"

"Over in the parking deck on Cox." Miranda says, putting her napkin on her now-empty plate, and finishing up her drink.

"I've got my car just a block away. Why don't we take mine over to the Peel so we don't have to find parking for *two* cars there." She says gregariously.

"Sounds like a plan." Miranda says, as the two women leave the restaurant for the concert.

Once they're in the venue, they find a couple of folding chairs at a nice distance from the stage. Not too close, and not too far out. Besides English, Barb used to teach music, so has a thing about finding the sweet spot in a venue. They chit-chat while they wait for the concert to begin. Miranda's uneasy, but figures it's just the noise, and closeness of so many people. Even though it's been years since the Covid outbreak, she still gets anxious in crowded places. The concert begins, and she stops paying attention to a prickling on her scalp. She relaxes and enjoys the concert. Intermission begins, and she and Barb are talking about school gossip, when she notices a red-haired woman staring in her direction; she gets the oddest impression the red-head's angry at her. She shakes her head, and goes back to the conversation with Barb, who's telling her how she had to rescue Miranda's substitute teacher earlier that day from her students, who were in quite a *rambunctious* mood.

The band comes back on stage, and Miranda and Barb turn around to watch them play; but Miranda notices the red-haired woman up front, standing near the stage, not watching the band, but staring right at her, and she gets chills down her spine. *What is it with her? Why would she be staring at me with such hostility? Hell, it's probably just someone behind me, or near me. Lord knows I've never seen...* her thoughts trail off as part of her realizes the woman looks *oddly* familiar, though she can't place her. She forces herself to focus on the band and ignore the woman. Soon, she's all but forgotten her as the band gets swinging, and people sing along.

She enjoys the rest of the concert with Barb, though she keeps getting an odd, tingling sensation on her scalp, and wonders if her Bellini was stronger than usual. The venue warms with so many people moving around, that the air conditioning has a hard time keeping up with the hot, muggy air. By the time it's over, Miranda's overheated, overwhelmed, and light-headed. The two friends head outside.

Barb says. "I'll drop you off at the parking deck."

Miranda gets an aversion to that idea and a strong urge to walk back. "You know what? I'm overheated and I'm gonna walk off the last of my drink. You go ahead home. You need to grade all those book reports my students were *complaining* about yesterday!" The two women laugh.

"All right, but you be *careful* walking back there! Stay in *well*-lit areas! My daughter got her purse snatched in town recently. Could'a been worse! Just lucky her purse is all they went after." Barb says and gives her friend a hug. "If ya need to talk, you've got my number, 'kay?"

"Thanks, think I just needed a break, but the concert and company helped a lot!" She smiles and heads toward Hilliard Avenue, and the four blocks back to Cox. She's about halfway there when that odd tingling returns. Without realizing it, she takes a 'short-cut' through the mostly dark, artist area of South Slope, rather than staying on the main road, where it's well-lit and well-travelled. She's passing through a darker section when she feels someone very strong grab her from behind, cover her mouth, and pull her into the shadows.

She tries to scream, but can't make a sound. She's surprised when she hears a woman's voice snarl in her ear. "I don't know how they turned you human again, or why you didn't run when you saw me, *Millie*, but your reprieve is over. Jason's looking forward to a reunion with you tonight." Even though the woman has taken her hand off Miranda's mouth and relaxed her grip, Miranda is paralyzed, and can't fight, speak, or scream for help. The world swirls out from around her, and when she can see again, she's in a dank basement, and she wants to retch. The red-haired woman from the club drags her painfully over toward a post in the corner, shoves her down on the floor, and attaches a black, metal manacle to her right leg.

She looks up at the woman looming over her, still unable to speak, but she can move enough to massage her ankle above the manacle. "Enjoy a little solitary time to think while you're waiting for Jason. Oh, and welcome back, *Millie*!" She sneers with a very unfriendly smile that makes Miranda do a double-take, as she realizes the woman has unnaturally long, canine teeth that make her shiver.

She digs into her pocket, looking for her cell, but it's not there. She thinks, *Millie? She CALLED me Millie? She thinks I'm my sister!* She's nauseous and dizzy as she looks around the room with an eerie sense of Déjà vu, finding the scene disturbingly familiar. The more recent dream she had about Millie being in some sort of dungeon floods her mind, and she realizes she's in the *same* place. "Holy *Shit!*" She says aloud, and scans the darkened room. She remembers the red-haired woman, and knows those extra-long canines, or fangs, are all too real.

Consolation prize

Miranda sits in the corner of the cold, dark cellar, knees pulled up against her chest with her arms around them. She can hear the occasional skittering of mice, or other denizens of the dark, and smell the moldy dankness of the surrounding room. Cold water drips on her arm from an old pipe covered in condensation, it makes her jump, and shiver from the chill. Miranda *knows*, beyond a doubt, her sister was here; not only because the woman spoke as though she's Millie, and she'd been with them before, including whoever this Jason fellow is, but because of her dream of *this* very room, from *Millie's* perspective. She desperately latches on to that dream thread, and remembers more of it. Other dreams of being kidnapped at her car, dragged here, and chained up hit her like repeated slaps to the face. She shakes from near shock as she relives her sister's terror. Eventually, she's so exhausted, she dozes off against the support pillar, despite the cold, hard floor, and the fear pervading her very being.

While she sleeps, more dreams surface; Sue and Colin's suppression undone by the evening's chain of events. She remembers the part about *vampires*, and being bitten by them, and she remembers other dreams she suppressed; dreams of Jason forcing himself on her sister.

Miranda shudders awake as she hears a door opening, and a heavy thudding of someone coming down the stairs. It's not the woman; she's certain of that. While it's dark in the room, the shadowy figure is larger, less curvaceous, and no long hair. The shadow also moves in a much more masculine fashion, and she knows it's whoever this Jason is. She's terrified he'll do to her, as he did to Millie. The dark form comes closer and hovers over her. She can make out hints of details in the dark. She can tell he's cocked his head to one side, and hears him sniffing. He crouches down to her level, staring at her. His gaze feels like a physical pressure and she can see a dark, shadowed version of his face. She steels herself for whatever he may do, knowing she's helpless against him.

He lets out a long, disappointed sigh. "You're *not Millie*, are you?" He says with gritty annoyance.

Miranda isn't sure if he's expecting her to answer or if it was just rhetorical, but answers him in a quiet, nervous voice. "No."

"Well, *fuck*! Philipa was *sure* you were Millie. She's good for a lot of things, but she *fucked* this up! So, what's *your* name, then?" He asks, coldly, without an ounce of compassion in his voice.

The reality of her situation, and the dream memories of her sister overwhelm her. "M...Miranda." She answers nervously.

"Well, Miranda, you *sure* do look like *Millie*! A few differences, no tattoo, longer hair, and something else, something subtle. Your smell, for one thing, and something a little less vulnerable." Jason had found Millie's memories of her husband, and his psychological abuse, as well as a couple of physical altercations in her memory, but he couldn't sense the same vulnerability in Miranda. "There's something familiar about your scent, however." Suddenly, he vanishes, giving her quite a start, and making her wonder if she's losing her ever-loving mind!

He ports back in carrying a purse with a USB cable hanging out the side. A purse Miranda knows all too well. She cringes, thinking, *Damn, that's the purse I got Millie for Christmas last year.* She's fuzzy-headed, and her heart breaks, thinking, *maybe Millie's dead, if this is the asshole that kidnapped her.*

Jason takes out a wallet, and flips through some photos, finding one of Millie and Miranda together at a birthday celebration. Jason laughs maniacally, and then pulls on the USB cord, dragging out the attached cell phone. He skims through her phonebook, and a wicked grin appears as he spots a familiar name. He clicks 'call', and Miranda's cell phone rings from a shelf across the room.

She thinks, *The red-haired woman must have taken it at some point, and put it out of my reach.* Jason's lopsided grin sends shivers down Miranda's spine again, somehow knowing Jason is disconcertingly pleased by his discovery.

"Well, *well*! This is quite a turn of events! You must be Millie's twin sister." He holds up the photo of the two women. "*Well*? *Are* you?" He sneers.

Barely audibly, Miranda replies, "Y...yes."

"Hmm, what to do with you, then? Well, you're human, so you *do* have one obvious use." He remarks, letting his fangs down so she can see them. She recoils, but can't go far with the wall behind her, and her ankle bound. Jason flops on his behind, and crosses his legs under him, staring at the terrified look-alike to his onetime charge. "I wonder, same genetics as Millie, perhaps they made you compatible, too?" Miranda can hear a sadistic-sounding chuckle under his breath. He says, "For now, until I figure out the best way to use you, perhaps just a *snack*." Jason lunges forward, pulling her close, pushes her head aside roughly, and sinks his fangs into her neck, with nary an effort to numb the pain. Miranda makes a squealing sound, but her mouth won't open to make a proper scream. He feeds on her, and gropes her body, knowing it will make her more afraid of him. He withdraws his fangs and pushes her back. Lightheaded from his feeding, She loses her balance and rolls backwards, banging her head on the metal water pipe.

Jason laughs. "I'll be back when I figure out what to do with you... *Miranda*!" He climbs the stairs and slams the door closed.

His bite still throbs. She tentatively touches the welts, shaking now she knows her nightmare is *all too real*. She realizes *this* is what Millie went through. She curls up into a ball, and leans against the wall, reviewing everything that's happened since the red-haired woman grabbed her. She realizes, *Wait! If they thought I was Millie, then they couldn't have killed her! She's out there somewhere!* That thought gives her some small comfort, even if her own future looks dim.

Miranda's left there, alone until the next afternoon. She struggles to get out of the manacle, even though she knows it's practically impossible. She's terrified, damp, and starving. She frequently checks the welts on her neck to prove to herself this is *not* another nightmare. Even though she feels them every time, they grow rapidly smaller. She's been hearing distant rumbles of thunder and wind outside, and while no rain has fallen yet, there's a sudden brilliant flash outside, and a nearly instantaneous, roaring boom right beyond the glassless, barred window. She lets out a startled scream. She's always been terrified of storms, but Millie loved them as a child, and their dad would have to drag her in from under the trees outside, soaking wet, to get her out of the storms. Miranda cowers in the corner, as the storm moves in and rages, until she hears the door open upstairs. A new set of thuds on the steps, lighter ones. A light comes on in the basement; one of those old, bare, single-socket, incandescent bulbs hanging only from a wire with a pull chain, now swings slowly back and forth, making shadows stretch and shrink along the walls around her. Now she can see the source of the footsteps: a woman with short, blonde hair is carrying a basin down the steps, along with some towels and rags. She also has a canvas bag. She cautiously comes over to Miranda, puts the water and supplies down in front of her.

"Miranda, I'm Alice. Jason told me to tell you to clean yourself up, and change clothes." She motions to the canvas bag. Those are some of your sister's clothes. He figures they ought to fit. Alice looks uncomfortable, like she can smell something unpleasant. The area around Miranda smells of urine, as they didn't give her any way to go to the bathroom. "When you're done, I'm to take you to him." Alice says. She unlatches the manacle, so Miranda can wash up and change clothes. Alice avoids eye contact, as she knows what awaits Miranda will *not* be pleasant.

Miranda complies, but feels awkward with Alice there. "Would you mind looking the other way. I've got to take these clothes off

288

to wash." Alice nods, and turns away. Once done, she digs in the bag, pulls out some clothes, and puts them on. There's a brush in the bag, so she brushes out her hair, though it's limp with sweat and oils from stress. "I'm done." Miranda says, despondently.

Alice looks at Miranda, and nods. She motions for her to follow her, then stops and turns to face her. "*Don't* fight him. It's *far worse* if you fight. Millie fought and he knew just how to make her stop; words from her *past*. Things her husband said to her. He took them from her mind, and turned them into weapons to quell her determination to fight, and then, *did* even *worse*." Alice motions for Miranda to go up the stairs first, remembering Jason told her she must watch her go up the stairs, or Miranda could attack her from behind, and try to escape.

Miranda goes upstairs, and through the door. The upstairs doesn't look much better than the basement. There are dim lights, and she can hear an old generator chugging away outside. The wallpaper and paint on the walls are peeling or flaking off; there are signs of water damage on the ceiling, and down one wall, and the carpet is matted and stained. Jason is sitting at a ratty old desk staring at a laptop, but closes it, and turns his attention to Miranda, just as large flashes of lightning shine through the window behind him, making him look even more sinister than he had in the dark. He stands, and motions for Miranda to sit on a tattered, old sofa. He joins her and she retreats to the far end of it.

He narrows his eyes, and screws up his mouth, trying to determine the best way to get what he needs out of Miranda, then asks, "I don't suppose you have any idea where your sister is, do you? Has she contacted you at all?" He leans in with a menacing smirk, and she can see hints of his fangs. Jason figures if Millie had sought help after escaping, who, more likely, than from her twin sister?

"No. I haven't heard from her in about three months. I'm worried about her." She admits, trying to avoid looking in Jason's crazed-looking, green eyes.

Jason edges closer to her, but she can't retreat any further away without getting up off the sofa, and suspects he would likely punish her if she did. "Do you know what I *am*, Miranda?" He asks, showing his fully fanged grin.

Miranda cringes and nods. "I know what you *appear* to be, though I don't know *how* that's possible."

"Would it surprise you to know your sister's like me, too?" He raises one eyebrow, and leans menacingly closer.

"She *is*?" Miranda gets vague flashes from Millie's perspective of having to bite people, and drink blood. She'd suppressed those memories completely before now, and she thinks, *Oh, God! It's true!*

"Yes, *Miranda*. Only certain, *very* special people can become like me, and your sister's one of them." He says, conspicuously licking his lips as he edges closer to her. Miranda swallows nervously, but doesn't say anything. "You see, it's a matter of being genetically compatible with a virus that transforms us. And since you're apparently Millie's *identical* twin, I'm betting there's a damn good chance you're compatible as well!"

"No... *No! Please!* I don't *want* to be like you!" She whimpers and sobs, but hears Alice's warning from the basement, only *in* her mind, telling her, *DON'T fight him!*

He gives her a sadistic grin, then says, "It'll only *hurt* until it's over, though, since I can't be one hundred percent certain you're compatible, I won't take as much blood from you as I usually would. If you're compatible, your transformation will, *unfortunately* for you, be slow, and probably *tortuous*. However, if you're not compatible, I still *need* you *alive!* You see, if I can get a message to Millie that you're alive, and I *have* you, whether you're one of us or not, I'm thinking it will encourage her to return to us! After all, we're her *family*." He motions to the other two women, Alice, who looks withdrawn in a chair across the room, and the red-haired woman she's learned is Philipa, looking sullen, and annoyed in another chair. Jason's not happy about the mistake she made, even though

290

he's found a way to make the best of it. "What I'll do with you afterwards remains to be seen." He gives her a wide, wicked grin, trying to unnerve her. Before she can say anything, he lunges forward, pins her down on the sofa, latches on to her throat, and painfully feeds on her once again. When he pulls back, he uses his left hand to hold her by the throat, and bites his right wrist. "Open your mouth, *bitch!*" He commands. Miranda can see Alice looking at her, eyes focused on her in concentration, and can actually hear her pleading with her in her mind, *Just do as he says!*

Miranda knows she can't win, and dreads what may happen next, but she opens her mouth, and he shoves his bleeding wrist against it. She tastes his blood going down her throat. At first, it makes her gag, but that quickly changes as she gets an overwhelming urge to drink more; a sure sign she's compatible, like Millie. She's weak, and her body feels immovably heavy. She hears Jason bark out a command to the other two women.

"Put her in Millie's room, and secure her!" He commands, and then vanishes, leaving the two women to pull Miranda up, draping one of her arms around each of them. They drag her to her sister's room, and put her on the bed, temporarily using zip ties to bind her there until they know for sure she's well into transition.

Philipa leaves the room, but Alice lags, and whispers in her ear. "If you'd fought him, he'd have gotten angry, and done a lot more than change you! Let him think he's broken you, and maybe you'll be spared his worst." Alice reassuringly strokes Miranda's face, glances around for Philipa, and leaves the room, knowing Jason prefers his new transformees to be alone and afraid while they change.

Jason ports into downtown Charlotte, looking for someone to feed on after giving Miranda his blood. He thinks, *her transformation will be slow, possibly days, but I can't risk her dying on the off chance she isn't compatible. She's not any use to me dead. Alive, human, or otherwise, I can use her; maybe get Millie to come back. Hell, if nothing else, she'll be a consolation prize, should Millie never return.*

Double the trouble

The next day, Saturday, Sue, Colin, Liz, Kari, and Tess meet up at an otherwise empty Inspiration Inc. They gather in Liz's office to discuss the situation. Sue's still tired, albeit not fully exhausted, as she was after her session with Miranda the day before. The stress and heavy psychic dream work really took it out of her, and even after eating and feeding, she wishes she could have stayed in bed.

Liz looks worse for wear, but sits with the others and pulls out her tablet. She taps on it a few times, and everyone else's tablets in the room let off pings, as information she has is shared with the group. "So, we have a dilemma, *yet again!* As you know, Millie and Miranda, being identical twins, and therefore genetically identical, were both tagged as potentials as children. That isn't always the case, as slight variations in epigenetic factors can lead to different expressions of the otherwise, identical genomes."

"I'm afraid, however, that isn't the biggest problem." Kari interrupts. "What Liz is avoiding saying is, despite your mental compulsion for her to go home last night, Miranda never got there."

Sue exclaims, "*Holy Hell!* What now?"

Liz looks exhausted and distracted, but says, "We just don't know. Maybe she met up with someone, and is spending the night with them, but it could be something more…." She trails off.

Tess completes her thought, "*Sinister?*"

"Liz nods. "I had Kari make calls to all the hospitals in the region this morning, and no one by her name or fitting her description has been admitted. We also checked the local morgues for unidentified bodies. Nothing!"

Sue shakes her head, and looks concerned, she looks up at Liz, and asks, "You're wondering if Jason came for her, aren't you?" She stares Liz down until she answers her.

"It's a distinct possibility, but it could also be something more *humanly* sinister. She could have run afoul of someone human. Maybe she went out for a drink before going home, and someone slipped her a micky. If so, *hopefully*, she's just sleeping it off somewhere, and not hurt or, or worse. I've asked Amy to work with our new IT guy, Ty, to see if they can hack into some of the local traffic and web cams to see if they can spot her or her car last night. We got her car info from the DMV server. They're also working on tracking her phone, but so far, nothing! It could be dead, or even intentionally turned off." Liz suggests.

Tess bangs her hand on the table in exasperation, then asks, "So, what do you suggest we do?"

Kari pulls out her tablet and brings up a list. "Tess, I want you to focus on evaluating her as you would a Lost Missioner or misfiled potential, in case we do find her. We may not have a choice but to turn her if Jason is after her, but the more we know about her, the better." Kari turns to Sue and Colin. "You two are the only ones who've had mental contact with her. I know Sue is relatively new, and isn't used to tracking down mental signatures, but Colin is. Work with her and see if you can track her down. When you've exhausted that route, Sue, I'd like you to help Tess out with research and evaluation."

"And what if we can't find her?" Sue asks, sensing an ominous energy in the room.

"If you can't pick her up at all, then either she's dead, or Jason has her and is masking her signature, human or not." Kari says bluntly.

Tess exclaims, "God *Dammit*! If Jason has her, I'm gonna freaking *kill* him!"

Liz nods in agreement. "I think we're all nearly ready for that option, even though our priority is always peaceful solutions. However, there is one more option you all are overlooking, but it's a precarious option, psychologically. Sue, you said the two of them have a natural, telempathic link, right?"

"Yeah, so Miranda was saying. I haven't confirmed that with Millie yet." Sue says, shifting uneasily as she knows what Liz is about to suggest. "You'd like us to see if Millie can find her, right?"

Liz lets out a long, tired sigh and nods. "And that's the precarious part. I know you talked to her about whether Jason knew she had a sister, and I assume, Tess, you did it in a way that you didn't give away the entire ball game?"

"I did my best. I asked her if Jason were to look for her, where might he check, and then I asked about family, and I thought she'd mentioned having a sister. She told me she made a concerted effort to avoid telling him about anyone he might hurt, like family or friends." Tess lets out a small, ironic bark of amusement. "However, she was tempted to tell Jason about her ex-husband, as he'd been such an asshole to her, he deserves to get some of what he dished out. But Jason clearly knew about him, because he used her fear of him against her. Fear, and things he'd said that were psychologically abusive. He must have read her mind."

Tess closes her eyes, and her stomach twists and turns, "If he read her mind about her ex-husband, he may well know about Miranda too." She suggests.

Liz puts her hand up to her forehead and massages the stress out of her temples. "All we can do for now, is what we've talked about. You all have your tasks, as do Amy and Ty. If any of you find anything, contact me immediately. It's not just Miranda at stake, but her sister's psychological health is at risk if she comes to any harm." Liz puts her tablet down on the table, sinks back into her chair, closes her eyes, and takes several deep breaths while everyone but Kari leaves.

Kari walks behind Liz's chair, and puts her arms around her from behind, hugging her. "You need a break, my *love*. I know you feel unable to take a break mid-crisis, but everyone's doing what they can. If you don't rest, I don't care how nearly immortal you are, Lissa Pedersen! You're gonna crash, and psychologically burn! Don't make me *sic* Sara on you!" Kari comes around in front of her, and sits on the edge of the table, tipping Liz's chin up to look at her. "We could take the weekend, and go up to our cabin in Grimsøysand (Norway). It's midnight sun season up there."

Liz let's out a small huff of a sound, and a slight grin of reminiscence. "*Javel*? We could... but Tess and Sue need *your* help, and I'm just afraid we'll return to full chaos." Liz loses all her normal buoyancy, like she's just used up the last of her reserves to get through the meeting. "But, it would do me some good to get home, I suppose. *Multer* (cloudberries) should be ripe around now, shouldn't they? It must be over 50 years since I took the time to pick any." Liz reflects.

"I'd say that settles it. Tess and Sue will be fine researching without me this weekend. I'll meet with them Monday morning, and go over all their findings. In the meantime, I'll port home, pack, and you need to leave that..." She points at Liz's tablet. "*here* for the weekend! *No work* unless it's an emergency!"

Liz pulls Kari's face down to her level, and gives her a light kiss, saying, "Deal!"

In vain

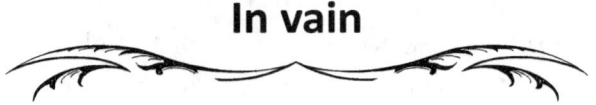

Sue and Tess research Miranda as much as possible during the weekend, while Liz and Kari take a much-needed break in Norway. They treat Miranda's case as though she's a Lost Mission or misplaced potential. Officially, she's listed as unavailable, as she was married when she was twenty-one; therefore, no further evaluation, other than her original Benefactor's evaluation, was ever done.

Monday rolls around, and Kari arrives at Inspiration Inc. early in the morning, without Liz, pathing to Tess and Sue, *I'm at the office. I'm ready to look at what you've found.*

Moments later, Tess and Sue port in, looking tired, and a bit sullen. Sue asks, "Did Amy find anything? Did she ever show up at home? Colin and I could *not* find her mental signature. We thought we found it briefly, but then it was gone before we could zero in on it. So, it may have been wishful thinking."

Kari shakes her head. "No, she still hasn't shown up at her place all weekend. Amy and Ty hacked into traffic cams, and ran a plate ID scan, but the only thing they got was one shot of her stuck in traffic, south of town, heading home. Unfortunately, none of the other cameras between there and her home ever recorded her passing by."

Tess sits back, looking frustrated. "Sounds like we may have to bring Millie in on this. Do you want me to talk to her?"

"Not yet. Give it a little more time. I'd rather not traumatize her if it isn't necessary. She has given no indication she can't sense Miranda, so I would guess she's alive, and there could be a mundane explanation for her not going home." Kari suggests.

Tess gets an odd expression. "Kari! If *that's* the case, then why isn't Liz sitting in on this meeting?"

Kari glares at Tess with one eyebrow raised, realizing she should have known she wouldn't be able to sneak that past Tess. "*Okay,* you've got me there. Liz is staying up North an extra day. She's been working nearly non-stop since before Jerusalem, and now, it's taking its toll. She doesn't *need this* on her plate right now!" She snaps. "She's leaving this up to me; so *just* let it go! Now, what did you find in your research?" Kari pulls out her tablet, and a stylus to make notes, doing her best to continue in a business-like fashion.

Tess and Sue look at each other, unsettled by Kari's reaction. Sue nods to Tess to take the lead, as she's the one who's been doing most of these evaluations.

"Neither Miranda, nor Millie... Melinda, were ever really considered beyond the Benefactor's original evaluations. Both got married young, and neither marriage worked out in the long run. Neither had any kids either. Miranda's marriage is unlikely to continue, as her husband has settled in with a woman several years younger than Miranda, and he seems to be quite..." Tess pauses, and sighs. "satisfied according to his Facebook posts. He rarely mentions Miranda, and when he does, he refers to her as 'the ex', and talks about being glad when the divorce is finalized."

Sue clears her throat. "They were seeing a marriage counselor last year, and Tess helped me tap into the therapist's records. I'll tell you one thing, if the APA (American Psychological Association) knew we could hack into confidential records this easily, they'd be *shitting* bricks! Anyway, he made notes her husband is suffering from a severe case of narcissistic personality disorder, and he believes Miranda, who he considers a basically nice, respectable person, would be better off on her own. Granted, these are his personal observations, and not what he's shared with them."

Kari's busy making notes on her tablet. "Okay, does Miranda have any other relationships in the wings? Any current love interests that could explain where she's gone this weekend?"

Tess sighs and rocks her head from side to side. "Not that we can see. From what we can tell, she's in no hurry to find anyone right now. Rather, she needs to find herself again after dealing with her husband, Joey, for a decade. Between teaching full time, and life with him, she has had little time to be herself."

Kari sits there, flipping the stylus back and forth in her fingers absentmindedly. "How about her suitability and adaptability?"

"She clearly has some basic psychic abilities, at least between herself and Millie. She's certainly got a telepathic bond with her. I'm sure, even though it's a twin situation, she can expand those skills if she's turned." Sue remarks. "As to adaptability, she's stressed between her marriage collapsing, and her sister missing, though Colin and I suppressed the conscious thoughts and memories about Millie's missing status. However, she's been adaptable in her life, and psychologically stable. The fact her sister is already one of us will help her adapt if we turn her."

Tess adds, "And I think it will help Millie to have her here as well. I'm not sure if we can break that twin bond as long as both of them are alive. Even if we can filter or mask it, there's a strong risk they may link up in a crisis, as they have their entire lives."

Kari looks thoughtful, and Tess can hear her tapping one foot on the floor anxiously. "Give me your findings, and I'll do a once over on them tonight with Liz. Don't contact her until *we* get back to *you*. And just to give you a heads up, I'm working on getting Liz to stay up there a couple more days." Kari looks at Tess. "She and Marc have one thing in common, they work, work, work, and rarely take a true break." She packs the information from their notepads neatly into a document pouch, and puts her tablet inside. "If you two will excuse me, I need to get back to Liz before she sneaks back here. If you all hear or find out anything, contact *me*, *not* Liz, immediately." She nods, and ports out.

Sue turns to Tess. "Well, someone's stressed out! Listen, I've got to head on over to the clinic. I told them I had a doctor's appointment this morning, so would be late, but I do have clients to see today." She reaches over and gives Tess a friendly hug. "Maybe, after we see Millie tomorrow afternoon, we can port over to my place, and hit the beach, burn off some of this anxiety. It's cooler than here, and according to the weather forecast, it's supposed to be brilliant weather!" She gives Tess a tired grin, and walks off to get Colin from his office before going to the clinic.

Tess leaves the office, and heads down the hallway. There are several human potentials about, so Tess heads back to Marc's office, closes the door, and ports back home.

***

Tuesday morning, there's an email to Tess and Sue from Kari.

> **Have convinced Liz to stay the week. She wasn't up to going over stuff last night, but we'll do it as soon as possible. Most likely, turning her is a viable option, assuming we find her.**

Tess spends part of Tuesday doing LM evaluations, but late afternoon, she ports to Medical to meet Sue. The two of them spend some time with Millie.

Sue sticks her head into Millie's room. "*Hey*! You're looking better! I hope you're feeling better too!"

Tess follows Sue in, carrying a paper lunch bag with her. "I brought you a treat! My partner, Marc, loves to bake, so I hope you like chocolate chip cookies!" She smiles as Millie perks up at the mention of chocolate. Millie eagerly reaches for the bag, opening it, and inhales the aroma from the Belgian chocolate.

Millie laughs. "You must have read my mind! I've been craving chocolate. Last time I had good chocolate was when my sister gave me some stuff she'd ordered from California. You know, one of those mixed 'nuts and chews' boxes." She's distracted and the two women both feel overtones of sadness from Millie.

Crap! She's thinking of Miranda! Don't let on you've run into her! But this could be an opportunity to feel things out about her sister. Tess paths.

Tess puts on her best 'surprised smile' and asks, "Tell me about your sister."

Millie looks at Tess, and her smile fades. "Miranda's my best friend. We're identical twins. I don't know how I'm going to explain all this to her. She'll think I'm crazy."

"I'm sure Jason didn't exactly tell you our rules, but we don't tell anyone human, unless they're likely to *join* us." Tess says, hoping she'll understand the reasons innately, but braces herself for a rebuttal.

Millie gets upset. "I've gotta tell her! How else can I explain why I look a younger and why I don't age? Didn't you tell me you knew while still human?" She asks Tess accusingly.

"Yes, but it was an extremely rare exception. I found out by accident, and they couldn't make me forget. It turned my life upside down, because until I accidentally got infected and turned, everyone assumed I wasn't compatible. I spent my time in limbo, stuck between humanity and the Apara. If I hadn't become one, I'd have grown old while all my friends stayed young. I'd have had a hell of a time finding new human friends, or even relationships, because I couldn't have told anyone any of this! Would it be fair to your sister to know, but still be human, aging normally while you remain young?" Tess is preparing Millie in case Liz says no.

Millie's expression goes sullen. "No, I guess it wouldn't." She's quiet for a minute, but then her face lights up from an 'a-ha' moment. "She and I are identical twins. If I was compatible, wouldn't she be too?"

Sue, sensing Tess feels awkward, chimes in. "It's possible, but until we know for sure, it's a moot point. Maybe if you give me your sister's name and information, we can look into it, though it may take a few days."

Deflated, she says, "*God*! I really *miss* her! Her name's Miranda Bartholomew, though our maiden names were Lisenbe, it's Cherokee.

Sue rips off a piece of paper from her notebook. "Here, write her address and phone number down, and we'll see what we can find out." She hands her paper and a pen.

Sue paths to Tess, *I wish we could tell her, but I think Liz and Kari would have our heads?*

Tess chuckles mentally, *No doubt!*

They continue to talk and spend time with Millie, who's fed up with being stuck in her hospital room.

They wrap up for the day, fill Sara in, and the two women head down to the lobby to port out when Sue asks, "So, what about it? You gonna come and hang out on my beach?" She gives Tess a huge grin.

"I would, but I promised Kari I'd get through a pile of LM potentials, but with everything going on, I'm behind. Maybe when I'm done, though, if the weather's okay." Tess gives Sue a hug, stands back, gives her a little 'bye-bye' wave, and ports out.

Sue ports back to Vancouver Island in Sanctuary, and literally ports in with a bang, as thunder rages outside. "Well, *Hell!* So much for a swim!" She complains. "Colin, are you home?" She bellows. She can hear heavy footsteps as he ascends the stairs from their basement.

"I'm here! Just checking some things downstairs. I heard from Tech and they're nearly done fitting a portal to your home, so soon, your neighbors may see you again." He leans over, and gives her a quick kiss.

"Really! That's wonderful! Do we need to move any of my stuff out of the way?" She asks.

He chuckles. "No, your stuff can stay where it is. Consider it storage for now. If you need to get your things, you merely think about entering *your* home when you open the door!"

"That's so *cool!*" She yawns. "I'd planned to hit the beach, but the weather isn't cooperating, even though the forecast said sunny and warm all day!" She gripes.

Colin gives her an amused look. "And just where did you see the forecast?" He asks.

"Where else? On one of the online weather sites." She says, as if he's being obtuse.

"*Love*, just because we are in the same geographic location as Vancouver Island, doesn't mean the weather will be the same here, as in the other world. So many factors to consider, including manmade ones." He reminds her.

"She looks puzzled and then gets it, "You mean like global warming and climate change?" She asks

"Yes, but even if they weren't factors, the currents and variables affecting weather are so complex, they would never match up entirely." He explains.

"*Damn!* I was really looking forward to a swim! It's been a *really*, long, hot day in Asheville. Hmmm, would you be horribly put out if I go to bed after dinner tonight? Sara wants me to pop in around 3 am our time, to talk about setting up a schedule, and a team to work with some long-termers after I'm done with the clinic in Asheville."

"That's fine. I've got to finish some reports. They've had me porting to tension hot-spots to get a feel for any impending problems. I need to sum it all up for our international team. Why don't I port out and grab something to eat?" He says and she nods. He ports out, but can hear her telepathic afterthought, *Surprise me with something good!*

Officially

Sue finds it hard to sleep, so after tossing and turning, she pulls out her laptop to check the local news and weather for Asheville. It's nearly 8 pm local time, so she pulls up the livestream of the 11 pm news on an Asheville TV station. Now that she's technically living in another reality, and on the other side of the continent, she makes it a point to keep track of 'local' Asheville news, so she stays in the loop because of work. She's only halfway listening when she hears:

> **A local elementary school teacher has gone missing. Miranda Bartholomew, of Skyland, was last seen by a fellow teacher Friday night at the Orange Peel. Barbara Robinson could not reach her during the weekend, and Ms. Bartholomew has not shown up at school either yesterday, or today. Police have checked her home, and it was locked with no sign of break-in or struggle. Her car was found parked in the Cox Avenue parking deck, which is where her friend said Ms. Bartholomew parked Friday night. If you've seen this woman or have any information about her whereabouts (Various pictures of Miranda flash on the screen) please contact the Asheville Police Department immediately.**

"Oh, Holy *Hell*! COLIN!" She shouts from the bedroom.

He ports in, sensing the urgency in both her voice and emotions. "What's wrong?"

"*We've* got a big problem. Miranda is now *officially* missing! As in, it made the freaking, local news report! I've got to get hold of Tess and Kari. *Holy Hell*! Colin, this means our worst fears for her might be true. *Jason* may have come for her." She suggests.

"You said Liz and Kari are in Norway, *right*? I'll pop over and let them know." He says and is about to port out, when Sue stops him.

"*No!* No porting in over there. Call Kari, or send her a private path. She doesn't want Liz stressed out any more than necessary." She explains.

Colin nods, and sits in a chair to focus on privately pathing Kari, while Sue reaches out to Tess. Sue grabs her cell and calls.

Tess answers and begins talking before Sue can say anything. "Hey, Sue, *perfect* timing! Been staring at my screen for hours going through potent..." Sue cuts her off.

"Sorry, no time for chit-chat! Did you watch the local, 11 pm news tonight?" She asks, anxiously.

"No, like I said, been staring at file after file for hours. Why? Is something *wrong*?" Tess gets a knot in her stomach at Sue's tone.

"Oh, *yeah! Very* wrong! It's official, Miranda's gone MIA, and it made the local news!" Sue blurts out.

Tess is quiet on the other end of the phone for a minute. "*Shit*, should I call Kari?"

"Colin's on it! Can we all meet at the office in a few? I think we may have to assume something's seriously wrong now, including the possibility Jason's got her." Sue rambles out.

They hang up, both get ready, and port into the office. Kari and Liz are already there, with Liz, looking frazzled. "Kari, Liz, I'm so *sorry* to have Colin disturb you in the middle of the night, but I didn't think this could wait."

They all head for the meeting area in Liz's office, settling in for a crisis session. Kari looks up at Sue. "You did the right thing. I understand you heard this on the local, Asheville news?"

"Yep, it was on the 11 pm broadcast, but they confirmed she's been missing since Friday night. She and a fellow teacher went to a show at The Peel, and that's the last anyone saw of her. They found her car in the Cox Avenue parking deck. So, whatever happened, must have happened between The Orange Peel and the parking deck, after about 10-11 pm, when the concert was over.

"*Okay*, give me a minute to make a call." Kari says, taking out her cell, and going out in the lobby so the others can talk. Ten minutes later, she comes back in, looking haggard. "*Alright*, I spoke to our guy in APD. He'll check the files in a few, but did say they think they caught a picture of her on a security camera from South Slope. There's been an increase in muggings lately, so they recently put up some new, hidden, surveillance cameras through there. I'm just waiting for him to check and send me the picture."

A couple of minutes pass, then Kari's message tone pings, and she pulls up the image. "*Helvete!*" She curses in Norwegian, and hands Liz her phone.

"Can't tell much from that!" Liz shakes her head, and hands the phone back to Kari.

"*Unfortunately*, I suspect Sue can confirm my suspicion." She passes Sue her cell, and she looks. Even though the images are grainy, she knows instantly who it is. "*Damn!* That's *Philipa* dragging *Miranda* into the shadows!"

Liz sits there, forehead leaning on the palms of her hands, shaking her head. She looks up, focusing on Colin and Sue. "If that's the case, we can assume Jason has her by now. I know you've already tried, but see if you two can get a fix on her mental signature now we know more. Granted, if Jason has her, his cloaking would explain why you haven't tracked her so far." She says with effort, as though her soul is exhausted.

Sue looks at Liz for a minute, sensing the depth of her exhaustion and depression, but doesn't say anything. She turns toward Colin, clearly worried about more than just Miranda."

He nods, knowing she's also worried about Liz, then says, "Let's go to my office, where it's quiet, and we can focus." Colin suggests.

They port over to his office, and she lies down on the sofa, with her head in his lap. "Think about what Miranda felt like when you were in her mind. Think about who she is, and then try to find her mind. I'll link with you. Maybe we can increase our sensitivity."

They try for about ten minutes. Colin can't sense her but Sue groans and says, "I *feel* her, but something's *wrong*. I sense *fear*, but no thoughts. I can't tell where she is, but she *is* alive. Something's off though, different."

The two of them get up, and head back to the others. Colin speaks up, "I couldn't feel her, but Sue could."

"I felt fear from her, and possibly pain. She just felt different, somehow. I can't put my finger on it though! Unfortunately, I couldn't get any idea where she might be." Sue's tone comes across as apologetic.

"It's alright. If Jason has her, what you're sensing could be due to his ability to cloak mental signatures, but if you're certain you *felt* her, at least we know she's alive." Kari sighs.

Liz mutters under her breath. "For now..." causing a chill to go down Sue's spine.

"Do you think he'll kill her?" Sue asks.

"He *has* killed before, but if he's taken Miranda, he must be planning to use her to ransom Millie out of 'hiding', or he's working under the assumption she, like Millie, is compatible. In which case, the 'differentness', may be connected with her being transformed, or in the process, thereof." Liz suggests.

Kari rubs Liz's arm. "Go on back, I can deal with this, *kjære*" Liz nods and ports out.

Kari turns to Sue. "Sorry, I could sense her getting overwhelmed. She insisted on coming. We had a good day yesterday, but this knocked the wind out of her anew." She looks down at her phone as her text message alert goes off again. "Our guy at APD is going to get the actual footage from the webcam. What he sent us before is just a still they pulled to try to ID them. I've also let him know something should 'happen' to the original before APD can do any digital enhancements on it."

Tess chimes in. "So, what do we do now?"

Kari shakes her head, "I don't know. If we can't find them, there isn't much we can do, not at this point. I'd say we should all try to get some rest for tonight, and brainstorm in the morning." She suggests.

"I'll try." Sue says, uncertain she'll be able to rest knowing Miranda's likely in Jason's clutches. "Maybe I'll dream about her."

"*Good* thought, Sue! *Literally*, keep an open mind, and let me know if you get anything. I'm going back to Liz for a few hours, but I'll be in by about 9 am." Kari sighs, and gets up.

Before she can port out, Sue interrupts her. "Liz's really hit bottom, hasn't she?"

Kari pauses and sits back down, letting out an exasperated sigh. "Yeah, she's been verging on this for a while. I think some of it's a delayed reaction from Jerusalem, itself, and the period where she thought she'd lost her brother. Even though we stopped all but the one bomb, she still feels like she failed. She's taken on a ton of guilt. She feels responsible for every single death, human and Apara alike."

Sue pulls Colin close, needing the contact. "Sometimes, I think the entire world is suffering from PTSD after Jerusalem. But you all, you were a part of it! And Liz was more than most, from what I've heard. If you want me to, I'll try to talk to her when she's ready. For now, let her rest as much as possible."

"*Thanks*, I'll keep that in mind. And *yes*, I think we've all been affected. How could we *not* be?" She gives everyone a half-hearted, exhausted smile, and ports out.

Sue turns back to Tess. "Any tips for helping Liz? You've known her a lot longer."

"Well, she's been working for the Benefactors for around 800 years, rarely taking a break. At one point, when she thought Peder was dead, she said something to me..." Tess focuses, trying to get all the words right.

> **"Even though we know we aren't truly immortal, time, and time again of getting wounded, shot or even put into stasis, our kind nearly always comes back. You get used to taking such injuries, or stasis incidents casually once it happens a few times. You never really expect to lose someone, because it so rarely happens, until now."**

"She lost friends she's known for hundreds of years. She nearly lost her brother, and I'm sure she hasn't stopped to work through her grief for any of her losses." Tess explains.

Colin inches even closer to Sue, putting his arm around her to comfort her. She thinks, *I've only been Apara for a few weeks, but I'm already thinking of being with Colin for a very long time. I don't know what I'll do if I ever lose him!* After a minute, she tells Tess, "I can see how that would be a problem. I'm falling into that trap myself. Now that I've got Colin back, and I'm *like* him, it feels so safe and secure now, like we'll always be together."

Tess sighs, and then says, "*Yeah*, I know. Part of me thinks that way, *but* I almost lost Marc in Jerusalem, so I'm still a bit iffy on the whole 'undying' part. If he and I hadn't formed a strong bond right before Jerusalem, I'd probably still be human, and alone."

"I'm beginning to understand why Colin suggested doing research into how death and grief, affect Apara." She says seriously and then gets a mischievous grin. "Of course, I suggested it would make a *kick-ass*, PhD dissertation, but he *nixed* that!" She nudges Colin with her shoulder to reassure him she's not serious.

Tess laughs and then says, "*Do* it *anyway!* Just don't *publish* it! Go through the process. The hypothesis, research, and writing it! The whole kit-and-kaboodle! You certainly can't be the Apara shrink for everyone, all the time! Others could learn from what you write."

Sue gets a quirky, half smile, and replies, "I just *might* do that! But after things settle down. Our priority, right now, is finding, and hopefully rescuing Miranda."

Tess yawns. "I've got to get back to Marc. I'll see you tomorrow, depending on when Kari gets in, and you're free from the clinic." She ports out.

Sue lets Sara know she's got to postpone their planning session. She and Colin say little, but are both deep in thought. Colin and Sue head home and to bed, holding each other until they fall asleep.

Reverse the polarity

Since Sue is working at the Clinic until 5 pm on Wednesday, she, Tess, and Kari plan to meet at 5:30 pm Asheville time, at the office. However, at approximately 12:15 pm, the three women all get an urgent path from Sara with a request to meet up there, as soon as possible. Kari asks Peder to stay with Liz, and ports in quickly, as does Tess. Sue leaves the clinic as soon as possible, cancelling her afternoon sessions. On her way out, she runs into her boss, Cheryl, a heavy-set woman with short, spiky, bleached hair, and oversized glasses.

"Sue, I *need* to talk to you." Cheryl says sternly.

Sue stops just short of the front door, takes a slow, controlled breath, and faces Cheryl. "I don't suppose it can *wait*? I need to get somewhere. It's an emergency."

"What *kind* of emergency?" Cheryl asks, tapping her foot impatiently.

"A cousin of mine is in the hospital. They just called, and they need me to come in as soon as possible. Some sort of psychological crisis, and they need me to help reach her." Sue dissembles on the fly.

"Don't they have their *own* therapists at the hospital to deal with her?" Cheryl purses her lips, annoyed.

"*Yes*, but my cousin isn't responding well to them. She *trusts* me. I'll work in my cancelled clients as quickly as I can, even if it means after hours arrangements, but this *truly* is an *emergency!*" Sue emphasizes. She thinks, *Hell with it! Next time, I'll just port out! Unfortunately, this is becoming a big problem. Between time zone differences, Apara responsibilities, and the clinic, I can't keep this pace up much longer.*

Cheryl shakes her head. "*Go*, but we're *not* done with this discussion. I realize you were sick for a while, but if you can't keep up with the pace, we may have to cut your hours until you're capable of carrying your load, or find someone else who *can*."

Sue's temper is a hair's breadth from boiling over, but she controls her anger and outward expression. She goes out the door, thinking, *I didn't damn-well have to come back at all, but I did, for my clients! Once I've seen them through this, Cheryl and her micromanaging ego can go to Hell!* She walks across the street and behind a building, porting away to Medical.

She arrives in the lobby atrium, and Sara's there waiting for her, pacing restlessly. When she senses Sue port in, she motions for her to follow her up the stairs. Sue rushes to catch up with the small woman. "*Damn*, Sara, you sure move quickly for your size!"

Sara stops, and faces Sue. "Kari told me Millie's sister is missing, and you think she's likely with Jason, right?"

"Yeah. We were supposed to meet later today for a planning session." Sue admits.

"Millie just woke up, inconsolable, from a nightmare. I suspect it was more than that, but only *you* can find out for certain!" Sara says, grabbing her by the wrist and moving rapidly down the hall with her.

"You think it's their link, don't you? Like they've reversed their link polarity?" Sue gasps out.

"I think it just might be, but I want *you* to check it out!" Sara picks up her pace as they get closer to Millie's room.

"Did she say anything? What did she dream?" Sue asks, worrying.

"I'd rather not bias you!" Sara says, and stops Sue right outside Millie's room.

Millie's distress oozes out of her room like some dark, pervading fog. "*Holy shit!*" Sue gets her empathic breath knocked out of her, and she must steady herself against the doorframe before going in. After a minute, she opens the door, and Millie's curled up in a ball, sobbing and shaking. She isn't responding to either Tess or Kari, so Sue sits on the edge of her bed, gently stroking Millie's back for a couple of minutes, reading her psychologically. Eventually, she speaks very softly to the distraught, young woman.

"Hey, Millie. I got here as soon as I could. Can you tell me what's wrong?" She asks gently, never stopping the stroking on her back. Millie's shaking violently, and nearly in shock.

Sue paths to the others in the room. *I'm going to have to try to reach her some other way. I just don't know how well it will work to go into her mind and dreams if she's awake, and since she's not human, like Miranda, I don't know if I can make her sleep by myself.* She gets up and goes over to a more comfortable chair in the room. She paths to Sara, *Is there any way you can calm her down? Maybe even make her sleep?* Sara nods and flips a switch on a small, spherical device next to Millie's bed.

Sara paths, *Don't worry, it's set to a frequency that will only affect Millie.* Sara shoos Tess and Kari out, and dims the lights in the room. Sue settles in and pictures tendrils of thought reaching out to Millie as she sleeps. In doing so, she feels those tendrils touch Millie's dream mind, and uses them to pull herself into her dreams. Sue watches and sees a woman's form on an old, stained mattress. She wonders if this is another of Millie's memories, as it's from the woman's perspective, until she notices the woman's arm lacks the tattoo on her wrist. Sue thinks, *Fuck! She's tapped into Miranda's mind. Miranda's ankle is bound by the same manacle and chain they'd used on Millie in the basement; only it's anchored to a heavy, metal ring in the floor.*

Sue says, "*Millie!* It's me, *Sue,* I'm here with you!" As she looks on, the view shifts, and she sees Miranda's body on the bed as a double image of the twin's faces, out of phase. Even though Miranda appears to be in distress, Millie is the one who speaks.

"Oh, *God!* He's changed her! She's like me now!" Millie cries out.

"*Holy Hell!* Millie, is this the same house you were in?" Sue asks.

The scene shudders as though there's an earthquake, and the image of Millie separates from her sister, and stands alone, looking down at her. She faces Sue. "Yes, this was my room once they let me out of the dungeon. Oh, *God!* We've got to get her out of here before...." She trails off, unable to project the words about what he might do to Miranda, and what he did to her. He must have taken her because of me! It's all *my fault!*" She wails, trying to lean in and comfort her sister, but Miranda can't feel her.

Sue puts her arm around Millie. "I know we've talked about this before, but do you have any idea where this house is? Maybe, if we knew, we could find a way to get her out of here."

Millie shakes her head. "No, he always ported me back and forth from there to wherever he needed me. He told me I couldn't do it myself. All I know is it must have been an old farmhouse because of the bins in the cellar. I also never heard any cars or anything, so it must have been far away from the main road."

Sue turns Millie to face her. "You're being here, connected to her, isn't doing either of you any good right now. Remember how we got out of the other dream? We walked up the stairs in the basement?" Millie nods, crying. Sue looks around the room for some symbolic exit. There's a window, but it's boarded up. "I want you to picture the window losing the wooden panels so we can see outside."

Millie focuses, and the boards rattle, but don't go away. Sue says, "Okay, let's try it a different way. Picture the wood being eaten by termites, becoming porous, and turning into sawdust." She tries, and slowly, the wood disintegrates, sawdust falling to the ground outside. "Now, we're going to go right through the glass. Just like we did with Jason in your other dream, and when we do, we'll be back in medical." She takes her hand, they walk toward the window, passing through it. Sue's eyes fly open, and she lets out a gasp, sitting up, back in medical. Millie's sleeping restlessly, unable to wake because of the wave generator. Sue slowly stands, feeling disoriented, but flips the off switch on the sphere. *Slowly*, Millie's eyes flutter open, but fill with tears as she sees Sue sitting next to her on the edge of the bed, gently rubbing her arm.

"He *did* it! That *jerk* changed Miranda! Oh, *God!* She must be *terrified!*" Millie sobs, her words interspersed with gasps of anguish.

Sue reaches over and pulls Millie into a hug. "I know, *hon*, I know. We're going to help her." She releases Millie from the hug, letting her lie down again, still sobbing. She paths to the others, **As suspected, Jason's turned Miranda, too. We need a plan; how to find, and rescue her, but I don't want to leave Millie alone right now.**

Sue senses the others' anger and frustration flaring to new heights. Sara opens the door and comes in, gently patting Sue on the back, and motioning her to move out of the way. She approaches Millie and gently holds her face in her hands. "*Rest...*" Millie struggles, but Sara's mind is too strong for her, and she falls into a dreamless sleep. Sara flips the wave generator back on to keep her out.

She looks at Sue. "*Well*, come on. She'll be fine for now, but we need to figure out what we can do to help her sister!"

The Invenir

The four women head to a conference room near Sara's office. Marc is waiting for them, and sits up straight as they come in.

"Marc, what are you doing here?" Tess asks as she sits next to him.

"Sara asked me to come. She thought my experience might help." He says, gently patting her knee.

Kari settles in by Sue, while Marc, Tess, and Sue stare at Sara expectantly from their seats around the small conference table.

Sara addresses Sue. "So, you've confirmed our worst suspicions?" She inquires.

Sue shifts uneasily. "I believe so. While it could have been a dream, it felt like the other dreams I had with Millie, except there was an added layer, which I believe, was Miranda's mind connected to Millie's."

"What did you sense from her?" Sara asks, carefully trying to elicit details from Sue's recollection.

Sue concentrates, eyes unfocused, as she looks back into her dream memories. "She was in pain, and upset, but I didn't sense the same overtones I got from Millie. I didn't sense he'd assaulted her, but she was clearly having a hard time coping with it all. I got the impression she's been there for a while." Sue shivers. "She was starving, like she needed to feed and hadn't. It was like Millie's dream you witnessed."

Sara curses in some dead language no one else grasps, but they all get the gist of it. "Yes, that would fit. Change someone, withhold their first feeding to make it more desperate, and traumatic, but also to bind her to him by stopping the misery."

"That was my impression, too. I didn't see anyone else there, so I'm guessing isolating her while she's in need is their intention." Sue ponders aloud.

Tess clears her throat, and then says. "Is there any way we can find her? I know he cloaks, but I don't want to see her victimized by that jackass!"

"If you had some control over your out-of-body talent, we might be able to use that, but I'm assuming it's is not an option at present?" Sara raises one eyebrow and looks pointedly at Tess.

"Unfortunately, no. I mean, it sounds like the same place I've been to astrally, but I've never gotten a fix on the location. I'm always just there, and then I'm home." Tess says apologetically.

Sara turns to Sue again. "I know Millie hasn't been able to give us a location. There's a way I could get there with her, but it would be too risky."

"Like what? What could you do?" Sue asks, feeling the urgency to not only rescue Miranda, but protect Millie from reliving Jason's abuse through her link with her sister.

Kari clears her throat and interjects, "When we port, we're guided by our minds. We slip into the membrane or veil between the realities, and out where we want to go. Newer transformees usually stick to places they've been to, or know, and have a sense of where that place is, just as you pointed out when we first realized Jason was the one who killed the three women in Atlanta, Richmond, and Charlotte; all places he'd lived at some point. However, we don't have to know where a place is on a map or relative to us. We can focus on people, landmarks, or even remotely viewed locations. In addition, any place we've been, we can find again, even if we don't know where that place is. Our minds keep track of where we've been through a GPS like ability, so even if we only picture it, we can port there again as our unconscious minds know where it is."

Tess's face lights up with understanding. "So, you're saying Millie could port back there since she's been there before?"

"Yes, she could, though he apparently hasn't taught her to port, so she wouldn't be able to do it on her own." Sara explains.

"Okay, so call out the troops and we'll all port in and get Miranda out and catch the lot of them!" Sue exclaims.

316

"Unfortunately, along with our ability to port, we develop the ability to sense when someone is porting in, meaning Jason would have time to grab Miranda, and he and the others could port out and re-cloak before we could get there, making us lose any chance of finding them that way." Kari admits. "It's possibly Millie could home in on Miranda, but only if Jason lets his cloaking slip."

Marc is tapping his fingers on the table. "While we need to capture Jason, Philipa, and Alice, I'd say our priority is getting Miranda out safely and as soon as possible."

"Agreed! I also don't want to risk taking Millie there to find her sister, on the chance Jason may somehow reclaim her. I suspect that may be part of why he took and turned Miranda, to use her as leverage to get Millie back." Sara elaborates while making notes on her tablet.

"Do you think he knows Millie's with us now?" Sue asks.

"I don't know. He may, but he may just think she ran away after being sent out to watch Colin and you in town. My guess is he had to teach her some cloaking before she was sent on her mission, so he may assume she's hiding somewhere, cloaked. It's hard to know, but that would fit with using Miranda as leverage to get her to come back." Sara sighs, frustrated by their current impotence in rescuing Miranda.

Tess sits back in her chair, looking frustrated. "Can't you just pluck the location out of her mind?"

"*Alas!* No! It doesn't work that way. It's not like getting longitude and latitude and writing it down. I could go with her, and then I'd know too, but I can't take the location from her unless she knows, consciously, where it is. I do, however, have an idea, and that's why I've asked Marc here as he worked to find the Jerusalem bomb." Sara nods to Marc. "I know you're not a true Invenir, but I'd like you to try to use the connection between Millie and Miranda to see if you can find her."

"That's not something I'm good at. I can sometimes track objects, but not people I don't know." Marc admits.

Tess and Sue look at each other, confused, then Tess inquires, "What's an Invenir?"

Sara gives her a half smile. "Sorry, that's an old term for a Finder or Locater; someone whose gifts include being able to find things or people. Some of them specialize in finding people, and they often work with the law enforcement around the world, or other ways where their skills can be hidden as 'good detective work'."

"What's the big deal then? Can't you just call one of them up and put them on her trail?" Tess asks, confused by Sara's hesitation.

Marc puts a hand on Tess's gesticulating hand and pulls her to face him. "*Love*, we lost most of our strongest Finders in Jerusalem. They were the ones on the front line, looking for the bomb."

"Weren't there any in the other cities?" Tess's voice is tinged by frustration, bordering on desperation.

"Yes, but once those locales were determined safe, they joined the rest of us in Jerusalem." He holds her hand in both of his, trying to send calming waves to settle her down. "In fact, that's one reason we haven't been able to find Jason. Yes, he is proficient at cloaking, but a few of those we lost were talented enough to see through it and find him."

Sue looks from Marc to Sara. "There have to be some left, right?"

Sara nods slowly. "There are some. Most are currently not on active duty as those who survived were some of the most severely injured, physically, as well as psychologically." She glances toward Sue, as they've been discussing working with some of said Apara. "That being said, Dimitrios may be up to the task." She gives Marc a questioning look.

Marc nods slowly. "He may be, at that."

Sara looks back at the two confused, young Apara. "Dimitrios is one of our older Apara. He's been a recluse for nearly 300 years. He lives on a small island between Greece and Turkey."

"300 years? Do they let you all just go off on your own like that?" Sue inquires while looking back and forth between Marc and Sara.

"He's a unique case. He was born in Pompeii, turned, and sent around the region as a philosopher and teacher, though one of his strongest skills is being a Finder. He was in Egypt when Vesuvius erupted in 79 A.D. He sensed something was wrong, but not what. By the time he ported back, most of Pompeii had been destroyed, and everyone he knew was dead. He took some time to grieve and eventually went back to his duties. He was living in France, when they rediscovered Pompeii in 1748; that's where I first met him. It brought back a lot of his trauma. He was thoroughly burnt out and petitioned to be released. He's been living on an island since then, but comes out occasionally, for worthy causes." Marc explains.

Tess touches Marc on the arm gently. "Do you think he'd consider this a worthy cause?"

"Very likely. He lost his sister in the eruption. I suspect saving a lost and endangered sibling might just appeal to him." He nods and says to Sara. "I'll go." He says and ports out.

"You two should go get some rest. I'll summon you when we're ready to plan further." Sara says, and the two women port to their homes.

***

A couple of hours later, Marc ports in at home and finds Tess on the sofa, asleep, with Mable sleeping on her chest. He lightly brushes her hair out of her face and she begins to rouse, dislodging an annoyed cat. "You're back? Did you get him?" She yawns, stretches, and halfway sits up.

Marc lets out a small chuckle. "Yes, after some major convincing! The situation with Millie and Miranda reminds him of his sister. He's at Medical with Sara. She asked me to collect you and bring you back. Colin and Sue are heading there too, as well as Kari, Liz, and Peder."

"Liz is coming in? Is she up to it?" Tess's face is full of concern as she thinks about how despondent Liz has been.

"Kari wasn't going to tell her, but Liz picked up on it anyway, and insisted on coming." Marc reaches a hand down to her and helps her up. "We'll grab a quick meal and then head back to medical. Do you need to feed?" He asks, out of habit.

"No, I did that before I took a nap."

***

Forty-five minutes later, the conference room is full, including one man neither Tess nor Sue knows, but they assume he must be Dimitrios, a man of middle stature, with dark, wavy hair, and doe-brown eyes with long lashes. His features are angular, and yet there's a softness to his expression. He's uneasy with so many people around him, and he's left a wide buffer of space around his chair. Tess and Sue both sense his psychological fatigue and loneliness, and look at each other, knowing they both have the same impression.

Liz stands, trying to look her normal, business-like self, something those who know her well can see through, but with Dimitrios there, she doesn't want to add her own depression to the mix. "For those of you who do not know our guest, this is Dimitrios." Liz extends her hand to him and he nods quietly, unused to the attention. "We've been discussing the situation and think we have a plan. Dimitrios thinks he can piggy back Millie's link with Miranda if you, Sue, and he link using psiamp."

Sue shifts uneasily at the thought of letting some strange man link with her mind, but Colin paths to her. *Don't worry, love, Dimitrios knows what he's doing. He'll merely use you as a bridge into Millie's telepathic linked dream with Miranda. I've known him almost as long as Marc has, he won't peek at anything he shouldn't!* Colin rubs her back reassuringly.

After a brief pause, Sue nods to Liz, who then continues. "This is stage one. We link in Dimitrios to help us find Miranda's location. Tess, I know you can't control your astral travels yet, but I want you there as well, under a *light* dose of psiamp. Maybe you'll get carried there in Dimitrios' and Sue's wake, which could potentially give us backup information." Liz nods to Sara to continue.

"Remember how you linked with Annie, and she pulled you out of body?" Sara recalls.

"Yes, but that was out of my control." Tess says uncertainly.

"I know. The initial part was, but I was able to talk you through it so you could separate your mind and see the area around Riverview Station, so you could give us location information like landmarks, descriptions and so on. I'm hoping this will recreate that incident, but this time, we'll be ready for it." Sara eyes her, and Tess knows Sara will not let her back out.

They plan for a couple of hours, and break down the plan into stages: Locate Miranda, rescue Miranda, and if possible, catch Jason and his two cohorts. It's now late in the day, and they take a break so everyone can get some rest for a few hours, and come back around 2 am local time. In the meantime, a still sedated Millie is moved to a larger room with three additional beds.

Once everyone is back, Sara begins. "Okay, Sue, you'll be linking with Millie, so you take the first bed. Dimitrios, you take the one next to Sue. And Tess, you're on the other side of Millie in that bed." She motions where each of them should go. "Sue, I'd like you to try, as you did this afternoon, to link with Millie without any psiamp. Once a link is established, I'll administer the psiamp to you, Tess, and Dimitrios. Marc, I want you to sit in the chair behind Tess. You'll have to help her if she goes out-of-body, as I did when she went to Annie's aide."

Marc nods curtly. "Will do." He moves behind Tess's head and gently kisses her forehead before settling into the chair behind her.

Sara dims the lights and reduces the wave generator enough to allow Millie to connect with her sister again, but not wake up. Liz, Kari, Peder, and Colin are on standby in the hallway, and Sara stays in the room to coordinate and monitor.

Sue uses relaxation imagery to calm herself and enter a state similar to sleep physically, but she's aware of her surroundings. She visualizes those same tendrils of energy she used earlier, touches Millie's mind, and is drawn into her dream world. She sees the same bedroom, but it's dark. There's blood on the grimy blanket on Miranda, and somehow, she knows it's human blood, and it's fresh, not previously bagged blood. Her mind flashes on the original dream Sara intercepted from Millie, and the terrified young woman he threw to her to feed upon, knowing he'd likely done something similar. She moves over toward the bed and can see Miranda's eyes are puffy from crying. Sue concentrates and watches for Millie to separate from her sister as before. She thinks, *that's odd. It's almost like a triple image.* The first image glows, vibrates, and fissions away from Miranda's sleeping form. It's Millie watching her sister sleep.

"Millie, it's me, Sue. Do you hear me?" Sue wants to reach out to her, but knows she needs to be patient.

The now separate form of Millie sighs, and backs up next to Sue. "She's not in any pain. She's dreaming too. After a minute, Sue feels Millie's tone change as she says. "She's dreaming about me!"

Sue looks back at Miranda, and sees an out of phase, double image, but this time, it fissions off and it's Miranda. The world blurs and changes, and the three of them are all sitting in Sue's office in the clinic. Miranda's back where she was as a client, and Millie is standing with Sue.

Miranda's eyes grow large as she exclaims, "Melinda!" and goes over and hugs her sister like she'll never let her go.

While the two women reconnect, Sue sits in her usual office chair and looks around. She thinks, *This is unexpected. It feels real, but we're not in my office, not really.* She realizes her office *is* a safe space, where she's in charge. She swivels her chair to face the twins. "Millie, Miranda, I don't know how much time we have, so please have a seat and focus." She motions, and sees there are now two seats, one for each of them, instead of the usual single chair.

The two women sit, and Miranda looks at Sue oddly. "I know you, and this place. The Clinic, right?"

"Sort of. We're all sharing a dream where we're currently in my office, but it's just an illusion. It's a safe space where we can talk, but I don't know how long this will last. Miranda, I'm physically *with* your sister. She's safe, but we need to find you now." Sue explains, hurriedly.

Miranda grows stressed. "What do you mean, not here. Where am I then?" But before Sue can answer, the windows looking out onto the street darken and change, becoming a window into the dark room where Miranda still sleeps. A tear rolls down her cheek. "I *don't* want to go back *there!*"

"Miranda, look at me, not the window." Sue says, and Millie takes her sister by the hand.

"Miranda, listen to Sue. She's trying to help us." Millie urges her sister to focus back on Sue, and not the Hell she'd temporarily escaped from.

Miranda looks at her twin and puts her other hand over Millie's, holding tightly around them, and looks her in the eye. "Please help me!" She pleads, both with her words and her eyes.

"Miranda, I'm trying to help you, so I need you to listen to me. You and your sister share a telepathic link. We know what he did to you, and now you're changed, your link with Millie should be even stronger than before. We're trying to find you, and think we can, *using* your shared link, but you need to be centered back where you are physically, so when we leave this place, and you go back, I want you to focus on where you are." Sue emphasizes.

"But I don't *know* where I am!" Miranda blurts out desperately.

"I know, but I want you to focus on yourself, in your bed. Center your mind on being there wherever there is. A part of you knows, even if you can't show us on a map. That will be our beacon to follow. And Miranda, remember, you *are not alone*, no matter how much Jason wants you to feel alone. Your bond with Millie is strong, and I want you to embrace it, knowing, in your heart, she's with you, as you were with her when she was going through this." Sue pauses, waiting for Miranda to process it all.

"*Okay, please* find me *soon!* I don't like how he looks at me, like I'm his to play with! One woman isn't much better! The other one, Alice, helped me. Told me not to fight him when he changed me. Earlier today, she told me what he and the other woman did to her when she resisted." She looks wearily back at the room through the office window, aghast at Alices tales. After a minute, she says, "I'm ready to go back." She says, wiping her tears and leaning over to hug her sister again.

Millie looks her in the eye. "We're going to get you out of there. I promise. It may take a little time, but we *will*! We'll meet in our dreams in the meantime."

Sue nods and the office dissolves in swirls of smoke and they're back in Miranda's room. Miranda's lying in bed, with Millie beside her, looking on. They feel an odd, warm feeling that grows into a presence. Sue knows it's Dimitrios and knows he has the location. "Millie, you can stay with her if you like, I have to leave now." Sue says, and faces the window to leave again, feels a familiar mind, and knows Tess is connected to them as well, though she can't see her. She pauses until she no longer feels Tess and Dimitrios, and wakes up in the hospital room. The first thing she sees is a wide grin on Sara's face and knows they were successful.

Strategy

Once everyone's fully awake, coherent, and the psiamp has worn off, they gather in the conference room. Liz stands and all eyes fall on her. "Alright, what did we find out?"

Sue begins. "It's the same place they kept Millie, and currently have her in Millie's bedroom, not the basement. It looks like an abandoned farmhouse, as there's some old furniture in it, likely a place where the owners died, and the property went to either the family or the state, but the house isn't worth renovating, so it's just been sitting there. Some of the windows are boarded up. He's got a generator hooked up for basic power. Other than that, I'm certain Miranda understands we're doing what we can to rescue her."

Liz turns to Tess. "Were you able to go out of body?"

"Yeah, Sue's right. It's an abandoned farmhouse. It's two stories tall with a root cellar. Most of the windows are boarded up, and part of the roof is sunken in. The house is far away from the road, and there's a lot of overgrown bushes, trees and grass which obscure the view from the road. I did see either a small river or a large creek, and mountains nearby. The building itself has a stone foundation, and is otherwise wood. There are two chimneys, one at either end of the house. The wood is painted white, but a lot has peeled or been worn away. There's a porch around two sides of the building." She re-counts as though she's taking a tour of the place.

"And you're sure you were there?" Liz queries.

"*Yes*! It felt like the time with Annie, just less distress." Tess confirms.

Sue speaks up. "Liz, I could feel her, though I couldn't see her. I felt Dimitrios, so I think that part worked."

Liz smiles subtly. "Dimitrios, do you have a location for us?"

The man shifts in his seat and clears his throat. His voice is gravelly and quiet, as though he rarely uses it. "Yes, they're approximately eight kilometers northwest of..." He looks at a map in front of him. "Lake Lure, North Carolina. I will share the coordinates with you telepathically, after the meeting." He looks uneasy being the center of attention, even briefly.

"Alright! It sounds like we've got a location. As Marc suggested earlier, the priority is to get Miranda out of there. If we get any of the others, that's a plus, but the main goal is her safe recovery. I'll be sending in some of our security guys to locations nearby on the chance there's any conflict or an opportunity to catch any of the others. All of them will be carrying neutralizer dart guns, so if all hell breaks loose, *try* to stay out of their line of fire!" Liz looks from one person to the next around the table.

Tess chuckles. "I *can* vouch for that! You don't want to get neutralized, and you *don't* want to deal with the after-effects of the antidote!"

Marc reaches around her back and pulls her a little closer to him, knowing how much of a struggle she's had regaining control after her own experience with the antidote. He turns to regard Liz. "What about an extraction team?"

Liz sighs. "I'd like to keep that as small as possible. I spoke to Amy before the meeting. She's volunteered, as her military training included stealth tactics, as well as search and recovery."

"I'll volunteer." Marc says, and Tess gives him a stare of horror, remembering Marc's last encounter with Jason, and the sound of his vertebrae shattering when Jason broke his neck. He paths to her, *Love, he caught me off guard that time; I'll be ready this time, and if I beat the shit out of the little weasel, I'm sure you won't exactly mind.* He sends the mental equivalent of a wicked grin, which quells Tess's unease.

Liz nods to Marc. "Great, I'll work on recruiting the rest of the team." She paths to Tess before she can speak up. *No, Tess, we're not putting you in that situation, not with your abilities still unstable, and your prior interactions with Jason.* She gives her a long stare with one eyebrow raised until Tess slumps down in her chair, sulking.

Sue is quiet at first, but they speak up. "Liz, someone she knows should be on the team, and seeing the only Apara she knows are her sister and myself..." She takes a deep breath and glances at Colin, knowing he'll probably object. "I'd like to go. Miranda knows me, both from the Clinic and from the dream meeting." She feels Colin tense up, and hears him path to her. *I don't want you anywhere you might get hurt! You're so new to this, he could easily get the advantage over you.*

Liz senses Colin's unease, but says, "She's right. Someone Miranda knows and trusts should be there, and it can't be her sister, not without risking Jason ending up with them both." She admonishes him.

"But Jason was after Sue as well! What's to keep him from grabbing her?" Colin's tone has a frantic edge.

"A couple of things; first, he didn't turn Sue, but he did turn Millie, and therefore sees her as 'his property'." She shakes her head at the antiquated attitude. "In addition, if Sue's going, so are you! *You* can play bodyguard." She gives him a lopsided grin, and waits for his response.

He looks down at the table, rubbing the bridge of his nose to ease his tension. "*Alright.*" He tells Sue. "I don't want you more than an arm's length away from me, do you understand me?"

Sue rolls her eyes. "Yes." She plays as though she's annoyed, but she knows he's only being protective because he loves her.

Liz sits back down, but continues to speak. "Marc, Colin, and Sue, Amy's waiting for you at the office. You four need to plan strategy and contingency plans with her." She turns her stare on Tess. "I need to meet with you and Dimitrios to get any location information you two have." Dimitrios is sitting next to Liz, so she gently lays a hand on his arm, and he almost flinches, being unused to physical contact after so many years alone on his island.

"Once I have the coordinates from you, if you choose, you can go back home."

He's quiet for a few seconds, then makes eye contact with Liz. "No, I would like to stay and help." Liz pats his arm with understanding. He's been alone so long, and while still uncomfortable around these people, it's been a long time since he's felt useful.

Marc, Sue, and Colin port out to meet with Amy. Liz motions for Tess to come closer. "I'd like to review your impressions, if you'll let me?" Tess nods, and sits in the now empty chair on the other side of Liz. Liz gently tips Tess's chin up to make proper eye contact, and Tess feels her slip into her mind. She trusts Liz as much as Marc, so there's no resistance, and no unconscious mental shields slamming into place. "Thanks, I'd like you to go over to Marc and the others. Share these images with them. If need be, share them with Marc, and he can pass them on."

"Will do." Tess vanishes, leaving Liz and Dimitrios alone in the room. Even Kari and Peder have gone off to talk to Sara.

"Liz closes her eyes, and Dimitrios gently touches her right temple with his fingertips. A flood of images, mental coordinates, and a visual location on a mental map flood her mind." She opens her eyes again and gives him a slight bow. "Thank you for helping us. I know you prefer to keep to yourself, but after Jerusalem, we have few Invenirs left, or who are in any shape to help us."

"It's my honor to help." He pauses. "I've missed companionship, so am happy my services were needed, but *don't* tell Marc! I made him grovel for my help!" He says with a twinkle in his eye.

"You know, you're always welcome! You're still Apara, and there is *always* a place for you!" She says, but he can sense the sadness and stress underneath Liz's normal, diplomatic leader façade.

"And you, Liz? I sense you wish to petition to be released, as I did." He covers one of her hands on the table.

"I'm just tired. The last year's been the most hellacious of my 800 plus years among the Apara! I've still got a few centuries before I need *that* kind of break, but some days are *harder* than others." She admits.

328

"And yet your family grows." He gives her a knowing look.

"Yes, it's good to have some of my charges back under my 'roof', as well as their partners." She admits.

"You finally got the eternal bachelor to settle down?" He laughs.

Liz chuckles. "Yes, Marc finally found someone who broke through his walls! She's quite special too. A bit of a prodigy, in fact."

"Yes, I touched her mind while we were all connected. I cannot say I've ever met someone quite like her." He admits.

"None of us have. She was misplaced in our database, but she found us anyway." Liz explains.

"You must not let this...this aura...this mood drag you down so much! Even with all the death and destruction, you have sparkling, new minds and energy around you! Take a break, care for yourself, and Kari, of course! But never forget to see the good and only see the bad! That is what I did! I've been a stupid ass and moped on my island for nearly 280 years! Perhaps it's time I consider coming back out from retirement, if you will have me?" He grins.

"Yes, of course! We *need* you! After this, I think I will get Tess, Sue, and Kari to keep an eye out for new, potential Invenirs, and who better to teach them than you!" She insists.

Ready, set: wait

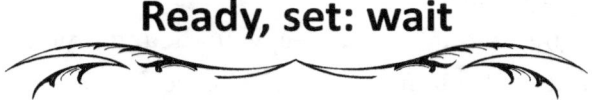

With Miranda's location identified, a team, and a plan ready to go, all they need is the right opportunity. To reduce the risk of Jason or the others sensing them porting in, grabbing Miranda, and disappearing into a sea of mental signatures, they must wait until Jason, and preferably all of them except Miranda, are out of the house. The fewer in the house with Miranda, the greater the chance they can get in and out with her.

Sue and Tess meet with Millie, who, while still upset Jason has turned her sister, is reassured by the renewed mental connection between herself and Miranda. Even after the telepathic dream ends, she senses a presence she's always known was Miranda in her mind, stronger than ever now they are both Apara.

"Millie, we need you to do something." Sue says.

"*Anything!*" She says enthusiastically, finally feeling safe and among friends.

"Next time you link with your sister in a dream, we need you to get her a message. We need to know if they ever leave her alone in the house." Sue explains.

"They left me sometimes, but usually, either Alice or Philipa was in the house to babysit, though they rarely ever sat in the room or watched me. Ask her. I don't know if they will do the same now, after I 'escaped'." Millie sighs.

Tess sits there, looking at Millie's Aura and can perceive a tendril of energy tapering off and connecting, loosely, with another, though she can't see where it's coming from. After a minute, she asks Millie. "You all had this link even when you were human, right?"

"Yeah, we'd often know when each other was sad, afraid, or needed help. Sometimes we'd finish each other's sentences, stuff like that." She shrugs.

"Sue told me Miranda could feel you, though it was weaker and different after we brought you here. The weaker is due to you being here in Sanctuary. Can you feel your sister in your mind?" Tess inquires, giving her a sideways glance.

"Yes, it was weaker for a while, and it almost faded to nothing while she was changing. But since that last share dream, I've felt a strong, mental connection. No words. I just feel her there, and it feels awesome!" A tear rolls down her cheek as she immerses herself in the connection.

Tess sits quietly, chewing on her lower lip, thinking. "Try reaching out mentally, like you were shouting across a field to Millie. Ask her if she can hear you. Maybe we don't have to wait until you two dream to find out when she's alone!"

"Good idea! Go on, lie back, and relax. I find it helps me when I picture the person's face, which, in your case, *shouldn't* be a problem!" She smirks.

Millie lies back on her double pillows and closes her eyes. She pictures Miranda across a field, like Tess suggested, and shouts, *MIRANDA! CAN YOU HEAR ME?*

She doesn't get an answer, but can sense a confused reaction from Miranda. "I think she heard me, but she's not answering."

"Can you sense any distress from her?" Sue asks, wondering if she might be dealing with Jason, or if he might somehow be stopping her from responding.

"No more than I have been." Millie shrugs her shoulders.

"Okay, try this. Call her name, tell her it's you, she's not crazy, and tell her something that would make her certain it's really you." Sue urges her to try again.

Millie closes her eyes, and pictures Miranda's face, her long hair hanging loose, and she's still manacled to the floor in the bedroom. *MIRANDA! It's Melinda! Millie. Remember when we were seven, and we kept tricking Ms. Frances in school about which of us was which? I think we nearly gave her a mental breakdown! Please, Miranda, answer me! I'm trying to reach you telepathically, without dreaming!*

After about fifteen seconds, Millie hears a tentative, *Millie? Is that really you? I thought I could feel you, but wasn't sure.*

Yes! It really, truly is me! We're working on rescuing you, but I need you to do me a favor. We need you to tell us if Jason and the others or just Jason, leaves the house. I'm sure he goes out to feed! He'll sometimes go out for several hours. Sometimes he'll take Philipa along with him, occasionally Alice, but often just him. Next time he goes out, try to reach out like this and tell me, okay? Millie paths.

I'll try! But what if he hears me talking to you like this? Miranda worries.

Millie asks Sue and Tess, "Can Jason or the others hear us when we talk this way?"

Tess replies. "If you aren't careful. You need to focus on each other, and imagine it being a narrow line or thin wire between the two of you, and only you. It can take some practice, but it's how you path privately."

Millie relays the info to Miranda, and they agree they will stay in touch, and Miranda will tell her when Jason's gone, and especially if she thinks he'll be gone for a while. They break connection, but still feel the reassuring presence of each other in the back of their minds.

Tess turns to Sue. "Now we're all on standby until the time is right." They say goodbye, and each go home to their partners, and coordinate with Liz and Amy as well.

GO!

They track Jason's comings and goings for a few days. So far, he's mostly ignored Miranda, and makes Alice go in with food, and other things, or take her to the bathroom. Miranda and Alice form a bond. Not friendship, but more like co-hostages, or co-victims. He makes Miranda feed from him, making her dependent on him.

Jason tries posting notes on Millie's Facebook page and even in online newspapers she might read like the ones in Asheville or Charlotte. Things like 'Hello, Millie, just wanted to let you know Miranda misses you' or 'Miranda says hi.', all in the hope she'll come back to him. In his mind, she is still his property, because he made her what she is.

Saturday night rolls around, and Jason's restless. He's had no response or even signs of life from Millie's social media. He calls for Philipa. "Let's go hit Charlotte! Find something to do, as well as someone to do, and feed on!" He gets a slimy grin on his face.

A few minutes later, Philipa comes out, wearing make-up, and her 'party clothes', as she calls them. As she would put it, 'Something to attract all the drooling, testosterone-morons!'

Jason commands, "Alice! *Come* here!"

Alice comes in quietly, subserviently. "Yes, Jason." She stares at the ground or her fingers instead of looking him in the eye.

"We're going out for the evening. You're responsible for Miranda, got it? If anything happens, or if she somehow escapes, you'll be punished." He gives her a slimy, lascivious grin. He knows she understands the implications.

"Yes, I understand." She stands there until they port out, then goes to her room and crawls under her filthy bed, scattering dust bunnies the size of hamsters everywhere. She moves a few under-bed totes with clothes and pulls out a plastic shoebox. It's her stash of 'sweets and treats' she'd 'lifted' the last time Jason took her out to feed, and gave her a little time to herself. She knew she couldn't get away. He'd find her and punish her, but she could do something to treat herself, and that was going to the nearest source of candy, Oreos, or sour cream and onion chips. She hides most of her stash under her bed, but leaves some out, which Philipa often purloins for herself, not realizing Alice's real stash is under the bed. She backs out and brushes off any mega-dust bunnies clinging to her clothes. With a grin, she rushes over to Miranda, hiding the box behind her back.

"*Miranda*! I've got a surprise for you!" She grins ear-to-ear and hops on Miranda's bed, sits cross-legged, and pulls the box out. "*Surprise*! Jason and Philipa went out for the night and left me to take care of you. I thought we could share some of my stash!" She pulls off the lid, and it's packed full of sugary decadence.

Miranda imagines this is something some of her students might have hiding under their beds, or in their closets, and almost cries. She tentatively takes a treat, and is about to stick it in her mouth when she realizes what Alice said. "They've gone out?"

"*Yup!* And when they go out on a Saturday night, it usually means a good three, four, maybe even five hours with *no* Jason or Philipa!" She grins and takes a treat.

Three to five hours? It's time! She thinks and sticks the candy in her mouth, and reaches out to her sister. *"Millie! It's time!!"* She tries to keep it short in case Alice might pick up on it. She likes Alice, and mostly trusts her, but knows she's afraid of Jason, and doesn't know if she'll tell him or not.

Millie paths back, *Time? Are you alone?*

Not alone. Alice is here. Jason and Philipa went out on the town. Alice says usually three to five hours! Miranda paths excitedly, but tries not to give anything away with her expression.

Alice pushes the box toward her. "Have some more!"

She takes a couple more and says, "Thanks!" smiling.

She hears in her mind. *Hold tight! They'll be there soon. Look for Sue. She'll be there with others! You can trust them!*

Fewer than ten minutes pass when Amy, Marc, Sue, and Colin appear in the room, startling the women, but mostly Alice. Marc creates a mental shield around Alice to keep her from reaching out to Jason, assuming her reaction hasn't already alerted him.

336

Sue reaches over and hugs Miranda. "Go with my friend, Amy, she'll take you to Millie!"

"But my leg!" She points at the manacle.

Amy gives her a big grin. "Not a *problem*, girl!" She grabs Miranda's hand and ports her out, leaving the manacle behind, still closed.

Sue turns to Alice, who is terrified, though Sue isn't sure if she's terrified of them, or of what Jason will do to her. "Alice, *right*?" Alice nods, trembling nervously.

"We're going to get you out of here. Come on!" Sue extends her hand. All the while, Colin's on guard in case Jason or Philipa returns, and Marc maintains his shield around Alice.

"*No*! He'll just find me and hurt me again!" Alice sobs frantically.

"We'll take you where you'll be safe from him. I *promise!*" Sue says, still holding out her hand.

"Alice hesitates, but takes it, flinging herself forward to embrace Sue like she might never let go.

Colin paths rapidly. *Need to leave, someone's porting in!*

Before they can port out, Millie's red-haired demon, Philipa, ports in. She and Jason felt something from Alice, followed by mental silence. Jason was distracted with a very willing blonde woman, and told Philipa to go check. Now Philipa is in the room, her eyes focus on the all too familiar face with hair matching her own. "Susie! So, it *was* you!" She spits out, using her childhood nickname, lets out a yell, and lunges for Sue and Alice.

Sue instinctively ports away from Alice for a split second; enough to dislodge her grip, phases back in and pushes her into Marc's arms. He ports out with her. She knows the moment she's been waiting for has come. Her arrogant, bullying cousin will never see it coming. She pulls back her arm, and hits Philipa in the jaw just as she reaches her, moving at full lunging speed. Philipa is flung backwards several feet, knocking her head into an old, iron radiator. She's disoriented, but still conscious, but so is Sue, from the impact. She lands on the floor, stunned.

Colin lunges toward Sue on the floor, ports her to safety, leaving Philipa alone to explain to Jason how she'd lost both of his other charges.

A few seconds later, Philipa, still sprawled on the floor from Sue's punch, senses multiple people porting into the house. As she's porting out, a female Apara with short, dark, curly hair ports in, and she feels something jab her arm before completely entering Limbo. She's disoriented, but exits Limbo to normal Earth reality near where she'd left Jason, losing control and careening into several garbage cans in the alley, disturbing Jason's feeding and fun. She's unimaginably weak, and has trouble moving. Jason lets his 'meal' sag to the ground, unconscious, and stomps over to berate Philipa, stopping when he sees the dart in her right arm.

"What the *fuck* happened at the house?" He growls as he pulls the dart out of her arm, careful not to touch the tip.

"My *fucking* cousin and an ambush happened." She says, weakly.

"Your *cousin?*" He crosses his arms and looks skeptical.

"Yeah, *Susan Burns*! I wondered when you mentioned her name as a target, but hadn't seen... since...teens." Philipa struggles to stay conscious.

"What was she doing at the farmhouse?" He drags her up on her feet, but her legs just fold under her weight.

"She, and others took... took Alice... and Miranda. Then others... came. Got away but... but..." She points at the dart in Jason's hand, no longer able to make her vocal cords work.

As Jason realizes what this means, not only has he lost two more of his charges, but their latest safe-haven is compromised, and the other Apara are, *no doubt,* in possession of his laptop and other equipment with information on various possible targets.

He bursts into a cursing fit, kicking one of the fallen metal trashcans. It flies twenty feet down the alley, clattering loudly as it collides with other cans, causing dogs to bark, and people to peer out of windows to see what the racket is. He looks down at the now unresponsive Philipa, realizing there was more than just a neutralizing agent in the dart. He takes her arm, drags her over to his chosen meal, healing the wounds on the woman's neck, and porting away with Philipa, leaving his unconscious, anemic victim lying in the alley, half-clothed.

338

Mission accomplished

By the time Sue and Colin arrive back at Medical, Millie and Miranda have been reunited, and the two are following Sara off to an examination room. Millie's not about to let Miranda out of her sight. A large, male Apara with an infuser full of neutralizer approaches Alice, who's still clinging nervously to Marc.

Sue steps in front of the approaching man. "I don't think you'll need that with her. She came willingly. She's a victim in all of this."

"We have our orders. She needs to be prevented from escaping. This will cut off all her abilities." The very stolid man says.

"I just think we need to extend her some good will since she came willingly. She's already a victim, taking away all her abilities will only make her feel more vulnerable." Sue says as she refuses to move out of the way.

Colin clears his throat. "Would a suppresser bracelet set to block porting be an acceptable alternative?"

The man makes eye contact with Colin, purses his lips, and nods. "You're responsible for her until I come back with one." He ports out.

Alice relaxes her hold on Marc. "Is everyone here a *vampire*?"

Sue turns around and smiles. "In essence, yes, but we don't call ourselves that. We're called Apara, and we won't hurt you, I promise." She extends her hand to the frightened woman. After a minute of nervous indecision, Alice takes her hand, and Sue guides her over to some chairs, and keeps her company while they wait. Colin follows along, but gives his partner some space, and Marc heads off to find Tess, Liz, and Kari to debrief.

"Apara? Jason said vampires." Alice says, having a hard time making eye contact.

In Your Dreams

"Jason would. Listen, he wanted you to feel isolated and afraid so you'd turn to him. I'm guessing, from what Millie told us, Jason said we were the bad guys?" Sue asks.

Alice nods. "He did, but I never really believed he was a good guy either, but I knew what he'd do if I didn't do as he said."

"You don't need to feel isolated any more. You've become part of a whole, new world, and we'll help you adjust to your new life and deal with what's happened to you until now." Sue keeps her tone calm, and sends calming, reassuring energy to Alice.

Alice asks timidly. "Is there no way to go back to my old life? Jason always said there wasn't."

"In that, he was telling the truth. We can't go back to being human, but that doesn't mean you can't be happy, and have a good life with us." Sue sees Annie and the large man coming back toward them, carrying a cent-opal bracelet. "Alice, they're going to put a bracelet on you to prevent you from porting out; disappearing on us, though I suspect you're glad to be anywhere but with Jason?"

"Ugh, definitely! He and Philipa are *awful!*" Sue senses some of the fear and shame in Alice for what they'd put her through.

Sue paths to the unnamed guard. *Let Annie do the bracelet! She's had enough of domineering men dealing with Jason!*

The guard gives her an annoyed look and pushes Annie toward them while dutifully watching Alice.

Annie gives Alice a timid smile. "Hi, I'm Annie. I just need to put this on your wrist and make some adjustments. It won't hurt or anything."

Alice tentatively extends her hand, and Annie places the bracelet on her wrist and locks it in place, taking out a tablet and clicking different settings to adjust what the bracelet restricts and by how much. Alice's nose flares as she recognizes Annie from earlier, and looks at Sue with an unspoken question.

Sue paths privately to Alice, *Yes, that's Annie Deng. Yes, she's still human and yes, she knows you were with Jason that night in the River Art's District, but she also knows you're a victim of his, as she is.*

340

Annie smiles. "You're all set! Sara will be out in a few to check you over. She's our doctor, and she's really nice. You'll like her!" Annie turns and trots back down the hallway.

Colin turns to the guard. "I don't think we'll need your services any longer. We'll stay with her until Sara's ready for her." The guard looks annoyed, but turns around and stalks off.

Colin paths to Sue privately, *When this is over, we need to talk.*

Sue looks at him, unsure what's on his mind, but senses, while proud of her for her work tonight, he's concerned about her.

***

Liz, Kari, Marc, and Tess are in the conference room going over what's happened so far, when Amy ports in, annoyed.

"What's wrong?" Tess asks.

"You know how it goes, *girl!* I've got some good news, and some *not* so good news!" She sets down her dart gun on a counter near the door, pointing away from everyone, and sags into one of the other chairs around the Table. "The bad news is we didn't get Philipa or Jason. The good news is, I think I neutralized Philipa just as she was porting out. I know my aim was dead-on and couldn't find the dart after she was gone, so I think I got her. But the great news is we got his laptop, other equipment, notebooks, and so on, with the names and information of those he has on his current wish list!"

"That's great news! Granted, he can get new equipment and try hacking us again, but we now have a data security specialist to secure our system against his hacking. If you haven't met him yet, his name's Ty Russo. Once that's secure, we'll sort the results of all your research, Tess, and share it out to the appropriate centers around the world." Liz leans forward in her chair. "Amy, did tech get that tracking compound into the neutralizer cocktail?"

Amy grins from ear-to-ear. "They *did*, indeed! Assuming the dart hit its mark, the compound will settle in her bone marrow and spine over the next few days, so it's permanent! We'll still have to be within about five miles of her to pick up the trace, but that's far enough away we can port in my guys on the ground to go after them when we're ready. He shouldn't be able to pick up on them porting in so far away, so maybe we can get the jump on them."

"What's left to do before we're ready"? Liz asks curiously.

"Sara's got some of her people working on a masking agent; once our guys are on the ground within a five-mile radius, he shouldn't be able to sense them as Apara, meaning they should be able to get close to him without him knowing they're there." She leans back in her chair and puts her hands behind her head, stretching, and cracking her back.

"So, all we have to do is figure out what area they settled in and set the trap." Liz lets out a long breath and relaxes a tad, knowing they may be close to resolving the biggest thorn in her side in centuries. *Once Jason's out of the way, we can focus on rebuilding our numbers more rapidly and doing what we can to stabilize the world.* She thinks.

Letting go

Once Miranda and Alice are settled in, and Liz has debriefed them, Sue and Colin port home. It's late, even on the West Coast; Sue slips off the protective body suit they made her wear, so she's just in a t-shirt and underwear, and flops down on the sofa, stretching out, exhausted, but satisfied she'd done her part today. Colin goes into the kitchen and comes back out with a tray of odds-and-ends food and two bags of blood.

"Before you pass out for the night, there are some loose ends to sort out." He gives her a lopsided grin as he sets the tray on the coffee table. She sits part way up, her feet bare and stretched out on the sofa, grabs a couple of ham sandwiches and devours them hungrily. "*Love*, we need to talk about tonight."

"What about it? I thought we got most of it talked out when Liz and co, debriefed us." She's still hungry, so grabs a big bunch of white, seedless grapes from the tray, pops them off the clusters, and stuffs them in her mouth.

"You do realize your cousin now knows you're one of us, don't you?" He sits on the sofa, moving her feet out of the way, and into his lap, then massages them.

"Yeah, I guess she does, what about it?" She gives him a confused look.

"Don't you think she's probably pissed off you decked her and rescued the women? I'm betting Jason gave her hell for letting that happen." He suggests.

She looks at him, annoyed, but can't help but relax as he massages all the pressure points on her feet. He continues. "As I understand it, she can be obsessive and violent, right?"

Sue shifts, pulls herself upright, and folds her legs under her on the sofa. "You think she'll want revenge, don't you?"

"You're the expert in psychology, and know her personally, what do you think?" He asks, scooting over on the sofa so he can cup her cheek with his hand.

"Unfortunately, you're probably right. What are you going to do? Get the guard from the hospital to be my personal body-guard?" She halfway jokes.

He rubs her leg gently. "I think you need to reconsider your job at the clinic. I know it's important to you, but if there's any place you're vulnerable, it's there. And worse, it sounds like she wouldn't care if there's collateral damage should she go after you there." Colin halfway holds his breath, expecting her to fight him tooth and nail, so is surprised by her reaction.

"Yeah, I've already concluded the clinic job isn't going to work anyway. Between time zones, Apara duties, and an anal-retentive, micromanaging boss, I can't keep up with everything, and that's the one thing that can go. I think I'll get on that dissertation project, though. Tess is *right*, I can't be a shrink to every stressed-out Apara, but I can help others learn to do this job." She grins.

"What about your clients? Were you able to help any of them?" He asks.

"Some, but I have some I never even got to meet with again. But then again, maybe I can meet them in their dreams, and do a little dream therapy?" She grins and yawns.

He leans over and kisses her. "Sounds like a plan!"

Meanwhile

Thanks to Apara scientists, their Benefactors have gifted humanity technology that will reduce radiation levels and allow more rapid reclamation of the lands in and around Jerusalem. While relatively small, the nuclear device contained a small payload of cobalt, leading to longer lasting, and more lethal radiation in the area immediately around the detonation site. In addition, because it was ground based, and not an airburst, the amount of radiation reaching the ground and contaminating the area was higher than if they had exploded a normal nuclear device in an air burst. The Benefactors, through well-placed Apara scientists, introduced radiation eating fungi. The melanin-containing fungi thrives on radiation, but in the process of consuming it, breaks it down into an inert form, drastically reducing the dangerous radiation period from as long as eighteen months down to about three months, while reducing the relatively mild levels of cobalt-60 in about seven months instead of decades.

Because of this, many of the original military volunteers, including Charlie Abrams, Amy's pre-Apara boyfriend, were moved from helping refugees forced out of the city; including building temporary housing, providing medical treatment, safe food, clean water, clothes, and other necessities to the displaced, to reclamation of the ruins within Jerusalem itself. Apara Scientists also provided anti-radiation medication so that workers can work without heavy suits to prevent radiation sickness.

The first stage is clearing debris, and any still contaminated topsoil to a storage and decontamination region in the desert, where additional treatments of the fungal cleaner may further clean the rubble, and much of that will eventually be recycled for new building materials. Charlie is on one team running bulldozers and removal trucks, working about five miles from the original detonation. Currently, they're working on an area riddled with both natural caves under the surface, and ancient, hewn-rock tombs. Tombs and caves discovered before the bomb are mapped, and GPS devices are used to keep the bulldozers and other equipment away from areas that could cave in from their weight.

It's early July, and Charlie's running a ground-sonar device to look for unmapped caves and chambers the GPS may not show. He's walking in front of one bulldozer by about twenty meters when he hears pings suggesting a sizeable cavern ahead. He radios the bulldozer driver to warn him, but the driver's listening to music in his headphones instead of listening to his radio, and doesn't get the message. Charlie tries to warn him off as he approaches, but he misinterprets his waving as a sign to come and deal with an enormous pile of rubble. As he hits the pile of rubble, the ground rumbles and shakes; a large hole opens about five meters ahead of the careless driver, who's barely able to stop in time, avoiding following the rubble into the newly exposed cavern. Charlie is not so lucky and slides down a stream of loose soil into the dark cavern below. He reaches the bottom, sore and scraped, and with a slight bonk to his noggin, but is otherwise uninjured. He scrambles around, finds his radio, and is relieved it still works.

"Central, this is Sgt. Charlie Abrams. Do you read me? Over." He repeats his hail three times before someone with a handset closer to the cave-in answers him.

"Roger, Charlie. This is Jefferson. I don't think your signal's reaching the base from down there, but I hear you, and will relay. Are you okay?"

"Yeah, a little bruised, including my ego, but nothin's broken! That dumbass on the dozer needs to go get a refresher course before he's let on that damn thing again!" He hears Jefferson guffaw. He pulls out a flashlight and tries to turn it on but it flickers. He tinkers with it, unscrewing the front and cleaning dust and sand out of the contacts, and closing it up again to get a steady light. "Jefferson! While I'm down here, I'm gonna try to get an idea what we're dealing with! How far it goes and stability."

Jefferson's quiet for a minute. "Ya sure ya wanna do that, boss? What if it ain't stable?"

"If it's not stable, it'll come down on my head one way or 'nother, so best we get something out of it! Try to find a stable enough edge to send down a rope ladder so I can get out if it don't cave in on top of me!" Charlie says, lax in his grammar so he can hide the fact he's a lot smarter than the rest of the grunts on the team. He can hear voices from above, work lights from the dozer shine down into the hole, and Charlie sees something deeper in the cavern. He moves forward carefully, moving his flashlight back and forth ahead of him. As he goes deeper into the cavern, he makes out manmade structures, including columns, archways, and hand-hewn doors that likely lead to burial chambers. A couple of chambers have what look like stone caskets in them, and there are various artifacts scattered around. He approaches one chamber and peers in over the casket, flashing the interior with his flashlight; he's startled by what he sees, and stumbles backwards, tripping over some ancient pottery on the floor and landing on his behind with a thud, raising ancient dust, and making him sneeze.

He gets up slowly, and goes back to the chamber for a second look, but what he sees just can't be possible. There's a body behind the stone casket. It's not ancient remains, but the intact, fresh-looking body of a woman. Her clothes are in tatters and burnt. The ends of her hair are blackened, but the rest of her hair is strawberry blonde. Her skin, what he can see of it, is pale, like she might be dead, yet her skin doesn't look burned, dried up and shriveled. He can't see her breathing, but she looks like she could open her eyes at any moment.

He tries to radio back to Jefferson, but he's too far in and doesn't get a reply. He retraces his route back until he can see the darkening sky of twilight through the opening to the cave in. He tries his radio again.

"Jefferson! You there?" He says, and wipes dust from the cavern off his face.

"Yo! I'm here, Charlie. Thought maybe we'd lost you there for a sec!" Jefferson's voice crackles over the radio.

"Nah, but I think I need the Commander down here and a medic. I found something I want them to look at. Did ya find a place to lower a ladder?" Charlie doesn't say what he's found. He's certain they'll think he's hallucinating.

Jefferson answers. "*Roger*, Charlie. They're anchoring the ladder right now and will lower it down. We'll set up a spotlight so you can see it. I'll see if the Commander's willing to come. Last I heard, he was entertaining a local tonight!" Jefferson makes a knowing chuckle as the local is a woman from a makeshift bar in the refugee settlement.

Charlie's annoyed. "Tell him he needs to get his *ass* down here, or I'll go to the Israelis! In fact, tell him they might want to send a rep down here too! I found something odd down here. Looks like an ancient burial chamber that's not on the maps, and I need them to come see someth'n down here, but only the higher ups and a medic, got it?"

"Whatev'r ya say, boss! Chief's not gonna be happy, but it's your *ass* if he doesn't agree it's important!" Jefferson replies. Charlie can hear Jefferson's outgoing call telling the Commander he's needed, and should bring the other people with him, but the signal from the reply is broken and mostly static.

When that stops, he radios back to Jefferson. "What's the status, man? Are they coming?"

"Yeah, yeah, though Chief's not happy. Says the only higher up from the Israelis is one of those damn spooks trying to find out more about the people behind this shit! They'll be there soon." Jefferson says.

A spotlight flashes across where Charlie's standing and when he shades his eyes and looks toward it, he sees a rope ladder flop down from above, swaying randomly along the far wall of the cavern. He goes over and finds a bag attached to the end with spikes, and uses those to anchor the lower end of the ladder. He's overwhelmed and sore from his fall, so heads over to a wall of the cavern and sits, leaning his back against the cool, damp, stone wall while he waits. He nearly nods off when he hears his commander's voice bark out loud commands to others around the hole. Charlie stands as they near the ground. His Commander,

Colonel Matt Stevens, a petite, female medic with short, black hair and olive skin, and a shifty-looking guy he figures is a Mossad agent near the bottom of the cavern.

His commander comes over and apathetically salutes Charlie. "What'd you find that's so all-fired important it couldn't wait 'til tomorrow, Abrams?"

"Sir, there appears to be a series of previously undiscovered tombs in that direction." Charlie explains, sensing his commander glare at him in the darkness.

"And that required my presence, a medic, and him?" He uses a thumb gesture to motion to the likely agent.

"I believe so, Sir. There's something there that shouldn't be, Sir." Charlie says. "And I think you need to see it for yourself, as you'll never believe me otherwise!" Charlie lets out an anxious sigh.

"Very well, lead on!" The Commander's voice is gruff, though there is a hint of curiosity in it.

Charlie leads them to the ancient tombs, warning them when there's debris they need to step over. The medic, Janna Baker, is following him closely, followed by the Israeli rep, and last, already out of breath, is the Commander. When Charlie gets to the tomb in question, he stops and waits for the others to catch up.

"I'd suggest the medic take a look first and do an eval, Sir." He turns toward Janna. "You'll have to climb up and over the stone casket. I'll help you, and then hold a light so you can see." He gives the small woman a leg up onto the ancient stone coffin. She crawls to the end and looks down into darkness. He hands her the medic kit, she takes out her flashlight, then shines it down, and gasps. "*Shit!* How'd *she* get down here?" Janna exclaims.

"Glad you see 'er too, ma'am. Means I didn't hit my head hard enough slide'n down to be seeing things that aren't there." Charlie jokes.

"No, she's *definitely* there, but how did she get here? She can't have been here long, not with that flesh tone!" Janna turns around so she can back down, feet first into the alcove behind the stone coffin.

Charlie takes one hand and helps ease her down, then climbs up and shines his own flashlight down to illuminate the scene.

The first thing Janna does is check for a pulse, but doesn't get anything, however, she notices all too quickly the body is warmer than it should be. She checks for rigor mortis, but there's none. In fact, if she didn't know any better, she'd have thought the woman was just sleeping, as her limbs are pliable, and skin's relatively warm. "This doesn't make any sense!" She exclaims.

The Israeli man, who has yet to give his name, comes closer. "What do you see?" He asks.

"Well, sir, there's a woman's body back here, but it's just not right! She's pale, like a corpse, but her skin is still supple, nearly flawless and limbs move easily. I'd guess the temperature down here is about sixty-five degrees now, with some warmth from the cave in, but has probably been a constant fifty-five like other chambers in this region. That being said, if she's dead, her body should be the same temperature as the surroundings, but it's at eighty-five degrees, Sir. If I were to have guessed, I'd have thought she'd *just* died, and it's too soon for her temperature to drop or her body to go into rigor, but that's impossible too! This chamber hasn't been explored before, meaning the only things we should find down here should be ancient, and any bodies just a pile of dust and bones!"

"Is there any way she could have been caught in the cave in?" The commander barks out.

Charlie looks at him and bites his tongue, knowing the Commander is not the brightest bulb out here. "No, Sir. There's no way a body could have come down the hole and gotten all the way in here! I came down with the cave in! If she'd been there, I'd a seen her!"

"Are you sure she's dead Medic Baker?" He asks.

"I'll check again sir, but I checked for both a heartbeat and pulse for about half a minute and found none. If you all will stay as quiet as possible, that would help." She suggests, puts a stethoscope in her ears, and listens for a heartbeat. This time, about twenty-three seconds in, she narrows her eyes and gets a surprised expression. She sits there, holding the stethoscope in place for nearly five minutes when the Commander makes a gruff noise and finds a half wall to sit on.

"Medic Baker, is she or isn't she dead?" The Israeli agent asks.

Janna pulls the stethoscope out of her ears. "Sir, I don't know how it's possible, but I did get a heartbeat! An incredibly slow and subtle one, and I also got a slight pulse to go along with it. We need to get her out of here and somewhere where I can hook her up to an EKG, and maybe an EEG and see what we're dealing with."

"Hm..." The Israeli says, and goes over to the Commander for a discreet chat. Charlie and Janna can hear the Commander's unhappy with whatever the Israeli agent wants, but eventually concedes. The Agent comes over to Charlie. "I want you to go and clear the area! Get everyone out of here immediately. Some of my people are on their way. They'll recover the woman... the *body*, and take her to a facility where we can get to the bottom of this. Sergeant, not a word to anyone of what we've found down here, and I'll need a list of anyone you spoke to before we arrived."

"Sir? I only spoke to Jefferson. Told him there were some tombs and stuff, and he relayed my messages to the Commander cause my radio wouldn't reach that far from down here." Charlie explains.

The agent narrows his eyes and continues. "You and the medic will accompany me, my men, and the *body* to the facility. You've been reassigned and won't be working on the reclamation any longer."

"Sir? I'm US army, I'm not under your jurisdiction." Charlie looks unsettled.

The Commander clears his throat. "Under the agreement between Israel and the international forces here to help, he can, and has conscripted you for this duty. You're in his hands now, Abrams; you as well, Baker. We'll forward your things along to whatever address he gives me." The commander looks uneasy as he informs them, like he almost fears the agent or is doing this under duress. "Come on Abrams! I'll help you clear the area." He pushes Charlie, who's about a foot taller than he is, back out into the open chasm toward the ladder. Once out of the agent's hearing, he says, "Look, Charlie, this is off the record. That guy's some kind of spook, and he's got a lot of pull around here. I think they're hunting more terrorists or somethin'. He wouldn't give me any details, but said it's all top-secret crap. You all have stumbled into somethin' they really want kept under wraps. You watch your back! And Baker's, too. But you've got to go with him, hear me?"

"Yes, Sir." Charlie says with a concerned expression. After a couple of second's hesitation, he gives the rope ladder a slight tug to test it before ascending to the top, followed by the Commander. Between the two of them, they clear out the entire reclamation site in twenty minutes flat. The Commander heads back to base, while an exhausted and bewildered Charlie carefully descends the rope ladder again and heads for the tomb. When he arrives, Janna's sitting on top of the stone casket, waiting, and the 'spook', as the Commander called him, is waiting impatiently, sending messages on some sort of device. Charlie wonders; *How the hell is he getting any signal down here?* But sure enough, Mr. Spook gets a reply and types away again.

Janna gets down from the casket and looks at Mr. Spook typing away, oblivious to both she and Charlie. Charlie leans forward on the stone casket and asks Janna, "Any idea what we're supposed to do now?"

"Yeah, I need your help. Her right arm is pinned under some heavy stones that must've fallen after she got in there. They're too heavy for me to move alone." Janna says.

Charlie motions for her to go on down into the alcove again, as he pulls himself back up onto it. He notes she's cleverly found a way to wedge her flashlight into a gap in the stone wall in the alcove to give them better light. The two of them lift stones and relay them to the other side of the alcove. When they lift the last, large stone out of the way and Janna looks back, she gasps and lets out a squeal of disbelief. Charlie tosses the stone into the pile and comes back over to her.

"What's wrong?" He asks her.

The young medic has her hand over her mouth trying to stifle her cries of disbelief, but she moves out of the way so Charlie can see and says, "Oh *Hell!* I really can't explain *that!*"

Charlie looks, and then rubs his eyes like maybe something is wrong with them, uttering, "Yeah, that's *definitely* not right." He reaches over and traces the woman's arm, which oddly enough is not bruised from all the rocks they'd just removed, but her arm runs toward the casket and ends, halfway up her forearm, embedded in the stone of the casket as though the rest of her arm might be found inside.

'Mr. Spook', hearing their exclamations, puts down his device and goes over toward the casket. "What's going on? Has there been any change in her condition?" He asks, wondering if maybe she was showing signs of waking.

"Not exactly..." Janna trails off.

"Oh man! This *shit* is mind bending, *Sir!* Her arm literally appears to be going through the stone casket! Not through a *hole*, mind you, but literally through the stone itself!" Charlie blurts out, still shaking his head.

Oddly, Mr. Spook isn't surprised by this discovery and goes back to his device and taps on it some more. Charlie and Janna look at each other like they don't know what to make of him. After another fifteen minutes, Spook looks up at them and gives them a disturbing grin. "Your ride is here. My men have arrived. They'll get the woman out. You two go on up and they'll take care of you." He says in a manner, while not menacing, that sets their nerves on edge.

"How are they gonna get her out if she's literally connected to that damn stone casket?" Janna asks. "Are they gonna amputate? 'Cause I don't know if she'll survive such a shock! Hell, I don't know how she's survived at all!"

"We'll take care of it, Ms. Baker. My guys have brought experts and tools and will take the utmost care in extracting our mystery woman." He says and goes back to his messaging.

Charlie and Janna are walking out of the tomb and toward the rope ladder when Charlie whispers to her, trying to look like he's not saying anything as several black clothed and masked, special service types descent the rope ladder and head in their direction. "Commander told me to watch our backs! Will do all I can to keep us safe. Just do as they say for now!" He whispers.

Janna nods and notices Charlie is speaking much clearer and more correctly than he had with the other men earlier. She files that observation away for later as they head to the ladder and hear voices from above. A crane arm is extended over the pit and what appears to be a body sized container is being lowered. She watches it descend while she climbs the rope ladder, and recognizes it as a quarantine capsule; the kind she's seen used in training videos for extreme viral or bacterial outbreaks such as Ebola.

Janna gets a sinking feeling in her stomach, wondering if she and Charlie have been exposed to something dangerous, or if it's all just precautionary. She reaches the top, and a black gloved hand reaches down and pulls her up like she weighs next to nothing, and leads her to one of several, all too stereotypical, men-in-black style, unmarked vans. She looks over her shoulder and sees Charlie, maybe fifty feet behind her being led by two guards toward the same vehicle. She's put in the van. The only windows are in the front, and her anxiety increases exponentially.

A minute or so later, Charlie joins her in the van, and a black clothed, but unmasked woman with short, dark hair and a scar on her jaw hands them both what look like ski masks. There are mouth and nose holes, but no eyeholes. Charlie rolls his eyes and shakes his head, but nods reassuringly to Janna to just put it on. He thinks, *Damn! I hate this cloak and dagger shit!*

Their van drives off, no one speaks a word, and there are no sounds other than the rolling of the tires over a rough, unpaved road. Eventually, the van stops and they're both pulled out by the woman with the scar; though they cannot see her, they can both smell the same perfume or something else fragrant, and know it's her. She guides them along and they can hear a gate rolling along and closing behind them. Charlie can tell Janna's getting anxious. He is too, but he'd learned to control his expression of such things.

As they're moved forward, they both feel smooth flooring beneath their feet, and sense a change in the temperature from warm, night air to an air-conditioned space. Their footsteps echo like they're in a long hallway. They're herded into an elevator. Charlie gauges the speed from the way the elevator feels and counts the seconds go by. When they stop, he estimates they're the equivalent of several sub-basements down in whatever facility they've been brought to. They're guided down several hallways, and through a door, which closes behind them. The woman pulls off their masks.

"You will both stay here." She says with a strong, Israeli accent. "Consider this quarantine time. You have everything you need here. A common room, multiple sleeping chambers, a kitchen, bathroom, shower, and even entertainment. There are clean clothes in the bathroom. You're both to shower before you settle in. Your current clothes are to be thrown down the shoot above the toilet."

Janna speaks up timidly. "Do they think we've been exposed to something dangerous?" She asks.

"Uncertain. Consider it a precaution. Scrub well, change clothes. Prepared food will be delivered shortly, though there is some in the kitchen to use at your convenience. Oh, yes, any mobile devices or other forms of communication must be turned over." She holds out a black, metal lined bag for them to put their cells in, and ties if off once they have.

Charlie eyes her suspiciously. "Are we some sort of prisoners or what?"

She cocks her head to one side and gives him a smile. "*No*, Sergeant. These are just precautions until we know what we're dealing with. This base is top secret, including its location, hence the masks. If you need anything, there will be guards outside this door, just ask them." She smiles, turns, and leaves before they can get in any more questions.

The two of them do as told, and settle in. Entertainment videos are available, as well as music, and games, but no live broadcasts. Being several stories underground, there are no windows, and unfortunately, no clocks either.

After about a week of this precautionary custody, both Charlie and Janna are getting worried. They'd taken to speaking generally while in the facility, knowing it is likely monitored, but both are aware this is not a normal situation. They've just finished watching some old 1990s sitcom series when the door opens, and both 'Mr. Spook' and 'Ms. Scar', as they refer to the unnamed pair, come into the room, carrying a metal briefcase.

"Please, don't get up. We're sorry this has taken so long, but we were not sure what we were dealing with, and still aren't." Scar says as Spook takes a laptop out of the metal briefcase. He pulls up some sort of slide show on the screen. "How much do you know of the terrorists, and the plot behind the bomb?" Spook asks.

"As much as anyone, I guess." Charlie says, dropping his country bumpkin dialect.

Spook gives him a curt nod. Because you two were there when the anomalous woman was found, and we wish to keep only the bare minimum in the loop at this time, our governments have made you representatives for your country in this matter. Dr. Zelkind..." He motions to the woman formally referred to as Scar. "and I will debrief you. As you may or may not be aware, Jerusalem was but one city around the world supposedly targeted last autumn. Over a dozen other cities, including in your own country were targeted, but the bombs there weren't completed." Spook can see the look of shock on both Janna and Charlie's faces. "I see you were unaware of this point. I was unsure how much your military intelligence might have passed on since you are in the service. Alas! Only the one here, in Jerusalem was completed and went off that night, though we are still uncertain why. Someone tipped off the authorities, though no one seems to know whom. While we did capture some terrorists involved, we suspect this was a much greater endeavor than we thought. Survivors reported an unusual number of people in and around Jerusalem lurking around suspiciously. Most people were too busy trying to get out of the city once the alerts went out, but we received several reports of people appearing and disappearing randomly. We installed a new webcam based, anti-terrorism network last summer, and all video is piped to this facility, which is well outside of the city, and underground as I assume you've surmised." He looks from Janna to Charlie and grins when he realizes they're on the same page. Video proof exists." Spook says, and starts a slide show of video clips showing people appearing, lurking around and then disappearing. Spook's not surprised to see gasps of disbelief from their two, conscripted, American, military guests.

Janna looks confused, and asks, "Sir, I'm sorry, what's the connection to the woman we found in the tomb?"

Before Spook can answer, Charlie has an a-ha moment and answers her, "It's the only way she could have gotten into the cave and the tomb. She was one of the people teleporting!" Janna's mouth drops open in shock.

Dr. Zelkind speaks up. "Very good, Mr. Abrams. That's exactly what we suspect. It also fits with the fact her clothing was clearly burnt and still carried some radioactivity, hence why we had you shower and discard your clothing. You'll be pleased to know our monitors have not picked up any signs of residual radiation from either of you." She smiles at them.

Charlie looks like he's trying to do a mental puzzle. "Do you think this woman was caught in the blast, did this disappearing act, and ended up in the tomb?"

Dr. Zelkind gets a pleasantly surprised look as Charlie shows he is more than just an Army grunt. "Good deduction, Mr. Abrams. Yes, we feel that is the most fitting explanation for not only her burnt clothing, but the fact her arm was literally phased through the stone in the casket. She must have rematerialized with the molecules in her arm phasing, and taking up the same space as the wall of the casket."

Charlie sits back, looking stunned. "Any idea how she did that? Is it some kind of classified tech or something?"

"We're not sure, but after examining her, we do not believe she is exactly...normal. In fact, we do not believe she's quite human." Dr. Zelkind drops that bomb and watches the reaction as a few brain cells in each of them appear to implode with the implications of this revelation.

"If she's not human, what is she?" Charlie asks.

Spook speaks up. "What do you know about vampires?"

Foreign Words List

Norwegian:

Faen i helvete!	Fucking Hell!
Helvete	Hell
Hva i Helvete?	What the Hell?
Ja	Yes
Javel?	Southern Norwegian slang that can mean a number of things, such as: well? What do you want? Oh, really?
Kjære, Kjæreste	Dearest one, my love, dear

French:

Faux pas	Mistake
Le Petit Chou	The Little Cabbage.
Merci beaucoup	Thank you, very much
Merde!	Shit!
Mousse Au Chocolate	Chocolate Mousse
Oui, mon Ami!	Yes, my friend.
Voila!	There!

UK English

Wanker	Slang: Jerk